GARAGE SALE DIAMONDS

Garage Sale Mystery Series

SUZI WEINERT

International Standard Book Number 13: 978-1-60452-065-1
International Standard Book Number 10: 1-60452-065-5
Library of Congress Control Number: 2014948214

BluewaterPress LLC
52 Tuscan Way, Ste 202-309
Saint Augustine, Florida 32092

http://www.bluewaterpress.com
This book may be purchased online at

http://www.bluewaterpress.com/GSD

Editing by Carole Greene

This is a work of fiction. All characters, organizations, and events portrayed in this novel are either products of the author's imagination or are used fictitiously.

LETTER TO MY READERS

Terrorism is not new. My story's about Middle-Eastern terrorism, but historically this tool has served conquerors, militias, governments, religions and Mafia-like organizations. The contest between power via intimidation and freedom to cooperate voluntarily continues in the 9/11 era.

My book is fiction but terrorism is real, affecting citizens of every nation. For open societies like ours, peaceful coexistence vs. the need for safety requires constant vigilance. Live-and-let-live philosophy works where groups live in relative harmony, not attempting to destroy one another.

With the remarkable technology of modern warfare, no person or place is safe from harm. Any nation's capital is a strategic target for attacks, so people living near Washington, D.C. recognize their particular vulnerability. Just such a suburb is McLean, Virginia.

All countries, cultures, societies and religions incorporate the full range of human behavior: kind or cruel, war-like or peace-loving, close-minded or open-minded, progressive or regressive and so on. Education and economics affect the global family. Rights of individuals vs. collectives continue to challenge the brightest minds. Since we all share the same planet, survival of mankind may rest on designing ways to live harmoniously on spaceship earth.

Thank you for reading my book. E-mail me if you like at Suzi@ GarageSaleStalker.com

~Suzi Weinert

PROLOGUE - PART A

Hearing insistent knocking on the front door of their dwelling in a remote Middle Eastern village, Ahmed obeyed his father's hand signal pointing the child to hurry upstairs. The boy scampered to the top step, pressed himself against the wall and peeked at the scene below.

Their heavy pounding unanswered, the intruders escalated to boot kicks and shoulder thuds against the wood to bash down the door. With triumphant snarls, four men burst into the home. Already on his feet, Ahmed's father lurched forward to protest their invasion; but they muscled him into a corner, punched him to the floor and took turns delivering vicious kicks to the helpless man's torso. Then one dragged Ahmed's father to a chair to prop his bleeding body upright.

The five-year-old cowered at the top of the stairs, staring open-mouthed at the horror below. An ear-shattering BANG echoed around the room. The child watched red and gray explode onto the wall behind his father. When the men stood back, the child saw a faceless man dressed in his father's clothes sprawled at the base of the wall beneath the dripping splatter. The men grunted and gestured among themselves. One pointed toward the foot of the stairs.

But Ahmed had already sprinted into the bedroom where his mother's eyes peered at him from her tear-streaked face above the infant she held against her heart.

Wide-eyed with terror, he whispered, "The men who hurt Baba are coming for us." Heavy footsteps thumped on the stairs as the boy spoke.

His mother reached a quick decision and moved faster than he'd ever remembered. In one swift, continuous motion she lay the baby on the floor, closed and locked the bedroom door, grabbed Ahmed's arm and flung him into the wardrobe. He heard her turn the key to lock it.

The sounds of the men knocking down the bedroom door penetrated the darkness where the terrified child shrank against the back of the dark armoire. He heard his mother talk to the men, then whimper as she begged them to spare her baby. The infant's hysterical cries stopped mid-wail. Ahmed's mother screamed.

He heard scuffling and the men shouting among themselves followed by a crude laugh. His mother's anguished voice rose decibels higher. "No, please!" she cried. The scrambling and grunting intensified as his mother's screams filled the air. Those screams changed to horrific shrieks of agony, sounds he'd never heard her make but knew came from her mouth because her voice was as familiar to him as his own. Ahmed heard her gagging, coughing and sobbing while the men laughed. Then one man shouted a command in a language he didn't understand. More scuffling. His mother's final scream halted as abruptly as the baby's had.

The boy heard another harsh command from the same man's voice. Then their shoes shuffled across the room, grew fainter and disappeared in footfalls descending the stairs. Then silence.

Paralyzed with fear, he pressed himself into a corner of the cupboard's inky blackness. But as the unbroken silence stretched on, he finally sat up, pressed an ear against the doors and listened with great care.

"Ummi?" he risked calling his mommy. No response. "*Ummi?*" he called louder. Silence.

He pushed his small hands tentatively against the wardrobe's doors. They wouldn't budge. Would his mother turn the key to let him out? Could she if she were hurt? How long should he wait?

Listening again but hearing no sound, he touched a foot against one of the wardrobe's two doors and pressed, jostling it a little. He listened again, heard only silence and pushed harder, this time with both feet. A thin vertical crack of light appeared where the double doors joined in the middle, but the lock's resistance held them. He listened again for any noise from the room. Nothing! Squaring his back against the rear of the wardrobe, he bent his knees and pushed with his feet as hard as he could. With a creak of wood and metal, the doors popped open.

The sight before him stunned Ahmed. His baby sister lay still in a circle of blood near the door, her eyes open but unblinking. His mother slumped across the bed's edge. Blood stained her clothing, pushed askew. Her bare legs stuck out from her twisted skirt.

He gazed open-mouthed, stupefied by the ghastly scene. What did it mean? His parents always explained unusual events, for he was only a boy. But unless they woke up...

Hearing no sound from downstairs, he eased himself out of the wardrobe and touched his mother.

"Ummi?" His small hand gently shook her shoulder. "*Ummi*?"

She moaned, feebly lifting the fingers of one hand. With difficulty, she opened her green eyes.

"Ummi," he urged. "How can I help?"

She moaned again. "The...baby?"

Ahmed looked at his tiny sister. "She...she doesn't move. Maybe she's resting."

His mother's eyes closed, pain and despair distorting her usually cheerful face. She struggled to form words.

"Your path...difficult. Allah...will guide you," she whispered hoarsely. "Seek...truth. Use...your mind to...sift what you see and hear. Think for yourself. Listen to your heart." A long pause. "Take care of Amina."

In the craziness, he'd forgotten his twin sister. Cousins from a neighboring village had picked her up only this morning to visit with their young daughters for a few days.

"Yes, Ummi," he answered obediently. "But...I don't know where to find her."

His mother gazed deep into his eyes. "Take care of her. And...avenge our undeserved deaths."

"Yes, Ummi. But how?"

"You will... know what to do when... the time comes. Kiss me... good-bye."

He pressed his warm lips against her cheek, exactly as he had kissed her so many times. He pulled back, but the usual loving smile he expected wasn't forthcoming. He buried his face against the familiar cloth of her garment, clasping her in a desperate hug, his little arms stretching around her as far as they could reach. At last he pulled back to look again into her loving eyes gazing deeply into his own, locking him in wordless communication forever connecting mother and beloved son. One moment he saw his image reflected in her moist pupils. The next moment their clarity blurred as her dying eyes unfocused, fading into a vacant stare.

"*UMMI!*" he screamed, first nudging her to wake up and then urgently shaking her. Instead, she slipped from the bed to the floor and lay in a lifeless, crumpled heap.

His anguished sobs of loss and fear lasted until dark, when at last he crawled back to the earlier safety of the wardrobe, closed the doors and began a fitful night's sleep. The following morning he again tried to wake his mother and baby sister, but even a five year old realized something irreversible had happened. He crept across the grisly bedroom scene, down the stairs, past the faceless thing dressed in his father's clothes and into the kitchen to find some food.

When Amina's visit ended in a few days, wouldn't the cousins bring her back? Wouldn't they explain what happened?

PROLOGUE - PART B

Two strange men arrived the next morning as Ahmed sat on the cooking hearth, gnawing a piece of bread. Forcing the resisting child to accompany them, the older one explained to the younger one, "When our cleansing team punishes troublemakers like this, we usually find the orphans in the kitchen. Hunger is stronger than fear." Older gave a mirthless laugh.

Younger politely emulated the laugh but with a nervous edge.

"You who I train," Older said to Younger, "do you see how we attack the snake four ways?"

"Four ways, Teacher?" asked Younger with respect. If this were another test, failure to answer correctly meant consequences.

Satisfied at this deference, Older continued. "First, we forever silence the snake's slander against our glorification of Allah, blessed be His name. Second, we take the snake's children to further *our* cause, not theirs — to become human swords for our crusade against all heretics here and in other lands. Third, this snake's punishment frightens the other villagers enough to look away and make no trouble for us now or in the future. Fourth, our cleansing team returns to bury the bodies before confiscating the snake's house and belongings."

"Ah...yes, now I do see, Wise One. But how do you explain to the children the murder of their parents, perhaps witnessed by their own eyes?"

Younger registered alarm at Older's initial menacing look but sighed with welcome relief when his teacher's disapproval changed to a smug response. "We tell them agents of the American Satan or the evil Jews committed this act. We say we rescued the children from those vicious enemies, the Unbelievers of the one true faith. We say we will teach these children the skills to deliver the vengeance due those enemies who destroyed their family."

"And now we take this new 'recruit' to meet his destiny?" Younger asked.

"You learn fast," Older said with approval. "Yes, at the madrassa boys receive intense religious instruction. When old enough, they learn fighting at the training camps."

"And the girls?"

"They have a different future."

"Different?" asked Younger.

But Older ignored his question, turning instead to the little boy. "Your name, child?"

"Ahmed," he managed in a frightened whisper.

"Speak up, boy," Older demanded gruffly. He repeated his name a little louder. "And what is this on your neck and shoulder?" Older pointed to a large maroon birthmark.

"Baba says Allah drew this mark on me to show my special importance to him."

Older processed this information uneasily. Allah's signs weren't always easy to understand. He studied the shy boy. Was he in the presence of a child bearing a holy mark or had a father invented this tale to comfort his blemished child?

"So what do you think?" Older asked Younger.

Younger thought fast. "Maybe we should watch the boy to learn more before we decide what his father meant," he suggested.

"But of course," Older agreed with a raspy laugh, hiding his own uncertainty.

* * * *

Not understanding their words when the men switched to another dialect, Ahmed stumbled along with his right hand clenched in Older's tight grip. Through tears the child looked back at his home, reaching his left arm in that direction as if his small grasping fingers could grab and hold forever the memories of his precious life there...precious until yesterday's madness changed everything he knew.

If they took him away, would he ever see his parents or his twin sister again? Staring at his home for the last time, the boy sobbed with such anguish that his steps faltered.

His head snapped back and he choked on his sobs when, cursing with annoyance, Older jerked him hard — toward a future he could not imagine.

DAY ONE

THURSDAY

CHAPTER ONE

THURSDAY, 9:31 AM

Jennifer Shannon grinned with triumph as she drove from the estate sale at the sprawling Rotunda condo complex toward her home in McLean, Virginia. Reaching that sale early, she stood third in line when they handed out numbers controlling how many shoppers entered the apartment at one time. Had she really bagged this unlikely treasure? A quick glance at the shiny contents in the shoebox nestled beside her on the passenger seat confirmed she had.

Was that a siren whining in the distance? She turned off the radio and lowered her window an inch to gauge the emergency vehicle's closeness. No, it sounded far away.

As she browsed this morning's estate sale in a spacious apartment, nothing caught her eye until she spotted the very silverware she needed – a stainless steel pattern she started years ago with four packages of eight place-settings, long before Oneida discontinued this Bancroft style.

What happened to all those missing forks and spoons remained a mystery. She'd rescued two from the trash where table-clearing "helpers" mistakenly scraped them along with uneaten food. But could that account for eleven disappearing?

The siren again, a little closer this time.

Only last week Replacements, Ltd, the magic source for discontinued china, silverware and crystal patterns, charged more for these eleven missing forks and spoons than she originally paid for eight place settings many years ago. And now ten place-settings glinted in the box beside her—fifty pieces for only $20! Even husband Jason should salute this fortuitous coup!

But that wasn't all. She'd also found the 20-lb exercise weight he'd asked for only yesterday. She filled many requests from family, friends and neighbors who knew about her regular treks to weekend sales, but finding this improbable item so fast beat all odds. Maybe now he'd stop irreverent references to her "garage sale mania."

The siren pierced the air again, triggering an automatic wish for the safety of her five grown children and their families. All lived within a two-hour drive of the McLean home she and Jason bought twenty-five years ago, their proximity to parents seeming a gift in today's mobile society. This nearness allowed frequent family gatherings, which she cherished.

She marveled that a marriage of two such different personalities could last forty-one years, but in the process she and Jason had morphed into a team. At sixty-one, she enjoyed good health, a close family, a loving husband, many friends and a financially comfortable life in upscale McLean. With their child-rearing responsibilities largely behind them, these recent years seemed the best ever. Well, except for her major foible: succumbing to the irresistible weekend lure of garage and estate sales. If Jason grumbled, comparing her "sport" to his golf and tennis brought silence.

She drove into her cul-de-sac, pressed a button to open the iron driveway gates and another to lift the garage door. As she climbed out of her car, the siren whine wafted even closer. Fire? Police? Ambulance? Trouble for someone, she thought, but at least help was on the way.

She shelved newly bought under-the-pillow gifts in a garage cupboard as later surprises for Grands who spent the night. Then she carried her remaining items into the house. As she loaded the sale silverware into the dishwasher to be sanitized, the siren sounded louder. Must be on her side of Dolley Madison Boulevard, the major road cutting through the center of McLean from the George Washington Parkway through Tyson Corner and into Vienna where it became Maple Avenue.

As she pulled clothes from the laundry room dryer, the siren wailed insistently. Was the engine hurtling past her neighborhood?

She stacked the laundry to carry upstairs but the siren's shriek stopped her. Looking out the front door's glass sidelights, she checked for tell-tale smoke somewhere in the neighborhood.

Now deafening, the sound penetrated the walls of her house as it roared into her community and, screaming louder yet, arrived on her street!

Was her house on fire? With a gasp she jerked open the basement door, sniffing for burn odors. She dashed through the house, fearing the acrid smell or billow of smoke. Detecting neither, she rushed out the front door. Covering her ears at the siren's shrillness, she stared open-mouthed at the sleek red-cream-and-silver fire truck and EMS ambulance circling the cul-de-sac in front of her house. They parked opposite her. The piercing siren stopped. Four firefighters poured from the big truck and two from the ambulance, disappearing around the other side of the engine.

After a final anxious glance to assure her own home wasn't in flames, she peered nervously at neighbors' houses around the circle and as far down the road as she could see. No smoke or flames. What was going on? She ran outside and skirted around the truck to find out.

CHAPTER TWO

THURSDAY, 9:46 AM

T he firefighters strode straight to the Donnegan house directly across the circle. She and Jason had known Kirsten and Tony Donnegan for at least twenty years. Their children grew up together, they shared family camping trips, the men went deer hunting each year and the two couples dined often at local restaurants. A practicing veterinarian, Tony was the kindly go-to person for neighborhood kids who found injured or orphaned animals.

What had *happened* here? Maybe a false alarm like the time their son burned microwave popcorn? The smoke had triggered their security system's fire alarm, alerting the fire department. The big engine had pulled into the cul-de-sac that day just as now. Those fire fighters had insisted on coming inside to assure themselves popcorn was the only smoke issue. Bless 'em.

Jennifer paused on the sidewalk. Her police detective son-in-law had warned their family that bystanders and gawkers often interfered with professional emergency work. But if her good friends had a problem, shouldn't she offer help? She raced across the Donnegans' yard to their front door.

Speaking to the first uniformed man she saw inside the doorway, she said, "I'm the Donnegans' neighbor and good friend from across the street. May I...?"

The fire fighter hesitated, but Tony saw her and called, "Jennifer, thank God you're here. Come in quick." She rushed to his side and he gripped her in a desperate hug. "It's Kirsten. She can't breathe." Jennifer's eyes followed his pointing finger to her friend lying on the floor. Kirsten's face looked ashen as several medics tried to revive her. One attached a heart monitor and took her blood pressure. Another listened to her lungs before starting an IV. Each reported aloud to a third man who stood aside, writing on a clipboard and giving periodic instructions.

Tony clutched Jennifer as the lead medic asked, "Sir, have you a list of her medications?" Tony's bewildered expression showed he did not.

Jennifer answered. "Yes, in her wallet. She and I each keep a list there. Where's her purse?"

Tony shrugged. He seemed confused. "I...I have no idea."

"Then I'll look." Jennifer found the purse in the kitchen, hurried to the living room and gave it to Tony. He fumbled inside before handing it back to her.

"Jen, could you please find it for them?" he asked in a thin voice. He turned to answer more questions from the lead medic.

"Please describe her symptoms."

"She felt tired the last few days and today woke up weak. When she finally came down for breakfast, she looked pale and said she felt clammy and cold. So I bundled her up here on the couch. When her chest hurt and she couldn't breathe, I..." his voice caught, "I called 911."

"Has she a history of heart trouble?"

"High blood pressure but controlled with medication. Isn't it on the list Jen gave you?"

A medic kneeling beside Kirsten said to the lead provider. "Uh-oh, she's going into V-fib."

"Start CPR," the lead medic directed, triggering a flurry of treatment activity. The one who identified ventricular fibrillation began CPR. A second medic applied two hand-sized stickers with wires attached to the heart monitor and injected epinephrine. "Prepare to shock."

"Step away from the patient," the lead medic warned. "The electric current could transfer the same cardiac shock to anyone touching the patient."

Tony clutched Jennifer as the shock jolted his wife's heart. The monitor recorded several audible beeps before the sound changed to an even tone.

"Asystole?" the lead medic asked and got a positive nod from the other techs. The lead radioed Dispatch. "This is now a CPR call. We're going to Fairfax ER."

One technician continued administering CPR, stopping compressions for only a few seconds as they placed Kirsten on the collapsible stretcher.

Tony cried out, "Is she going to be all right?"

The lead medic touched his arm to calm him. "The hospital is equipped for the care she needs right now, so we're taking her there."

"Can I ride with her?"

"Sorry, Sir, we don't have room. But we'll give your wife our best professional care, and Fairfax Hospital's ER is the only level-one trauma center in northern Virginia. She'll be in good hands."

"I can drive you to the emergency room, Tony," Jennifer offered.

This quieted him, as did the apparent reassurance of Jennifer holding his hand tightly. "All right."

"By the way, I'm Lt. Sommer. A captain who's the EMS Supervisor may come by later to talk with you or he may send a policeman to gather all the facts."

Tony frowned, "Why...why police involvement?"

"Just routine, Sir. Don't be surprised if you see one or both of them."

Jennifer hurried across the circle to get her car as Tony watched the crew wheel the stretcher to the ambulance and collect their equipment. She stopped behind the ambulance. Tony climbed in.

The ambulance pulled out first, lights flashing, siren shrieking. The fire truck's powerful motor revved to life, preparing to return to the McLean station house. Jennifer followed closely as the ambulance swept through the neighborhood, but when it hurtled through a red light at the first intersection, she knew she couldn't keep up. Though she drove in the same direction as fast as she safely could, the shrill siren gradually faded and evaporated as if it hadn't existed at all.

CHAPTER THREE

THURSDAY, 10:31 AM

In the Middle-East, before his arduous journey began, Ahmed remembered looking up sharply when a skinny, rifle-toting soldier rushed into his tent.

"The Great Leader wants you, *now.*" Such commands required instant response. Anxiety gripped Ahmed as he grabbed his weapon and hurried to the big tent. Little good could come from this.

"Permission to enter, Great Leader?"

"Come in, Ahmed."

Complying, he stepped in upon the worn Oriental carpet and stood at attention before a tall, thin bearded man with steely eyes.

"At ease, Ahmed," the leader said as the soldier before him tried to imagine what rule he'd unintentionally broken. "How would you like to command a secret operation in the United States?"

Ahmed hoped his jaw hadn't dropped open in surprise. "It is an honor that you even consider me for such a mission, Great Leader."

"Your excellent martial skills, quick mind, unquestioned devotion to our cause and obedient submission to Allah, peace be unto His name, have not gone unnoticed. I think these qualities qualify you as the operative for this critical assignment. I chose you among others similarly adept because of my faith in your abilities plus your allegiance to me personally. Don't disappoint me."

"I offer my energy and my life to you and our cause, Great Leader."

"Well spoken, Ahmed. Facilitators along your journey will move you from this camp to a destination in the United States where you will lead a cell of men in an explosive event to terrorize the Great Satan's world. You and those other men will sacrifice your bodies, but your martyred names will touch all Muslim lips and assure your direct path into Paradise."

"I thank you and my ancestors thank you for this great honor to our humble name."

"Besides my detailed instructions, you must prepare to improvise if rocks block the path of your intended plans. You've demonstrated ability to invent new solutions while keeping your eye on the goal, leading us to believe you can handle this situation, however it unfolds. Life doesn't always follow our plans and, in the end, the only one truly in charge of what happens is Allah, bless His name."

"As always, Great Leader, you speak truth and wisdom."

"Good. Now here's what you will do..."

CHAPTER FOUR

THURSDAY, 10:41 AM

As the fire/rescue ambulance sped toward INOVA Fairfax Hospital, lead medic Lt. Nathan Sommer watched his team take turns administering CPR to an unresponsive Kirsten Donnegan. The EKG attached to her emitted a flat green line. Sommer knew bringing a patient back from this stage was next to impossible. He counted on CPR coaxing enough oxygenated blood to her brain to keep her alive until the hospital ER could attempt to restart her heart.

"Heads up," the driver announced; "five minutes out. You might want to call the ER."

"Thanks." Sommer dialed the hospital ER on his cell phone. The five-out call gave ER staff three time-saving pieces of information: treatment thus far given by EMS, update of the patient's current condition and their imminent arrival at the hospital.

When the ambulance raced up to the hospital's emergency entrance, Sommer jumped out to accompany Kirsten as other professionals arrived to rush her gurney inside. While the rest of his team stayed in their vehicle parked close by, he wouldn't give up, pumping her chest as the gurney rolled until ER personnel took over.

Inside the hospital he watched the Code Team take over and leap into action: intubation, IV drugs and continued CPR. A smile crossed Sommer's face when he heard the heart monitor begin to beep. The beeps rallied, sounding as if she'd make it. But then the steady beeps straggled unevenly and soon evolved into a monotone buzz. This dreaded sound, indicating flat-line pulmonary activity, launched more frantic measures to activate her heart...but without success.

At last, the attending physician stood back. He sighed, dejected at losing this battle. "Note the time of death," he said to a nurse in a barely audible exhale.

Sommer stood transfixed. Despite their training, modern equipment and his team's heroic efforts, their patient was gone. He knew they weren't to blame, but it always hurt and he was a poor loser.

He thought about what had transpired in this case. EMS never left a dying or newly deceased person at the incident location, in this case, Kirsten's house. They transported the patient to the nearest hospital ER. Important reasons justified this. They saved their share, but when they didn't, this action spared the family the traumatic moment of death. Also hospital staff could make the patient presentable before the family came to grieve. On-call grief counselors could assist, if needed.

But there was more. The ER doctor's staff could call the patient's personal physician to determine whether a death appeared natural. If so, the patient's doctor signed the death certificate. If not, they requested autopsy. For heart attacks absent heart-disease history, as in today's case, the radio dispatch Sommer made earlier to his headquarters would alert the EMS supervisor to consider sending a policeman to interview the family and neighbors.

As lead medic, Sommer felt responsibility for the outcome because he ran the calls. His years of experience and refresher training enabled him to quickly evaluate the big picture in each situation. He directed the unfolding second-to-second patient emergency, giving calm orders to the other techs. Every emergency call needed one person in charge to coordinate the team. His job: make quick but correct decisions, coordinate efficiency and move fast. Time was never on his side. He needed to stay hands-off to direct the call and record developments. For Sommer, letting other techs do the work was the hardest part. If the run was shorthanded, he relished the occasional chance to pitch in hands-on to save a life.

Sommer walked out of the ER toward the ambulance. He hated telling his crew their patient died. Sure, on the drive back to the station they would critique what took place. They always did, searching for insights from this experience to improve the next run. Today's by-the-book performance delivered their patient to the ER alive, suggesting a job well done. But as seen-it-all surgeons sometimes phrased it, "The operation was a success but the patient died."

He tried—his whole team tried—to leave disappointment at work when they went home. But the job rolled on... The sheer urgency of attempting to save lives during the next five calls would overshadow the memory of this loss and reset their resolve until the next successful rescue rebalanced the scale.

CHAPTER FIVE

THURSDAY, 10:57 AM

Jennifer comforted Tony at the hospital when they learned Kirsten's fate. Surprised that he seemed to handle this devastating situation better than she could, she dried her tears to phone Jason, explain the situation and ask him to meet them there. When he arrived at the ER, he found the two of them sitting, shoulders hunched, in a hospital room where Kirsten's body lay in a bed next to their chairs. Jason put a sympathetic hand on Tony's shoulder.

"She's gone, Jay..."

"We're here to help any way we can. Have you told your children?"

"Not yet...."

"Do you want us to drive you home where you can do that?"

"I guess that makes sense," Tony agreed.

"Jen, shall we both drive Tony home in my car and come back later for yours?"

"Absolutely."

Ten minutes later Jason drove while Jennifer sat with Tony in the back seat. She caressed his hand to comfort him and lend him her strength. Though silent, he seemed grateful. Tears dampened his face as he gave her what seemed grief-stricken looks but, except for a few ragged sighs, he controlled his emotions and squeezed her hand.

Jason noticed Adam Iverson's unmarked police car in front of Donnegans' house.

"That's right," Tony recalled, "the lieutenant said a supervisor or policeman might come by. Glad it's your son-in-law Adam."

"Hello, Sir." Adam shook Tony's hand. "I'm very sorry to hear about your loss."

"Thank you, Adam. When Kirsten and I attended your wedding a few months ago, I didn't imagine I'd see you next under these bizarre circumstances."

"Right, Sir. I know this timing isn't good, but could we talk for a few minutes about what happened so I can fill out a report?"

Tony frowned, contemplating him a long minute before deciding. "Sure, Adam. Come on inside. Your parents and I were about to call my kids. This won't take long, will it?"

"No, Sir, it won't," Adam assured as the two of them walked toward the Donnegan house.

Jason called after them, "Tony, when you finish, let us know if we can help."

When the Shannons entered their house, Jennifer hurried to answer the ringing phone.

"Hi, Mom. It's Hannah."

"Hello, Honey. What a nice surprise to hear from the little bride. Everything okay?"

"Oh, yes. Everything's wonderful. Sorry not to call oftener, but Adam and I are still so wrapped up in each other we haven't made much time for the other people we love."

"Not to worry. We all understand. But I'm afraid we have some bad news. Kirsten Donnegan collapsed and died this morning. We just saw Adam, who's across the street for a police report."

"Oh, Mom, I've known her since I was little. What a blow for their whole family. Was she sick?"

"No, very sudden and unexpected."

"How awful. I called to see if you and I could have lunch today. Are you up for that, given the situation? We could talk and you could fill me in about what happened to Mrs. D."

"Hang on a minute, Hannah." she turned to Jason. "Could you take the afternoon to help Tony but drop me at the restaurant beforehand so Hannah can take me by the hospital later to get my car?" He nodded. "Okay, lunch sounds great. How about Pulcinella at 12:30 if you don't mind dropping me by Fairfax Hospital afterward to pick up my car?"

"Glad to, Mom, and you picked a favorite restaurant. Just like old times. See you there."

"I'll make a reservation in case they're extra busy today. Love you, Sweetie."

"Love you, too, Mom."

Jennifer glanced at her watch. If she hurried she could dress quickly, meet her daughter on time, get her car and multi-task several errands afterward, including buying ingredients for the casserole dinner.

CHAPTER SIX

THURSDAY, NOON

When Jason returned from dropping Jennifer at Pulcinella, Adam knocked on the Shannons' door.

Jason invited him in. "Are you still on duty or would you like a beer?"

"I'm still on but thanks anyway. Post-rescue follow-up isn't my usual job, but I was headed this way anyhow and know the family so I volunteered. If you have a minute, could I ask you the same questions I did the other neighbors?"

"Sure, Adam, but what's this all about anyhow?"

"In cases like this, we try to rule out foul play while the deceased is still at the hospital—whether the death looked suspicious in some way. So, how long have you known the Donnegans?"

Jason did the math. "About twenty-one years."

"And during that time did you witness friction or violence between them?"

"Just the opposite. They're well-liked in the neighborhood and from everything we saw, devoted to their children and each other. He's also a respected member of the community. You probably know he owns a popular veterinary practice."

"That matches accounts from other neighbors. My last stop is Mr. Donnegan's office to talk with his staff. If that checks out, my work here is over."

"Any progress on developing the Yates property?"

Jason recalled walking some of the fifteen acres of valuable farmland located on the McLean/ Great Falls border, land that Adam had inherited from the Yates estate when he became the only surviving heir. During his first six years of life, when Adam was called Mathis Yates, his parents had abused him and his younger brother, Ruger. Jason understood that Adam's emotional survival of these horrific childhood experiences required him to totally repress those early years.

"That's just what I wanted to speak with you about. We have impressive offers from two developers. We're studying them to make the best choice. Both allow us to subdivide the property but still keep one terrific lot for building our own house.

"Good for you, Adam. Take your time. Choose well."

"Would you give us your opinion about our finalist? We'll also ask my other new dad for his input. With so much at stake, we want to pick the best option."

The "other new dad," Jason knew, referred to lawyer Greg Bromley. Greg's youthful romance thirty-five years earlier with Adam's mother, Wendey, had produced an unwed pregnancy she feared would ruin Greg's budding law career. To protect him, Wendey had eloped in a loveless marriage with Tobias Yates. She'd discovered too late that her husband was an abusive monster who, for years, terrorized her and the two hapless children.

"Of course, we'll share our knowledge and experience," Jason assured him. "I can look at your project as an engineer and Greg can as an attorney."

Adam smiled in gratitude at his new father-in-law. "Thanks, Sir...er, Dad."

"You're welcome, Son." After farewells, Adam left.

I like that young man, Jason thought. He and Hannah make a fine young couple even though each brings some baggage to their relationship. Hannah needs to trust men again after ex-boyfriend Kevin broke her heart with his cheating, and Adam must face his awful childhood trauma if and when it surfaces.

He hoped their marriage would survive whatever lay ahead.

CHAPTER SEVEN

THURSDAY, 12:33 PM

Hannah's reference to "old times" at this restaurant conjured Jennifer's memories of family meals there before their children grew up to lead their own lives. At a Shannon son's wedding rehearsal dinner in the Pulcinella party room, the owner's gifted friend, operatic tenor Antonio Salvatore, had provided the evening's entertainment. Not everyone received such treatment. They were truly blessed.

As Jennifer pushed open the restaurant's heavy front door, one of the owners hurried to greet her.

"Mrs. Shannon, good to see you again! Your daughter is at your favorite table by the windows."

"Thank you, Moe. We're looking forward to a wonderful meal, as usual."

As they approached the table, Hannah jumped up to hug her mother.

"So glad you thought of this, Hannah," Jennifer said as Moe seated her and moved away. "Is our little bride still a happy girl?"

Hannah beamed. "Oh yes, Mom. It's almost embarrassing how much Adam and I are in love."

"Wonderful. So if you're a happy girl, you must want to talk about something else."

"Yes, but first, what happened to Mrs. D this morning?"

Jennifer told her the whole story and they shared dismay at Kirsten's passing.

Finally Jennifer asked, "So why did you suggest lunch together today?"

"You know we live in Adam's bachelor apartment, the one attached to his mother's house. It's private and in a good neighborhood close to downtown McLean, so it offers many advantages. But from the start we thought it temporary until we found our own place."

"Does this mean you're house-hunting?"

"We want to stay in the McLean area. We both grew up here, Adam's police work is here, both our families live here. My last year of college at George Mason is nearby. But what real estate agents call 'upscale, affordable McLean' may be upscale but it isn't affordable, at least for us just starting out. Rents are steep. Buying is out of the question. For our budget, prices are astronomical. So Adam's decided to subdivide and sell some of his inherited property on Winding Trail Road. His new dad, Greg Bromley, helped him start a corporation to offer the land without revealing Adam's name. Developers drool over such prime real estate between McLean and Great Falls. When he sells it, we'll have money to buy or build our own house."

"That makes financial sense."

"True. So we visited the old farm to evaluate the situation. Mom, it's beautiful and peaceful there. Unlike downtown McLean where we live now, it's fresh and open—like countryside. You know how I've loved nature since childhood. This place has unusual birds and wildflowers. At night, away from the lights of town, the sky is filled with stars. We both love the location."

Hannah's obvious excitement touched Jennifer. She remembered early days when she and Jason had viewed the world and their life in it with just such idyllic eyes. Anything you wanted enough and worked together to achieve seemed doable when you combined energies with this incredible person you loved so much. She smiled, encouraging Hannah to continue.

"We talked with a developer who showed us how the fifteen acres could be divided into six two-acre lots and one three-acre. He suggested we keep the bigger piece for building our own house one day. According to him, our three acres and new house would be on the choicest part, which happens to be the site of the old Yates house where Ruger lived as a child."

"Oh?" Jennifer tried to hide sudden discomfort. Was Hannah's failure to mention that Mathis also lived his early years there a glaring oversight?

"Yes, because the land slopes in such a way that if we build near the top we'll have gorgeous views in several directions and good water run-off. Adam's already knocked down most of those old weathered sheds except for the barn and hen house."

Frightening images of the old house swam into Jennifer's mind. The awful place where many had suffered and she'd expected to die after her capture. With conscious effort, she changed the subject. "After college graduation will you job hunt?"

"Yes, I'd like one in the McLean/Tyson areas so we'll both live close to work. That's part of the new 'green' strategy. Rather than gas-guzzling, time-wasting, environment-polluting killer commutes, my generation hopes to work near home."

"Commendable. So you've prepared a resume?"

"Not yet. My income isn't needed at the moment, and I want time to work on our other plan."

"...your other plan?"

"Mom, we're going to move into the old Yates family house on the property. We'll be on scene to make important decisions about where to build the new house before Adam decides which acreage to sell. We need that clearly in mind before he signs with a developer. Since Adam already owns the land, the price is right. We'd have all the benefits of the McLean and Great Falls communities but could still raise a few chickens, plant a garden and eat organic vegetables we grow ourselves. Control over food quality is important because we think the toxic stuff sprayed on plants and fruit bought in groceries explains a lot of illnesses and diseases. We could create our own special world. We're so excited, Mom. It's a dream we can make come true."

Jennifer felt as if she'd been punched. Her daughter and Adam in that wretched house of horrors day after day, week after week?

Hannah paused her animated chat, fork in midair, to stare at her mother. "Mom, what's wrong?"

"I agree with everything you said about food quality—even though you didn't warn me you were stepping on your soapbox." She tried a nervous laugh then looked directly at her daughter. "I'm just trying to absorb this...this.... You...you're not concerned about living in a place where such dreadful things happened generation after generation?"

"Mom, you of all people don't believe in haunted houses. It's just an inanimate building—walls and a roof—with no control over who lived there or how they behaved. It isn't infected with poison. We'd get rid of *everything* inside, which is right up your alley because we'd want to have a huge garage sale and then refill the house with quality second-hand furniture."

Jennifer drew a sharp breath. Should she share her apprehension with this daughter so focused upon a single course of action? What was her responsibility here? Each person deserved freedom to make decisions and learn from mistakes. But informed decisions stood the better chance of success. Shouldn't a parent try to spare his child pain or danger when possible? The more puzzle pieces Hannah had, the clearer picture she could make.

To avoid Hannah's needing to repent later, shouldn't someone warn her before she plunged ahead?

CHAPTER EIGHT

THURSDAY, 1:07 PM

L ooking across the table at her daughter, Jennifer wondered how best to explain her concerns. She composed words in her head then blurted them before she changed her mind. "You're right, Hannah, a house is an inanimate building. But this isn't just any old house. It's where Adam, your husband, endured terrible abuse for the first six years of his life."

"Good second-hand furniture makes sense since we only expect to stay a few months. You and I could have fun giving a big garage sale to get rid of what's there and afterward shop together for replacements. Our tastes differ, which is normal for different generations, but you know all the resources, and I can make the selections. And if Adam goes to law school as his new dad suggested, we'd live on my new job's income until the other acres sell."

Jennifer stared at her daughter. Had Hannah missed what she said about Adam's torture at the house or chosen to ignore it? She thought about Ruger's experience at the farm. Did his similar plan to start a new life there prompt him to comb local garage sales to replace his hated mother's belongings? If so, his plan didn't work. Purging the house didn't purge its horror for him.

How could she share this connection and her resulting uneasiness with Hannah? She reached across the table, touched her daughter's hand and looked directly into her eyes. "Honey, didn't Adam tell us repressing those awful childhood memories allowed him to move forward and develop into the balanced person he is? What if living in the house reawakens those torturous memories? Doesn't 'repressed' mean the experiences still exist, just buried deep in his mind until something jars them out?"

Hannah's gaze dropped to focus on her plate. A tear spilled from the corner of one eye. "Oh, Mom, I don't want anything to threaten our happiness together, especially a risk we take voluntarily. Adam and I talked about this, and he's convinced bad vibes from the past can't change the person he is now. I'm nervous because I don't want anything to hurt someone I love, but he thinks our plan is logical and practical. He thinks country living would be fun and eco-sound. I admit that the idea of using the old house startled me at first, but I'm not the bold visionary he is and, of course, I want to support his ideas. At best, the plan seems like a harmless, quaint way to spend a few months in a beautiful country setting."

"But..."

"...but frankly, Mom, I'm nervous about anything that might threaten our life together."

Moe reappeared. "Dessert for you ladies today?" They shook their heads and Jennifer produced a credit card from her purse.

"Oh, Mom, what should I do?"

"Honey, this is one of those dilemmas life keeps handing out. You make the best decision by learning as much as possible about the situation. Sometimes you get it right, sometimes you don't. If you don't, you try again."

"You're not going to tell me what to do, are you?"

"Of course not, Honey. This is your life. But I'm glad you're not overlooking anything affecting your best choice. And here's an idea that might influence your decision."

Hannah's eyes widened. "What?"

"A house safety inspection. You'd want one if you bought a house. They only cost a few hundred dollars. The inspection checks the electrical system, plumbing, foundation, roof, chimneys, drainage, HVAC and water heater; even radon gas and carbon monoxide. A farm's tests should also include well water and septic tank."

"Adam told me Greg Bromley—I still have a hard time calling him 'Dad'—advised him not to invest in structural repairs since the old house will be torn down for rebuilding. So if it isn't safe, I can't imagine Adam would want us to live there."

"Well, there you go."

"Oh, Mom, thanks. And by the way, guess what?" Hannah flashed her winning smile.

"I give up."

"Adam took me to a shooting range to learn to fire weapons. Police work teaches every person should know how to defend himself, so it's a sensible skill to learn. He thinks isolated living on the fifteen acres means I should know how to protect myself if it's ever necessary. Turns out I'm a pretty good shot with a pistol." She groped in her purse, withdrew and unrolled a target showing a silhouetted human form perforated with holes centered about the head and chest.

Jennifer remembered Hannah as a little girl, holding up her latest proud triumph: a Girl Scout badge, a report card with straight A's, a tennis trophy...and now this.

"Impressive, Hannah. What a many-talented gal you are!"

She grinned at her mother's approval. "Before we go, I almost forgot to ask—any family news?"

Jennifer thought. "Your sister Becca comes home from Virginia Tech for Thanksgiving break on Saturday. She invited Tina McKenzie to join us for the family event on Thursday."

"How's Tina recovering after her awful experience with Ruger Yates?"

"Plastic surgery repaired her outer wounds and counseling's working on her inner ones. I guess we'll learn more when we see her at Thanksgiving."

"And my siblings?"

"Kaela and Owain are about to take a needed business-and-pleasure long weekend get-away. Guess who's babysitting their three kiddos while they're gone?

"Mom, you're a saint."

"Back to Thanksgiving, Dylan's family and four kiddies are coming as well as Mike and Bethany. And we've invited Adam's mother, Sally Iverson, and his new dad, Greg Bromley. And, of course, we'll extend an invitation to poor Tony Donnegan. How about you and Adam?"

"Absolutely. What can we bring?"

"Appreciate the offer, Honey, but if I shop for one item I might as well get them all. One of these days, I may ask you children to take over, but not yet. Coming home should be a relaxing treat for you with your busy lives."

"Mom, you make coming home something very special." She stood and hugged her mom. "Now, let's go get your car."

They left the restaurant arm in arm.

CHAPTER NINE

THURSDAY, 2:32 PM

Dressed in shabby, filthy clothes, Ahmed accepted exhaustion from the tormenting hardships along the way. He balanced it with the exhilarating thought that he'd reach his final destination *today*.

The difficulties during these past dangerous, miserable months swam through his mind as he recalled how one designated accomplice after another handed him off to the next, moving him invisibly from the Middle-East toward his pre-arranged destination in North America.

Before leaving his country, he'd felt a surprising personal hesitation when the Great Leader ordered him to shave his luxuriant natural beard and crop his hair. He understood the need to disguise identifiable Middle-Eastern characteristics for this mission. Compared to the excruciating training to endure torture if captured, this simple cosmetic gesture was nothing. Yet, relinquishing this cultural sign of masculinity dismayed him even though he admitted sadly that Allah's path for him excluded any expectation of a woman in his life. He needed no handsome beard to signal his maleness.

Still, he needed respect among his male peers with whom the beard showed both his dedication to Allah and his virility. Fortunately, he'd been told to wait until the night before departing on his mission to remove his beard. The further he traveled from his homeland, the less this lack of facial hair set him apart from others.

Instructions to let the beard stubble reappear while he traveled to the U.S.A. created an unkempt-look which, together with his dirty, worn travel clothes, achieved a decrepit appearance signaling potential human predators this wasn't a man worth harassing. Tolerating the filth served its critical purpose even though Ahmed's religion reinforced his personal preference for cleanliness. He chafed at this disgusting daily desecration, although the ruse served his mission well.

First a series of small boats, then freighters, moved him down waterways from the Gulf of Aden through the Red Sea to the Mediterranean. Then a particularly uncomfortable cargo ship tossed him mercilessly for too many days across a stormy Atlantic. He ventured out only at night in seasick desperation from his sequestered, claustrophobic cabin.

At last the vessel entered the Gulf of Mexico, depositing him at a port where others removed him from the ship in a cargo box they conveyed to a warehouse. More facilitators moved him in a series of clunker vehicles across scorching Mexican wasteland. They delivered him to a coyote who prodded him through a rancid, decaying, rat-filled tunnel beneath the U.S. border into Texas.

Once he was delivered inside the Texas line, others picked him up and drove him to a seedy motel where he showered away the travel stench in a cleansing lasting until the shower's cascading hot water ran cold. He winced at again donning the filthy clothes, but with only days to his destination, he had forced himself. Their critical importance to his larger objective meant under no circumstances could he leave these clothes behind. The safest way not to lose them was to wear them.

A variety of trucks and cars drove him for days on end through Louisiana, Mississippi, Alabama, Georgia, the Carolinas and into Virginia. Every step along the way pointed him toward a certain house in a certain town where he would carry out his destructive mission, and, praise be to Allah, he would reach that destination before this day ended.

When the panel truck in which he rode the last stretch stopped for fuel, he shaved away his beard stubble at the gas station's restroom sink, washed his hair and cleaned his face, neck and armpits with damp paper towels. Later, hidden from view in the back of the panel truck, he changed into clean clothes after carefully placing his worn travel garments in his suitcase.

To prevent this driver from knowing his final destination, the truck dropped him in front of the McLean Safeway store, where he phoned his host to pick him up.

CHAPTER TEN

THURSDAY, 4:02 PM

Jennifer returned from lunch to find Jason at home. "How's Tony doing?"

"Rough afternoon. Telling his kids was hard. I overheard their reactions to their mother's death on the speaker phone. Heart-breaking, Jen! Then we called funeral homes and picked one. He wants a small funeral, family only, but you have to jump through most of the same hoops as if it were public. The funeral director's a pro, with lists of what needs to happen."

"Like?"

"Like writing her obituary and deciding which newspapers should print it, asking someone to give a eulogy at the service, picking a casket and selecting a cemetery or columbarium. Then planning the church service, musician and a reception for mourners there afterward. They'll make a slide show — with today's technology, it'll be a Powerpoint — of Kirsten's life with any photos he gathers. I'll help him when he and the kids work on that tomorrow. This afternoon at 3:30 we meet his pastor to make church arrangements. What a grim education, Jen. This convinces me we should work out a lot of this in advance so our kids — or whichever one of us is left — won't need to wade through it while confused and grieving."

"Okay, it's on our to-do list. By the way, what's a columbarium?"

"A place to store a deceased person's ashes. Tony's having Kirsten cremated." At his wife's stricken expression, he added, "What's wrong?"

His words stunned her. "But that's impossible. She and I talked about this just a few weeks ago. Neither of us wanted cremation. How could he not know that about his own wife? You know exactly what I want."

"True, because we talked about this when my parents died, but maybe they didn't."

Kirsten's voice echoed in Jennifer's ears: "Burial is definitely my choice. I shudder at the idea of cremation. If you have a preference, Jen, tell Jason now so he'll know what you want. Tony knows exactly how I feel about it."

Surely Tony wouldn't ignore Kirsten's wish unless...unless he had a reason? But what? A crime needed motive, method and opportunity. Sure, spouses had opportunity because they lived together. But absent motive and method, scratch opportunity. Why in the world would Tony want Kirsten dead? Could their behind-the-scenes life differ that much from the façade they presented?

Without a body, Jennifer realized, nobody could investigate external evidence like bruising or internal evidence like poison. EMS techs might not see signs of trauma because they saw Kirsten clothed except for her chest, but hospital ER crews had a full-body view.

Then she chastised herself. What kind of disloyal tangent was this? Both Donnegans were long-time, trusted neighbors and friends.

Jason tapped her on the arm. "Jen, you have that thinking-look, a look that makes me uneasy."

"Jay, he's making a terrible mistake." She picked up the phone. "I need to set him straight."

Jason gently eased the phone from her hand and put an arm around her shoulder. "Honey, it's too late. The funeral home cremated her thirty minutes ago."

A tear spilled onto her cheek. "How could he? Why would he? Something's wrong. She told me they discussed this. He wanted cremation but she didn't. What's going on here, Jay?"

"Look, I don't know the answer. Maybe she thought they discussed it but they didn't? Or she said it but he didn't hear it. Or he's so upset and confused with her sudden death he forgot that conversation? Or he accidentally checked the wrong box on the form at the funeral home? Whatever the explanation, it's over, Jen. There's no undoing it. Should you torture him with recrimination by telling him he made a terrible mistake or should you let it go?"

"Oh, Kirsten, I'm so sorry this happened to you," Jennifer whispered to her departed friend.

"Jen, Kirsten's problems are over. She's gone. Does it matter now what happens to her remains?"

"It's not right. When we make our funeral plans in advance the way you suggested, let's write it all down. Please promise me you'll respect my wishes."

"Honey, you know I will. We trust each other. We love each other. You'll follow my choices and I absolutely promise to follow yours. Now, let's dry those tears and think good thoughts."

She sniffled but changed the subject. "I guess you're right." She busied herself in the kitchen. "By the way, I rushed off early to the estate sale and only scanned the classified ads. Any big news in the morning newspaper?"

"Mainly more terrorism attacks around the world, mostly the Middle-East and Europe this week. At least the powder keg hasn't exploded in the U.S. again since 9/11. McLean's probably one of the safest places around, with the CIA and Homeland Security right here."

He thought a moment before adding silently to himself, or the most dangerous....

CHAPTER ELEVEN

THURSDAY, 4:16 PM

Still uneasy about Kirsten's cremation, Jennifer tried to shift focus. She scanned *The Washington Post* Jason handed her and picked up on his comment about terrorists attacks. "Why don't Muslims follow their religion and just let others do the same?"

"Some do, but it seems to me every religion's fundamentalists concentrate on the word rather than the spirit. In poor, desperate and illiterate populations, the masses are easily guided by whoever interprets holy writings for them. Islam has no corner on that. Fundamentalists tend to be fanatics or extremists, convinced that if they're right, everyone else is wrong. They see a them/us power struggle ending in a mandate to convert or dispose of *them*. Without separation of church and state, religious brainwashing starting with toddlers is reinforced by their churches or mosques, schools, government and social culture. They know nothing else."

He paused, noted his wife was still listening intently—a behavior he counted on—then finished offering his perspective. "For Muslim fundamentalists, even questioning Islam is severely punishable blasphemy. Without exposure to other ideas, their way seems the only way. You're a believer or a non-believer, no in-between categories. And this isn't even original. Remember the Salem witch hunts? Remember the Inquisition?"

"But Jay, you said yourself, Islam isn't *all* radicals. When radicals come to this country, aren't they exposed at last to new ideas? How can they miss other ways of thinking and acting?"

"Don't oversimplify, Jen. Even in the U.S., where citizens can read anything they like, attend any church they wish and question all religions, many stick with their original religious exposure from the cradle to the grave. Their parents' religious values influence them even if they question them later. Imagine growing up where church and state are combined. To draw a group even closer together it's handy to invent a scapegoat to hate, some guilty person or group who deserve loathing. You see that at work even in sports where the other team's athletes are the 'bad guys.' Right now the Jews, Americans and British fill this need for radical Muslims. Even if we understand how radicals get that way, we can't allow them to murder the opposition to further their cause."

"You're right, Jay. I love how you always think these things through." She changed the subject. "By the way, please tell Tony I'm bringing dinner tonight. I feel so sad for them. When his children go back to their own worlds after the funeral, he'll live all alone in a big empty house. How will he do it? Jay, I can't imagine life without you."

Jason walked over and pulled her into his arms. "Jen," he soothed, "Kirsten would appreciate what a true friend of hers you are to help Tony. You got him through the emergency room ordeal, and you'll watch out for him in the weeks ahead. Of course, you're affected by what's happened; you've been an integral part of it. We both have." He kissed the top of her head. "We have lots of wonderful years ahead of us." He sang a few bars of "Don't worry, be happy" accompanying the lyrics with uncoordinated, off-beat body sways.

His antics made her smile. She hugged him close. "Thanks, Jay, for understanding."

"Hey, isn't that what we do for each other?"

"Do you want me to come along to help plan the church service?"

"No, I think we can handle it. His kids arrive this afternoon, and they want to be together as a family tonight. Speaking of family, what did Hannah want at lunch today?"

"She and Adam are moving into the old Yates house while they subdivide his property." Jennifer explained her concerns and her home-inspection advice.

"Well, they're young and eager..." he said with a far-away look.

"...and idealistic, imagining nothing could change their happiness."

"We can relate to that, can't we?" he chuckled. "Well, maybe not the young part any more..."

She nodded, thinking of Kirsten: warm and lively one minute, cold and dead the next. "We better value each moment and people precious to us. Like you, dear Jay."

He chuckled. "I love you too, Jen. Nobody gets more out of the moments we're on earth than you. You hit the floor running every day."

"Are you up for dinner at Kazan tonight?"

"I'll be more than ready for a pleasant evening by then. Turkish food sounds just right. I hope Zaynel is serving my favorite doner kebab tonight." He looked at his watch. "Well, gotta go get Tony." She waved as he closed the front door behind him.

Jennifer sat still, thinking about their conversation. Her mind wandered back to the Donnegans. Was Tony's decision to cremate Kirsten accidental, as Jason suggested, or deliberate? If deliberate, what could he possibly need to hide?

CHAPTER TWELVE

THURSDAY, 4:39 PM

A few minutes later Jennifer stepped onto her front porch, waving as Jason and Tony pulled away in her husband's car. She inhaled the warmth of this rare summery November day. Looking across at Donnegans' house, she wondered which of Kirsten's children owned the unfamiliar car parked in his driveway. From years as neighbors, she knew the children. Should she sympathize now or let them marshal energy for the ordeals ahead? She'd wait until she took dinner over later.

Not a thoroughfare, their cul-de-sac drew few cars other than residents', but nice days like this invited foot traffic. A man walked a dog around the circle, saying "hello" as he passed. A child whizzed by on a skateboard. A jogger raised a hand of greeting as he huffed around the sidewalk.

Along the front yard's wrought-iron fence, she spotted several dead, scruffy plants, an eyesore in an otherwise tidy yard. Why not take a few minutes to cut them back? She got garden gloves and plant scissors from the garage and knelt, snipping the spent stalks. Focused on clipping, she jumped when a deep male voice said, "Hello, Jennifer. You seem busy."

She looked up to see a neighbor who lived a few blocks away. He regularly walked this route, and they often chatted over-the-fence when she was outside as he strolled past. They'd exchanged names, as casually-meeting neighbors do. She stood to greet him. "Why, hello, Larry. Thank goodness you happened by. My old bones don't kneel very long any more."

He laughed. "With old bones myself, I sympathize. What a perfect fall day for a walk—so warm, so beautiful. And how are you. Jennifer?"

"I'm well, but do you know the Donnegans across the street?" He did, explaining Tony was their cat's vet. Jennifer told him about Kirsten and he spoke of his own experience with families at his temple who had lost loved ones.

"So you're Jewish?" He nodded. On impulse she said, "Good. Then maybe you could help me better understand this old hatred between Arabs and Jews. Jason and I were talking about it earlier, and I have to admit more ignorance about all this than makes me comfortable."

"I'll help if I can."

Jennifer put down her gloves and shears and leaned against the fence. "The media describe terrorism escalating in the Middle-East, and 'Arab Spring' hasn't turned out the way our country hoped it might. Iran's involved through Hezbollah and they're Persian. If any of them plays a nuclear card, the world's at risk. Do you know how this ancient Arab/Jew feud began?"

"A very weighty subject, but I can tell you what I know."

"Thank you. Shall we sit on the front porch to talk? May I offer cookies, coffee, soda or wine?"

Larry chuckled. "You've made an offer I can't refuse. And I'm not even Italian." They laughed as he settled himself on a porch chair.

"What would you like?"

"A glass of water would be fine," he said.

She returned with water and brownies for them both. Jennifer told him what went through her mind as she'd pruned bushes.

"To outsiders, Arabs and Jews appear more alike than different. They share the same genetic origins in the same part of the world with similar traditions and culture. Both Muslims and Orthodox Jews separate men and women at social or religious gatherings, and the women cover their hair with scarves. Both groups practice circumcision. Neither group eats pork. They share many holy places. Why not brotherly comrades instead of arch enemies?"

Larry gave a wry laugh. "Well, don't forget real brothers often fight. Remember Cain and Abel? But some biblical history might help answer your question. Judaism was well established for several thousand years before Jesus came onto the scene. After that, Muhammad gave birth to Islam in 610 CE in Saudi Arabia. He wrote down religious wisdom he said he received from Allah, the one God. He drew heavily upon Jewish tradition, which he interpreted and modified from Torah stories for use in his Quran. The one-god idea was already a pivotal Jewish concept, though ours wasn't named Allah. One important biblical story Muhammad changed concerns Abraham, a patriarch acknowledged by both Jews and Muslims, who called him 'Ibrahim.'

"The Holy Scripture describes Abraham as an obedient man of great faith who talked often with God. God told Abraham he would be the father of many nations. This seemed unlikely since he and his wife, Sarah, who Muslims call Sarai, were old, well beyond child-bearing years. But with this prophecy in mind, his barren wife Sarah offered Abraham her Egyptian serving girl, Hagar—Muslims call her Hajar—saying, 'Consort with my maid; perhaps I shall have a son through her.' We might view this now as an ancient surrogate pregnancy."

"Isn't the Abraham story from the Book of Genesis?" Jen asked.

Larry nodded. "Yes. It's the first book of the Torah as well as what Christians call the Old Testament. Hagar, so the story goes, had no choice in this and when she conceived she despised Sarah. Jealous of Hagar even though this was her own idea, Sarah got Abraham's permission to punish her maidservant. When she did, Hagar ran away from her mistress into the wilderness. An angel found her by a stream and asked why she was there. Hagar explained. The angel told her to return to her mistress and submit to punishment, for she would bear eighty-six-year-old Abraham a son and name him Ishmael. The angel said this son's descendants would multiply until there were too many to count. So Hagar returned, took the punishment and bore a son. When Ishmael was thirteen years old, God told Abraham to circumcise all males in his household to show their covenant with God. So, ninety-nine-year-old Abraham followed this instruction, which included himself and his son Ishmael."

"Ouch!" Jennifer cringed. "This must have seemed an extraordinary demand."

"Yes, but Abraham obeyed, as always. Then God told Abraham his wife would bear a son to be named Isaac, so when Ishmael was fourteen years old, Abraham 100 and Sarah ninety, she had her first baby and named him Isaac. They circumcised him at eight-days old, per the covenant with God. When Isaac was weaned, Abraham threw a celebration feast. At this event Sarah noticed Hagar scoffing at this favoring of Isaac over Ishmael. You see, no such party happened for *her* son although born first. Jealous again, Sarah asked Abraham to 'cast out this bondswoman and her son; for the son of this bondswoman shall not be heir with my son Isaac.' Upset about this, Abraham consulted God, who said to go along with Sarah's wishes, for God would make nations from both these sons. So next morning, Abraham gave Hagar food and a skin of water and sent her with Ishmael into the wilderness."

"Not too different from today's soap opera tales, is it?"

"No, but this story isn't over. Hagar wandered the desert of Beersheba until her food and water ran out. Resigned to death, she shaded her dying son under a shrub. She walked away — to avoid seeing him perish — and wept. But God heard her son's cries and sent an angel to Hagar saying God would make a well of water to save and protect the boy for his future. They lived in the wilderness until the boy grew up and eventually married an Egyptian wife Hagar found for him."

"A happy ending, then?"

"Not yet. Before Hagar and Ishmael were kicked out, God tested Abraham's faith with another startling order: to sacrifice his son as a burnt offering to God. Muslims and Jews agree about this event but not about which son he tied down on the sacrificial rock. As Abraham raised his knife to obey God by killing his son before lighting the sacrificial fire, a ram caught his horns in a nearby bush. God said to sacrifice the ram instead of the son. Abraham had again proved his faith. God promised to multiply this son's descendants 'as numerous as the stars in the sky and the sand on the seashore.' He added other special blessings. But was this nearly-sacrificed son Isaac, as the Jews record in the Torah, or Ishmael, as Muslims claim in Muhammad's Quran modification?"

"I see the problem. Were these Abraham's only sons?" Jennifer asked.

"He fathered more children, but these two 'first' sons create the schism between Judaism and Islam. Biblical scholars disagree about some ancient writings and what they really mean. Some think them more legend than gospel. Sumerian rules of succession at the time apparently upheld the rank of a son born to a first wife as greater for inheritance than a son born to a second wife or concubine. Sumerians also upheld that a child born to a relative of the man ranked higher than to a non-relative. Some scholars think Sarah was Abraham's half-sister, which would give Isaac the birthright no matter if Ishmael was born first. Others think 'sister' is a generic term in that culture for any female relatives. Then Muslims point out God said elsewhere that marrying a sister was an abomination, making Ishmael the rightful heir, so even more confusion."

Jennifer nodded. "I see. Three great monotheistic religious nations sprang from Abraham just as prophesied. Judiasm through Isaac in Torah, Christianity through the Jewish prophet named Jesus in the New Testament, and Islam via the Prophet Muhammad's Quran version of Ishmael's Arab branch."

"Yes. Once Muhammad reinterpreted Abraham's story, Muslims hated Jews for their cruel treatment of Hagar and her son Ishmael. Both were significant figures in their religion. But don't forget that geo-political reasons also play strategic roles, compounded by ethnic and religious differences. Consider, as part of the picture, that current uprisings in the Arab world are not about scriptures but about land, politics and economics plus Islamic opposition to Westernization. Similarly, the nation of Israel isn't biblically driven at this point but fighting for survival. It no longer boils down to just a theological debate."

Jennifer shifted in her chair. "Taking-what-you-have-that-I-want is as old as the caveman who found death a quick, permanent solution for anyone disagreeing with him. And he could steal his victim's property afterward as further incentive."

"Religious zeal and a God's presumed blessing to take-what-you-want, destroy-all-who-disagree, avenge-past-injustice — real or imagined — and blame scapegoats... All this nourishes a recipe for terrorism. Rewards with virgins in paradise and awed respect for martyrs on earth further this madness. Islam is not only a religion but an entire social, political, cultural, legal and military ideology."

"What happened to 'live-and-let-live'?" Jennifer asked.

"Ah, that's the real puzzle. But how can we 'get along' with radicals single-mindedly focused on destroying Israel and, now, western cultures of Europe and America?"

They pondered this question silently. Jennifer sighed. "Larry, I'm impressed by your knowledge. You've given me new insights. Thanks for taking time from your walk to tell me about this."

"My pleasure." He stood, eyeing the last brownie.

"Please take this for the walk home," Jennifer urged. "By the way, I'm curious. How do you happen to know so much about this subject?"

"Well, it just so happens that at the Reform temple I mentioned, I'm the rabbi."

CHAPTER THIRTEEN

THURSDAY, ALMOST MIDNIGHT

A hmed bolted upright in bed. Sweat dampened his body and the sheets on which he slept. His frightened eyes swept the room until he realized the horrific memory of his parents' deaths before his eyes was the painful recurring dream. Distant in both time and location from that experience thirty years ago in the Middle East, he slept tonight in a house in McLean, Virginia.

A glance at the clock confirmed he'd wakened in the middle of the night. He shook his head with grief at his father's execution, his mother's adored but deathly-still face and the murdered infant. Would he ever purge these ghastly childhood images? Yet, didn't their murders provide the root cause for his sitting tonight in McLean: avenging their undeserved deaths as his mother wished?

He turned on the bedside lamp, shuffled to the bathroom and doused his face at the sink. Filling a glass with water, he sank into the upholstered armchair, drained the glass and looked around the room he'd first entered this afternoon. A wallpaper border of animals circled the wainscoting, suggesting a child used this room previously. When he'd shoved his battered suitcase into the closet earlier tonight, a box of toys pushed to one end confirmed that theory.

Smaller than numerous mansions he'd driven past to reach this McLean neighborhood, this house fit well into its surrounding residential development. Though modest by McLean standards, it contrasted grandly with his simple accommodations in the country he'd left only months ago.

Mahmud, his host, welcomed him warmly at the Safeway this afternoon. "Your room will be cleaned daily, your laundry washed and your meals prepared. Eat with my family or in your room." Due to fatigue this first night, he chose the latter and settled into his new, final abode.

Now at his McLean destination, he'd start the long-awaited action. Mahmud, and other "sleeper" comrades placed here decades earlier, had assimilated into this community to await their destiny—and now that time had arrived.

"Have you mail for me?" Ahmed asked his host upon arrival and was handed two letters and a package. All were addressed to Tom Johnson in care of Mahmud's McLean address. In his room Ahmed opened the box containing the promised thirteen untraceable cellphones. With one he'd communicate only with the Great Leader. Cell members would get ten, he the eleventh and an extra. The package came from Dearborn, Michigan, one letter from Columbus, Ohio, and the other from New York City. With trembling hand, he opened the two letters. They divided the list of the local sleepers' names and contact data. None knew each other until Ahmed assembled them. If compromised, this ensured no one learned all from one envelope and only "invisible" Ahmed knew how these cell members fit a larger plan.

He phoned Abdul first. Although the man didn't know it yet, their first meeting would take place at his warehouse tomorrow. Abdul must scramble to clear out employees for this secret session. Once Ahmed established this gathering's location, he phoned the other names on the list, again using the special code word to ensure their attention.

"Our friend Scarab asked me to contact you..." He waited while this profound information registered before adding, "about a meeting tomorrow morning at 9:00 at this address—he read Abdul's warehouse location. "Scarab wants to know you will attend."

"Yes," they all responded with surprise but no hesitation. Finishing the nine calls, he relaxed.

Ahmed's plot to glorify Allah, peace be upon Him, would unfold at their target. He'd perish while striking the Unbelievers with his lethal sword. This room, then, was his last earthly home.

The clock read 12:08. Though he needed sleep after his arduous two-month trek over sea and land, the upsetting nightmare had jolted him wide awake. So be it—a good time to hide the entrusted treasure he guarded with his life during each leg of his perilous journey to McLean.

But where?

He studied the room. He could tape the packets to the back of the dresser or behind the bed's headboard, both too heavy to move during routine cleaning. He could pull up a carpet edge, flatten the packets, tuck them beneath and re-attach the rug to the existing tack strip. He could tape them under a drawer, not noticeable unless one lay on the floor to look upward from directly beneath the pulled out drawer. He opened the closet door. His gaze fell upon the box of toys. He pulled it into the room and, given the hour, quietly emptied the contents onto the carpet.

Unfamiliar with American playthings, he gasped at a nude Barbie doll tumbling from the box along with her toy furniture and clothes. Did American boys look at such dolls? Is that how their irreverence for women began? Or was his host's child a daughter? He reached for a second doll, this one dressed in simple Middle-Eastern clothing. He studied its wisp of black hair mostly hidden by the hijab, its dark eyes and soft cloth body. The sight of this toy ignited a nearly lost childhood memory of his twin sister playing with a doll remarkably similar. She visited a cousin that terrible day in his homeland, sparing her the grisly killing scenes he witnessed, scenes still haunting his dreams. When she left home that morning, he had no idea he'd never see her again, but the sight of this doll evoked an instant connection with her. Had she survived? If so, where was she now?

His mother's last words echoed in his mind, foretelling Allah's guidance in his life. "Look for his signs." Had she predicted his Allah-directed rescue by the two men following his parents' brutal murder by depraved American Jews? Had Allah guided his placement at the madrassa by those two men, his graduation to combat training at the tough Yemeni military camp, his selection by the mullah for schooling in the English language and, later, elite special-forces school? And was Allah's final gift the Great Leader's selecting Ahmed to lead this suicide mission?

Was tonight's frightening nightmare of his childhood, followed by the poignant discovery of this doll from the past at the moment he sought his treasure's hiding place, an accident or an omen?

He examined the doll with new interest, opening its clothes for closer inspection of the cloth body beneath. Yes, he could slice open the fabric, remove some stuffing, hide the packets, cover them with a piece of the batten, stitch the cloth together again and replace the clothes to disguise the surgery. Then he would place the doll out of reach behind his suitcase on the closet's top shelf.

A smile creased his lips, the first he'd allowed himself during the two months of grueling travel to this house in McLean. He took a small sewing kit from the dresser where he'd unpacked his belongings.

Removing scissors, he snipped at stitches in his filthy, travel-worn clothes, tediously collecting the gems secreted into the garment's seams and hems.

This accomplished, he removed seven sheets of soft jewelry paper hidden in his suitcase's false compartment. He counted the collected stones twice to assure he'd found them all and divided them into equal groups. Putting ten stones aside, he folded the rest into the jewelry paper to form six packets. Then he wrapped the remaining ten stones in the seventh piece of jewelry paper and placed it on the desk. Crowding diamonds together risked scratching against each other, which lowered their value. But for the number of packets he must hide, less was more.

Scissors in hand, he cut a three-inch slit in the doll's soft torso, inserted the diamonds and sewed the gash shut over the hidden packets. Viewing his handiwork with approval, he dressed the doll with clumsy hands. Women and girls touched dolls; men of his culture didn't sully their masculinity by doing so. But he pushed away his distaste. Terrorism was a male province and this mission demanded whatever means were necessary for success.

This job finished, he next wrote his name on an envelope, sealed the smaller package of ten stones inside and pushed the envelope to the back of the desk drawer.

Ahmed sighed with relief. He returned to bed. Exhaustion combined with accomplishment at solving his first challenges in McLean allowed him to drift into immediate, dream-free sleep.

DAY TWO

FRIDAY

CHAPTER FOURTEEN

FRIDAY, 7:02 AM

Ahmed awoke hungry the next morning. He dressed and went downstairs. His host met him at the bottom step. "God's blessings upon you," he said. "So, Important Traveler, is your room comfortable?"

"Blessings also upon you. Yes, it is. Thank you for your hospitality, Mahmud."

"Come." He led his guest to the dining room where they took seats at a table set with two places. "First, breakfast and then shall we go to accomplish your tasks today?"

"A good plan," Ahmed agreed.

"*Heba,*" Mahmud shouted impatiently toward the closed kitchen door. It opened quickly to reveal a woman carrying a laden tray. She wore the hijab, a scarf framing her face and hiding her hair. Mahmud ignored her. His host's wife? With downcast face she served coffee, cream and sugar.

"Coffee?" Mahmud asked his guest.

"Yes, thank you."

"Pour," Mahmud directed. Her loose-fitting floor-length clothes disguised her shape, leaving only her hands and face visible, as in the Middle-East. Seeing her gaunt, down-turned face, Ahmed thought she looked fifty, about Mahmud's age. She placed pastries and fruit on the table, took the empty tray to the kitchen and closed the door.

"For me to understand your household, she is...?"

"My servant. I bought her from a Turk I met a month after I arrived in the U.S. He bought her from someone else who got her from someone else and so on. She works hard and does everything I want her to do." He gave Ahmed a significant look. *"Everything* I want her to do."

Surprised, Ahmed grasped this meaning and then thought of the irony. No woman would ever grace his life or his bed, and this man had two.

"Her wage is food and a sleeping room in the basement, so I list her as a dependent for taxes. She cooks, cleans house and launders clothes, which pleases my wife. And she does not speak."

"No tongue?"

"They don't punish blasphemy that way in this country. I don't know why she's silent. But in a household with four women," he gave a thin laugh, "one not talking is a blessing."

"Four women?"

"Yes, here they come now," he said as two women and a child entered the room. To them he said, "This is Ahmed, who visits us for awhile." He turned to his guest, "This is my wife, Zayneb. She is Muslim-American, born right here in Fairfax County. We met at a mosque in Falls Church twenty-four years ago and married a month later. This is daughter Khadija, who is twenty-three years old and here's my dear little daughter, Safia, who is five. Come, Safia, and sit on my lap."

The wife wore a demure long-sleeved blouse, ankle-length full skirt and no make-up. Ahmed thought her pale Nordic coloring and high cheekbones produced a regal look, enhanced the more by the hijab framing her face. His indoctrination taught repulsion for American women, but he found her modest in demeanor and striking in appearance.

The little daughter had her father's dark eyes and black hair. Neither she nor her sister wore the hijab. Khadija's hazel eyes and lustrous light brown hair reflected a mix of her parents' genes. Ahmed tried not to gape at the unmistakable female contours revealed by the older daughter's slacks and loose sweater. He stared, marveling at her beauty.

Unlike the submissive shyness and downcast glances his culture equated with femininity, this young woman's hazel eyes looked directly into his as if looking deep into his mind...into his heart. In his country, men and women not of the same family didn't touch in public, so he fought shock as she boldly approached and shook his hand in the American manner.

"Welcome to McLean." Her sweet voice, lovely face, warm smile and the unexpected feel of her soft hand triggered a flood of longing so unexpected and powerful Ahmed feared he could not hide his spontaneous reaction from anyone in the room.

CHAPTER FIFTEEN

FRIDAY, 7:34 AM

A hmed tried not to stare at his host's beautiful daughter. Aside from the family women he knew as a small boy, until arriving at this home he had little proximity to females. From ages five to twelve he'd endured long days in the strict, all-male madrassa where memorization of inflexible religious rules reinforced Islam's rigid Sharia law. Islam was heritage, in your genes, like your nose shape or skin color. This wasn't a choice. Destiny assigned you to this religion, your ultimate Muslim identity. Even doubting Islam was a sin. Reading other religions' holy books, if they could be found, meant grave heresy and severe punishment.

The mullah identified devoted, obedient Ahmed as an alert boy. He sent the thirteen year old to an all-male Yemeni terrorist camp to train for military skills. Impressed with his quickness to improvise auxiliary solutions when primary solutions failed, the commandant selected him for the competitive special-operations hierarchy. This brought him to the attention of the Great Leader, who finally chose him to lead a part of this brilliant, long-planned suicidal strike against America.

Hate lessons during those formative years included pictures of heathen American women wearing disgusting, skimpy clothes and garish makeup. Yet inwardly, powerful emotions warred between Ahmed's learned revulsion for such blatant decadence and a natural curiosity about women and their seductive magic. After all, most Middle-Eastern men took one to four wives, to discover what forbidden mysteries lay beneath their flowing robes. The brashness of Mahmud's daughter shaking his hand should affront him. Instead, her touch left an electric tingle upon his palm.

"Hello, Ahmed," Zayneb spoke from across the table, her polite smile not reaching her eyes. "A blessing that God kept you safe during your travels. How was your flight?"

My flight? Good, Ahmed thought, Mahmud told her nothing of his real journey here, never mind his purpose. "It is a pleasure to meet you." He repeated the memorized, respectful phrase before adding, "My trip was long. I am glad to arrive at last. Thank you for your hospitality."

"Will you take breakfast with us now?" Mahmud asked his wife.

"Thank you, no. Friday mornings I drive Safia to school and stay to assist her teacher. We already had a bite in the kitchen." She gave Ahmed another superficial smile. "Welcome to our home."

"Thank you very much." He recited the expected response.

"Sorry, but my youngest and I must leave now for the school. Please excuse us." Zayneb left holding Safia's hand.

"Thank you for inviting us to join you for breakfast this morning, Baba," Khadija said. Her father frowned disapproval as she put food on a plate, sat at the table and turned toward Ahmed.

"Your English is good. Where did you learn to speak our language?"

"In the madra...in my school and later at special language camps," he answered.

"Would you like to learn more?"

"Yes, I would." His answer surprised him. Why improve his language skills when he'd be dead in a week?

"Watching television is a good way to hear and practice the language, especially the news channels. Did you notice the TV on the wall in your room?"

"Not yet, but I will make a point to do so when I return upstairs."

"If you like, maybe I can help also. I teach ESL at a nearby community college."

"E...S...L?"

"English as a Second Language. I teach my students to speak and write English plus practical skills, like filling out a job application. I also teach them about our culture because life here may be very different from what they're accustomed to in their homelands."

Mahmud frowned harder. He allowed women at the table after his own twenty-four-year exposure to American habits, but this high-ranking guest came straight from a different Middle-Eastern culture. Khadija's refusal to behave according to Sharia law, the cornerstone of Muslim life, angered her father and must horrify Ahmed. He felt rage that his daughter embarrassed him in front of this honored visitor with whom he would soon shape a violence of such proportions all American lips would speak their names.

"Khadija, *enough!*" he shouted with authority. "Our guest has no time for this. His schedule here is busy. His English is excellent and..."

"No," Ahmed interrupted on impulse. "To know more is wiser than to know less. I accept your daughter's gracious offer, Mahmud."

As Khadija's face lighted with enthusiasm, Ahmed marveled at the length and thickness of her eyelashes and the way her soft hair brushed the delicate skin of her face. Could the others hear his heart's loud pounding inside his chest? Shifting self-consciously in his seat, he hoped the motion distracted Mahmud from noticing his strong reactions to the man's daughter.

Mahmud's look of surprise at Ahmed's reaction froze into a rebuffed and disapproving scowl. They ate in silence until Khadija looked at her watch, sipped the last of her coffee, stood and announced, "I'm off to class. Back about one o'clock. See you all this afternoon."

Her father grunted annoyance and Ahmed said, "Safe travel."

He felt as if a piece of him left the room when she did.

CHAPTER SIXTEEN

FRIDAY, 7:47 AM

As Khadija's car pulled out of the driveway, Mahmud volunteered to Ahmed, "The others have gone and Heba's in the kitchen where she can not hear us, so we can speak openly."

"A Muslim-*American* wife, Mahmud? How did this happen?" Ahmed's own training forbade unnecessary social mingling with the enemy, never mind *marriage*.

Rather than apologize, Mahmud allowed his smug expression to suggest an opposite story. "In truth, it's genius. Although I executed the task brilliantly, I can't take credit for originating it. Years ago, when the Great Leader placed me in this infidel country, he instructed me to find an American bride. Imagine my disgust at this unthinkable duty. But marrying an American put me in the quick-line for American citizenship and proved to everyone here my willing integration into this life—a life you and I know is entirely false." He gave an ironic laugh. "Who would suspect this 'Americanized' Muslim man is actually a terrorist?"

Recognizing the strategy's cleverness, Ahmed said, "I see we all play needed roles here. And have these twenty-four years of integration changed your dedication to carry out our mission? Speak truly now, for this is essential."

Mahmud's face sobered. "If anything, my resolve grows ever stronger. You have no idea how hard this is. Every day I am torn between acting like a perfect American husband or killing my wife. My life is a nightmare! Only a strong man could endure the madness.

"And she's not even pretty. But the homely ones are easy targets, wanting husbands to validate their worth. She insists on some independence, and when I give her the discipline she deserves, she threatens to leave me. American men, she argues, don't treat women that way. Then I show her newspaper stories proving this untrue. Many American men beat and even kill their women. But I cannot risk doing this during my assignment here in case someone calls the police. I must blend into this filthy culture to avoid all suspicion. I cannot draw attention to myself until Allah, blessed be His name, calls me soon for our great mission. "

"Stones fill your path. I see that," Ahmed agreed. But how could this man think his wife plain? "Your wife is homely?"

"Ugly. Her color is washed away: white skin, blue eyes and the hair beneath her hijab is yellow." He flinched. "She's not at all our kind. Never would I willingly choose her for a wife."

Mahmud spoke with such venom that Ahmed didn't doubt his sincerity. Odd, because the very differences he loathed fascinated Ahmed. He remembered his father's delight in his mother's unusual green eyes, perhaps a genetic gift from early European plunderers or European women brought centuries earlier as gifts for powerful Sultans or Caliphate rulers.

"In this country the wife's family expects no dowry. Imagine! None! Coaxing her to marry was easy, at least for a clever man like me, but living with her is impossible. She disgusts me every day. First, the way she looks. Second, she wears only the hijab, not a veil. Third, she won't stay at home under my protection and control." He shrugged. "Unlike our homeland, this degenerate American society fails to combine laws and customs with religion to enforce a man's sovereign power over the women in his household. Even so, many American men correctly regard women as inferiors." Mahmud laughed. "Some of their own religions, especially those called 'fundamentalist,' instruct men to rule as undisputed, respected heads of families...just as we do."

Ahmed cleared his throat. "Your wife's manner and dress show Muslim modesty..."

"Yes, but she's not our kind of Muslim woman. She goes to meetings in the community and helps at Safia's school. I insist she account to me where she goes and what she does. She drives a car, unheard of in our homeland. She *questions my decisions*, or did until I punched that notion out of her." Mahmud gave a conspiratorial grin, confident any Muslim male understood his mandate to flex control upon household members defying his will.

Inwardly, Ahmed winced. His own father lifted no hand to harm the beloved, beautiful creature who was his wife.

"The final insult: she prevents conception. Oh, she denies this but what else explains we have only two children in twenty-three years of marriage? We should have at least ten."

Ahmed nodded gravely.

"Zayneb is her Islamic name; she was called Phoebe before. She changed names when she converted from Protestant to Muslim because she correctly recognized the greater wisdom of our teachings. She joined Islam on her own. When I show her the Quran teaches a wife's total submission to her husband, this sometimes works to my advantage."

"And how is that?"

"I remind her *she* chose this path and my dominance is a vital part of the religion she selected. Confronted with this as her decision, I needn't force her to obey. She forces herself."

Ahmed thought if this were true, Mahmud would complain less, but he said nothing. His host filled the silence. "Zayneb inherited this house when her parents died." He gestured around the room, "Well-built, large house, four bedrooms, good neighborhood. If she dies, as her husband, I inherit it all." An ancient Bedouin gleam glittered in his eyes. "And she *could* die," he held his hands as if choking someone, "because *accidents* happen all the time."

Ahmed made no comment, but his host's message was clear.

Mahmud changed the subject. "Look, the Americans have a saying, 'the right tool for the right job.' Zayneb is such a tool, needed to build the convincing structure to hide me...and you...until we complete our holy mission. She doesn't know, but she is our cover."

"And your children?"

"Ah," Mahmud hesitated. "They are merely daughters, yet the fruit of my seed. The older one is lost to American ways, but the younger is devoted to me, and I admit special fondness for her."

Covering emotion in his voice, he added with conviction, "In the end, the little one is still another tool, yet one I leave with regret when you and I soon reap our rewards in Paradise. For our God, glory to His name, I will gladly give my life and all I hold dear...including my youngest child."

Ahmed wished the joy of fatherhood could touch his own life. He pushed this thought aside. He gave his host a long look. The man's words rang true, but something about him — a man integral to their mission — didn't feel comfortable. Did Mahmud care more for his own glory than God's?

And what of Mahmud's desirable older daughter? Why would a god put devilish temptation in Ahmed's path at the very time his final sacrifice for his god was at hand? A test or a sign?

"Come, we have work to do." Mahmud rose and Ahmed followed his lead. "May I respectfully suggest we buy American clothes for you today, so you blend in? And have you a list of the other places you wish to go today?"

"Yes, I will show you in the car."

"Come," Mahmud gestured, "see my yard." He opened the dining room's French doors and they stepped out. Ahmed saw none of this when arriving at the front of the house.

"This is the back deck. I installed the high fence for privacy. Many tall trees for shade. Over there, I built two raised gardens for flowers. Two more such gardens will go over here when I find time to build them." His expression grew serious. "But I guess that isn't likely now, is it?"

In the politeness characterizing host/guest rituals in their homelands, Ahmed said, "Your house is solid and welcoming. Your yard is an oasis that brings peace to eyes fortunate enough to see it. Thank you again for your hospitality, Mahmud. Now would you like to show McLean to me?"

As the garage door closed behind the men's departing car, Heba peeked out from the kitchen. She'd listened to all they said.

CHAPTER SEVENTEEN

FRIDAY, 7:53 AM

Zayneb's troubled face reflected inner turmoil as she drove toward Safia's school. She'd known for years her husband didn't love her, but today she faced her situation with cold objectivity.

How young, naïve and idealistic she was twenty-six years ago when she felt teenage fervor to develop an identity of her own, distinct from the parents she loved. Repelled by typical rebellious symbols like dyed spiky hair, weird clothes, tattoos or drugs, she chose a different way to distinguish herself from her parents' generation. At age nineteen, she'd changed religions.

Baptized in infancy into a Protestant denomination, she decided as an adult that their trinity doctrine confused rather than simplified her concept of one god. When a fellow student explained Muslims worship one god, she investigated. Right or wrong, the change to Islam seemed more a deity name-change than a concept-change. Islam valued her gentleness, shyness and modesty. Both religions spoke of a caring god who oversees human life and desired behavior. Good followers of both obey God's rules in their holy book as interpreted by church, mosque or temple leaders. Rules and prayers differed, but all posed a path for living a good and worthwhile life.

She liked the concept of women wearing a hijab, loose clothing, long sleeves and low hems to encourage Muslims to judge each other by their character, not their looks. Modesty played an important role in this attempt at equality. Absent overt sexual attire or behavior, the theory held, men and women could treat each other as fellow human beings rather than objects of desire. Protecting women struck her as the equivalent of valuing and honoring women, much as her father cared about her safety and welfare. She didn't consider protecting might lead to controlling or that denying Muslim women education in some parts of the world relegated them to a state of arrested development. Women without skills, education or personal freedom tied many into roles as child-bearing domestics living at the mercy of their protectors.

In Zayneb's middle-class American world, this "lateral" conversion seemed daring and original yet safe. Rather than devaluing her as a woman, she thought respectful devotion to a strong, kind future husband appealing. She envisioned him much like her own father—a good-natured, intelligent, gentle man who loved her unconditionally while encouraging her education and the discovery and expression of her talents. She converted to Islam.

Soon after her conversion she'd met Mahmud. She winced now, remembering her pathetic vulnerability as he swept her away with his foreign good looks, attentive courtship and vows of adoration. Never pursued so ardently, she blossomed under his flattering attention. Thinking back, she cringed at how her trusting, eager cooperation facilitated his courtship. His sharing her passion for Islam further elevated his importance then. With a convert's zeal, she felt marriage to an *authentic* Middle-Eastern Muslim showed her new God—and the world—her dedication to Islam.

Confident of his love at the outset, Zayneb realized after the first months that something was wrong. Not just indifferent toward her, he seemed repelled. Assuming this displeasure her fault, she tried recapturing his love with a tidy home, appealing personality, careful grooming, memorable meals, submissive demeanor and bedroom eagerness. Pregnant by then with their first child, she used every means she could think of to right the marriage. She offered him her entire self and all she owned to underscore her trust in him and commitment to their future. This included agreeing to his repeated request to legally combine their assets, despite her earlier promise to her now-dead parents to keep the inherited house where they lived always in her name—for her protection.

When attempts to win back his love failed, her new religion reinforced submission. She resigned herself to accept responsibility for the painful consequences of her mistake. This was Allah's will. She knew not all marriage commitments worked. Even in America, where people could marry for love rather than family-arranged marriages between virtual strangers, fifty percent ended in divorce. She'd tough it out.

For years she'd lived with her bad decision, but the night he first beat her, she decided two things: to escape his control and to leave with her children.

Zayneb knew Mahmud's stern, strict, quick-tempered and humorless demeanor offended many, like Roshan next door. For years Zayneb excused his traits, hoping he loved her in his own brusque way. She realized every culture included those who were kind or cruel, cheerful or grumpy, polite or rude, thoughtful or opinionated. Islam had no corner on that universality. Marriage everywhere included the luck of the draw.

She knew her husband adored their younger daughter but had turned stone cold toward Khadija. Zayneb also chafed at her husband's stinginess and shivered at the cruel streak surfacing more frequently. Now fully recognizing the pathetic quality of her marriage, she'd still walk the path forced by her earlier choice, but she'd begin walking it her way.

With her house in both their names, under Virginia law he'd get half in a divorce. They couldn't divide the house, so she'd be forced to sell it to pay his half and leave the familiar neighborhood where she grew up with her family and many friends. At twenty-three, daughter Khadija could fly on her own wings, but not little Safia. Zayneb would need a job to support her. And where to live? Mahmud could pay little alimony or child support. He financed their marriage with salary from his job, and she guessed he hid part of it from her.

What had she gotten into and how to get out? Besides her consideration of the practical aspects of leaving him, she feared the way his temper flared into violence if he thought she questioned or defied his authority. Many honor cultures punished disrespect by disfigurement or death. This profile fit Mahmud. The public rejection of her divorce filing would embarrass him in front of his friends. Would he, perhaps with their help, hunt her down to exact revenge? Could she and her girls survive these retaliations?

Should she take Heba with her when she fled? Surprised but not displeased twenty-four years ago when her new husband arrived with a mute servant, Zayneb believed his story of kindly rescuing this poor woman with nowhere else to go. Now the woman was part of Zayneb's household as well. She'd discovered Heba's quick intelligence and over the years schooled her in the three R's—partly to simplify household teamwork and partly from pity for the woman's hapless plight. Heba's gratitude for this kindness evolved into grateful loyalty.

No, she couldn't abandon Heba.

And what of this visitor? For years Mahmud told her if Middle-Eastern visitors arrived, his culture expected him to open his home to them. But in twenty-four years no visitor came until now. Who was he and why was he here? And what about his obvious interest in Khadija?

"Ummi, are you okay?" Safia asked her mommy.

"Yes, fine, Safia. I'm just thinking about lots of things. I bet you do that sometimes, too."

"Yes." The child bubbled with smiles. "Right now I'm thinking about garage sales tomorrow. See these signs on all the streets in our neighborhood? Could we give a garage sale at our house, too?"

"Your father would not allow it." They drove in silence as each considered this. Having no money of her own forced Zayneb to beg her husband for every household penny. Besides controlling her spending, he reveled in interrogating and humbling her in this way.

Though she couldn't conduct her own sale, Zayneb made a plan with Roshan, who lived next door. Originally from India, Roshan and her husband had settled in this neighborhood thirty years earlier. Zayneb's parents befriended them the first day and, over time, became close. When Roshan's husband died suddenly a few years later, they encouraged her to stay in McLean, which she did. "Auntie Roshan" took then twelve-year-old Zayneb under her grandmotherly wing. Years later, she continued this loving role with Zayneb's children — to Mahmud's vocal consternation.

In her British-Indian accent, Roshan told Zayneb, "For the garage sale you gather clothes that don't fit, books and toys your children don't want and household things you don't use. Three-times good luck to get rid of things — to clean out the old, get money to buy new things and to recycle." Zayneb smuggled over many items Auntie next door would sell for her tomorrow.

"Could I also bake for the sale?" Zayneb asked. Roshan agreed with delight. So, while ostensibly baking for her family, she quintupled recipes, packaged cookies in Ziploc bags, tied each with ribbons from a spool Roshan gave her and spirited them next door.

As she drove, Zayneb reflected on recent events. Ahmed arrived yesterday, on Thursday afternoon. At breakfast today, her husband said they would be gone much of the day. Her husband never told her when he'd return — to keep her waiting, ever anticipating his arrival. While she helped this morning at Safia's school, she asked Heba to search through the house for saleable items no longer used. Back home at noon, she saw the woman had gathered a few more things, including the box of toys from Safia's old room, now occupied by Ahmed. Zayneb priced the toys and hustled them to Roshan before her husband returned. The sale began tomorrow at 9:00.

CHAPTER EIGHTEEN

FRIDAY, 8:58 AM

"We arrive in two minutes; prepare the door." Mahmud spoke into a cell phone. As they approached the warehouse, the automatic garage door lifted to admit them. The others had parked elsewhere in the vicinity and walked to the meeting place. Embedded in the U.S. for so many years, the men Ahmed met today chafed for action.

Mahmud opened the door into the office. "This is our honored guest, Ahmed, and I am Mahmud." Abdul identified himself and welcomed them to his humble business facility.

"Come," Abdul bowed slightly and, with a graceful wave of an outstretched arm, indicated the direction they should go. Folding chairs formed a circle in the next room.

Eight men stood respectfully as Ahmed entered the warehouse main room with Mahmud and Abdul. Shades covered all main-floor windows to insure privacy; industrial fluorescent lights bathed the room in harsh commercial light.

"As-salaam alaikum." Ahmed pronounced the traditional greeting. "Wa alaikum as-salaam," they responded. Abdul indicated the prominent chair for Ahmed. When he sat, so did the others. The group shared enough Arabic to read the Quran but due to their differing dialects, ironically they conversed in their new common language: English, though peppered with certain Arabic words all recognized.

Ahmed sat ramrod straight. "You were sent to this country many years ago for a specific reason. That fulfillment is at hand. If you are *not* willing to answer the Great Leader's call, speak now and depart before we talk further."

One man stood, fidgeting nervously. "My name is Ali. Like you, I am Muslim. Like you, I acknowledge Islam's inevitable world domination. Unlike you, I think Islam will triumph in our religious takeover of the United States without terrorist acts but in a bloodless coup where we eventually outnumber them. During my quarter century here, I've studied American culture. I think we can move forward together side-by-side under their democracy until time puts us in charge. Dictatorship doesn't always serve people best. Meantime, we observe how they create their high standard of living and ask: what can we borrow to improve our own countries?"

Ali shuffled his feet as he looked at the men he'd just seen for the first time. He rushed on, his words tumbling out before he lost his nerve. "As directed by the Great Leader twenty-five years ago, my family and I assimilated into this culture; my children attend their schools, my wife shops in their stores. We live as peaceful Muslims in their land. Because of the secret nature of this mission, I discussed my reluctance to join you with no one, not even the imam. Our clandestine situation forced me to figure this out myself, begging Allah's wisdom and guidance, blessings upon His name. He has shown me a clear path for my thinking and my actions. Your task is yours, but mine is different although still in devoted service to Islam. While in this new country with my family, I will learn all I can about their schools, science and economic success, to improve our lot in the Middle-East. It is with sadness, but certainty, I choose not to join you. May Allah guide your steps in all you do to further His true intentions."

He looked around the room, inviting their understanding. Nobody moved.

"Go then," Ahmed said amicably. When the man left, an uneasy silence filled the room.

"Anyone else?" Some shifted in their chairs but no one spoke. "Then may Allah, praised be His name, smile upon the jihad the ten of us remaining will shape today to honor Him and all Islam," Ahmed intoned reverently. The rest murmured approval.

"As you are aware, until now we were a little-known splinter group of Islam, the religion destined to rule the world. Our mission in northern Virginia will hasten Islam's world-wide acceptance in the United States. Rather than wait a thousand years for this gradual inevitability, we will accelerate Islam's path to victory by attacking and crushing our ancient enemies the Jews and, now, the evil American Satans whose warlike meddling disrupts our nations. The CIA and Homeland Security headquarters, both in McLean, will earn public humiliation when our attack explodes outside their very tents. We will shock Americans where they feel safe and join other activist units to shatter their resolve. They will know beyond any doubt they cannot escape their ultimate Islamic fate. Allah, peace be unto His name, blesses our actions and sacrifice with joy in his Paradise."

Wanting his own attention, Mahmud said, "Ahmed brings us an underground Taliban video to remind us of our task here." He pushed the DVD into a machine Abdul had been asked to provide. The others exchanged mumbles of surprise as the TV screen sputtered to life.

Background gunfire and chanting male voices sounded as actual war footage of bloody carnage filled the screen. Uniformed U.S. soldiers and military vehicles exploded in graphic detail as body parts and broken machinery spewed into the air. The capture and abuse of American soldiers in desert-storm-camouflage outfits preceded their being dragged through villages. Intact bodies of those not already beheaded were strung up for further mutilation. The film's Islamic background voices praised fallen fellow heroes and invited more sacrifice.

A robed figure stepped forward and faced the camera. "Powerful oppressors come from all directions. We use what skill and weapons we have to destroy their tanks and planes; yet even when we set the infidels on fire and burn them to ashes, they do not stop, coming in even greater numbers. But if these heathens kill me as I fight for our cause, then pick up your gun and follow in my footsteps when I am no more. In the end, Islam will prevail."

When the shocking visual and ear-splitting audible violence stopped at the video's end, the men in the warehouse jumped to their feet, fists in the air, cheering as if at a sports event.

Gratified at the film's electrifying effect upon them, Ahmed smiled. When they quieted he spoke. "Thank you for your loyalty to our cause and for waiting patiently for many years to pluck this forbidden fruit from our enemy's tree. Our jihad will create a catastrophe killing more than died at the World Trade Center in 2001 and unleash a wave of terror earning great respect for our religion in all American minds. We shall smite the Infidels with Islam's sword, showing their pathetic vulnerability in our hands. We shall avenge Osama bin Laden's vicious murder and their cowardly drone attacks on leaders of our heroic fighters. We shall prod the enemy with a hot poker. They will tremble at the name of Islam."

Cheers and stomping filled the room.

"The Great Leader instructs me to reveal to you more extraordinary news. At the exact time of our attack, simultaneous strikes by other units in a town in every state across the U.S.A. will happen. This will create both a local and a national atmosphere of sheer terror."

Again, the men cheered and gestured. Ahmed thought if they'd held rifles, as they would in their native countries, at this moment they'd fire them again and again into the air.

CHAPTER NINETEEN

FRIDAY, 9:33 AM

Ahmed waited for silence. The men looked at him expectantly. From years imbedded in American culture, they knew far more of local life here than he. However, he came directly from the Great Leader, whose inspired long-range vision placed each of them here in the first place.

"From information provided me by the Great Leader, I know who you are, but you do not know me or each other. To safeguard our project, we will use first names only. I will introduce myself first. My name is Ahmed. When I was a small boy, American Jews came to my village to murder my family before my eyes. Men from our secret sect rescued me, educated and cared for me at their madrassa. Later they sent me to learn specialized military and language skills. Our Great Leader honors me to lead this group to implement the plan he's crafted like an artist for forty years, a plan attracting rich funding from Middle-Eastern and certain other governments who recognize his brilliance. Because of Americans' atrocities to my family, I will punish these infidels twice: once for the glory of Islam and once for the deaths of my parents."

He gestured for the next man to speak.

"I am Muzamil. Sent to this country thirty years ago, I worked for rail transportation. My uniform, credentials, knowledge and industry associates give me access to trains and Metrorail. Ineffective security exists for freight cargo, including hazardous material. Exploding them in pre-determined locations insures severe damage or biochemical contamination lasting far beyond the event itself. Security for passenger trains is similarly lax. Luggage isn't electronically screened or visually inspected. Even with security, many passengers board trains at unmanned depots such as Fredericksburg, Virginia. Detonating hidden bombs as a train passes through a tunnel or over a high trestle would create a railroad disaster crippling routes and frightening riders for years afterward."

Ahmed nodded approval before turning his eyes to the next man.

"Abdul is my name. After fifteen years as trusted foreman of a big HVAC company, I started my own business. I have access to air circulation systems in office and government buildings. My uniformed crews and I fit in everywhere and can use our access to infuse ventilation systems with bio-weapons or deadly gases or place demolition explosives to blow workers to bits while destroying computers, files and creating chaos."

"Mustafa here. For twenty-five years I worked with janitorial teams providing cleaning services in civilian, government and military office buildings, factories, schools and shopping malls. I am now supervisor. Nobody questions our presence in any commercial venue. My uniformed workers and I could install bombs to destroy buildings, office machinery, records and personnel."

"My name is Mahmud. My business is commercial and industrial painting. Painters are needed everywhere, so we go everywhere. Our company uniforms and equipment are tickets inside most buildings where we can place explosives or whatever is needed."

"I am Mohamed. The U.S. government trained me to monitor and ensure computer security and prevent hacking. I have top-secret clearance. I can create considerable chaos in government, military and civilian computer systems even without a cyber-bomb. With such a bomb, and rumor has it several kinds exist, this country will fall to its knees. The advantage is useable infrastructure ready for our takeover. Only their technology and way of life it supports are destroyed."

"Call me Faheem. A licensed semi-trailer truck driver, I learned my trade with major companies. I did well enough to buy my own rig plus four more. Explosives packed into my trucks can detonate in tunnels, on bridges or underground parking garages of office buildings, with horrific results."

"I am Basheer. I worked my way to management in a gun shop chain and can get my hands on most weapons. More important, I am an accurate sniper, as are my associates, to serve you well."

"Jabbar here. I work in a government chemical laboratory but have my own well-stocked lab at home in my basement. I can create toxic gases and poisons for the others here to deploy and can get bio-hazardous material for use if desired."

"My name is Aziz. I am a construction foreman. Commercial work and road improvement exist all over Fairfax County. My crew and I are accepted without question wherever we go. We use heavy equipment, useful for destruction as well as construction, and know strong and weak points in buildings for Semtex, and other explosives, to insure maximum damage."

Pleased at their array of talents and careers, Ahmed smiled. "Thank you. Our Great Leader's plan uses all your skills for this jihad, our holy war against the Unbelievers. We will strike on the day after Thanksgiving. They name this 'Black Friday,' a day with meaning to American people which exemplifies their twisted devotion to materialism. But Friday also has great meaning for us: our day of the week to worship Allah. Our holy war on His holy day is the ingenious thought of our Great Leader."

"And what is the target?" asked one of the men.

Ahmed smiled. "A very large shopping mall in northern Virginia. Because shopping is an American mania, stores are everywhere. Our attack will cause Americans fear when they shop for their needs and wants, and they spend few days without visiting a store. Shoppers will cram the mall on this date. Many thousands will die. The plan is brilliant."

Several cell members exchanged cautionary glances. Finally Aziz managed the courage to respond. "I speak with total respect for you and our Great Leader, but my company has constructed many malls and worked on expansions of others such as the Tyson Corner Shopping Mall, which almost doubled in size in 2005. Is the Great Leader aware security systems in these malls are super-sophisticated? To protect huge Black Friday crowds, the mall's management greatly increases existing security personnel plus Fairfax County policemen, both uniformed and plain-clothes. Individual stores, responsible for their own security, also ramp up their security on Black Friday. The mall's state-of-the-art camera systems miss little. Management's suspicion for any irregularities will be on highest alert."

Abdul added, "Individual stores in large malls must provide their own HVAC, but concourses rely on body heat in the winter. This is no problem since daily foot traffic in huge malls is about 55,000 shoppers a day. Chill systems cool common areas in the summer, but this is November. Extra security on Black Friday seriously limits my normally easy HVAC access."

"Thank you both for your information. I will report this to our Great Leader, although I do not question his choice."

Ahmed looked at the group. "We will each make a farewell video for TV stations to receive after our strike. Write down your message to our enemies so you will be ready. We meet again here tomorrow morning at 10:00 to make the videos. Do you all understand?"

They assured him they did. Regrettably, the nervous Ali, who humiliated himself by revealing his traitorous cowardice and leaving before the meeting began, could not be allowed to live.

"Abdul," Ahmed signaled him to approach, "I have a special assignment for you..."

CHAPTER TWENTY

FRIDAY, 10:32 AM

Veronika Verontsova paced the living room of her Great Falls estate. Her long, gray hair, gathered in a braid at the back of her neck, framed a winkled face from which alert brown eyes surveyed her world. Wearing a shawl over a blouse tucked into an ankle-length skirt, she looked more like a wizened gypsy than a member of the once-powerful Russian aristocracy.

Pain in her temples warned of a vision soon, but not until the special scent filled the air. Strong emanations today trembled with danger, yet she couldn't identify the source. Sinister energy pulsed nearby, yesterday's faint uneasiness more insistent today.

"I'm almost ninety years old," she muttered aloud to the empty room. "I hoped these glimpses into the future would ebb long ago, but if anything, I've learned to coax more details from the unwanted scenes invading my mind."

She smiled, remembering how innocently the discovery began. As a child, she'd loved playing outside in the gardens surrounding her family's estate in Russia. She'd felt keenly alive outdoors with sunshine kissing her skin, breezes stirring the leaves to whisper around her, insects buzzing as they spiraled along on their pollen mission, and the distinct scents of flowers, especially lilacs. They drew her powerfully when first she inhaled their perfume.

At age four, on a glorious spring day, she buried her face in clusters of the fragrant lavender blossom spikes she'd picked, breathing their intoxicating lilac fragrance minute after minute until she felt light-headed and melted into another world. Although she lay in her garden with her nose in the lilacs, she "saw" a ship sinking into the ocean. The heady sensation of two dimensions excited her, and she repeated her secret "looks" other places by inhaling the inebriating lilac scent every day they bloomed. Soon she didn't need the actual flowers but only the memory of their perfume to peer forward in time. She didn't summon these pictures. They just happened.

Today's vision in Great Falls, Virginia, was as strong as her first recorded experience at age five in the old country, when the beloved family dog failed to return from the woods at dinnertime. Speculation permeated the household from the salons upstairs to the servant quarters below.

Her mother tucked her into bed that night, comforting her child with the thought "Baron" would return by morning. But during the night, Veronika smelled lilacs and, in her dream, saw Baron pursued by a bear. She watched the bear sink predatory claws deep into their pet's flank and drag it closer for the kill. As she watched, the bear's jaws closed on Baron's throat. The dog's legs raked the air fiercely, then twitched and finally hung limp. Releasing the dog's neck, the bear sank his fangs into his victim's belly.

Veronika awoke to her own screams in the middle of the night. Her nursemaid already stood at her side when her mother rushed into the room. "Nika, my little Veronika, what is it, Darling?"

The child couldn't believe she was in her bed rather than in the woods near the violent attack. "Baron is dead," the child sobbed. "I saw the bear kill him. Now it waits for whoever comes next."

"It is just a bad dream, Precious. Baron will return tomorrow. Now go back to sleep, Little One."

Veronika lay back on her pillow. "The bear waits where the path forks near the giant oak tree. I saw him looking for the person who comes next.

"All right, close your eyes. I'll tell Papa about your dream. We'll talk more about it at breakfast."

A bear *did* wait next morning for a servant sent to find Baron. Alerted by the nursemaid's story of the girl's dream, he carried a rifle. He found Baron's remains in the bushes beside the path as the bear rushed at him. The servant later insisted the child's vision saved his life.

Baron was but her first shared vision. A month later she smelled lilacs and "saw" her mother's lost ruby earring beneath a bookcase. Later, when a gardener fell ill she "knew" he wouldn't recover. As the years passed, dozens of examples of her "gift" taught family respect for her sixth sense.

News of Veronika's visions spread through the household to neighbors and finally to town.

Aristocrats, merchants and peasants came to the house, begging the child's help to find a missing loved one or a valuable lost article. Her parents did their best to shield her, but several bribed servants brought her messages about mysteries, which the child then solved, increasing her mystique.

One day she overheard her parents talking. "Well, is she prescient about these events or does seeing them cause them?" blustered her father.

Her mother laughed nervously. "Rudolph, you do go on so. Don't be ridiculous. She's just a beautiful child with a rare gift. You should be proud of this, as I am."

Her father harrumphed, downed his whiskey and said no more. But this conversation frightened Veronika. Had she the power to make bad things happen? Nursing this fear, she didn't know what to do when in her mind's eye she "saw" her mother thrown from a horse. Veronika "saw" the doctor standing over her mother's bed, shaking his head sadly.

"Don't go riding today," she begged her mother. "Please stay with me. I...I need you here." But her mother said she'd return from the ride soon to spend the afternoon with her daughter. "Don't go," the child sobbed. "I saw your horse rear and you fell off and you...you died."

Stopping in her tracks, her mother gazed into her daughter's eyes. "Is it true you saw this vision?"

"Yes, yes." The girl twisted the strand of beads at her throat until it broke, scattering jewels across the floor. "Please, Mama."

"Well then, I think I'll change my plans and stay with you after all."

This experience introduced Veronika to the notion her gift might prevent calamity. But in this case she merely delayed fate, for a year later her mother was thrown from a horse and killed.

Months after her mother's death, she pounded on the door of her father's study. When he opened it she wailed, "I see men in uniforms marching with guns toward our house. What should we do?"

Her father jumped to his feet. He'd anticipated this possibility since last year. "Quick, tell nurse to get your travel bag and hurry. Meet me at the back door as soon as you're ready. We'll leave in fifteen minutes. Wear the disguises we practiced."

Soon their loaded car sped across the countryside and eventually to a wharf where they boarded a boat for Europe. There her father said, "Here are pictures of three ships: one sails to Spain, one to Africa and one to America." He showed them to her. "So, my little Seer, which one do we take?"

She sniffed and as the lilac fragrance touched her nostrils, she saw them aboard one of the ships. "This one." Tapping the picture, she chose America, with no idea what that destination implied.

Now Veronika sank her old body into a comfortable living room chair and thought about her eighty-some years in Great Falls. When she'd first arrived, farms and woodlands stretched in all directions with a few simple country stores at crossroads. At age ten, she'd attended boarding school while her father built their new mansion on his prosperous horse farm. Later she graduated from Georgetown University and afterward married a wealthy man, who moved into their mansion on the estate. In time, she *knew* her husband spent time with other women, even before shown the facts. After she divorced him, she knew the day before it happened he would be mortally wounded by an enraged husband. She felt no remorse.

She was almost sixty when her father took an extended trip to Russia, returning five months later with a young bride, who disliked Veronika on sight. This stepmother considered Veronika a threat to her power and the eventual inheritance of her new husband's wealth. Two years later, baby Anna was born to that union. The new wife's hostility toward Veronika increased. Her father always showed devotion to his older daughter, a situation angering the new wife even more.

That spring, when a hundred lilac bushes blossomed around the estate, Veronika knew beforehand her stepmother would fall ill and die soon. With no children of her own, Veronika welcomed the chance to "parent" little Anna, but the child had a mind of her own, hungering for excitement resulting in constant trouble at school and risk-taking at home. In elementary school, Anna invited dares and took every one. In high school, she drove too fast, partied too hard, drank too much and wrecked her car numerous times.

Veronika knew when he failed to appear for breakfast one day that her father would die before nightfall. His Will gave Veronika the estate and a money settlement to Anna, who left immediately to visit her mother's relatives in Russia. She sent no word for five years but reappeared one day, now a sly, seductive beauty who asked to live at the estate. Veronika agreed so long as she caused no trouble.

"I sell real estate now," Anna explained, but her older sister thought this far too tame for the adrenalin rushes Anna craved from living on the edge. Anna often stayed away for days, even weeks, with no explanation.

Veronika pulled her shawl around her shoulders and sniffed the air. Did ethics apply to prescience like hers? Was hers a gift or a curse? Should she intervene or ignore? Did it make a difference? Her warning not to ride only delayed her mother's death while telling her father about the approaching soldiers changed the outcome.

Veronika sank back into the chair and closed her eyes. A faint aroma of lilacs drifted around her. She breathed deeply to shut out distraction, allowing the vision to come. A group of men sat in a circle, their faces twisted in cruel exuberance. Some spoke oddly-accented English. She knew they plotted violence and death...death to thousands. Hate gleamed in their eyes. She recognized a few words as they spoke. This danger lurked near but not in Great Falls. Was the setting a warehouse? What explained their foreign-accented language and use of those specific words? Her eyes opened wide as a sudden, powerful cognizance dawned: terrorists!

She sat up in the chair. How could she prevent this danger from growing? Call the police? Say she had a vision with no specific leads to trace? Absurd! Yet if she did nothing, she felt certain monstrous results *would* happen. Minutes passed as she struggled with options.

At last she stood, gathered her purse and car keys, primed the security system protecting her home, climbed into her car and headed for the police station.

CHAPTER TWENTY-ONE

FRIDAY, 11:46 AM

When Veronika entered the McLean District Police Station on Balls Hill Road, the on-duty policeman sitting behind bulletproof glass indicated a phone on the wall. She picked up the handset and put it to her ear.

"What can we do for you, Ma'am?" he asked from behind the protective window.

"I'd like to speak with the person in charge—the chief."

"Sorry, he's not here now. If you tell me what you need, maybe I can find someone to help you."

"I...I know about something very dangerous that will happen soon."

The reception cop tried to size her up and balance this against staff on duty at the station. "Just a minute, please." He pressed a phone button and spoke briefly, his conversation muted by the heavy glass separating them. Into the lobby phone he said. "Please have a seat. He's on his way."

Veronika sat down and looked absently at newspapers on the coffee table. Picking up a copy of the *McLean Connection* weekly edition, she turned the pages idly, glancing with little interest at the articles until she stopped short at the photo of three smiling women. One woman in the picture drew her total attention. She closed her eyes, trying to grasp why.

"Hello, Ma'am," said a deep, pleasant male voice.

Startled, Veronika's eyes blinked open as her concentration diverted from the photographed woman to her reason for coming to the police station.

"I'm Detective Adam Iverson. How can I help you?"

She stood, still clutching the newspaper and told him her name. "Have you a place where we could talk more privately than this waiting room?" she asked.

"Of course. Come on back to my office." He held the door open and she preceded him down the hall. "It's the last door on your right." As they entered his cubicle, he held the back of a chair to comfortably seat this elderly woman before settling into his own chair behind the desk.

He noticed her age and the dignity with which she moved and spoke, yet her clothes and hair-style looked as if she'd stepped out of an old European painting. Noting her nervousness in the unfamiliar police setting, where law-abiding citizens often felt uncomfortable, he began with small talk to put her at ease. "Fall's a beautiful time of year in Virginia. Do you live nearby?"

"Yes, in Great Falls."

He pushed the small talk another minute until she seemed calmer. "What brings you here today?" he asked in a friendly voice.

"Detective, this will sound strange to you, but I am clairvoyant. Since childhood. Not always right but right way too often for coincidence."

Geez, he thought, freezing the smile on his face. Another kook with a rambling tale I must endure while I have better things to do. No choice but to hear her out. Maybe she'll surprise me with something after all.

"I don't believe much in coincidence," he said.

Taking this as encouragement, she continued. "The last two days I've felt growing dread about something terrible starting to happen close to us, somewhere in northern Virginia. Not Great Falls but perhaps McLean or Vienna. It will bring death to thousands of people."

"Have you had this feeling other times or other places?" he probed.

"Nothing like this." Her hands twisted together in her lap. "In a vision today, I saw ten men sitting in a circle. They're foreign but not Oriental or African, yet dark-complexioned. By that I mean no blue eyes or blond hair. They wore American clothes and contemporary haircuts."

"So...they could be any group of Americans?"

"No. Some spoke accented English but peppered it with words from a tongue I didn't recognize. I speak English, Russian, German, French and recognize many Slavic words, but I am here because of two words they spoke which I have heard before."

Interested now, Adam asked quickly, "And what were they?"

"Allah and jihad."

CHAPTER TWENTY-TWO

FRIDAY, NOON

A dam considered various implications of Veronika Verontsova's two loaded words. He studied her carefully.

"You may think me eccentric," she continued, "bringing you unverifiable information, but add it up as I did to see why I'm here. Try to put yourself in their position. Terrorists seek inventive ways to attack us, and we've avoided a major incident killing thousands of people since that horrible 9/11 incident in 2001. Their lack of success must increase their frustration and resolve. Osama Bin Laden's death at American hands further outrages them. My clear look at the men, my certainty that danger emanates from them and something awful will happen nearby—all frighten me. Alerting the police is my first step, because you have direct lines to Homeland Security. If you don't intend to contact them, tell me whom to call and I will. I don't think we have much more time, maybe only a week, before they commit this terrible act."

The wrinkled old woman's sincerity convinced Adam she believed every word she spoke. And what if she was correct? If threat of such danger lurked in Fairfax County, police needed to know.

"All right," he said. "Please give me your contact information so we know how to get in touch with you. May I see your driver's license?"

"Of course." As she fumbled in her purse to retrieve the ID, the newspaper in her lap fell to the floor. She placed her license on Adam's desk, retrieved the newspaper page with the photo and spread it out. A wave of connection again washed over Veronika as she studied the smiling woman's picture. "Detective, I found this in your waiting room.

This woman is about to become involved in the danger. I'm sure of it." She turned the photo 180 degrees for Adam to see and pointed to the person about whom she spoke. "This woman..." She pointed to one of the three heads in the picture.

Adam's jaw dropped as he stared at the face in the photo. He read the picture's caption: "Darla Clark, Jeannie Meyer and Jennifer Shannon plan McLean Newcomer's luncheon at Great Falls restaurant L'Auberge Chez Francois." Her finger rested on the photo of his new mother-in-law.

Veronika watched Adam. "Your expression says you know this woman."

Adam gave a nervous smile and changed the subject. "Who's acting like a detective now?"

"The caption gives her name. I must talk to this Jennifer Shannon. She may help me better understand the danger confronting us. I can find her in the phone book, but if I approach her without introduction, I may upset her as I did you."

Adam cleared his throat to buy time as he sorted out this development. "Why don't I tell her about our meeting and give her your contact information? If she wants to talk to you, she'll call. You'll recognize her name when she does."

"Thank you, Detective."

"No, I thank you for coming to the station. Here's my business card. Phone me with any more information about this."

He walked her back down the hall, but before she went through the waiting room door she turned to shake his hand. "Goodbye, Detective." Sniffing the air as if savoring an aroma, she stared at him, extracted her hand from the farewell gesture and looked at her fingers as if she'd never seen them before. "I...I see information about you. A new wife? An important career decision soon? A farm with a harmless old house that isn't harmless at all, not for you. Proceed very carefully right now, young man."

And then she was gone.

Adam stared as the door closed behind her. When surprise at her personal comments about his life wore off, he frowned. How could she know this about him? He'd dropped by the office this afternoon for a few minutes only to pick up a case file. But as he prepared to go home to help Hannah with the revamping at the farm, reception asked him to take this walk-in. His interview with Veronika Verontsova was pure accident. No way could she have researched him in advance, never mind personal insights not in any public records.

So how could she know?

The detective shook his head, trying to make sense of it. How should he take what she'd said today? Was she a well-meaning, dignified lunatic? More troubling, was she for real? He reached for the phone then hesitated. Not understanding this himself, how could he explain it to Steve, a police buddy who'd recently left the McLean station to join Homeland Security? By itself, a single potential clue like this might appear irrelevant; yet alongside other pertinent clues it might fit a meaningful pattern. Nutsy as he feared this would sound, Steve *should* know. He punched the number.

CHAPTER TWENTY-THREE

FRIDAY, 1:06 PM

K hadija returned from morning classes, pleased to find Ahmed back also. Her father had gone to his workplace for an hour.

"Have you finished lunch?" she asked. He nodded. "Then have you a few minutes to look at the textbook I use for teaching? I brought an extra copy for you to keep if you'd like to read more later."

"Thank you. I will read the book with pleasure." Pleasure hardly described the thrill he felt. This gesture proved she thought of him at least once that day, whereas thoughts of her squeezed everything else out of his mind. And now this gift and her request to sit with him. He could hardly believe his good fortune.

"Then let's go to the living room and I'll explain it. Here, sit by me so you can see when I turn the pages." She eased onto the couch, patting the seat beside her.

Ahmed complied and, as he settled next to her, his nostrils filled with her fragrance. Was this haunting aroma perfume or perhaps a scented soap used to wash her hair? She wore no hijab. He marveled at her long hair swaying smoothly about her shoulders as she talked with animation. He breathed deeply, savoring the wonder of her closeness.

Though they sat apart on the couch without touching, Khadija's profound nearness to Ahmed overwhelmed him. Conscious of this physical proximity as she talked about her ESL textbook, he concentrated hard to focus on her words rather than her closeness.

"Besides language and grammar, I teach my students practical skills like applying for a job. I also tell them about life in our country so they know better what to expect." She traced a slender finger across the title on the workbook's cover. *"American Ways, An Introduction to American Culture."* Turning to a marked page, she read. "'Until we are confronted by a different way of doing things, we assume everyone does things the same way we do and thus our own culture—our values, attitudes, behavior—is largely hidden from our view. When we spend time analyzing another culture, however, we begin to see our own more clearly and to understand some of the subtleties that motivate our behavior and our opinions.'" She asked, "Did you understand this?"

"It says my Middle-Eastern culture seems normal to me until compared with another way of life."

"Yes. If you can't read the whole book, at least try Chapter Two about traditional American values and beliefs." She turned to the chapter and pointed to a heading. *"Individual Freedom.* I tell my class this means the right of individuals to control their destiny without interference from a ruling noble class or government or religion or any other organized authority."

He tried to absorb this. In Middle-Eastern culture, government, religion and education reinforced identical doctrines: submission to Allah, the one-and-only God who held everyone's destiny in his hands.

"Individual freedom" meant a Muslim's choice to obey Allah or not. If you strayed, Sharia Law clamped hard on transgressions. Holy men interpreted Allah's rules and "signs." Good Muslims accepted these interpretations. Subtle variations existed among Shia, Sunni and other Islamic factions, but all agreed upon submission to one God as understood through the words of his prophet, Muhammad. All non-Muslims were Infidels. Therefore, everything Ahmed heard, saw and learned in his life thus far corroborated these as absolute truths. All else was heresy.

"The price paid for this freedom is self-reliance," she continued. "That means individuals must rely on themselves or risk losing freedom. Americans believe they must stand on their own two feet because their destiny is in their hands."

Ahmed shifted uncomfortably. During his conscious adult life, compliance earned praise in his country. They valued obedience and stringently discouraged questioning. Physical punishment might follow humiliation in front of classmates for questioning authority. The military camps he attended used similar social and physical deterrents to discourage independent thinking.

Khadija turned a page. *"The Third Value* is equality of opportunity. That means everyone has an equal chance to succeed in America. Everyone can better himself because there is no fixed condition for his whole life."

"What does this mean, 'no fixed condition'?"

"Some cultures stifle upward mobility." Seeing his confused expression, she amplified. "In some cultures, if the father is a farmer or tailor or baker, his son must be also; then his son's son and so on. They have little opportunity to rise to something better. So a farmer couldn't become a teacher or a shopkeeper or a doctor. In America, with determination and hard work you can pursue any profession you wish. You might start poor, but with hard work you might become rich."

Ahmed knew nothing of his own family. What was his father's occupation? Without photos to reinforce childhood memories, he could hardly remember his parents' faces. The school where the two men took him didn't name his original village. From age five, he'd survived at the whim of those housing, feeding and indoctrinating him, learning early to please or suffer consequences. What future might have awaited him at home if his parents had lived?

Khadija's voice brought him back to reality. "Here's the *Fourth Value* I teach: the cost of equal opportunity is competition. So, if everyone has an equal chance to succeed in America, then it's their duty to try. Competition is part of growing up in America."

In Ahmed's madrassa, youths competed to memorize verses from the Quran while learning the 3-R basics. In training camps, they competed with weapons, mastering skills for recognition and advancement. He didn't know how this applied to business.

"*Value Five*," Khadija pointed to the heading on the page, "is material wealth. Americans want to achieve a better life and raise their standard of living for themselves and their children. The quality and quantity of a person's material possessions are a measure of social status."

Muslims accepted their condition as God's will. Changing it challenged Allah's plan. Ahmed owned no material wealth. He never had. Allah provided for his needs at every juncture. His small exposure to merchants offered little understanding of accumulating tangible wealth.

"We're almost at the end. *Value Six:* the cost of material wealth is hard work. Most Americans believe in the value of hard work. They see material possessions as a reward for their work."

Ahmed had no possessions, but he understood hard work in schools and training camps to earn Allah's blessings.

"This is the last one, the *American Dream*. It's the determination by American parents to provide their children with a better life than their parents were able to provide for them. According to this philosophy, with hard work, courage and determination, anyone can prosper and be successful."

The melodic sound of her lilting voice entranced him. He didn't want this interlude to end. Her pleasant smile, graceful movements and unmistakable femininity fascinated him—against his will. But with this thrill of awareness and desire came confusion and anguish. She was the daughter of a colleague who would enter Paradise with him in a matter of days. What was wrong with him?

"Would you say more about this American dream?" he asked in spite of himself.

"All right. In a land of freedom like ours, you can choose your religion, question authority, say what you think and do what you want so long as it isn't a criminal act. You can marry any adult you can coax to agree. Education is free from kindergarten through high school, and afterward you can work your way through college on a campus or on-line at your computer. You have opportunity to educate yourself, learn skills, choose a job, work hard and achieve a good life for yourself and your family. Individuals are valued over groups. Do you understand this 'freedom'?"

"Perhaps not."

Her smile dazzled him. "Don't worry. Many of my students come from countries with cultures very different from America's, so your answer is not unusual."

In the camps, Ahmed had met men from others lands such as Syria, Egypt, Pakistan, Saudi Arabia. One said he was Lebanese-American but he spoke their language and mentioned none of these "values" Khadija described. "From what countries are these students in your class?"

"This semester's students are from the Congo, Ghana, Mexico, Colombia, Brazil, Korea, Senegal, India, Pakistan, the Dominican Republic—and one is Polish. Do you know of those places?"

"Some."

She unfolded a small world map tucked in the back of the book to show her students' countries.

Added to her lyrical voice and undeniable womanly appeal, his host's daughter displayed knowledge and accomplishments that astounded Ahmed.

"Do you agree with anything the book says?" she asked. Confusion showed on his face.

"In America you don't need to agree. You might, but only after you decide for yourself. Freedom lets you make your own choices, but with freedom comes responsibility. To think what he wants, an American must reason things out for himself, decide what is true by using his mind and his heart to process information. He must think for himself and live with the results of his decisions."

Like a thunderbolt, Ahmed heard his mother's parting words: "use your mind and heart." Now nearly identical words came from Khadija, a girl her father dismissed as "lost to American ways." How did his mother know such things in a village so far away? His radical sect found such talk disrespectful. How could his mother know about freedom? Why would Americans murder his parents if their ideas sounded so similar to their own?

"Ahmed, are you all right?" Khadija put a concerned hand on his arm. The warmth of her palm, the gentle touch of her slender fingers produced a visceral reaction. How could a woman so lovely acquire enough knowledge to teach at a college? In his country, a woman of twenty-three years would have married years earlier and have many children with the man to whom she belonged.

"Sorry, I...I was, how do you say, making the day-dream?"

"Something good?"

"Something...from childhood." He changed the subject. "Thank you for the book, Khadija." There, he said her name out loud. "I will read it."

"You're very welcome. If you have questions, I'll try to answer them."

"Goodbye, Khadija," he said.

"Goodbye to you, also." She stood, smiling.

As she walked from the room, he felt an acute loss. Lengthy mental indoctrination prepared him to follow religious orders given in Allah's name, blessings upon Him. Training camps prepared him to construct and plant improvised explosive devices, to fire guns, trigger grenades, launch rockets and survive gas attacks. Torture prepared him to withstand painful enemy interrogations. But nothing prepared him for the primitive, irresistibly magnetic attraction of a desirable, available woman to a normal, healthy man.

CHAPTER TWENTY-FOUR

FRIDAY, 1:39 PM

His action-packed first twenty-four hours in McLean had recharged Ahmed's energy, but now he felt grateful to retire to his room. Khadija's explanation of her textbook both stimulated and confused him. Her book in his hands felt like a tangible extension of the beautiful girl whose smile and grace drew him with such magnetism.

Men in his country might dismiss their responsibility for such a reaction as the woman's fault, eluding blame by arguing she used her wiles to entice him against his will. But Ahmed saw this self-serving argument as one to avoid blame.

Each generation must replace itself with children, requiring men and women to find and embrace each other. In his culture, family-arranged marriages often forced newlyweds to face mates for the first time on their wedding day. Adjusting to this stranger, who they might not even like, superseded any concept of attraction or love. Not so with Khadija, to whom he felt profoundly attracted both physically and intellectually.

With reluctance, he lay the book on the upholstered chair in his room.

To push Khadija from his mind, he took out the maps he and Mahmud had obtained that day. On the bed he spread open the large map of the State of Virginia and located McLean. Next, he opened the book map of northern Virginia. The front page showed how the collection of inside map pages fit together like puzzle pieces into a whole picture. He turned the pages to McLean and searched until his finger touched the location of this very house.

He then familiarized himself with the target location, studied routes to it and formed a plan.

Next, he opened the desk drawer and assured himself the envelope containing ten diamonds remained where he'd left it.

Smuggled into the U.S., Ahmed had forged ID papers for emergency use only. To the American government, he did not exist. He intended remaining invisible. He knew well how to operate cars but wouldn't drive to avoid risking any inadvertent stop by police, through his own error or another's. Thus his host would chauffeur him where he needed to go. The downside of this inconvenience meant Mahmud had access to information sooner than Ahmed preferred.

The more time he spent with Mahmud, the less he liked the man. Team members needn't like each other to work effectively together, but it helped. Ahmed thought his host smug and cocky, a braggart who craved limelight and took credit for more than he contributed. Yet the man also possessed critical knowledge and skills for the task ahead. Thus Ahmed couldn't exclude him but didn't relish his proximity while driving.

As he removed his shoes and opened the closet to put them away, he did an anxious double take. Where was the toy box? A twinge of panic coursed through him. With a trembling hand, he reached high to inch his suitcase forward on the closet shelf. The doll lay right where he'd left it.

Relief flooded through him at the sight, but, to be sure, he pulled the toy down and opened its clothes to check the slash he'd stitched together. No change. A gentle squeeze of the doll's torso confirmed the packets still inside.

Good. Just as he'd left it.

He tucked the doll safely again behind his suitcase, turned on the bedside table lamp and opened Khadija's textbook. The Table of Contents listed twelve chapters. He flipped to the end: 296 pages total. Every page required concentration because of the language difference and because these new ideas seemed more foreign than the words themselves.

He read all afternoon, finished half the book and laid it aside. These new developments—what did they mean? If Allah had indeed prepared him for this terrorist assignment in McLean, why distract him with this lovely young woman and her information about America? Was it a test? If meant to heighten his resolve for his task here, why did it have the opposite effect? Was the longing for a wife and children he would never have on earth meant to increase the greatness of his sacrifice? Would the reward of virgins in Paradise compensate for this loss on earth? Was he to ignore the girl and her message or was he to listen and learn? What did Allah want him to do?

His mother's last words foretold Allah would guide him, to look for His signs, to seek truth and to use his mind, to think for himself and listen to his heart. Were her words a map from Allah or well-meant but irrelevant ramblings of a dying woman? If he listened to his heart, was this powerful attraction to the girl a sign pointing him in a new direction?

He longed to court her, marry her and raise their children. Impossible if he exploded himself into a million fragments within a week. How to resolve these two powerful influences pulling him in opposite directions?

To seek truth, to use his mind, to think for himself—how did that apply here? From childhood he'd blindly accepted Islam as the one true religion and pledged himself to it, as did all Muslims he knew. But he inherited this by default, not as a deliberate, independent choice like Zayneb's conversion. Did other religions mentioned in Khadija's book also think they understood the only truth? All couldn't be right at the same time, so some must be wrong. According to Islam, they all were wrong, whatever else they thought. Yet believers of those other religions must think Islam wrong? Who was right?

Yesterday a TV news broadcaster discussed demographics. "And so," he said, "as the Muslim population grows faster than the residents in the countries they've adopted, like England and Denmark, they will eventually take over without firing a shot." Even among Islam's faithful, some approved radical extremism and some did not. If an Islamic future was inevitable, would killing women and children now hasten the world's acceptance? Would their planned terrorist attack prove to non-believers the futility of resistance?

Ahmed hadn't felt the pangs of such bitter confusion since he was five years old.

CHAPTER TWENTY-FIVE

FRIDAY, 1:46 PM

Wrapping an under-the-pillow-gift in newspaper for the soon-to-arrive Grands, Jennifer reached for tape as the phone rang. Instead, she grabbed the receiver.

"Hi, Mom," said Hannah's familiar voice. "Have you a minute to talk?"

"Absolutely."

"Because I have news. We did the home inspection. He came only a few hours after we called yesterday, bringing a checklist covering basement to roof inside and more outside. The original structure is over a hundred years old with some updates along the way, so dozens of criteria don't meet current code. But when Adam explained we only want to camp there a few months, the inspector said even this ancient house offered more protection and amenities than a tent."

"What did he say about the water, septic and electricity?"

"All okay, if we don't overload the electrical system with too many appliances. Well water is good quality, but he suggests we recheck it monthly for the short time we're here or use bottled water if in doubt. Septic works, so it's a go. We made the snap decision to move in."

Jennifer heard the caution in her voice. "Happening fast, isn't it?"

"Yes, we started yesterday. I'm here in the kitchen on Winding Trail Road. Adam's excited and I am, too. We've ordered baby chicks for next week—to start a hen house."

"What about your plan to sell the furniture there and re-decorate the entire place?"

"We're on it. Adam's off-duty police buddies were wonderful. A bunch of them pitched in to empty the house, and they even painted some of the rooms, including that dreadful cellar. They had to dismantle the awful human torture crate to get it up the steps. What did you call it?"

Jennifer flinched at the memory of a demented Ruger Yates imprisoning her in the crate. "They...their family called it the 'confinement box,'" Jennifer said in a voice becoming fragile.

Missing this change of tone, Hannah continued. "They worked until midnight last night and came back again today. We stashed our garage-sale stuff in the barn and trashed the rest. Then I cleaned the place inside. We brought Adam's bedroom furniture from the bachelor apartment at his mom's house and put a card table and chairs in the kitchen. We're using paper plates and plan to sleep here tonight. Mom, this is so different and such fun!"

"I...I can hear you're excited. Let us know if we can help. You know we're baby-sitting Kaela's children this weekend, but they don't come 'til 4:00. Meantime, I wrote down craigslist and newspaper ads for local garage sales if you want to visit some. I can make you a copy or look for things you need. Just tell me what and I'll phone you if I find something promising."

"Thanks, Mom. Would you like to come by to see our progress?"

She hesitated. Could she finish the rest and this, too, before the Grands came? "I'll dash by but can't stay long because I'm still getting organized for the weekend."

"Why not bring over the copy of the sales you mentioned around three o'clock and I'll give you our look-for list? Since we live here now, you know where to find me."

"Got it. Love you, Hannah."

"Love you, too, Mom."

Unfolding more newspapers, she finished wrapping the Grand's gifts, put a name on each one and marked them for Friday, Saturday, and Sunday nights. Three Grands times three nights meant nine presents + three for in-the-car. She counted the finished packages and had it right.

A glance at her watch confirmed that, if she hurried, she could make it to the farm and back in time for the Grands' arrival at four o'clock. Locking the house, she jumped in her car and sped toward her daughter at the house she'd hoped never to see again.

CHAPTER TWENTY-SIX

FRIDAY, 1:59 PM

Déjà vu gripped Jennifer as she turned her car into the driveway at 3508 Winding Trail Road. She hadn't been back since the wee hours of that awful night when she showed police the horrors she discovered while Ruger Yates had imprisoned her here. She felt her heart accelerate. Could she handle returning to this place where she'd once expected to die?

She inched forward up the driveway, reliving her headlong race down this very gravel path, gasping for breath, dreading that her maniacal pursuer's fist might stretch out to grab her.

At the top of the driveway, where the level parking area spread between the house and barn, her hand trembled on the door handle. She sat behind the wheel, fighting to regain control. Had she the courage to enter this dreadful house, never mind accept Hannah's decision to live here?

A rap on the window jerked her back to reality. She forced herself to look out the car window, fearing Ruger's evil leer. Instead, Hannah's eager face smiled through the glass.

"Hi, Mom. Your car door's locked."

Jennifer fumbled for the "open" button. Hannah jumped in, leaning close for a hug. "I know you can't stay long but hope you have time for a quick tour to see what we've done."

Jennifer knew what had happened to her here was her problem, not Hannah's. Her daughter shouldn't pay for her mother's inability to discard the past. She forced a convincing smile and said as brightly as she could, "Okay, let's have a look."

"Since we're outside, you'll notice the sheds are gone except the chicken house. The barn's big enough for both our cars plus the old furniture from the house we've kept for the garage sale, but in this case a 'barn' sale. Here, I'll show you." They peered into the structure's dim interior, lighted in daytime by sunshine from open windows and doors.

A good place to start, Jennifer thought. Never there, she held no bad memories of the barn. As they turned toward the house, she asked, "Have you set a date for this sale?"

"No, we wanted to check with you, our resident expert, to pick a day you might help us price it in advance. Some pieces look antique — like the old sewing machine, wringer washtub and farm tools. Here we are." She opened the back door. "Welcome to our new home."

They entered the laundry/mud room where the dog had guarded Jennifer. The kitchen, newly painted, looked bright and cheerful. A card table and chairs stood under the window. "There's no furniture in the other rooms, Mom, except for one bedroom, but I can tell you our plans for them."

Hannah led the tour and, as they moved through the house together, Jennifer thought the empty rooms gave the place an open, almost inviting look — one she hadn't expected — untarnished by the previous furniture she'd cleaned and dusted during her captivity.

"Here's our bedroom." Tastefully furnished with an attractive bedspread, rugs, lamps and TV, it lacked only window curtains. In the bathroom, aqua and yellow towels, rugs and shower curtain created a cheerful décor. In the room where Ruger had kept his exercise machinery, Hannah said, "We kept a few pieces of the equipment for our gym."

Jennifer gazed about. Should she tell Hannah about the closet's ceiling trapdoor to the hideous place where Mathis and Ruger endured imprisonment? No.

They approached the last room of the one-story house, the room where Ruger did his "important work." He hadn't let her clean this room, but as the rest of his Spartan house revealed little about him, she surmised that he'd kept his secrets here. Police sealed that room, awaiting forensics, when she'd returned with them the night of her escape. Still curious, she looked in now with interest. The clean, freshly-painted corner room had two windows facing overgrown foliage outside. Noting scuffed floorboards along one wall, Jennifer remembered what police had said they found beneath them.

"This will be our office, with two computer desks and some book shelves. As you know, we plan to buy gently-used furniture, but some pieces might also work temporarily in the new house we build until we can furnish it properly. Okay, that's it for the upstairs. Ready for the basement?"

Feeling a catch in her chest, Jennifer looked at her watch. "I'm getting short on time, maybe..."

"Mom, this will only take a minute."

"Well..."

Hannah led the way, opening the basement door, and Jennifer descended the stairs slowly behind her daughter. At the bottom of the stairs she realized the room had been transformed. Cream color paint brightened the walls and stairs. The six puny low-watt bulbs had been replaced with simple hoods over brighter bulbs. The grisliness gone, this room might serve a wholesome purpose.

"Remarkable what you've accomplished, and so fast. Impressive, Hannah."

"Remember, Mom, this is only temporary until we subdivide the property and start construction of our very own house; we think a couple of months at most. But I'm starting a vegetable garden now, positioned so we can still use it near the new house. We'll grow most of our own food and raise chickens to control the organic quality of the food we eat. As I told you before, it's the new craze, Mom."

Returning to her car, Jennifer exchanged her garage-sale ad info for Hannah's "look-for" list.

"Forgot to add a mirrored medicine cabinet — you know, the over-the-sink kind. The old one has deteriorated, and a new one will help me get my makeup on straight."

"I'm on the alert. Love to you and Adam, too. Thanks for sharing your vision with me."

"Oh, Mom. You *do* understand."

Jennifer couldn't push away her powerful intuition: Hannah might live here okay, but what about Adam? He grew up in this hellhole of misery and abuse. True, they'd dramatically altered the overall appearance, but would this also change his repressed childhood terrors? He'd avoided any recollections while living with his adoptive parents, but could he continue to do so in the very place where he'd endured the nightmarish treatment? Might some simple experience trigger a hideous memory, allowing other memories to wash over the dam to engulf him?

Jennifer started her car.

"Oh, wait. I almost forgot." Hannah dashed into the house, emerging with a large framed item she carried to the car. "It's the painting Ruger took away from you. We saved it, so you're getting the last word again, Mom."

Putting a corner of the frame on the ground, she spun it around to reveal the finished side: a seated nude woman, her back facing the artist, her loose hair cascading from the top of her head down to her shoulders, below which arched the feminine curve of her back.

Jennifer froze. Could she handle this last tangible evidence of her experience with a madman? Could she bring herself to hang the picture at home, a haunting reminder of this nearly fatal episode in her life? Before she could protest, Hannah slid the painting into the back seat and closed the door.

Robot-like, Jennifer shifted into reverse. To break the painting's hypnotic spell, she made herself look out the window, smile at Hannah and mouth "thank you" since the glass muffled her voice. She looked at her watch. The Grands would arrive in fifteen minutes. She needed to hurry.

CHAPTER TWENTY-SEVEN

FRIDAY, 4:03 PM

Driving home purposefully, Jennifer rushed into the house to receive the arriving Grands, only minutes away if on time. What a busy Friday and hardly over yet.

These particular Grands chose to sleep together in one room when visiting, so she added a roll-away cot to their bedroom and placed a small stuffed animal on each bed as a welcome.

Moving fast, she was setting places for five at the round wicker table in the sunroom when the bell chimed. The door opened, accompanied by squeals and scuffles of children.

"We're here!" they called.

"Wonderful. Let's have a hug." She embraced the children and then Kaela and son-in-law Owain. "So, you're off for a romantic long weekend?"

"A two-fer," Owain explained. "We're parlaying my business trip into a personal vacation."

"Thanks, Mom, for taking on the children. Here's our contingency info: where we'll be and our pediatrician's number. Bedtime's nine but earlier if you can swing it. They can take their own suitcases upstairs if you tell them what room they're in. Milo's still having trouble saying his 'r's, but the speech therapist says he'll outgrow it so just ignore."

"Have you any objection to my taking them to a few garage sales tomorrow?" Jennifer asked.

"Not at all. They'd love it." Her daughter looked around. "Where's Dad?"

Jennifer told them about Kirsten, or "Mrs. D" to them. "Dad's helping Mr. D and the kids select photos for a slide show and finalizing other arrangements. He should be home soon."

Owain looked at his watch. "Well, we better get a move on. We need to drive across the mountains to The Greenbrier in time to settle in before the big dinner tonight."

After quick farewells, Jennifer showed the children to their room. "Could we play in the yard until dinner time?" one begged.

"Yes, but stay inside the fence. If you see spider webs in the tree house, use a stick to poke them out before you play there," Jennifer instructed as they swooshed past her down the stairs.

Heading downstairs herself, she heard the front door open. Jason walked in looking grim. "How was it?" she asked.

"What a struggle." He sighed. "Tony and the children—we all had tears in our eyes going through family pictures. The service is Sunday afternoon at his church. Am I ever glad to come home to find you alive and feisty as ever."

"Missed me, did you?" she teased. "The Grands are in the back yard if you want to say hi. Adam and Hannah moved into the Yates house." She described the home-inspection, the macabre house's transformation with paint, and the garden-and-chicken plans. "You know I feel uneasy about Adam in that house."

"Yes, but let's hope you're wrong, Jen." He laughed. "Ironic, isn't it, how the pendulum swings? One generation moves away from farms to strike it rich in cities. Then the next, born in the city, thinks living from the land is the way to go."

"Becca phoned to remind she's coming home from Virginia Tech for Thanksgiving vacation this weekend. Hard to believe our youngest is a senior this year."

"With the last one nearly out of college and that financial drain almost over, maybe we can do some traveling?"

"Fantastic idea. I'm all for it. Have you anything in mind?"

"Maybe another cruise?"

"I salute that idea." She placed her hand to her forehead then swirled it away. The three Grands dashed into the kitchen, giggling.

"We're getting hungry," announced eight-year-old Christine.

"Is it almost dinner time?" asked six-year-old Alicia.

"Look, I have a cut on my awm," pouted four-year-old Milo, lifting his arm to flash the proof.

Jennifer diagnosed the wound as a scratch. "Grandaddy can bandage it, Milo. He might even find one with Angry Bird pictures on it. Too early for dinner, but how about a snack of apple slices?"

As the three followed Jason out of the kitchen for "doctoring," Jennifer heard one ask him in a plaintive voice, "Do we need an actual cut to qualify for an Angry Bird bandage?"

She couldn't hear Jason's reply but wasn't surprised when they each returned sporting a bandage.

CHAPTER TWENTY-EIGHT

FRIDAY, 5:06 PM

With Ahmed's instructions clear in his mind, Abdul checked the address as he drove north on Route 123 into Vienna. He must make no mistake about this destination.

He didn't like this assignment but knew someone must undertake it. Once Ali left their group, he became what Americans call a "loose cannon." No choice but to eliminate him. Surely the man realized shunning their cell earned a death sentence to punish his unforgiveable disregard of the Great Leader's mandate—and to ensure his silence about their imminent mission.

Though he must kill Ali, Abdul respected the man's courage in speaking up, explaining his decision and electing to withdraw. After all, the man might instead have gone through the motions, pretended to participate in their cause but deliberately fail at his role in their grand mission. What would Abdul himself do under similar circumstances? he wondered.

Impossible, Abdul decided, for he understood Allah's plan for him and saluted this honor with every fiber of his being. What explained Ali's confusion when Islam made it so clear? Allah is the legislator. Allah makes laws. Men must obey Allah's laws only, no other rules. This is the *opposite* of democracy, where people make the laws. One day Sharia Law would bring all men together, accomplishing Allah's will as revealed by his Prophet Muhammad, blessings upon him.

Abdul patted his concealed pistol and felt for the switchblade but liked best the thin garroting rope if circumstances allowed its use. His problem: controlling where the execution took place.

Ali would know the reason for Abdul's visit the moment he saw him. Would Ali try to escape his fate? Perhaps carry a concealed weapon himself? Abdul suddenly realized a risk of this assignment was wasting his own life before their jihad. But what choice had he?

Once he identified Ali's house, he'd park elsewhere to case the place from a safe distance. If Ali left his house, Abdul might follow in the car to do the job elsewhere. Otherwise, he'd ring Ali's doorbell; when he came to the door, Abdul would persuade the man to leave with him to protect his family from further danger. To save them, he'd probably agree.

But if not, least desirable was gunning down Ali in his own home while his family watched, for then he must shoot them all. At least the silencer wouldn't alert neighbors to the carnage taking place. But discovery of the bodies created its own problem if investigating police figured the terrorist connection. But could they? Their careful precautions should prevent such a link.

Prompted by the GPS voice, Abdul made another turn onto Ali's street. He'd drive by once to see how the man's house fit the neighborhood grid. Almost there. It should be in the next block.

But even before the house numbers verified his conclusion, Abdul's mouth opened in disbelief.

He stared at the charred remnants of a house burned to the ground! He drove past, checking the house numbers on either side of the scorched remains for absolute certainty it belonged to Ali.

Parking a block away, he sat still, absorbing this new information. Had Ali killed his family, committed suicide and burned the evidence rather than face the assassin he knew would come? Or did this distraction disguise their departure?

He needed more information. But how to get it?

A youth walking a dog made his way down the block, pausing as the animal sniffed a hydrant. Abdul lowered his driver side window as the boy approached. "Hey, young fella, is that a burned out house in the next block?"

"Yeah," said the boy. "Terrible thing. Whole family burned to death. Two of the daughters were my age. We rode the same school bus. The whole neighborhood watched it happen this morning."

"Do they know how the fire started?"

"Yeah. We all heard the explosion and the house burned so fast it was mostly gone when the fire trucks arrived. They blamed a gas leak and checked every other house in the neighborhood, but the rest are all okay."

"Any survivors?"

"No, they carried out five body bags. Wiped out the whole family. An awful thing." The impatient dog jerked his leash. "Gotta go, Mister."

"Thanks, Kid."

Abdul turned his car around, retraced his way back to the house, parked by a neighbor's curb and snapped a cell phone picture of Ali's destroyed home. With his untraceable phone, he'd inform Ahmed. Tomorrow's newspaper would surely feature its own photo story of this local disaster.

But one kid's story wasn't enough. He called to a woman raking leaves in her yard along the sidewalk and then a man repairing his curbside mailbox. Both told close versions of the same story, right down to the five body bags. Driving from the housing area, Abdul felt considerable relief. He'd accomplished his unwelcome task without risk, exposure or firing a single shot. He thanked Allah for smiling on him this day.

CHAPTER TWENTY-NINE

FRIDAY, 9:03 PM

At dinner with Mahmud's family, Ahmed could scarcely stifle his longing glances toward Khadija. Her charming smile, her graceful movements, her delicate hands—she fascinated him. Because of his bleak future, this woman could never belong to him, yet his attraction to her intensified every time he saw her. Did the way she smiled back acknowledge his interest? Under other circumstances, he would speak to her father about a marriage contract, but with his death a week away, he struggled to push away her alluring distraction.

As Ahmed excused himself after dinner, bidding polite farewells to those at the table, Khadija touched her napkin to her lips and stood also. "I must work on my lesson plan for Saturday's class," she announced, gliding gracefully out the door. Mahmud glared as the two left. Zayneb studied her plate, hoping their attraction would not point Khadija toward the same wrong path she'd chosen. Worse, what if her daughter should emotionally substitute this attentive foreigner for the father whose love she could never win?

Ahmed placed a hand on the stair's newel post, motioning Khadija to precede him up the flight. In a friendly gesture, she placed her graceful palm atop his hand and asked, "Did you read any part of the book I gave you?"

Electric currents shot up his arm from the feel of her hand on his. The powerful, strict taboo forbidding touching between men and women not of the same family seemed impossible to shake. Amazed that his voice sounded normal instead of the strangled words he expected, he answered,

"I read half and will finish the rest tonight." He needed to say more to lengthen the time they stood together. "How...how do you summarize this American culture you teach, this freedom?"

She thought a moment and gave him a beautiful smile as the answer came to her. "Question everything—everything you've been told or taught. Don't let anybody do your thinking for you. Use your own mind. Discover your own conclusions and, when you do, act on what you have learned. If not, you're just somebody else's robot."

Intrigued by her words, with a boldness he hardly believed, he placed his other hand gently atop hers. She didn't pull away. "Could...could you please give me an example?"

Several possibilities crossed her mind before she picked one. "Okay. You know about the 9/11 events in this country. Their handlers brainwashed those terrorists into thinking they'd earn the world's respect while glorifying their god. In fact, the world sees them as maniacal radicals murdering innocent, unprotected men, women and children with no chance to fight back and in the name of an equally crazed religion. In war, armed soldiers can defend themselves in a fair fight. But in terrorist attacks, victims have no chance, so killing them is easy. Not brave but cowardly. Men allowing others to use them to accomplish such awful acts aren't thinking for themselves; they are slaves to manipulators who waste their lives in this shameful way."

Stung by her words, Ahmed recoiled. She saw this change immediately, wondering how a simple truth produced this unexpected effect. To soften her words she focused her hazel eyes upon his. "If we think for ourselves, we will know what to do when the time comes, and it may be very different from what we thought was right when others manipulated us."

At that moment Mahmud lurched into the room. They disengaged their hands on the banister just in time. "What's the delay?" he growled. "Why are you lingering here?"

"I have a stone in my shoe." Ahmed fumbled with his foot, allowing Khadija to reach the top step before he followed at a respectful distance. Mahmud snorted unmistakable anger.

Moments later, Ahmed closed his bedroom door and clutched his head in his hands as if to prevent his brain from exploding out through his fingers. He'd arrived in McLean crystal clear about his life's mission and confident about commanding this assignment with skill for the sole glorification of his god. But this delicate, intelligent woman threw open the door to a hornet's nest of new thinking.

He sat heavily on his bed, logically and emotionally disoriented. His head swam. The last of the structured world he thought he knew had changed at the bottom of those stairs.

As he hung his clothes in the closet to prepare for sleep he double-checked the doll, right where he'd left it behind the suitcase. He lay down on his bed, forearm covering his eyes, trying to put it all together, but the enormity overwhelmed him. He felt a wave of fatigue. He'd face those problems tomorrow. Sitting up in bed, he opened Khadija's book to read the second half, as he'd promised her. But after the first few pages, the open book fell aside as his eyes closed and he drifted into a fitful sleep spawning a disturbing dream.

He and Khadija smiled on their wedding day, pledging themselves to each other before their friends and their god. Next they were alone together in their home. Nothing stood in the way of their hungry love and its long-awaited expression. But as they kissed, men from the terrorist cell pounded on the door. Ahmed and Khadija dashed up the stairs to escape as the men splintered the door and burst into the house. Mahmud led the men as they thundered up the stairs after the newlyweds. Ahmed and his bride rushed into the upstairs room, locked the door and hid in the wardrobe. They heard the room's door smash open, feet shuffling, voices shouting and furniture banged about. Mahmud said, "We're leaving explosives for you to strap to your body. You know your duty. We're ready to complete our task. Come downstairs wearing the bombs or we'll kill you both and finish the job without you."

He heard the men leave. He tried to get out of the wardrobe but found it locked. He leaned back and pushed with his feet to open the doors. When he reached back to pull Khadija out with him, she was gone. Instead she lay on the bed, covered in blood, her legs sticking out from her twisted skirt. He ran to her and shook her. Her eyes fluttered open. They were green, not hazel. He leaned close to hear her whisper, "Seek truth, use your mind, think for yourself and listen to your heart." As her dead body slid to the floor he realized next to her lay the still, small body of their baby. How could they have a child on their wedding day without consummating their love? Yet there lay their tiny infant in a pool of her own blood, eyes staring.

Horror, confusion and agony of ripped-away love formed an anguished cry that rose in his chest and erupted from his mouth. "NO!" he heard himself scream.

Jerking him from this tormented sleep, the loud rapping on the door was real this time. Ahmed blinked as he rose onto his elbows. His body felt clammy. Mahmud's voice called from the hallway. "Ahmed, are you all right?"

"Yes," he groaned. "Another bad dream, that's all. Sorry."

After a moment, he heard his host move down the hall. He sat up to look at his watch: 9:05. Still haunted by the dream, he picked up Khadija's book. He would finish it tonight.

CHAPTER THIRTY

FRIDAY, 9:09 PM

After rapping on Ahmed's door in response to his guest's outcries, described as another nightmare, Mahmud walked further down the hall to his daughter's room and knocked on her door.

She had just pushed her lesson plan aside, leaned back in her desk chair and rubbed her eyes when she heard the knock.

"Khadija?" Her father's stern voice caused her to sigh. What would he belittle her about this time? "I must talk with you. *Now*, Khadija!"

Could she stall him until morning? No, he'd pound on the door until she let him in, getting angrier by the second. And when angry, he could turn mean.

"All right." With resignation she unlocked her door.

Mahmud stepped inside, closed the door and spoke in a low, forceful voice. "Khadija, I want you to *stay away from Ahmed.* This is a direct order. This is my house and he is my guest. He is here on important business and is not to be distracted. You are five years past your eighteenth birthday. I fulfilled this country's legal requirement to provide for you until then, although you disappoint me every day. I let you stay on here out of charity but need only an excuse to throw you out of my house, so don't even think of disobeying this order. Stay away from Ahmed. Is this clear?"

For years she'd wanted to leave this house to share an apartment with a girlfriend, but the fear on her mother's face when she spoke of moving stalled that plan. To her father she said, "I have shown your visitor good manners. How long is he staying?"

"That is none of your business. He is my guest and he will stay as long as I want him to stay. A lot longer than *you'll* stay if you dare disobey me. Do you understand what I want?"

"Yes, I know what you want," she answered. But was it what she wanted?

"Good. And you understand the consequences if you fail to obey me?"

"I hear you." Unblinking, she returned his intimidating stare. Grinding his teeth with rage, he stormed from her room. She closed and locked the door after him before sinking onto her bed.

No tears flowed; her emotional wounds had long since scabbed over. Their failed relationship began way before she ignored his demands to wear the hijab, use no makeup and wear loose-fitting, body-disguising clothes. He'd already stopped caring about her by the time she'd started first grade. Devastating as this rejection felt to a little girl yearning for her father's affection and approval, at least her mother's love had never wavered. For this she owed her allegiance.

Khadija remembered being rocked on her mother's lap. "It's not our fault," she soothed her child. "Your father...he doesn't know how to show his love for us. You are precious and intelligent and beautiful. Let's try to forgive him because he can't seem to help himself."

Seven years later, thirteen-year-old Khadija showed her father her straight-A eighth grade report card. Rather than praise, his words cut hard. "What an insult! This shows you obey your school but not me. In my house my word must be law, but you argue, pretending to ask reasonable questions. You defy me. You're lost to Islam. You're...you're a filthy American." He spat out the last word. "Legally, I must allow you in my house now, but unless you respect my wishes, that will end one day. And look at you," his lip curled in disgust. "You even look like your mother."

When 9/11 stunned America in 2001, Khadija and her mother gasped in horror at the TV scenes unfolding, but her father seemed delighted. He exulted in the planes exploding the skyscrapers. When the smoking buildings pancaked to the ground, he jumped to his feet with a grin and a triumphant fist in the air. Khadija and her mother exchanged startled looks at this display.

Khadija understood how a naturalized American citizen might feel dual loyalties to his native country and his adopted one, but her father's reaction showed no affection at all for the U.S.A.

She forgot his anti-American behavior until another incident ten years later. After the stunning news of Bin Laden's death on May 1, 2011, her father moped for days, becoming more irritable than ever. Only little Safia escaped his verbal wrath. Khadija shared her country's post 9/11 concern about safety from terrorists, foreign or domestic, but clearly her father did not. Was her father's distaste for the U.S.A. and his family merely that of a discontented Middle-Eastern ex-pat—or something else?

She knew passion for a foreign cause had compelled Irish-Americans to donate funds to the IRA. Jews in America helped those in Israel. Was her father's loyalty similar? Yet those other causes didn't wreak havoc on American soil while Islamic radical extremists did. Was her father aiding such terrorists? Circumstantial evidence pointed in that direction. But if so, was it for terrorism in the Middle-East or here in the United States?

Why couldn't he be more like Ahmed? she wondered. Both men sprang from Middle-Eastern roots, but their guest liked her even though her father did not. Ahmed listened attentively to her ideas and asked questions about American culture. This built confidence that she *could* appeal to a Middle-Eastern man after all, just not to her father.

She wanted to punish her father for wounding her with his rejection. Withholding her affection didn't get his attention since he didn't love her anyway. Defying him did. Even such negative attention felt better than no attention at all. Would Ahmed defy and punish her father?

A plan formed in her mind. She'd return Ahmed's obvious interest in her. If trust developed between them, perhaps she could ask him to find out if her father covertly aided terrorists.

Khadija sat upright as a daring new idea struck her. What if she married Ahmed? She smiled at the satisfying slap-in-the-face this would deliver to her heartless father.

DAY THREE

SATURDAY

CHAPTER THIRTY-ONE

SATURDAY, 6:32 AM

After his chilling dream the night before, Ahmed realized how cherished this beautiful creature had become. So real was his nightmare—from the happiness of marriage to Khadija to the ghastly home invasion and her sickening murder—that he arose early on Saturday morning needing assurance she still existed. He dressed to appear by 7:00 at the breakfast table in order not to miss her, but as he put on shoes a rustling noise caused him to turn as a note slid under his bedroom door. He retrieved and opened it.

> *Ahmed,*
> *My father tells me not to talk to you again but I think we have more ideas to discuss. If you agree, let us meet at the McLean Library today. You can walk there in 20 minutes. I enclose a map, but if you get lost, ask anyone for directions. Since you attend to business during the day, I suggest 4:00 this afternoon. Please hide your "yes" or "no" answer under the blue flowerpot on the table at the end of this upstairs hall. Thank you.*
> *Your friend,*
> *Khadija*

He inhaled sharply, realizing he'd held his breath as he read the note. She was alive and he'd see her again—today! A smile of relief crossed his face, followed by a quick frown. Had this occurred in his homeland, honor directed him to give the note to the girl's father for proper reprimand of her immodest behavior. But not here, not now...

Hurrying to his desk he tore a sheet of paper in half, wrote "yes" and folded the note into a small square. Opening the door, he looked both ways before easing into the empty hall. The table stood near the top of the stairs. He paused, tucked the note under the flowerpot, made sure it didn't show under the edge and continued down the stairs.

He joined Mahmud at the dining room table as Heba brought breakfast. Zayneb and Safia entered a short time later, but to his great disappointment, Khadija did not appear. In a foul mood, Mahmud criticized everyone except his guest for real or imagined demerits and particularly Heba's breakfast—the coffee too strong, the eggs too dry, the fruit not ripe, the pancakes under-cooked. The food tasted fine to the rest, but no one contradicted him to alleviate the servant's shame at this verbal lashing.

When Mahmud threw his napkin into his syrupy plate and stalked from the room, awkward silence enveloped the table. Then Ahmed cleared his throat and said to Heba in front of Zayneb and Safia, "Your breakfast tasted very good. Thank you." Did he see a tiny flicker of appreciation before she disappeared into the kitchen? Hard to tell since she always averted her face.

Certain Mahmud couldn't hear, Zayneb whispered, "Bless you for that kindness. She's worked twenty-four years for our family." She wanted to add how, during those years, she'd discovered and engaged Heba's bright mind. But such knowledge would infuriate her husband and this stranger, Mahmud's kinsman, might reveal her secret if he knew.

Ahmed excused himself from the table and found his host in the garage. "Shall we leave in twenty minutes, Mahmud?"

Still testy, the man asked, "Where do we go today and what time is our meeting?"

"Nine o'clock in a church parking lot in Arlington. I'll enter their car, which will leave immediately. You wait three minutes then drive around until I call you with my pickup location."

"You are our leader. We can't control your safety once you're in their car. Is this wise?"

"Today's meeting is important but with little risk. The next meeting is more serious because we strike the deal and the third meeting perhaps dangerous when we make the trade. I will remind them any failure to cooperate as agreed earns deadly consequences." Ahmed left to go upstairs.

On the way to his room he looked under the blue flowerpot. His note was gone. In his room he took the envelope from his desk, assured himself the packet of ten diamonds lay inside and strapped to his leg the leather-sheathed knife bought the day before. He stood, smoothing his pant leg over the weapon to conceal this protection.

Downstairs, he climbed into Mahmud's vehicle. As the men drove away at 8:00 they passed neighborhood front yards strewn with sale items. Shoppers spilled from cars coursing through the subdivision. Ahmed couldn't believe the transformation from yesterday's quiet residential streets to today's purposeful lines of cars clogging their streets. Strangers roamed sidewalks and crossed lawns to shop the community sale's merchandise.

"What's this?" Ahmed asked in surprise.

Already in a bad mood, Mahmud ranted. "This idiotic American custom disgraces our home. Look—our once dignified neighborhood streams with traffic and herds of strangers roaming like camels across our lawns. At least in the Middle-East we have the sense to create market places."

They stopped for gas at Old Dominion and Chain Bridge before driving into North Arlington to re-con the meeting site. Parking nearby to study the situation, they agreed the small church's parking lot seemed surveillance-free. "Those we meet don't want attention any more than we do."

Troubled, Mahmud asked, "Should I know who they are if...in case something goes wrong?"

Ahmed thought this over. "They are Russian. Record their license number, but I expect no trouble at this meeting. I don't know where they intend to drop me after we talk or how long this will take; probably thirty minutes or less. I will call your cell phone with that location."

"If it is not a place I know, with an exact address my GPS will find you. Shall we drive the neighborhood until it's time for the meeting?" At Ahmed's nod, Mahmud started the car.

CHAPTER THIRTY-TWO

SATURDAY, 8:00 AM

Zayneb stood at the window as the car disappeared from view, before hurrying into action. She'd check the house one last time for saleable items, for this opportunity to make money was rare. In each room she looked under beds, through drawers and in closets, collecting items in a plastic bag. She hesitated at Ahmed's closed door then opened it resolutely to continue her search.

Yesterday, Heba had removed the toy box from this closet. No stray playthings lay under the bed. Curiosity prompted her to open several drawers and touch the contents to better assess what threat their mysterious guest posed. Uncertain about the man's visit or what to expect from him next, she looked under the pillow and mattress for a weapon but found none.

High in the closet, a doll's foot stuck out from behind the guest's suitcase. She pulled over the desk chair and climbed up to nudge his valise forward. She extracted Safia's old doll and repositioned the case. Examining the dressed doll, she thought it saleable and added it to her bag. Ten minutes later, the doll joined her other for-sale items on a blanket spread in Roshan's yard.

Doubting Zayneb had money to take her daughters to other sales, Roshan pressed cash into her god-daughter's hand. "Here, take this. If you must, pay me back later from your earnings here."

Zayneb wanted to protest, but this cash advance seemed a blessing. She ugged Roshan and thanked her before hurrying home with a big smile.

"Guess what," she said to her daughters, "let's walk around to see the sales. Maybe we'll find a little surprise for each of you."

Safia giggled her delight but Khadija asked, "Would Baba approve?"

Zayneb hid the nervousness in her laugh, "Let me deal with your father. You two do not need to upset him with this information. Do we agree about that, girls?"

"Yes," they chorused.

Zayneb clutched at this chance for harmless fun with her daughters. If Mahmud found out, she knew he'd give the girls a tongue lashing.

Her punishment would be far worse.

CHAPTER THIRTY-THREE

SATURDAY, 9:05 AM

At the exact meeting time, Mahmud's car drove into the church parking lot where a car waited. "May Allah bless you, praised is His name," Mahmud said as Ahmed walked to the other vehicle.

That car's window lowered as he approached. "Are you here to look at a ring?" Ahmed asked.

"Yes, a diamond ring." The code words matched. The driver spoke with a heavy Russian accent. "Get in the back."

Mahmud watched Ahmed enter the car and saw it glide away. He counted three minutes and left the lot, deciding to stop en route for coffee and a snack while he awaited Ahmed's call.

Inside the Russian's vehicle, a male driver and another man sat in the front seat, but to Ahmed's surprise, a woman waited for him in the rear. "Hello," she said in unaccented English. "You may call me...Natasha."

She offered her hand, which he shook. "And you are...?"

"You may call me...Mustafa," Ahmed invented, noting her slight body, expensive clothes and European features.

"Good. Have you something to show me, Mustafa?"

He passed her the envelope from his shirt pocket. She eased it open, spread the jewelry paper and glanced at the diamonds. Pulling a jeweler's loupe from her purse, she held it to her eye to examine several stones. "Boris, can you park where I'll get direct sunlight?"

As Boris obliged, she made no small talk. A few minutes later the car maneuvered so sunshine streamed in her window. She studied each gem with her loupe. "How many?"

"Three hundred, similar size, same quality as promised in advance. Guaranteed."

"And you want...?"

"Three million American dollars." Ahmed read no reaction in her face or body language. "You were sent our list: part cash plus certain explosives and weapons. I have a copy of that list with me if you'd like to see it again. We understand such armaments present no problem for you."

She matched this new list against the original and locked eyes with Ahmed. "Three million?"

"We know and you know these diamonds are more valuable than this amount. A bargain for you. I'm told you recognize a special deal when you see one. We can approach other buyers, but we talk to you first for three reasons: First, our organizations have made mutually satisfactory deals together before, so a good record exists between us. Second, you are a good fit for our interest in a combination payment, part cash and part military ordnance. Third, we share mutual common enemies: the United States and Israel."

Natasha gave him a disarming smile. "When?"

"Immediately."

"You have my attention, Mustafa, but someone else makes this decision. We must test these diamonds in our lab to be sure. In twenty-four hours we will use the phone contact already established to speak further about 'the ring.'"

"Thank you, Natasha."

"Boris," she instructed the driver, "our meeting is over. Find a comfortable place for Mustafa to wait for his ride."

Fifteen minutes later Mahmud found Ahmed sitting on a bench in Cherrydale.

"Where to next?"

"To make our videos for American TV with the other cell members at Abdul's."

CHAPTER THIRTY-FOUR

SATURDAY, 10:01 AM

Dodging shards of glass scattered across the kitchen floor, Jennifer rinsed a trickle of blood from her hand and pressed a towel hard against her palm to hasten clotting. Aware of the room's deathly silence, broken only by the ticking wall clock, she looked up. Across the room, three pairs of eyes riveted upon her from open-mouthed faces frozen with morbid fascination. This situation needed a fast positive spin. "So... what exactly happened here?" she asked her visiting Grands.

Christine took the lead, talking fast. "Milo wanted a drink and pushed a chair over to the counter and climbed up on it to get a glass but the glasses were stacked in the cupboard so tight on that little wire shelf and when the shelf jiggled as he reached for one, a lot of glasses fell out instead."

"And," Alicia added, "some broke when they fell on the counter and some rolled off and smashed on the floor. Milo didn't mean it, Gran. Nobody could stop them once they started falling."

Christine cut in again importantly. "And because I was the only one wearing shoes, I walked through the pieces of glass to rescue Milo and carry him over here where he'd be safe."

Four-year-old Milo hung his head with guilt. "I'm sowwy, Gwan," he apologized.

Jennifer smiled. "I know you're sorry, Milo. You didn't mean to do it. Accidents are strange because they happen without warning. A good accident might be finding a dollar bill on the sidewalk, but a bad accident might be dangerous, like breaking this glass into sharp pieces."

"Would you like an Angry Bird bandage, Gran? I know where they are," Christine offered.

"Yes, Chris. Thank you. Have you thought of becoming a doctor someday?" The girl nodded. When she brought the bandage, Jennifer asked her to put it on the cut. "Tell me: what can we learn from this?"

"Broken glass is dangerous," volunteered Christine.

"It's so dangerous it can even cut *grownups,*" added wide-eyed Alicia.

"I was twying to be a big boy and get a glass all by myself," explained Milo.

Jennifer soothed, "I understand. Lucky I was close in the next room to hurry in when I heard the crash, but what if I hadn't heard it?" The youngsters exchanged nervous looks, unsure of a "right" answer. Jennifer helped them out. "Is it safe for children to clean up sharp pieces of glass?"

The three stirred uneasily, thinking a practical side of this solution meant avoiding discovery.

"The safest idea," Jennifer supplied, "is getting an adult's help to solve a dangerous problem. We'll solve Milo's problem this way. My bad decision was gathering up pieces of glass with my hand. You see what happened." She held up her bandaged hand. "My good decision is using paper towels to brush them off the counter and into the wastebasket like this. Notice I'm wearing shoes to protect my feet just as Chris did. Next," she indicated the broom and dustpan, "we'll sweep up every piece we see. Then to make sure we don't miss any tiny pieces, I'll vacuum the floor so it's safe to go barefoot here again. Okay, what will you do next time about broken glass?"

"Call an adult," said Christine with confidence. Seeing Jennifer's approving smile, the other two chorused the same answer.

Alicia looked confused. "Is this today's 'learning surprise'?"

Jennifer laughed. "No, just an *extra* learning surprise. Okay," she repeated, "call an adult to help you solve a dangerous problem like this one. Now you each get a drink and a cookie. Then off to play while I clean up here. Did you have fun going to garage sales with me this morning?"

Their happy faces, rapid nods and enthusiastic murmurs confirmed they had.

"Could we do it again tomorrow?" Christine asked.

"Maybe. Now since it's raining outside, please take the toys you bought at today's sales downstairs to the playroom." Chatting happily, they bustled down the carpeted steps.

CHAPTER THIRTY-FIVE

SATURDAY, 10:16 AM

Jennifer's mind wandered as she vacuumed the remaining glass slivers from the kitchen floor. Forty years ago she and Jason began their family, producing five children in eleven years. Now all were grown, four of the five married and the fifth finishing college. Her bonus: ten little Grands. She thought of the three Grands' excitement at this morning's garage sales. Like her own young children, they enjoyed this bargain-hunting fun, and each found special treasures.

Jennifer's zeal for these sales finally overcame the understandable fear after her terrifying abduction and narrow escape last year. Surviving the nightmarish hell-hole she stumbled into while following a seemingly harmless garage-sale sign, she vowed never again to attend such sales alone. With second-hand sales gaining popularity due to the economy's slump, her desire for mutual protection wasn't difficult to solve, as shoppers flocked to them.

Besides local weekend garage and estate sales, she often visited the "Treasure Trove," McLean's long-time successful consignment shop benefitting Fairfax Hospital. Two newer consignment shops also made her list: "Betsy & Cornelia's" on Chain Bridge Road and "The Treasure Shop" in Chesterbrook's strip mall, which benefitted Vinson Hall residence for military seniors. Annual standbys included certain McLean and Arlington church bazaars.

Some friends scoffed at her garage-sale hobby, but she found the sales entertaining and practical. Today, for example, she armed each Grand with five dollars before they piled into her Cadillac Crossover for the adventure. She reviewed the notebook listing sales attended each day. They'd stopped at one big community sale offering scores of treasure-finding opportunities.

Seeing this as a useful budgeting lesson, she said, "Remember, this is your money now. You might buy one thing for five dollars or five things for a dollar each. You decide how to spend it."

Digesting this, Alicia asked shrewdly, "Gran, if I don't buy anything can I still keep the money?"

"Yes," But Jennifer knew this unlikely as she stopped at the first sale and they all jumped out.

"Let the fun begin," she said as the children scampered in search of toys. While examining merchandise herself, she kept a close eye on the children. Her trauma with Ruger Yates honed her sense of caution. Better safe than sorry with beloved Grands to protect.

During their tour of the many sales, Milo bought four life-like dinosaurs and a pop-up picture book about them. The book retailed for $22 but a delighted Milo paid only $1.00. At that sale, Alicia bought an unusual doll and at another a doll bed with sheets and a pillow, the right size for her new doll. At yet another she found a case for storing the doll. All this and a dime left.

Christine spotted a velvet-lined jewelry box with a pirouetting ballerina twirling to a music box melody. At other sales she added bracelets, a ring and hair clips. Last, a brush, comb and mirror set in a lovely case to groom her dolls and herself.

Jennifer found a $30 pair of artificial topiary trees in terra cotta pots for each side of her front door. But the timeliest discovery of the day was a $5 wood-framed bathroom medicine cabinet for Hannah—new, with the original bill in the box.

She must call Hannah about that find. Jason should return from golf any minute, and she needed to plan lunch for them all. She opened the refrigerator when a thunder of footfalls pounding up the basement steps distracted her. The Grands rushed into the kitchen, breathless and wild-eyed messengers of volatile news.

Their normally high young voices rose to even shriller falsettos as they all shouted in varying decibels: "BROKEN GLASS."

CHAPTER THIRTY-SIX

SATURDAY, 10:29 AM

Grabbing broom and dustpan, Jennifer hurried after the Grands, who careened ahead down the stairs. "Are you wearing shoes?" she called ahead. "Please don't touch the glass until I get there."

Except for windows or light bulbs, she could think of no breakable glass in the playroom. Turning right at the bottom of the steps, she noticed each child had staked out a play area on the big rug. Alicia pointed. Her doll's undressed body lay on the floor amid a splash of glinting pieces of glass.

"Careful," Jennifer cautioned. "Let's take a look." At first glance, these twinkling glass fragments looked different from the jagged irregular pieces in the kitchen. She knew tempered glass shattered in sheets, but could glass shatter into uniform lumps?

Mindful of the lesson upstairs, the Grands gasped as Jennifer brushed a tentative finger lightly over a few of the pieces as she investigated the situation. "Christine, please run up to the kitchen desk drawer and bring the magnifying glass. It should be right on top."

The child rocketed away, returning breathless to give it to Jennifer. Trying for an even better look, she pointed to the corner. "Alicia, would you please bring the flashlight plugged into the wall socket at the bottom of the steps? This light just isn't bright enough."

Alicia spun away to get it for her grandmother. Jennifer focused the flashlight beam under the magnifying glass until clear, enlarged images focused. The children sensed something amiss when she gasped.

"Gran, what is it?" Christine asked.

Jennifer moved the magnifier across the pieces several times.

"What's wong, Gwan?" asked little Milo's troubled voice as Jennifer stared at the scatter of glittering globs on the rug and floor. What she saw seemed impossible. Diamonds?

Jennifer sat down on the rug. "Children, these don't look like regular glass. These look like special glass used for jewelry. But where did they come from?"

Christine answered quickly. "They came out of Alicia's doll."

"Is that right, Alish?" To the girl's affirmative nod, Jennifer asked, "But how? Bring the doll and show me."

Alicia took a deep breath to propel the excited rush of words tumbling out. "A boy in my class at school, his name is Tommy, he had an operation in his chest but the doctor left something inside when he stitched it up and it made Tommy sick so he had to go to the hospital again to get the thing taken out and when he came back to school at recess he pulled up his shirt and showed us his stitches." Out of breath, she inhaled quickly before racing on. "So when I undressed my new doll, I saw stitches across her chest just like Tommy's and when I squeezed her body I felt something inside just like what happened to Tommy. I didn't want it to make her sick like it did Tommy so I broke the thread to get it out and when I pulled her chest open, folded papers fell out and the glass chunks fell out of them."

"Actually," Chris revealed, "she opened the papers to see what was inside and then they fell out."

"Since this happened without warning, then is it an accident?" asked Alicia.

Jennifer recalled her explanation of good and bad accidents. "Yes, I guess it is but a strange accident indeed. The good news is they aren't sharp and can't hurt you the way most broken glass does. See." She let each child hold one to confirm this. "Let's collect them all with a lump-of-glass hunt like an Easter-egg-hunt. We'll crawl around looking everywhere with sharp eyes to find them all. Milo, could you please bring a container from the toy box big enough to hold all these little pieces?" He hustled on his assignment, returning with a plastic bucket.

"Perfect, Milo. Thank you for finding just the right holder. Okay, put the ones you find in your own pile and at the hunt's end we'll see who found the most."

They scurried around, retrieving sparkling gems that had skittered across the floor. The girls found many and Jennifer surreptitiously placed a few near Milo's fingers.

"Look, I found some, too, Gwan," he crowed, placing two gems in his "pile."

Wanting to search more thoroughly on her own, she said brightly, "Thanks, children. Good job. Let's see. Looks like Chris gets first prize for the most, Alish gets a wonderful second prize and Milo gets the thrilling third prize. Why don't you all run upstairs to watch the special movie I rented for you while I get your prizes and sew the doll back together?"

She followed with the bucket of gems and the doll as the children rushed upstairs to the media room, found places on the couch, snuggled against welcoming pillows and pulled fleece throws over them. Starting the DVD, Jennifer guessed they'd remain enthralled for at least an hour. Putting the bucket and doll on the kitchen table, she started back downstairs but stopped, hearing Jason's voice as he came in the front door.

"Hello," he called. "The victorious golfer has returned."

They hugged, but one look at her face signaled a problem. A man learned a few things about his wife in forty-one years of marriage. "So," he said tentatively, "have you survived the Grands today?"

"Oh, Jay, I'm so glad you're home. Where to begin?"

"Some excitement this morning?" He braced himself for a hold-onto-your-hat tale. She recounted the broken-glass-in-the-kitchen saga and the diamond story. She showed him the sparkling gems in Milo's plastic bucket. Jason rolled a few around in his hand. "They look real enough," he said. "You think more might still be downstairs? Let's grab flashlights and have another look." He found several more stones and, using a chopstick from the toy box, she slid another two from the narrow space beneath a heavy bookcase.

Back upstairs, Jason examined the doll's incision. "Jen, what's this?" He extracted four more folded paper packets. They exchanged bewildered looks as he eased the packets open. Sure enough, diamonds twinkled inside each.

He stared at his wife incredulously. "You say these came from a garage sale, Jen?"

"I know it sounds incredible, Jay, but...yes, they did."

CHAPTER THIRTY-SEVEN

SATURDAY, 10:40 AM

"What explains this?" Jason wondered aloud. "If someone hid the diamonds inside this doll to protect them, how did it end up in a garage sale?"

"Jay, aren't you assuming they're valuable? They might be glass beads or rhinestones or zircons. But isn't the mystery kind of exciting?"

"Exciting? It's *bizarre!* We need to figure this out."

She nodded, his response calming her a bit. They checked on the Grands, ensconced in the media room, before spreading out the evidence on the glass-topped wicker table.

"How many do you suppose there are?" she speculated.

"If you count the loose ones from the basement, I'll count these in the packages."

"Wait!" she said. "Let's pour each batch onto a paper plate to separate the groups. Easy to count and they won't roll away." He nodded, she brought the plates and they counted. "Let's see, this first package has fifty," Jason counted. "And 86 came from the floor."

"Fifty each in the second and third pouches. Here, you count the last one."

"Fifty here also."

"So the four unopened packages hold 50 diamonds each and the other two probably did also. Since the two packets spilled on the floor should equal 100 but since we found only 86..."

"...the other 14 might still be downstairs."

"Six pouches times 50 in each equals 300 stones."

"...assuming we find the missing 14."

"Geez!"

"Isn't this wild?" she laughed. "They're big stones. If they're real and each is worth even $3,500 times 300." She grabbed the kitchen desk's calculator, punched in numbers, read the total and giggled. "Just over a million dollars! It's like winning the lottery, Jay."

"Jen, Jen. Calm down."

"You're right. Let's think this through. Two possibilities: they're real or they're fake. Maybe just 'paste' as the British call that brilliant-looking lead-glass composition stuff."

"Yes," he agreed. "We need to know which."

She brightened. "It's Saturday morning. Stores are open. If you watch the Grands, I could take some stones to a local jeweler. Learning their value is critical to deciding what to do next."

Planning on a relaxed Saturday watching sports on TV or working in the garden, Jason frowned. "Well, I guess I could. You wouldn't be gone long, would you?"

"Back in an hour, tops."

"Well...okay then."

She grabbed her purse. "How should we organize this?" She focused on the stones. "They all look the same, but what if some packages have fakes and some reals?"

"Let's put one from each group in a different Ziploc bag. I'll put a post-it note number from one to five on each pouch and we'll magic marker that same number on the corresponding Ziploc.

"But didn't we find six pouches?"

"Well, yes, but two packets mixed together when they fell out on the floor."

"You're right."

They followed Jason's plan. She put the Ziplocs in a large manila envelope, hiked her purse strap over her shoulder, jingled her keys and started for the garage. "About Grand-sitting, it's easiest to entertain them inside, but if you decide to garden they could play near you in the yard. Just keep a close watch on them, please, Jay. I couldn't face their parents if anything happened to them on our watch."

Did her last warning words hang in the air after she left or was it only Jason's imagination?

CHAPTER THIRTY-EIGHT

SATURDAY, 10:57 AM

Jennifer pulled out of the driveway onto the street before realizing she had no exact destination. A jeweler, yes, but which one? She ticked off the factors in her mind. She promised Jason to return in an hour so it must be close. She didn't want the jeweler to know who she was yet — she wasn't sure why, but anonymity seemed smart — so she must pick a store she rarely frequented.

Tiffany's stood off Route 7 while Tyson Corner Shopping Mall and Galleria housed many impressive jewelry stores. But there she'd need time to find a parking spot in the lot or garage on a busy weekend shopping day. She'd face a long walk into the mall from her car. Besides her time constraint, she didn't know the value of the stones in her purse. What if she were mugged? No, she'd drive into downtown McLean and park her car right in front of the store she picked.

BLUMENTHAL & SONS, she read above the door. Inside, a large display case of estate jewelry distinguished it from stores selling only new jewelry. This suggested they bought as well as sold.

The only customer at the moment, she smiled agreeably at the two jewelers behind the counter. "How many Blumenthal sons are there?" she asked cheerfully.

"Actually, three but one became a lawyer so that leaves two. My brother and I manage the store and our father, who's been in the business over sixty years, still comes to work almost every day to run our repair shop."

"Then you were both born to the business, so to speak?"

"I guess that's right," said the tall brother. "How may we help you today?"

"I hope you can tell me the value of some gems."

"We'll help if we can. Do you want a written appraisal?" the short brother asked.

"No. For today, just a ballpark idea of their worth."

As she extracted the five plastic bags from her purse, "Tall" produced a velvet-lined tray from behind the counter and "Short" helped her line up each stone with its corresponding numbered bag across the tray's plush expanse.

Each of the brothers pressed a loupe to one eye, picked up a stone and squinted at it. A long moment passed as they turned the stones in their fingers for a thorough visual inspection. Putting them down at last, the brothers exchanged looks before focusing on Jennifer. Saying nothing, they each picked up a second gem and repeated the same process, eyeing her afterward with more curiosity. Tall gave the fifth diamond a cursory glance, apparently deciding it matched the others. Laying their loupes on the counter, the brothers again exchanged meaningful looks.

"Well," said Short, "these are real diamonds, all right, and high quality. They're almost too perfect, virtually flawless, which is unusual enough to suggest they might be man-made." He chuckled. "When something appears too good to be true, it often is. I'd like to do some tests to be sure."

"Tests?"

"Yes, first I'd put the diamond in an electronic color meter, an enclosed compartment showing how light comes through the stone. The light reveals the stone's color range. Then I'd use a binocular diamond scope to reveal even more clarity. Think of it as a microscope that shows much more detail than this ten-power loupe. Last, I'd check the diamond's thermal conductivity."

Noticing Jennifer's eyebrows furrow, he explained. "Diamonds conduct heat better than anything, five times better than the second-best element, which is silver, so most diamonds show high thermal conductivity and most imitations don't."

"May I take a look at the stones with your loupe?" she asked Tall.

"Of course." He handed it to her and she imitated his earlier one-eyed squint until the diamond swam into focus. This magnification, much greater than the desk magnifying glass she'd used at home, revealed the diamond's myriad tiny, tilted flat surfaces.

"You're probably noticing the facets," Short volunteered. "Basically, the more facets, the more surfaces to catch light and the more light refracted, the more it sparkles and shows its fire. The facets are the diamond's cut. When we say 'cut' we don't mean the shape of the diamond, we mean the craftsman's skill in transforming the raw stone to release its brilliance and beauty. When a diamond is cut to ideal proportions, all the light entering from any direction is totally reflected—refracted—through the top and dispersed into a display of sparkling flashes and rainbow colors."

With the loupe's magnification and the store's bright illumination, she did indeed see light and colors dancing in the stone as she twisted it about. "Amazing," she marveled. "How many of these surfaces, these facets, can you get on so tiny a stone?"

Tall said, "Your stones aren't tiny. The original standard for hand-cut diamonds was 58 facets, but then gem cutters developed a King Cut with 86 facets and a Magna Cut with 102. The latest, a Dutch patent, uses modern machine cutting technology to create 121 facets."

"Remarkable," Jennifer allowed, still staring at the diamond with the loupe. "All my diamond jewelry pieces were gifts. I liked their sparkly appearance in beautiful settings without thinking how they were made. Their value to me was that someone chose them to surprise and please me. But now I'm curious. What makes a diamond valuable?"

Short laughed. "Do you want the technical explanation or the holistic version?"

Jennifer smiled. "How about holistic first?"

Short became serious. He selected one of Jennifer's stones. "A 'perfect' diamond similar to this one is awesome because it's sixty-five million years old. It survived the trauma of originating inside an underground volcano that pushed it up through alluvial pipes only to be buried under soil or rock or river eddies, where it might have been ground by giant glaciers. This tumbling through nature's washing machine was just the first step in the history of this diamond because it takes, generally speaking, three tons of mineral ore—or earth as it's called—to yield one carat.

"Diamond cutters are human and all humans make mistakes. It could have fallen into inexperienced hands. But the cutter of this diamond knew what he had and used all his experience, knowledge and talent to execute a totally professional job. Even though we'll never know who he was, his profound signature exists on this stone."

"So nature created this from our living planet, but man released its beauty and brilliance." Tall summarized. "Three amazing things converged to produce the breath-taking stone we see here: First, that it ever survived the overwhelming stresses of nature like millions of years of heat and extreme pressure. Second, that since they're hard to find this was ever discovered and dug up, and last, that it happened to fall into the hands of a cutter so remarkably skilled he coaxed the flawless beauty out of what's really a chunk of carbon."

"Wow." Jennifer clapped her hands. "You love what you do and it's contagious. Now I'm almost afraid to ask about the technical part."

"Never fear, we know that, too." Short grinned.

CHAPTER THIRTY-NINE

SATURDAY, 11:15 AM

"What makes a diamond valuable?" Tall repeated Jennifer's question and smiled patiently. "How much time have you to learn?" He chuckled. "Okay, there are a number of criteria but let's start with the unique combination of their four Cs."

"Four Cs?"

"That's right. I've already mentioned cut, which is the most important of the four Cs. The other three are clarity, carat and color. Clarity is about naturally occurring inner flaws called inclusions; the fewer inclusions, the greater the brilliance. The size, nature, location and amount of inclusions determine a diamond's clarity grade and affect its cost. The eleven grades of clarity inclusions we measure range from none, minute, minor, noticeable and obvious. The clarity grade of your diamonds," he gestured toward the velvet tray, "appears to be none."

Tall added, "The next 'C' is carat or the unit of weight for diamonds. One carat is 200 milligrams. A carat is divided into 100 points, so half a carat would have fifty points.

"The last 'C' is color. This impacts price the most." Tall continued. "Even diamonds which appear colorless actually have slight tones of pale yellow to brown. But other colors are also possible, like blue, green, orange, red and even black."

Jennifer hoped her face didn't show the amazement she felt. "I had no idea but, thanks to you, I do now."

"Well," Short chuckled, "the four Cs help, but the jewelry part of the diamond industry is pretty complex. We've been exposed to it since childhood but learn something new almost every day."

Tall picked up the tray. "So let me take these into the back room to weigh the carats, measure their height and diameter with a gauge and do the other tests I mentioned. Then I should have a ballpark idea for you. Please excuse me for a moment."

"Thank you." Jennifer wandered around the shop, looking at twinkling diamonds and other jewelry gleaming in the pristine display cases. But after five minutes she felt impatient and then uneasy. What took so long?

A few years ago the *Washington Post* had reported the arrest of a jeweler in Great Falls whose customers accused him of switching their valuable gems for inexpensive substitutes. As that story made the rounds, friends told her how hard reputable jewelers work to develop a trusted relationship with their clientele. She knew nothing about this store. Were they switching her stones in the back room? Were they checking her gems against lists of stolen property? Would police swarm in at any moment to arrest her? Would they even believe her honest garage-sale explanation? She tried unsuccessfully to curb her overactive imagination.

Just then the brothers returned to the counter with an older man who carried the velvet tray. "This is my father, Abraham Blumenthal. May I ask your name please?"

Jennifer blanched. She wanted anonymity with politeness since they'd given their time and knowledge to evaluate her "broken glass."

"Betty," Jennifer surprised herself by saying.

Abraham nodded. "Betty," he began, "it's not uncommon for someone to bring a jeweler a box of what they think is costume jewelry with some fine pieces of real jewelry mixed in. Good jewelry could be found in a bag in the pocket of clothes bought at a second-hand sale. Sometimes people buy the contents of a storage locker and find valuable jewelry tucked among the junk. You have five exceptional diamonds here. With their one full carat size, their D-grade colorless color, flawless clarity and ideal cut, they are probably in the upper one percent of quality stones. These are some of the finest diamonds I've seen during my years in the business."

"D-grade for color doesn't sound exceptional," Jennifer said. "At least, it wouldn't be in school."

"This is a totally different system. Diamonds are rated from D to Z, with most falling between D and J. D is the highest color in this system."

"I see." Jennifer tried to hide her surprise at her gems' high rating.

"May I ask how you happen to have such fine stones?"

Uh-oh, what to say now? Blurt out the truth? She studied the counter, groping for an answer. "It's a long story," she managed. They gave her a penetrating look but seemed to accept this as she recovered her poise. "Could you please tell me their value?"

"You have five stones, similar but not identical. Three are slightly larger but they are matched in the sense they're of the same quality and cut and so may be from the same source."

"...and their value?"

"Appraisal value of the three largest is about $11,000 each and the other two about $10,000 each. That's their appraisal value, which is your cost to replace them, if lost. Their over-the-counter value would be less."

"I don't understand. Isn't the value constant?"

Tall prepared to answer, but his father spoke instead. "Please forgive my bluntness, but allow me to explain with simple economics. Businesses like ours operate for profit. If we paid you $10,000 for a stone we later sold for $10,000, we made no profit to pay overhead like rent and salaries. Soon we'd be out of business. So if we sell this stone to replace a $10,000 appraised diamond someone lost, we must buy that diamond for less than $10,000 in order to make a profit. What you put here on the tray retails for about $50,000. We'd offer you less to make our profit, but we are willing to negotiate with you to buy your diamonds."

Jennifer smiled, showing her appreciation for his candor and business lesson. "Thank you for explaining." Although she and Jay had found 286 stones so far, if the remaining fourteen turned up as calculated, they'd have 300. Factoring that even number proved far easier as she mentally multiplied $10,000 times 300 stones. Over three million dollars? She struggled to hide her reaction to this staggering information.

"One last question." She spread open one of the papers that had wrapped the diamonds. "Does this paper have any watermarks or other identifiers to verify its origin?"

Father and sons examined it. "No. Looks like standard jewelry paper. Unlike writing paper, you notice it's very soft and pliable—to protect stones from scratching. These papers come in various colors, usually pastels, but nothing about this distinguishes it from other jewelry papers."

Learning more from the paper was her last clue, one going nowhere. With a sinking feeling, she realized now whoever owned these valuable diamonds must want them back. Did they know she had them? Could they? If they found out, to what lengths would they go to retrieve them?

Sobered by this thought, she politely thanked the three jewelers, put her diamonds in their numbered bags and the bags into the manila envelope. She fought a rising paranoia. Darting an anxious look outside the shop's large windows at the distance from the store to her vehicle, she dashed to her car. Once in the driver's seat, she locked the car's doors. Troubled by her strong intuition to take these precautions, she winced at the irony of this positive windfall already involving dangerous negatives.

Fifteen minutes later she pulled into her own garage, lowered the automatic door behind her and rushed into the house. Hoping not to alert the Grands, she hurried to find Jason in the kitchen.

"Well? What did you learn?"

"You won't believe it, Jay. Hold onto your hat..."

CHAPTER FORTY

SATURDAY, 11:40 AM

"Not 'hold onto your hat...,'" Jason moaned, "a phrase I've grown to fear." He sank heavily into a chair and added in a mock whimper, "I'm almost afraid to ask..."

"First, are the Grands busy so we can talk?"

"Yes. Saturday morning cartoons."

She described her jewelry store experience. "Now that we know the five diamonds they examined are real, do we assume the rest are, too?"

Jason leaned his head back and closed his eyes, considering. "Seems logical, wrapped together in those packages. And if they are real, should we start treating them like the $3,000,000 they might be worth? Right now they're stuffed in a kitchen drawer. I could put them in the wall safe upstairs until we figure out what to do next."

"Wait, maybe not. Unless the owner of the diamonds is dead, Jay, won't he want them back? I have a feeling the stones shouldn't stay here at the house. Maybe a bank lockbox is a smarter choice, where they're safe, away from the house and in a public place."

"Hmmm, I hadn't considered that, but maybe you're right. Is the bank still open?"

She checked the kitchen clock. "Yes, until noon on Saturdays. If I hustle, I can just make it. She grabbed a clean sock from the stack of laundry on one end of the dining room table. "Stuff the diamonds in here. The lockbox key is in the den. I'll get the car out of the garage. Meet me in front of the house with the key and the sock. Please hurry, Jay. We haven't a minute to spare."

Moments later, she drove purposefully toward the McLean Bank, arriving at 11:52. Years earlier, the Shannons had picked this local bank instead of the branch of a major chain. Feeling less like a number and more like a remembered-client, they knew most employees by name and appreciated the small-town feel and attention of the staff.

Jennifer swerved into a spot in front of the bank and hustled out of the car. Clutching her purse into which she'd stuffed the sock and key, she rushed inside.

Surprised to find no other patrons in line, she moved directly to a teller's window. "Hello, Millie," she said, slightly out of breath. "May I get into my lockbox, please?"

Millie glanced at the clock. "Hello, Mrs. Shannon. Looks like you're here with scant minutes to spare." She chuckled. "I'll ask Heather to help you with your safety deposit box. Have your key?"

"I do."

Ignoring proximity to closing time, Heather smiled pleasantly and led Jennifer into the vault housing safety deposit boxes. A separate area, this section was not in view of the lobby.

"May I ask you to sign in?"

"Of course. This step authenticates my signature in addition to producing the key, right?"

Heather nodded. "The bank allows only authorized owners to access their lock boxes. This cross-check system is a proven tool." Though she knew Jennifer, she still compared today's signature with previous ones on her box's ledger page. "Now, may I have your key, please?" Jennifer held up her personal key and Heather supplied the bank's key. Together these keys unlocked the box. Heather pulled out the long, thin metal drawer.

"This privacy booth has a shelf for the box while you're working here. When you finish, just come to the front of the vault so we can secure the box together."

"Thanks, Heather. I know you're about to close for the weekend and promise I won't be long."

Jennifer had no need to examine the wills and other documents already in the box. Adding the sock of diamonds, she closed the box's lid and alerted Heather she'd completed her task.

"That took no time at all," Heather marveled. "Would you like an M&M?" She held up a small bag. "These are my mini-weakness."

"Who can resist Mars, Inc's most famous invention?" Jennifer took a bunch.

"You know they don't operate like most businesses."

"What do you mean?" Jennifer asked.

"They don't advertise their location the way most companies do. Their headquarters building is just down the road on Elm Street but so low-key you can hardly find it. And their fortune comes from making outstanding products the old-fashioned way, not from sneaky insider deals like some wealthy big businesses."

Jennifer popped another M&M into her mouth and nodded. "For giving the world these outrageous chocolates, they deserve every penny."

Jennifer was the bank's last customer of the day. When she left, Heather activated special automatic door locks. Most patrons didn't know the doors that appeared to push right open were always electrically locked until an employee pressed a button temporarily releasing them for each approaching customer. This made it easy to exclude someone sinister. The employee's challenge: distinguishing customers from criminals.

CHAPTER FORTY-ONE

SATURDAY, 12:16 PM

Certain the Grands waited impatiently for lunch, Jennifer phoned Jason. "Hi, Hon. This diamond stuff played havoc with my morning schedule. I'm leaving the bank now. McDonald's is only a few blocks away. How about bringing the kidlets and I'll meet you there for lunch? Okay, fifteen minutes? Great! I'll stake out a table since Saturday noontime gets busy. Maybe ask the children what they want so they're ready when they get in line? Good. Thanks, Jay."

When Jason reached the restaurant with daughter Becca also in tow, Jennifer's eyebrows arched in surprise. After hugs all around, Becca said, "I left Virginia Tech early and, with light weekend traffic, made it in about five hours. Dad and the little ones were just leaving as I arrived, so here I am."

"A wonderful surprise, Honey."

They ordered and gathered around the table Jennifer saved. "Here are extra napkins." She put a pile in the center as they munched their lunches. Christine put her hand on Jason's arm. "We love visiting you and Gran because you let us do the fun things our parents don't allow."

"Oh? For example?" Jason didn't want to break enough rules to earn less access to his Grands.

"We're usually stuck with food that's 'good' for us." She wrinkled her nose. "And we watch *educational* TV instead of cartoons."

Alicia nodded. "Yeah, and we don't get under-the-pillow gifts at home."

Milo stuck in his two-cents. "And we don't have Angwy Bewd Bandaids at home."

The two little girls and Becca sat on one side of the table with Milo sandwiched between his grandparents on the other. Suddenly all on Becca's side of the table held their sandwiches still, focused on something those facing them missed. Jen, Jason and Milo twisted in their seats to see a man writhing on the floor.

Sitting on the end of the bench, Becca jumped to her feet, grabbed the unused stack of paper napkins from the table, rushed to the man and pressed them between his teeth just before he went into full seizure. By this time, the McDonald's staff and several patrons had dialed 911. Sirens blared almost immediately from the fire station less than a mile away.

Becca still knelt by the man when the EMTs strode in. "What happened?" the lead medic asked the pretty girl. Becca told him. He stared at her as other medics monitored their patient's vital signs and started an IV. In a few minutes their patient sat up, dazed.

A medic touched Lt. Sommer's sleeve. "Nathan, what's your call? Take him in?"

Pulled back to the present, the lead medic broke his stare at Becca and knelt beside the ailing man. "How do you feel now?"

"Not...not so good."

"Are you epileptic?"

The man shook his head. "No. What happened to me? Where am I?"

"Have you ever had a seizure before?"

"No."

Nathan Sommer made the decision. "Fairfax ER," he directed his team.

"I know that EMT," Jennifer told Jason. She wiggled out of the booth and crossed the room to her daughter. The medic stood aside as his team loaded the man onto a gurney. "Becca, where did you learn how to help that fellow on the ground?" her mother asked.

"A girl in our college dorm is epileptic. She taught us what to do if she had an episode."

"That's Lt. Sommer, the medic who tried to save Kirsten two days ago." Jennifer turned to him. "Thanks for all you did for our friend."

"We do our best but..."

"...but you can't always win." Becca finished his sentence. At his inquisitive look, she added, "My roommate's boyfriend is a firefighter. He told us about his team's good days and bad days."

"And you are?"

"Becca Shannon. This is my mom." She dazzled him with her most engaging smile. "I wonder, any chance if I could bring some nieces and nephews to the fire station to learn about engines and ambulances?" She pointed. "Those three little cuties there?"

His look followed her pointing finger. "Sure, how about his afternoon? I'll show you around myself...if we're not on a call."

One of the firefighter/medics appeared at the doorway. "We're ready," he said impatiently.

"See you later today." He held her glance a moment longer and was out the door, the retreating siren the only reminder of what had taken place.

Well, well, thought Jennifer. Becca's back for thirty minutes and already has a date.

CHAPTER FORTY-TWO

SATURDAY, 1:30 PM

At home, Becca settled the children at a table with crayons and coloring books. "What's *that?*" she asked as Jennifer stuffed cotton balls into the doll's torso and threaded a needle. Her mother told her the whole story. "Mom, that's too wild. Are you keeping the diamonds?"

"We haven't figured out yet what to do. Any ideas?"

"You don't know who they belong to so you can't return them. The owner doesn't know who bought them so they can't find you. I'd say they're yours. It's like winning a sweepstake, Mom. Will you buy a new house and new cars? Will you take exotic trips? Will you give the money to your children while they're young enough to enjoy it? Hint-hint."

Jennifer laughed. "The diamonds are safe at the bank for now. We know five are valuable but not the rest until they're appraised. So their total worth is still uncertain. She changed the subject. "Were you just flirting or will you take the children to the fire station today?"

She giggled. "Maybe a little of both. He is kinda cute, don't you think?"

"And maybe married with a herd of his own children?"

"Oh, Mom, you're so out of it. He's a good-looking guy with an exciting job. Sure, I'd like to know more about him. And don't forget, you introduced us." She laughed. "Besides, with kids chaperoning, how can I go wrong?"

"We're tired of coloring. Could we do today's learning surprise now?" asked Christine as the children brought over their completed pictures. "What are you both laughing about?"

"Aunt Becca made a joke. Here's your doll, Alicia, all well again. I think Aunt Becca plans today's learning surprise. Would you like to learn about fire engines?"

"Yes," they chorused with smiles and wiggles.

Twenty minutes later, Becca piled the children into her car and off they drove.

At the station, they knocked on the locked office door. A fireman behind the desk walked over to open it. "May I help you?"

"Is Lt. Sommer here? He said to bring my nieces and nephew this afternoon for a mini-tour."

"Come in. I'll see if I can find him." He spoke into a phone. "Nathan, you have company in the lobby.... What?... A pretty young lady with three little kids.... Okay. I'll tell them."

"Have a seat. He'll be right along."

"Remember," Becca warned the little ones," if we hear the fire alarm while we're here, the firefighters stop whatever they're doing, hurry to their fire truck and speed away to put out fires and save lives."

"They go to it, but I'd wun away if it gets too hot," Milo stated, his mouth firm.

"I'd put the fire out," Alicia announced.

"I'd call 911 to get help," Christine said. "What would you do, Aunt Becca?"

"I'd turn the situation over to a professional firefighter like Lt. Sommer, and here he is. Ta-da!"

Nathan came across the lobby, smiling broadly, a bit embarrassed by Becca's flourishing intro. "Welcome to the McLean Volunteer Firehouse. I'm Nathan Sommer and you are..."

The children introduced themselves, delighted with the attention.

Becca winked at Nathan. "When grandchildren visit my parents' house they're subjected daily to a 'learning surprise.' I took over that assignment for today. What can you teach us all?"

"Our mission..." He began the formal description but then dropped to one knee and continued at the children's eye level. "We have three important ways to help people. First," he held up one finger, "we fight fires in houses or cars or stores or big office buildings or woods or anywhere they happen. Second," he held up another finger, "we try to rescue and help anyone we find in trouble there. Some firefighters also are emergency medical technicians who work sort of like doctors to help injured people. Third," another finger lifted, "we teach people fire safety so they learn what to do if fire happens near them and how to prevent fires before they start."

"So let me hear you: what are the three things they do?" Becca reinforced Nathan's lesson as he noticed again why she'd drawn his interest earlier at McDonald's. The blue eyes, the silky hair, the animated face—pretty and competent.

"They teach us safety," said Milo.

"And they put out fires wherever they happen in all kinds of places," said Alicia.

"And they help injured people," Christine said. "Did you know I want to be a doctor when I'm big?"

"If you want to, you should try to make that happen," Nathan encouraged.

"If you have girl firefighters I might want to be one." Alicia made this up on the spot.

"And I'm going to twain dolphins," Milo revealed for the first time.

"Do you already know how to train them?" Nathan smiled.

"Not yet, but I will when I'm weady to do it." Milo's smile flashed conviction that dreams and reality blend seamlessly in a four-year-old's mind.

Nathan laughed, giving Becca a knowing look. "Aren't kids wonderful?"

"Do you practice with a bunch at home?"

"No, I'd need a wife for that, but I had a lot of fun with brothers and sisters before we grew up."

"Big family?"

"Six kids."

"Only five at our house. I was number four. And you?"

"Also four." He looked into her eyes and grinned. "Another connection?"

"Could we see the fire engine and ambulance now?" Christine asked.
"Sure."

They moved from the lobby into the garage bay. "Our McLean Volunteer Fire Department started almost a hundred years ago, in 1921. This new fire truck has room for six firefighters. It's thirty-five feet long or about the same length as a school bus. Let's climb up to take a look inside." They did and investigated the ambulance next. "This is where I ride and this is where we put an injured person."

After the tour, they no sooner returned to the lobby than the penetrating call-alarm blared. The Grands gaped as firefighters rushed from many directions to board their engine.

"Gotta go." Nathan grabbed his uniform jacket. "May I call you later, Becca?"

She handed him a slip of paper on which she'd written her phone number. "I'd like that."

"Good-bye, kids. Thanks for visiting." In a flash, he was through the door, inside his vehicle and all business as the engine and ambulance careened from the station, sirens howling.

"Wow!" Becca said.

"Wow!" the children agreed.

CHAPTER FORTY-THREE

SATURDAY, 2:02 PM

"Hello, Adam?" Jennifer held the phone. "Please tell your beautiful wife that I bought a great medicine cabinet for her this morning at a sale. It's new with tags still on the box and only $5. I think she'll like it. When will you pick it up? Okay, use your key. I'll leave it in the entryway if we go out.... What did you say? What do I know about psychics? Not a whole lot. What do you know about psychics?... You'll tell me later. Uh-oh, now my curiosity's up. Bye."

Jason wandered into the kitchen. "Where is everybody?"

"Becca's taken the kids to the fire station. She's checking out a firefighter under the pretense of a learning surprise for the children: Lt. Sommer, the medic-in-charge for Kirsten."

"Is he better than Becca's last one?"

"The gnarly dude with the tattoos, goatee and motorcycle?"

"No, the one after that." Jason conjured a mental picture. "Mr. Mundo, the egotist, the Big Man on Campus, the guy who knew everything and thought the world revolved around him."

"At least he had decent clothes." She laughed and changed the subject. "Back to the diamonds. When Becca asked me earlier what we plan to do with them, I realized we haven't had time to talk about it together. Now that we have a few minutes while they're out..."

"Okay, what's on your mind?"

"If we're right, we're missing fourteen stones. We could look for them downstairs before the gang returns. Knowing some are real, we assume they all are, but should a jeweler look at every one?"

"Yes, but is it safe for you to carry three million dollars' worth of loot from the bank to the jeweler and back again? Do we need an armed guard or will I do?"

"I always feel safe with you, Jay." She kissed the air in his direction. "But now it's 'loot'?"

"Well, what would you call a windfall of 286 top-quality diamonds?"

She ignored that. "With locked car doors and only the two of us knowing the plan and the value of our cargo, what could go wrong?"

He shrugged. "Cars get highjacked just for the vehicle, not what's inside. Adam reminded us police consider people vulnerable most of the time. You're your first line of defense. Stay alert to avoid bad choices leading to bad consequences." He sighed. "But there's the bigger problem."

"What?" she asked.

"Your record for garage-sale consequences got spotty this last year, don't you think?"

Her surprise showed she had no clue. "What do you mean?"

"Well, the serial killer before—and now this."

"Okay...maybe you have a point," she said slowly. "Let's think this out logically. Why did somebody hide the gems? Are they legal or illegal? Was hiding them in the doll like putting them in a safe if you don't own a safe?"

Jason looked serious. "Or if illegal, once they're discovered missing, consider two more possibilities: the owner wants to walk away from them to avoid criminal connection or he needs them back for some illegal buy or payoff. Maybe drug involvement. Diamonds are international currency, same as cash, Jen."

"That's right. Didn't that Holocaust Museum tour say during WWII when Germans made Jews leave home with one bundle and the clothes on their backs, they sewed diamonds or gold into their clothes instead of taking worthless paper money."

"Diamonds are small, virtually indestructible, easy to transport and hide, and valuable everywhere. But what has that to do with this, Jen?"

"McLean has a large foreign population with colleges, embassies, commerce, military and government. Cultural exchange is another draw when foreign sports teams or musicians or dancers visit this area. Maybe this is someone's nest egg to start a new life after defecting from a dangerous homeland. So even if smuggled in illegally, these diamonds might serve a positive purpose. Wouldn't returning them to that owner seem fair?"

Jason stared at her, a pained expression clouding his face. She knew that look.

"Jay, what is it?"

"Jen, Jen. Once again your garage-sale craziness puts us in potential danger. I...the whole family...we've barely recovered from the Ruger Yates nightmare. If these hidden diamonds are illegal, wouldn't the person who innocently finds them face vengeance from the angry owner who needs them back?" He looked into his wife's eyes. "Wouldn't that person be *you*, Jen?"

"But..."

"Worse, maybe they want their illegal diamonds back but not the witness who knows they exist."

"You're scaring me, Jay."

"They'd have to *eliminate* that witness." He sighed, catching the fear in Jennifer's eyes. "I'm sorry, Honey, but maybe I need to scare you to protect you, to protect our family. You look for good in people, but the existence of prisons proves not everyone's a good person. We read about crime daily from the media, so criminals walk among us. Even if we found the owner, which seems improbable, with your explanation, returning the diamonds is a good deed. With my explanation, your reward could be death. If I'm right, are you willing to risk your life and the family's safety for these diamonds?"

She slumped in her chair, unhappily following his logic.

"Look, Jen. I don't know why packages of diamonds fell out of this doll or whether a good person or a bad person hid them there. I don't know if they're legal or illegal, whether the person who put them there wants to avoid knowledge of them or wants them back no matter what it takes. I don't know whether the person who put them there is alive or dead or if these diamonds are a blessing or a curse. Guess what, you don't know either."

"You're saying we're novices playing marbles with the big boys."

"I'm saying our first responsibility is protecting our family — the opposite of ginning up danger."

"I hear you, Jay, but we can't make the diamonds go away. This can't 'unhappen.' We're two sensible people who need to figure out what to do next."

"We're two sensible people with absolutely no experience here."

"Should we consult Adam? Wouldn't a police detective know about stolen property? Maybe someone reported lost diamonds. If so, we'd find the owner right away."

"Consulting Adam's a good idea. What about also phoning Greg Bromley? He's an attorney who's now part of our extended family."

"Great. We'll learn more about the legal side of finders-keepers."

"Didn't you forget something?" Jason's voice sounded bitter.

Jennifer looked up. "What?"

"Losers, weepers..."

"Oh, Jay...."

He knew he'd upset her. While he believed every word he said, seeing his usually exuberant wife so forlorn — and knowing his words caused it — caught at his heart. He put his arms around her. "I love you, my precious Jen." He kissed her before looking deep into her eyes. "That's why I don't want to lose you. If you're in danger, I want to...I need to protect you. We're involved in something we don't understand, maybe good news or maybe bad news. The good outcome is easy, but we...I need to prepare for the worst outcome."

He reached for her hand. "Would you agree we must be extra cautious until we know what's going on? Cautious at home about locking up, setting the security alarm and knowing who's outside before opening the door? Cautious when we're out: making good choices and picking safe surroundings." She nodded. "Okay then," he deliberately changed the subject. "How about going on a diamond hunt?" Gently, he pulled her to her feet, put an arm around her and guided her down the basement stairs.

In shadowy places on the floor around the basement furniture and rugs they found three more glistening gems.

CHAPTER FORTY-FOUR

SATURDAY, 2:45 PM

Returning home rekindled Mahmud's anger over his neighborhood's earlier garage sale. As they drove into his garage he muttered, "At last, our community returns to normal." He changed the subject. "Did you learn what you needed to know on our shopping mall trip today? Does their map help?"

"Yes, with layouts of stores, but it shows no offices, utilities or loading docks."

Ahmed appeared preoccupied and as they pulled into the garage. He surprised his host, saying, "I will make a walk around the neighborhood now for exercise."

Caught off guard, Mahmud said, "Shall I go with you?"

"Thank you, no. I will see you next at the meal tonight. What time is dinner served?"

"Seven o'clock."

"Good. Thank you."

Mahmud sensed something amiss as Ahmed went to his room. A walk around the neighborhood? Where would he go? Who would he meet? Mahmud yearned to be at the center of events, not left out like a goat in the field. But he couldn't insist on accompanying Ahmed, and stalking him from a distance would make Mahmud look foolish.

With no satisfactory solution, Mahmud's frustration blossomed into anger. He kicked at the railing as he stomped up the stairs toward his bedroom. Pausing in the doorway, he eavesdropped on his wife and Safia talking in the bathroom.

"When I was a little girl, my mother cut my hair in this very bathroom. I sat on the same vanity stool in front of the mirror where you are right now. I wore a plastic cape around my shoulders like this one you're wearing. We're even using this same comb and scissors because they were an expensive set that lasts a long time."

"Why aren't all scissors the same size and shape?"

"They're shaped for their job. These barber scissors are long and very thin with sharp points. Your school scissors are short and blunt to cut paper but not hurt a child. Our kitchen scissors are heavy and strong to cut vegetables or meat."

"Why did your mother cut your hair in this room, Mommy?"

"We pretended we were in a beauty shop. She removed the scatter rugs just as we did so sweeping up clipped hair was easy. Now, we're almost finished. How do you look?"

Safia smiled her pleasure and Zayneb gave her daughter a hug. But their pleasant moment evaporated when Mahmud stormed in shouting, "Out. Out, both of you. Now."

Hurrying to comply, Zayneb dropped the comb and scissors atop the toilet tank and prodded her daughter toward the door.

"Shall I sweep up before...?" Zayneb asked.

"*OUT*," he bellowed, a ferocious expression on his face. They scurried away as he slammed the bathroom door behind them.

* * * *

In his room, Ahmed tried to control his excitement. He'd leave now to explore the library vicinity before meeting Khadija at 4:00 PM. He studied her map, pocketed it and left the house.

Arriving early, he strolled in the park near the library, past playground and tennis courts to a woodsy path, where he sat on a bench. Teenagers nearby flung plastic discs through the air into a chained net on a tree, walked a short distance and repeated this into another chained net. They disappeared into the woods, but the on-going clank of chains signaled the game continued. A few minutes later, two men about his age came by, carrying more of these flying saucer discs.

"Hello," said one. "Would you like to play a round of Frisbee golf with us?"

Normally shunning filthy infidels like these, people his team would soon kill in great numbers, Ahmed's curiosity surprised him. What were Americans like? He doubted Paradise offered this Frisbee golf. Ahmed liked games. He knew Iran invented the world-renowned game of chess.

What could he lose by learning more about his enemy? "Yes, thank you, I would."

"I'm Maury and this is Bob. Do you know how to play?"

Ahmed shook their offered hands, American style. "My name is... Albert. I do not know how to play but I would like to learn. However, I must be at the library at 4:00. Will we have time?"

"Yes, because the game is quick, easy and fun. We'll teach you as we go along."

In friendly sports, men could build pleasant camaraderie during an hour together. They cheered each other's scores and consoled if they missed. When they finished the game, Bob noted "Albert" still had five minutes to reach the library, only a few steps away. "Here, take my business card," said Maury, "in case you want to play again sometime."

"Morris Rosenblum," Ahmed read the card aloud and stared in shock. "Are you a Jew?"

Maury laughed, "Well, that's one of the things I am." He studied Ahmed. "Are you an Arab?" he asked good-naturedly."

Ahmed thought fast. "Until I become an American," he lied.

"Great. People in America learn to get along together. Sports and solving common problems together are two good examples. Think about the effect 9/11 had on us, uniting us all."

These words hit Ahmed like a slap across his face. Was Maury right? The terror Ahmed's cell planned only a few miles away was to weaken American's resistance to Islam. Was the opposite possible? Uneasily, he studied his watch. "I...I must go now. Thank you for this Frisbee game."

CHAPTER FORTY-FIVE

SATURDAY, 3:55 PM

Inside the library, Ahmed crossed carpeted floors in this newly refurbished building filled with people of all ages. He stood at the wall of windows overlooking the park he'd just left, thinking of the astonishing goods arrayed at two supermarkets Mahmud included on today's trip to McLean, the mega shopping malls at Tyson Corner and the endless bustle of cars. How could he explain the contrast between this luxury and the life he'd known? Were these products of the evil Satan or something desirable to be understood and reproduced in his country?

"Hello, Ahmed." Khadija's sweet voice spun him around. "Do you like our McLean library?"

"Yes. Thank you for inviting me to see it." And to see you, added his unspoken thought.

"Anyone can select and read books right here. Fairfax County residents can get a library card to take home books or audios or movies. Computers are over there. Librarians help you research a topic or find a book or guide you in other directions that interest you."

"Khadija, I think my country has no women like you: intelligent, kind, accomplished; a professional teacher and yet a modest female. Men and women cannot be friends there, but you have offered friendship and knowledge to a stranger from a far-away land. This is new and confusing for me, but so pleasant that I look forward to every minute I see you."

"Ahmed, you're my father's guest but you show interest in America. The coincidence that I teach American culture gives us a special way to connect. Did you finish the book I gave you?"

"Yes, last night. Please understand these new ideas shake the world I know."

"But do you like the ideas?" She indicated chairs and they sat down.

He tried to balance the familiar predictability of his homeland's unchallenged dogma against the stimulation of new ideas here. What he'd seen and learned in McLean made him doubt the Middle-Eastern tales told to him about America. Did that label him weak or even a traitor? If so, should he reveal this now to anyone? "My mind is asking many new questions."

"Intelligent minds always ask questions. How to improve the quality of life for more people around the world. How to improve cooperation among countries. How to share peace to improve their economies. How to use money to stop famine or cure diseases instead of funding wars."

He'd not considered such issues but thought about these goals. Was this an American trick to pretend peaceful interests while arming for victory when others laid down their guns? America was engaged in active "peace-keeping" wars with deadly weapons in other countries this very minute. He spoke carefully. "What if someone knows his way is the true and only way; that others must change to his religion and if they resist... he must be certain they conform?"

She asked, "How did he learn his is the only way? Did he figure it out himself or did someone tell him? Usually, a child's parents teach him the same religion they were taught to believe. The child hears more of this at his church or mosque. Then he joins the church, often in a ceremony approved by friends and family who believe this same religion. The child may even attend church school or a religious college, reinforcing those same ideas. Where church and government are not separated, laws may uphold the same religious doctrines. This happened in Europe for centuries. That's one reason the American revolutionaries insisted on separation of church and state."

"This is hard to imagine."

"If everyone around him agrees about a religion, a child thinks it must be true. But later, as an adult, he may think for himself. His lifelong indoctrination may be so strong he sticks with his early religion. Or he may look for something else. This happened for my mother. As an adult she left her childhood religion and converted to Islam. In the same way, a Muslim might decide to convert because that one-and-only 'true' religion doesn't satisfy him."

"Questioning God is blasphemy."

She nodded. "Yes, I understand the need for such a belief in many cultures. That teaching conveniently prevents people from exploring new ideas. If I try to push my religion on you against your will, I deny you freedom to make your own choice. I might try convincing you my religion is better than yours, hoping you'll change your mind and convert, but in America I can't force my will on you. Here, people can keep their religion or change it or choose none. You'd need a police state to deny individuals freedom of thought and religion."

"But what if God is on my side?"

She laughed. "Every religion thinks God is on their side. Which one is right?"

"God knows what is true."

"Whose god? Each of the many religions feels confident theirs is the only true one, so who knows which one really is? Is it decided by war? Is it decided by terrorism?"

"Islam demands submission to God and also teaches men's and women's roles in society."

"Ahmed, in my country, my education and work at the college label me a useful, productive citizen who found and developed her talents. But in your country leaving my house unchaperoned each day, driving my own car to work and wearing no hijab would brand me a loose woman with no marriage prospects. I might be stoned there for the very behavior that's valued here."

"Meeting you shows me my culture's narrow view of women. Are marriages arranged here also?"

She laughed. "No, but if we love our family we hope they approve of the person we choose."

"I suppose you look for a young man your age?"

"I look for an intelligent, attractive, kind man who will love me as I love him and who wants to make a happy family with children. When I find that man, age is not important."

Ahmed choked back a near sob of helpless despair, disguised as a loud cough. Set on a narrow terrorist course by the Great Leader, he hadn't acknowledged the powerful hunger for a fulfilling family life. But meeting Khadija, he ached for the love of this beautiful woman and the children they could create and enjoy together. He heard himself say, "Would you consider a man my age?"

"To me, age is less important than the vision we share."

"Orphaned early, I never had a real family of my own, but now I long to do so."

"When your business trip here ends, won't you return to the Middle-East to find a bride?"

He stared grimly at his hands, unable to reveal his life-ending assignment only a week away.

"Freedom means choices. You can change your mind if you're on a path you don't like."

This innocent woman couldn't know the penalty for changing his mind meant death at the hands of his cell, who then would implement their terrorist mission — with him or without him.

CHAPTER FORTY-SIX

SATURDAY, 5:03 PM

Preparing to leave after an hour at the library, they paused in the foyer. Khadija said, "If you like our country and our culture and want to stay when you finish your business in McLean, might you consider applying for citizenship? You're already here, so it's very convenient."

Convenient? How could he tell her he sneaked into this country without documentation and harbored violent intentions? *Impossible* described his situation better.

"Some foreigners who find themselves here defect, requesting political protection if they fear death or persecution at home."

Ahmed stared at her blankly.

"If I drive home now and your stroll takes twenty minutes, we'll arrive separately. My father forbids me to talk to you, so I may not be allowed at meals any more."

He stared at her back as she walked to her car.

Pondering their conversation on the stroll back, Ahmed returned to the house and went to his room. Looking over his target maps again, he felt a sudden pang of aversion for the task he'd trained to complete. When his plan ignited, innocent women like Khadija and children like Safia would perish in horrible ways.

He flipped through a few TV channels. He forced his mind again toward the magnitude of the assignment before him and of the treasure entrusted to him to fund those plans. On impulse, he checked the closet shelf again. Reaching up, he pushed his suitcase to the right and, not seeing what he sought, pulled it forward off the shelf. His eyes widened in disbelief. No doll! He shook his head to clear his vision before staring again at the very spot where the doll lay yesterday.

Where was the doll — with the critically essential diamonds stuffed inside?

He unzipped his suitcase and fished his hand through all its pockets. Frantic, he probed every inch of the closet. He even studied the closet ceiling for hidden access but saw only seamless, solid wood with uniformly aged white paint. He spun around the room, opening every drawer, ripping covers from the bed, jerking off the mattress, pushing furniture away from walls. He even searched the small refrigerator and microwave.

Red-faced from exertion, he sank onto the bed, his head in his hands, and moaned. After a few moments he heard a rap on his bedroom door.

"Who is it?" he croaked hoarsely.

"Mahmud. Are you all right, Ahmed?" Although thinking 5:30 an odd time for a nap, he asked, "Another bad dream?"

Ahmed rushed to the door and jerked it open. "Come inside quickly," he said. "We have a serious problem."

Mahmud glanced around the disheveled room, eyebrows lifted. "What is it? Can I help?"

"I...I found an old doll in this room and I...needed to protect something valuable so I sewed it inside the doll and put the doll on that high closet shelf behind my suitcase." Anguish filled his voice. "Now the doll is gone!" He jumped to his feet, grabbed Mahmud's shoulders, shook him and growled, *"We must find that doll!"*

Startled by Ahmed's behavior, Mahmud pulled back to stare at his guest. First, the nightmares and now this crazed tantrum in a torn-apart room. Had his guest gone mad?

"The doll was here this morning. Someone in this house took it. Was it *you?*"

"As Allah is my witness, peace be upon His name, I know nothing about this!"

"Then find the person who does," thundered Ahmed.

"I will question my wife and report back to you."

"No." Ahmed shouted. "Bring her here. I will question her myself."

"As you wish." He disappeared down the hall, returning with a frightened Zayneb. Ahmed eyed her wildly, "Where is the doll from behind my suitcase in this closet?"

Zayneb dared not tell the truth. She quivered with fear at reprisals from her husband's normal bad temper. This would trigger his full rage, amplified by embarrassment in front of this guest he sought to impress.

With trembling voice, she told a variation of the facts that might save her life.

"When cleaning your room, I found my daughter's old doll. I should have removed it when we prepared this room for you. My child no longer uses that doll and I knew a garage sale took place next door. Because charity is one of the five pillars of Islam, I donated the doll to the sale so another child could have it."

"*Where is the doll now?*" Ahmed bellowed.

She fought a sob as tears streaked her cheeks. "I do not know but I will find out. The information is next door. I will run there to learn the answer."

"Go then. *Hurry!*"

Zayneb pivoted and rushed from the house. She knocked frantically on Roshan's back door and nearly fell inside the kitchen when the door opened. "Roshan," she sobbed, "the doll I brought this morning — what happened to it?"

"Why, I sold it and have all your money here. You did well."

"Roshan, help me, please. My husband must never know you sold items for me. I said I donated them to you for charity. I wanted this garage-sale money for my children. Mahmud gives me so little, even when I beg him...even when he..."

But she pushed other anxiety away to face the urgent problem at hand. "Our guest is desperate to get it back. I must produce the doll before they hurt me or my children." Zayneb collapsed in sobs.

"Oh, no!" Roshan's alarm at Zayneb's plight triggered an instant desire to protect her. She hugged her god-daughter. "Let me think. So many visited my sale today. But who bought what? Here, sit down while I finish my tea and think about this. Would you like some?"

Tears spilled from Zayneb's eyes, but she struggled to remain polite. Her future depended upon Roshan's recall. "No tea, thank you. They're furious next door and wait now for information about the doll. I am desperate for you to remember anything about who bought it."

Roshan drank tea, deep in thought. Friendly encounters with neighbors when she walked her little dog, Izzy, had sharpened her memory for details. Zayneb twisted impatiently in her chair.

"I think...it was the older woman with several small children; maybe a grandmother because of her gentleness with them. She asked how I got to McLean from India and why I had the sale today. She liked my story and her interest in me gave me interest in her. Yes, the things they bought included the doll. They walked to the curb and got into...a white van."

Roshan drained her cup. "Something about that van...what was it?" She tapped a finger. "Ah, the license tag. When the woman turned her car around in my driveway, I read her license plate. "Something catchy. No numbers, just words. Two words." She snapped her fingers. 'Yard Sale,' that's it."

"Praise Allah. Oh, Roshan, thank you. The finger points away from me. I may live 'til tomorrow."

"Zayneb, if you're in danger let's call the police? Do you want to stay here with me tonight?"

"No, thank you, but pray for me, Roshan," she cried and rushed out the back door, across the lawn and into her own house where Mahmud and Ahmed glowered as she entered her kitchen.

She blurted out what she learned about the doll's buyer.

"You stupid piece of camel dung," her husband hissed. "I'll deal with you later." He turned his back to her and faced Ahmed. "Come, let's go to my computer."

They entered his office and closed the doors.

CHAPTER FORTY-SEVEN

SATURDAY, 5:32 PM

M ahmud sat before the computer, searching the internet in his home office to connect the license plate info with the name of the doll's new owner.

"They block this information for most people, but I have special links to access what we want. Ah, here it comes: this tag belongs to a white Cadillac SRX, a crossover. The owner is Jennifer L. Shannon with an address in McLean." He copied it and gave the note to Ahmed.

"Come, let's see where she lives." Ahmed led the way toward the garage.

Their GPS guided them to her subdivision. "Big houses," Mahmud observed as they drove through the community to a T in the road. "This is her street."

"Her car must be in the garage," Ahmed speculated as they drove by her house.

"In cul-de-sacs like this anyone not a resident stands out and two other houses face the circle to see all that happens here." Mahmud drove back down the street. "Shall I pull over?"

"Yes. Show me where we are on the book map." Ahmed turned on his pen flashlight. "Does this green area indicate parkland behind the house?"

"Yes," Mahmud brightened. "People in this country often protect the back door less than the front." He tapped the map. "Our best access should be from the back, but it's getting dark."

Ahmed studied the map. "Drive to the other end of this street." The road ended in another cul-de-sac at the community's pool and tennis court.

Ahmed pointed. "There's the path into the parkland. We must not walk through anyone's yard to draw attention. Let's circle her cul-de-sac once more and count the houses on this side of the street so when we approach through the woods we'll know which one is the back of her house."

"Should we risk parking in the neighborhood while we investigate?"

"No, we'll park on the main street outside the community and walk back. Bring two flashlights."

Twenty minutes later they crouched at the edge of the dark woods outside the Shannons' wrought-iron back fence. Mahmud nudged his companion. "Perfect! No one but those inside the house will see us if we approach from these woods. Do we go in tonight?"

"No, we need a plan." They worked their way out of the darkened parkland woods with difficulty, cursing the early dusks of fall. Back at their car, they plotted while driving home.

"We must get the doll back in a way that doesn't endanger our primary mission. We cannot draw attention to ourselves as individuals or to our cell," Ahmed reasoned.

"Perhaps you don't know how police operate in America. If the one who breaks into the house to steal the doll is caught, police will question him in jail. Homeland Security might become involved if they question our names or Middle-Eastern looks. If we kill people in that house, the police will certainly hunt us down. Their 24/7 search for us would limit our movements at a time when we have much to accomplish."

"Tell me about this woman who lives next to you, the one with the sale in her yard yesterday."

"Roshan? She's known Zayneb and her family since my wife was a little child. She is like a mother to Zayneb."

"Could Zayneb ask her to go to this house to ask for the doll? She could say selling the doll was a mistake and the little girl it belongs to cries for her toy."

Mahmud chuckled. "If they give her the doll, they solve our problem. If not, we find another way. If Roshan goes, no one identifies any of us. You are shrewd as any Bedouin, Ahmed."

At home, the men ordered Zayneb into Mahmud's office and closed the door. Her frantic, wild-eyed expression reflected fear for her life.

"Go to Roshan. Say she must help you. Tell her to go to this address to get the doll back because it was sold by mistake and a child mourns for it. Find a new doll at a store, one that Roshan can offer to substitute for the old one she brings to us. Do you understand?"

She trembled. "Yes...yes, I understand."

"Here is $20 for the new doll," Mahmud said. "Toy stores are still open Saturday night. Go with her to buy one quickly. If the family won't accept the trade, return the new doll to the store and bring me the money. Do you know exactly what to do or must I tell you again?"

"I do...I know what to do."

"Then go," Mahmud bellowed.

She fled.

CHAPTER FORTY-EIGHT

SATURDAY, 6:00 PM

Zayneb pounded on Roshan's back door and when it opened, fell sobbing into her neighbor's arms. She begged Roshan to help her get the doll back, repeating what they told her.

"What have I done?" she wailed. "I just wanted to make life better for my girls by earning a little money. How could I know our guest needed a doll I thought nobody wanted?"

"Oh, my beloved child. You're the daughter I wish fate had given me. I've watched you blossom and grow next door since you were tiny. Your girls have become my grandchildren. I am old now, but my fondest dream is to see you safe and happy before I die. You haven't felt happiness for years. Now you're not even safe with your dreadful husband. Yes, I'll help any way I can."

"Thank you a thousand times, dear Roshan."

"And now we'll play a small trick on your cruel husband. I have an unusual doll from India, one I played with as a child. We'll substitute my doll for the one we get and you keep the $20 to do something nice for your girls."

Zayneb smiled through her tears at her precious god-mother's love and understanding.

"I'll show you my doll to see if you agree. If you do, we'll be on our way."

Not a baby doll, Roshan's toy looked more like a teen dressed in brocade clothes with tiny mirrors sewn into the fabric. This was a doll any child would cherish with wonder.

"How beautiful she is," Zayneb marveled. "You're sure you're willing to give her up?"

"Absolutely. This good cause becomes my doll's destiny, one much more interesting than the bedroom closet." Roshan wrapped the doll in tissue paper and placed her in an empty shoebox before hugging her surrogate daughter.

"Now, off we go." They got in the car and studied the address. "I think I know this neighborhood but to be sure, my portable GPS will zero us in." She plugged the device into the outlet.

"I didn't know you had one. Is it new?"

Roshan laughed. "Very new. I bought it this morning at a neighbor's garage sale. She showed me how to use it and this is my first chance to try."

The GPS worked well. Twenty minutes later they arrived at the Shannons' house.

"Good, lights in the windows mean someone is at home and the porch light is on also. Shall we go together?"

"Mahmud didn't say if I should. I don't dare make a mistake."

"Then stay in the car. I'll get you if I need you. Wish me luck."

Zayneb smiled. "Better than that, I wish Allah's blessings upon you for success because," she sobered, "...because success is critical."

Roshan patted Zayneb's hand for reassurance, climbed out of the car, carried the shoebox to the porch and rang the bell.

CHAPTER FORTY-NINE

SATURDAY, 6:30 PM

"**W**here's Becca?" Jason asked his wife as they sat down to supper with the three Grands.

"Off to dinner and a movie with Nathan Sommer."

"His idea or hers?" Jason asked. Jennifer shrugged. "Well, let's hope he's a step up."

He sat down with the children and Jennifer served their dinner plates. They'd eaten only half their food when the doorbell chimed.

Jennifer excused herself and peered out one of the glass sidelights to the porch. Their afternoon discussion about caution left Jennifer wary. The woman outside looked vaguely familiar but not someone she knew. On the safe side, she called, "Jay, could you please come here a minute?"

When he stood beside her she pointed outside. "We don't know her. What should we do?"

"Well, we're here together and my cell phone's in my pocket. Let's find out what she wants."

Cautiously Jennifer opened the door half way. "Hello," she said.

"Hello. My name is Roshan Witherspoon. You visited my garage sale this morning. You may remember we chatted and I told you I was born in India but married an Englishman in London and we moved to America."

Jennifer smiled recognition, pulled the door wide and said, "I do remember you, Roshan. Won't you come in?"

"Thank you, yes, but only for a minute because I'm here with a task. My next-door neighbor asked me to sell some things for her this morning at my yard sale, including a doll bought by a little girl with you. Turns out my neighbor made a big mistake; the doll wasn't for sale after all, and now the owner is very upset. If you're willing to return it, may I offer to substitute this doll which the little girl might consider in exchange?" She indicated the box in her hands.

Jennifer and Jason exchanged quick looks. Had answers to their questions about the diamonds walked right in their front door? Would they learn what they wanted to know?

"Please, let's sit in the living room while we talk." Jennifer led the way. "You say this doll belongs to your next door neighbors? Have you known them long?"

"I've known the wife since she was a little child and now her two daughters are like my own grandchildren. The doll belongs to her youngest daughter, a first-grader."

Roshan didn't mention the diamonds. Perhaps this woman knew nothing about them, unlike the neighbor who owned the doll. "Was the toy valuable?"

"No, I don't think so. Just a plaything their little girl loves and wants back."

"How did you know how to find us?"

Roshan recalled her pleasant conversation with Jennifer and noticing her unusual license plate as she drove away. "The men next door used that information to find your name and address."

Jason frowned. Once public information, this personal data was privileged now. His suspicion grew. "Do you know anything more about the doll?"

"What more do you need to know?"

"Well, I think we'd like to meet the owner," he suggested.

"Not a problem," said Roshan good-naturedly, "she's outside in my car. May I bring her in?"

The Shannons exchanged glances. Was this wise? Would this help get to the bottom of the story or invite raw danger inside their house? Clearly, the diamonds' owner knew the Shannons had them now and wanted them back.

"Yes," Jason's decision surprised Jennifer. "Please do bring her in."

They accompanied Roshan to the front door and waited while she brought Zayneb to the porch and introduced her before they all returned to the living room.

The woman looked frightened, not like a mother recovering a beloved doll for her child.

"Your hijab is lovely," Jennifer observed. "Are you Muslim?"

Seeing Zayneb's anguish, Roshan spoke for her. "Her name was Phoebe when she was Protestant before converting to Islam about twenty-five years ago. Remember how Cassius Clay became Muhammad Ali? Well, Phoebe took the name 'Zayneb.'" She sighed. "That's what she's asked friends to call her for this last quarter century."

"What can you tell us about the doll?" Jennifer asked the young woman.

Zayneb wrung her hands. Too scared and tormented to invent a story, she knew she must get the doll before returning to those madmen at home. Nothing rang like the truth. "The doll belonged to my little girl but she hadn't played with it for a long time. It lay in a box in the room our guest occupies. I found it high on a shelf there this morning and put it in Roshan's sale. But our guest became," she blanched at the memory, "terribly upset when he discovered the doll gone and sent me to find it. So here I am." She lost her composure. "Please, please let me take it back to them."

"To 'them'?" Jason asked.

"Yes, to my husband and his guest."

"Who is the guest?"

Roshan started to rebuke them for so many questions but wanted to hear this answer herself.

"I don't know. Years ago, my husband said if a countryman visits the U.S. we would welcome him into our home. No one came for twenty-four years — until two days ago."

"So your husband is not born in America like you?" Jason asked.

"No, he's from the Middle-East, like our guest."

"And their names?"

"Why all these questions?" Zayneb protested. "Would you please just kindly return the doll?"

Jennifer smiled guardedly. "First, we must ask our granddaughter if she's willing to make the trade. Second, we'd like to know your name."

Close to panic, Zayneb conceded in desperation, "My husband Mahmud's last name and mine are the same: Hussein. Our guest is Ahmed. I don't know his last name."

"Thank you. Now excuse me a minute while I bring the little buyer."

Jennifer left, returning with Alicia, who clutched her doll protectively. "I've explained the situation to her but the decision is hers. Would you like to show her the doll you're offering to trade?"

Roshan held the shoebox toward Alicia. The child removed the lid and rustled the tissue aside. "Oh," she breathed before the rest saw what lay inside. "This doll is beautiful." She lifted it out for all to see, then looked at her first purchase. "Are you sure your little girl will love this one again?"

Roshan spoke, "We are sure."

"Then I will trade," agreed Alicia, cradling her exotic new doll from India.

A gasp of relief escaped Zayneb's lips. She covered her face with her hands to hide her tears.

"Are...are you all right, Zayneb?" Jennifer asked with concern.

Far from all right, Zayneb recovered quickly. "Yes, yes. When I return the doll, all will be well."

But in her heart, she knew this was a lie.

CHAPTER FIFTY

SATURDAY, 7:17 PM

When the two women left moments later, the Shannons stood as if rooted in the foyer, confused by what they'd heard and what it meant.

"Oh, Jay. What will this Ahmed *do* when he finds the diamonds aren't inside the doll?"

Moving fast, Jason locked the front door and hooked the safety chain. "I'll set the security alarm and double-check door and window locks throughout the house. It's dark now so we'll close all the blinds. Probably not necessary but why take a chance? You do this floor and I'll do upstairs."

He didn't add that he would load his pistol and put it in his pocket.

They hustled to secure the house and returned to the table. "Sorry to interrupt our meal," said Jennifer, not wanting to upset the children. "Back to where we were before the doorbell rang." But the children wanted to talk about the doll trading.

"Do you think someone will come with a trade for my jewelry box?" Christine wondered.

Milo pouted. "I won't twade my dinosauws for anything, no matter what somebody bwings."

"Then we won't let that happen. Your dinosaurs are safe with you." The boy smiled his relief.

"When we finish dinner, could we have our under-the-pillow gifts early?" Christine asked.

"Instead of when you go to bed?" Jennifer asked with mock surprise.

"We won't have time to play with them then because we have to go to sleep. We'd have to wait until morning to enjoy them," she explained.

Alicia added, "You could still call them under-the-pillow-gifts but not put them under the pillow."

"Well thought out. Okay, just a minute." Jennifer went to the laundry room cupboard, selected the surprises planned for that night and brought them to the table.

Stretching out the excitement, Jennifer asked, "Is there someone here named Christine?" A hand went up and she put a newspaper-wrapped present into it.

"Anyone named Alicia?" She distributed the second gift. Anticipating what came next, Milo wiggled in his chair.

"Anyone here named Bill?"

"*Bill?* Not Bill. It's Milo."

"Anyone here named Milo?"

He jumped up, nodding, to accept his gift.

"All right," Jason instructed, "open them at the same time when I count to three."

Afterward, Jennifer gathered up the pieces of torn newspaper. "Now how about taking your new toys to the playroom?" The children bustled down the stairs.

"A glass of wine?" Jason offered." Jennifer nodded. He poured two and handed her one. They sipped in silence, each lost in thought.

"What should we do, Jay? When the men learn the diamonds are gone, will they come after them and after us? Bad enough that we're here, but what about the children? Should we go to a hotel?"

Jason snapped his fingers. "I have an idea." He grabbed the phone and dialed. "Hello, Adam? How would you and Hannah like to spend the night at our house? Yes, I know it's a strange request but it's important; we need to talk with you about something. Sure, ask Hannah what she thinks.... You'll come? Great and this may sound even stranger, but do you have the police cruiser at home tonight?... Good, would you mind driving it over here and parking in front of our house? Thanks. Yes," Jason laughed, "I will have a good explanation."

CHAPTER FIFTY-ONE

SATURDAY, 7:41 PM

"Zayneb, are you in danger?" Roshan asked with concern when they returned to her house.

"I...I don't think so. But if anything ever happens to me, please find a way to watch over my girls, especially little Safia. And if...if the worst should happen, tell the police what you know."

"Your talk frightens me. McLean has safe houses where abused women get help and guidance. Or we could call the police to stop him or put him in jail. A restraining order would keep him away from you. Let me help you make a better choice. At least stay with me tonight. Or if you think he'd come after you here, I'll give you money for a hotel until you decide what to do next."

"Thank you, dear Roshan, for caring so much. Getting the doll should solve their problem. Your help tonight made that possible. I must go now." She hugged Roshan and hurried out the front door to her own porch.

The men waited at the door as Zayneb arrived. Mahmud snatched the doll from her. "Is this it?"

Ahmed nodded as his host passed him the toy. He squeezed the doll's soft torso for the hidden packets. Feeling none, he jerked open the doll's clothes and tore apart the newly stitched seam. He fought for control. "What was hidden is gone. But where?"

Mahmud grabbed his wife roughly by the arm, but Ahmed put up a warning hand. "Tell us exactly what happened at that house."

"Roshan went inside. I stayed in the car but they asked to meet me also. Roshan took me into their house. The husband and wife were friendly. They said their granddaughter who bought the doll should decide whether to trade it for the substitute doll we brought. The girl said yes, gave us this doll and we brought it straight home. I did exactly what you told me to do."

"You removed nothing from the doll yourself?"

Zayneb looked stricken. "Of course not. I held the doll on my lap during the trip home while Roshan drove. It did not leave my hands for one minute."

"They handed it to you in the way it is now?"

"Yes, the granddaughter carried it to us in the living room from the kitchen and gave it to me when she took the new one we brought."

"Anything else we should know?"

"As Allah is my witness, I did what you asked and I told you everything that happened."

"Go, then, and wait for me upstairs."

The raw anger in Mahmud's voice scared her but she obeyed instantly. She heard the men close the study door as she hurried up the steps.

Trapped by circumstance, Ahmed had no choice now but to confide his plight to Mahmud. "Hidden inside the doll were packets containing 290 highest quality diamonds. Add ten more I left with the Russians this morning for their expert to assess and the total is 300. From the Great Leader's own hands, I brought these stones nearly 10,000 miles sewn into my ragged clothes. When the Russians phone me accepting the diamonds, they'll expect the remaining diamonds to pay for the weapons, arms and vehicles needed for our attack. That meeting is Monday morning. We have until then to produce the missing stones."

Mahmud pondered. "What hands touched the doll after it left your room? Zayneb took it to Roshan's sale next door. Would she remove the stones? I don't think so. She is too simple a woman to think of that. Then the Jennifer woman and her grandchildren took the doll home. The people in that house must know where the diamonds are. Shall we confront them tonight? We can invent a story about how you own the diamonds and ask for your property back. They may choose to return your property the easy way or we can wrest it from them the hard way."

"And what if they deny knowledge of the diamonds or admit they found them but refuse to return them? This is a fortune worth millions of dollars," Ahmed pointed out. "They'll want to keep it."

"So what next? We can't get the diamonds back if we don't confront them, but when we do they will tell the police. So we must kill them. There's no other way."

Ahmed sighed. "Yes, you are correct. But when the dead family is found, you said police will search tirelessly for us. Yet how could police trace our connection?"

"Wait. Finding diamonds would seem big news for this family," Mahmud said. "How many others have they told? If those others tell police about the gems, they'll know the family's dead because someone wanted their diamonds back."

"But even if they know why the murders happened, how can they know who killed them?"

"Tonight they met Roshan and saw Zayneb. If others are told of this, police can follow that trail."

"Get balaclavas to cover our faces and two silenced-pistols from your basement stash. Let's solve this tonight."

Thirty minutes later their car nosed into the Shannons' residential community and down the dark street toward their house. Lights on behind their shade-drawn windows indicated the family was at home. As they approached, Mahmud uttered a strangled cry. "Allah, why do you curse us when our mission is for your great glory?"

They stared, frozen, at the police cruiser parked in front of the house.

CHAPTER FIFTY-TWO

SATURDAY, 8:32 PM

"**M**om, this diamond story you've told us would be unbelievable for anyone but you," Hannah said, noting nods also from Adam and her father as they sat on the sun porch.

Adam cleared his throat. "As it turns out, this may be part of an even bigger picture. What do you know about clairvoyance?"

"Now there's a segue for you," Jason chuckled.

Adam smiled. "Just hear me out before you decide. What do you know about clairvoyance, Dad?"

"Not much." Jason searched his experience. "I've read psychics-for-hire scam gullible people into paying for pronouncements or predictions. Some skillful psychics make clients dependent enough to fear making decisions without the psychic's input—that input available only for a fee. Or the psychic weaves a story about the client but leaves out the punch line, which the client must pay more to hear. Believe it or not, these charlatans can gather devout followings."

"What about the other kind who don't charge, don't want publicity and are more puzzled than proud of their visions?"

"We could look it up on the internet, but the dictionary might give us a quick answer." Jennifer grabbed the one above the kitchen desk. "Okay, let's see what Merriam-Webster has to say. '*Clairvoyant:* unusually perceptive, having the power of discerning objects not present to the senses.' Okay, next we'll try *psychic:* 'of or relating to the *psyche;* lying outside the sphere of physical science; sensitive to nonphysical or supernatural forces.' And here it defines psyche: 'the soul, the self or the mind.'"

"How about 'premonition'?" Adam asked.

Jennifer flipped pages. "'*Premonition:* previous warning or *presentiment.*' And presentiment is 'a feeling that something is about to happen.'"

"So, it's all murky, unscientific stuff?" Hannah speculated.

"*Science.*" Jennifer flipped more pages. "'Knowledge covering general truth or the operation of general laws especially as obtained and tested through *scientific method.*' Which points us to scientific method: 'the rules and methods for pursuit of knowledge involving finding and stating the problem, the collection of facts through observation and experiment and the making and testing of ideas that need to be proven right or wrong.'"

Jason rubbed his chin. "Well, it's no surprise that I look at this as an engineer since I am one. Science regards paranormal stuff mostly as bunk because of inconsistent testing results. Tests must be repeatable to qualify as new discovery."

"How did they test, Dad?" Hannah asked.

"One study hid shapes and symbols in one room and asked blindfolded psychics in another room to identify what was pointed to. Some scored better than others but the results were spotty and nowhere near 100 percent. Another study had a blindfolded psychic press a button when he thought someone behind him was staring at him. The government investigated ESP and paranormal communication with Stargate and other military intelligence studies. They reported mixed conclusions, but who knows if they revealed what they really learned?"

Hannah shifted in her chair. "Why this clairvoyant-talk? Aren't we figuring out the diamonds?"

Adam smiled. "Open-minded detectives look at all clues to see how they might fit together. Police get cases where someone 'feels' or 'senses' something's wrong, and investigation shows they were right. So we try to consider it all, to figure what's relevant and what isn't. What I'm about to tell you seems weird—or it did until tonight. Normally, I wouldn't divulge a name relating to police business, but when you hear my story, you'll know you would have found out anyway."

They exchanged curious looks. Jennifer smiled at Hannah's obvious pride in her husband, now the center of attention.

Adam described Veronika Verontsova's visit to the police station and her vision. "Seeing your photo in the *McLean Connection* upset her even more. She insisted you're involved somehow in this danger near McLean. She thinks talking with you might help her better understand her vision.

She noticed your name under the newspaper picture and said if I didn't give you *her* phone number she'd get *yours* from the phone book and call you anyway. Then just before leaving, she had vibes about me: said I had a new wife, considered a career change and lived in an old house on a farm." He omitted her warning of danger for him at the house. "Weird or what?"

Incredulous, Jennifer said, "You're kidding about this, right?"

"No, Ma'am." He extracted a paper from his pocket. "Here's her number if you want to phone her. I ran her name through NSIS but nothing came up. If you meet her, consider a public place, not her house or yours, to stay on the safe side until we know how she fits in."

"Actually, she fits in pretty well," Jennifer mused. "Add her story to what we learned earlier tonight and you get something like this: this guest from another country, I forgot his name..."

"Ahmed," Jason supplied.

"...Ahmed had access to diamonds, which he hid in the doll. Unknown to him, Zayneb put the doll in her neighbor's garage sale. We bought it. Roshan remembered my license plate, which the men next door used to learn my name and address."

Adam frowned. "They'd need a privileged computer link for that."

"We'd never have found the diamonds except for the freak coincidence of Alicia's curiosity because of a classmate's botched surgery."

Adam looked thoughtful. "You say Zayneb told you her husband and his guest both come from the Middle-East. Maybe they're peace-loving, but if we factor in the clues in Verontsova's vision, maybe they're not. Maybe they have a very different agenda for the diamonds to fund."

"Terrorism?" Jason guessed. They all sat silent, considering the chilling impact of this logic.

"Whatever their motive, they clearly want the diamonds back. They're convinced you have them or know where they are. If desperate enough, they may *persuade* you to return them."

Hannah looked uncomfortable. Were here parents vulnerable again? "This is very scary talk."

"Yes, it is, because potentially this is a very scary situation," Adam confirmed.

CHAPTER FIFTY-THREE

SATURDAY, 8:47 PM

Jennifer broke the tension by looking at her watch. "It's time to put the Grands to bed."

Jason stood, "I'll do that tonight, Jen. You catch your breath. Which story shall I read to them?"

"How about more chapters in the book I started last night? It's on their nightstand. After this, we have one more night to finish it before they go, so judge accordingly."

"We're going to run upstairs to unpack and get settled," Hannah said. "Back in a little while."

Alone in the living room, Jennifer leaned back in the easy chair. This had seemed like an extra long day, yet it wasn't even 9:00. She'd just closed her eyes when she heard light tapping on the front door. Peering out the sidelight she saw Tony illuminated by the porch light.

"Too late for me to drop in for a glass of wine?"

"No, Tony, of course not." She gave him a warm hug, locked the door and reset the alarm. "You and the children make it through the day all right?" she asked as they walked to the sun porch and sat at the table. She knew Tony liked the same wine she did and poured two glasses of pinot noir.

"Yes, a lot for the kids and me to get ready for tomorrow's funeral. We've been busy. I just didn't want another minute to go by without... without thanking you for driving me to the hospital and for the dinner you brought last night. You're a beautiful person and a precious friend. I told this to my kids and thought I ought to tell it to you, too." He put his hand over hers affectionately.

"Let us know if there's anything we can do to make this a little easier for you or the children."

"Just be here when I need to hear a friendly voice. Is that Adam's car in front of the house?"

"Yes, they're spending the night."

"Still happy little love birds?"

"Definitely."

He looked into her eyes. "Do you remember those days when you couldn't wait to be with the person you love, couldn't wait to touch them, when your heart jumped each time the phone rang, when every word they spoke seemed magical?"

She smiled. He must be reliving his early life with Kirsten. How sad to face future years without his loving companion. Maybe he'd eventually find someone new, as had many widowed friends who married again. But mere days after his wife died was way too soon to mention this to Tony.

"Will you do anything differently when your children go back to their own lives in a few days?"

"My vet business is well established and I like my job, so that will continue. Kirsten's sudden death traumatized the kids, so I'll try to support each of them."

He downed his wine. "Got to go. Just had to drop by to let you know how much I... appreciate you and Jason."

He pulled her to her feet and they walked to the foyer. "Maybe you'd be willing to take me to one of those garage sales some weekend so I could learn the ropes. Seems like a shame to reach my age and know nothing about them."

"Sure, if you're serious, why not? But aren't you at the clinic on Saturdays?"

"Geez, you're right. Well, we'll have to think of something else then."

Emotion clouded Tony's face. He hugged her goodnight. As she eased out of the embrace his lips touched hers. She couldn't hide her surprise. "Just a little kiss between old friends?" he murmured. An act of loneliness, she thought. He kissed her again, his passion proving this no accident.

Confused, Jennifer gently extricated herself from his arms. He must be more fragile than she realized after his wife's death. She thought how deprived of love she'd feel if Jason died. Would any expression of affection seem better than none at all? Under other circumstances, this pleasant man might appeal to her as a date or suitor were she single. But now she chalked up his behavior as a widower's lonely despair. Yet in that one instant her friendly neighbor and long-time friend had introduced a new dimension to their relationship — an uncomfortable one — at least for her.

She opened the door and shooed him outside. "Sleep well tonight. We'll see you tomorrow," she called as he walked away.

As she locked and chained the door, she realized the chain would stop Becca when her key opened the door later tonight. She dialed her daughter's cell phone. "Let us know when you get home so we can unchain the door.... Why? Oh, just a new wrinkle in the diamond saga. We'll tell you all about it when you get home.... By the way, Hannah and Adam are spending the night. They're in the bedroom next to the Grands. See you later."

Jason came down the stairs. "We did the whole ritual. They even told me their best thing that happened today and their good deed. It turned into a marathon."

"Good work and thanks. The day's events have worn me down. I'm really tired. How about you?"

He nodded. "A hectic, unusual day for us both — and mostly an emotional roller coaster."

"Then let's ask Hannah to let Becca in when she gets home later. They'll want to talk until late anyway but can sleep in tomorrow, whereas I'll be up early with the Grands."

Upstairs, Jennifer removed makeup while Jason tapped on Hannah's door, delivering the Becca message. By the time Jennifer finished at the sink and dressed for bed, Jason dozed with the TV clicker in his hand. She removed it gently as she slipped into bed beside him. He didn't stir.

As she lay awake in the dark she wondered idly what it would be like if Tony lay next to her instead of her husband. She considered the huge effort to start over with a new person, essentially a stranger. She'd invested so many years in discovering and accommodating Jason that they'd become like two working parts of one unit, two halves of one whole. Over their forty-year history, many shared memories and jokes were known only to the two of them.

Sure, Tony was a pleasant, appealing man, well known as a friend but unknown as a companion. But for her, attraction went beyond logic, appeal or availability; it involved the heart. The comparison of these two men only pinpointed how much she loved Jason.

As he slept curled on his side, she gently spooned against him, feeling the slumbering warmth of his familiar contours until sleep's relaxation at last softened the smile on her face.

CHAPTER FIFTY-FOUR

SATURDAY, 9:33 PM

At Mahmud's house, Zayneb prepared for bed, turned out the lights and lay awake. Would her god spare her or punish her effort to deceive her husband by earning money at the sale?

An hour later she heard the bedroom door open. Lying on the pillow under the covers, she stared into the room's blackness, alert for every sound. She heard Mahmud shuffle across the room and approach the bed. Please, Allah, touch his heart with gentleness and love.

Instead he hissed, "Your ugliness disgusted me for years and now your pig-brained stupidity brings shame and catastrophe upon my house. Not only does this terrible trouble you made humiliate me before my guest and other countrymen, but worse, your blundering affects the course of history."

Seconds later a punch thudded into her slight frame, but his words had bruised her as much as the blow. He pulled her from the bed, slapping her back and forth across the face and punching her body as she cowered away from his blows. He dragged her into the bathroom and slammed her against a wall. As she scrambled to gain her footing he punched her in the stomach. When she doubled over, he jerked her back, spun her around and twisted her arm up high behind her back until a cry escaped her lips.

She knew he hated it when she cried out. Weakness, he called it. She tried to endure the hurt in silence, but the pain squeezed out sounds she couldn't gulp back.

Now he bent her backward over the sink. She stared bug-eyed at the ceiling as his fingers closed around her throat. She twisted and turned as her hands clawed ineffectively to loosen his. She couldn't budge his grip on her neck. She grabbed something from the vanity to hit him back, a liquid soap dispenser, but he wrested it from her. Roaring his anger, he jetted a stream of the liquid into her eyes. The intense stinging beneath her eyelids produced involuntary thrashing to dispel the irritant.

"My eyes," she screamed. "Water, please..."

"You want water," he roared. "Try this." He wrenched her away from the sink and forced her head into the toilet. He held her there until she writhed and gurgled. As he pulled her to her feet, wheezing and coughing up inhaled water, she knew he would kill her this time.

In an act of primitive desperation she flailed her arms. The fingers of one hand closed over the scissors left earlier on the toilet tank. As he lurched to fling her into the empty bathtub, through a blur of soap-film she followed an instinctive desperation to survive, stabbing the sharp steel toward him again and again. Amid the grunting chaos of their struggle, she doubted it even touched him. Weak with pain and despair, realizing she couldn't win against his strength and vicious determination, she crumpled toward the floor to welcome death. Her last thoughts were of her daughters.

But he jarred her yet again, this time his entire weight pinning her to the tile. Then, as suddenly as his rage toward her began, the onslaught stopped. She could scarcely breathe with his weight upon her, compressing her lungs. Gasping for air, she finally pushed away this chest-crushing burden. Zayneb stared in confusion as he rolled aside and lay inert beside her. She made no sense of what she saw.

Her husband lay immobile on the tile floor, a bloody scratch across his cheek, an oozing puncture above his left eye and more blood on his neck. But then she spied the unbelievable: the closed handles of the long, thin scissors stuck out of his ear.

She sobbed, unable to believe she'd survived the terrible beating and unable to process the baffling scene before her.

She dragged herself to the tub faucet to flush the burning soap from her eyes. She felt dazed. A sudden, overpowering wave of fatigue and pain swept over her, shutting her down. She crumpled to the bathroom floor and passed out.

Zayneb wasn't sure how long she lay in the bathroom. As lucidity returned, stabs of physical pain and emotional misery confirmed she still existed. She sat up with enormous effort. What had happened here? She put a reluctant hand on Mahmud's arm and shook him. No response. She tried again without result. Staring at him and at the awful thing sticking out of his ear forced shocked recognition that her husband lay dead. Her face paled in terror.

What...what had she done?

CHAPTER FIFTY-FIVE

SATURDAY, 11:01 PM

In another room of the house, Khadija lay under her covers, eyes open wide. She thought of Ahmed. Was her attraction to this older man genuine or only a way to infuriate her father? Or maybe both? Troubled, she tried to fall asleep.

In the basement, Heba curled in her bed, stifling sobs, for Mahmud had visited her earlier that night with lust on his mind. She knew not to protest when he attacked her. Those men the human traffickers forced her to endure had no affection in mind during those endless, repulsive encounters. Neither did he. These physical and emotional torments began when her innocent childhood changed forever at age eight. Mahmud had shared her with his friends when he first owned her, as had the Turk, but those liaisons stopped when he married Zayneb. For twenty-four years, only Mahmud pushed his way, uninvited, into her room.

But from the start Zayneb showed Heba kindness. First she changed Heba's sleeping place from the dirty, blanket-covered mattress Mahmud tossed in the basement room to a comfortable bed. Thanks to Zayneb, her few belongings no longer lay in cardboard boxes, but now in a bureau beside a night stand, a lamp, a small desk, a chair, a television and books.

Zayneb taught her literacy. Heba learned to trust and care about this gentle woman. Heba thought if this were a Middle-Eastern Muslim household where a man could marry four women, as sister-wives she and Zayneb would share a very similar relationship as they did now but with one notable exception: Zayneb knew nothing of Mahmud's carnal visits to the basement.

Ahmed lay awake also, his panic at the diamonds' loss slightly assuaged by finding the doll buyer's house. But the police car parked in front signaled new problems. Had she given police the treasure or merely told them how she got it? Had she asked for police protection? Needing to produce the gems for the Russians, he must get the stones very soon. He pondered how to do this. He'd likely get only one chance.

Ahmed winced at sounds from the next room, aware of Mahmud's temper and knowing his own accusations triggered the man's anger toward Zayneb tonight. But what choice had he? Their mission's success hinged upon retrieving the diamonds.

The comfort of blaming others for one's mistakes appealed to Ahmed as it did to everyone. His culture's logic simplified this justification. A woman's stupidity had lost his diamonds, derailing a plan grander than anything her mind could grasp. Her mistake earned retribution, which her husband correctly meted out to teach her a lesson and regain control over his household.

But truthfully, he thought, she wasn't guilty. *He* chose the diamonds' poor hiding place, ironically thinking using the doll was a positive sign from his god. What purpose could Allah intend by twisting the rope of events to destroy the funding for Ahmed's mission to glorify Him?

And now gentle Zayneb endured punishment he earned instead. He wanted to find a way to make this up, but how was that possible in the short time they had left?

Guilt about Zayneb's situation and frustration over his love for Khadija forced his focus back to the doll. He lay in the dark, wracking his brain for a scheme to get the diamonds back from this Jennifer Shannon tomorrow. But how?

A rap on his door snapped him back to reality. Might it be Khadija? He opened his door. But it wasn't Khadija. For a moment he didn't recognize this battered specter as his host's wife.

"Zayneb? What...what is wrong?"

He could scarcely make out her frail voice speaking through damaged lips. "Please help me."

He hesitated. "A moment while I get my jacket." He owned no robe but could not emerge in his nightclothes. He reappeared wearing shoes and his overcoat.

She led him through her bedroom and into the bathroom, where an unnerving scene lay before him. Ahmed gaped in astonishment. In a million years, he did not expect what he saw.

"It was an accident. He smeared soap in my eyes. I couldn't see where the scissors went."

Ahmed knelt to take Mahmud's pulse but the staring eyes, open mouth and blood oozing from the impaled ear confirmed his condition. Ahmed had killed men himself and seen many corpses, but this bizarre accident with the scissors caused him pause. If she'd tried deliberately to stab her attacker in the ear, she couldn't have. Only a freakish twist of fate explained such violation.

"I will call the police now to tell what I have done," she mumbled.

Ahmed stood quickly, his voice firm. "No, Zayneb. Thank you for offering this but it is not...it is not a good idea. I will take care of everything. I...I have a plan."

But he did not.

CHAPTER FIFTY-SIX

SATURDAY, 11:37 PM

Ahmed could not allow police into this house to investigate a murder. Identifying and interrogating them all as witnesses or suspects would destroy his carefully crafted anonymity and, perhaps, their plot. No, he must deflect this unnerving development as if it had never happened.

His mind raced, exploring and rejecting possible solutions.

"Have you another one of these, Zayneb?" He pointed to the shower curtain liner.

"Yes, I will bring it."

"Tonight we wrap him tight in this plastic and tomorrow we will bury him. We tell family and friends he returned to his homeland. You make no missing person report requiring police investigation because he told you he was going overseas, just not when he will return."

Hearing this, her bloodshot eyes widened. Ahmed methodically checked the dead man's pockets, removing all identification and jewelry. "Turn your head away," Ahmed directed as he extracted the scissors and dropped them in the wastebasket. "No evidence if the body's ever found."

Together they wrapped him in the shower curtain, sealed it with adhesive tape from the medicine cabinet and dragged the resulting bundle to one side of the bathroom.

"Very little blood spilled on the floor. Clean it so the grout between these tiles looks the same as the rest."

"Who will run his painting company when he doesn't go to work?"

Ahmed considered this. "Has he a foreman? A good one?"

"I think so, but he speaks little to me of his business."

"Don't worry. I will find out and tell that man to take charge for the immediate future until Mahmud returns. You think how you will convince your family tomorrow. Our stories must be identical. Meantime, lock this bathroom door and allow no one in but yourself until we move him."

"Would it be safer to do it tonight in darkness when most are asleep?"

She didn't realize he must think of a safe place to dispose of a body and at the moment had no idea where that might be.

"Your idea is correct, but tomorrow night instead of tonight. I go now for sleep. You also. We will talk again tomorrow."

As she closed her bedroom door, he moved along the hall, past his room, down the stairs and out the back door for fresh air. He sat on the porch steps, his mind on overload, and pulled his coat tighter against the chilly fall night. He thought of his dead host: this had been his home, his family, his business, his life. Now the man was gone forever. He certainly hadn't died a hero's death, but was he in Paradise anyway? What would happen to his family when Ahmed and the rest of the cell died martyrs' deaths in a few days? What would happen to beautiful, bright Khadija? Who would hold her and love her? What fortunate man would create children with her?

He pulled his heart away from Khadija to focus his mind on urgent problems. He must recruit another driver from the cell tomorrow. He must decide on a plan to wrest back the diamonds. He must plan their sensitive mission and, absent this dead co-conspirator, accomplish it with only nine men. He must finalize negotiations with the Russians and put in place the inventory and cash they'd provide in exchange for the Great Leader's treasure.

Now, if all that weren't enough, he must figure out where to bury the body lying upstairs.

He stared around the pleasant yard. The few homes he'd seen in his country weren't like this one, but his narrow life experience—school, camps and classes—allowed little time in residential areas. Mahmud had lived an enviable life compared to his. His own life could unfold differently with Khadija in it, but that was impossible for a martyr. The Great Leader would counsel material joys of the flesh paled against the honor of glorifying Allah and changing history. He'd counsel only a selfish, small-minded donkey preferred a temporal wife and family to the keys to Paradise and the lasting fame of a martyr furthering the noblest cause.

Ahmed gazed at the lush grass, the six-foot wooden fence surrounding the property, the swing set with slide and tree house, the numerous trees and even some flowers still blooming in the raised gardens. And then, something clicked in his mind.

DAY FOUR

SUNDAY

CHAPTER FIFTY-SEVEN

SUNDAY, 6:30 AM

Jennifer wakened early after a good night's sleep and stretched lazily in the king-size bed. She rose quietly, without disturbing Jason, peeked in at the sleeping Grands down the hall and padded downstairs to collect the fat Sunday newspapers from the front yard.

She brewed coffee and nuked bacon in the microwave. As delicious hickory aromas filled the kitchen, she poured a coffee, slid the newspapers from their plastic bags, located the classified section and turned to garage, moving and estate sales.

Most sales were Saturday only. The Sat/Sun combos would be well picked over and very few in her area were Sunday only. One in Vienna looked promising but of no interest to children. A no-go today. She turned to another section, got a pencil and started the crossword puzzle but found concentrating difficult. The diamond dilemma intruded upon her thoughts.

On impulse she grabbed the phone book, looked for Mahmud Hussein but found nothing in McLean, despite trying different spellings for the last name. Roshan Witherspoon wasn't listed either. She wanted the location of Roshan's house because, if what the two women said was true, Zayneb and "the two Middle-Eastern men" lived next door. Jennifer remembered the name of the community where the sale took place, but it included hundreds of houses.

She'd sipped coffee when an idea popped into her head. At that very moment, the Grands appeared, hungry for breakfast.

Serving waffles and juice plus the bacon, she said, "Children, we went to so many sales yesterday I can't remember where Alicia bought her doll. Can any of you remember that house?"

The children looked thoughtful as they munched breakfast. Milo said, "They all looked alike."

"He's right," Christine said. "They did because we thought about the toys, not the houses."

Alicia agreed.

"Well, if you remember anything about that house, please be *sure* to tell me. Okay?"

They all nodded.

"This is your last day visiting us. Your parents pick you up tonight. How would you like to have two learning surprises today instead of one?" She smiled at their eager response. "Then after breakfast," she said with enthusiasm, "we'll do the first one early today. Who'd like to take a walk in the woods with me?"

"We would," they cheered and Christine added, "We love to do 'woods walk,' Gran."

"Where are our collection buckets?" asked Alicia.

"In the garage. Who knows what nature study we'll find today to show Granddaddy?"

Christine danced around her chair. "Do we have to go home when Mommy and Daddy get back from their trip?"

Jennifer laughed. "Haven't you missed them?"

"I don't miss them," Milo announced over his juice glass.

"No," Alicia said, "because we don't get under-the-pillow-gifts at home the way we do here."

Jason shuffled in stifling a yawn, "Did someone say under-the-pillow gifts? Do I get one, too?"

The three children giggled at this preposterous suggestion. Christine chided, "Granddaddy, you *know* only grandchildren get them when we spend the night at your house."

"Oh, no. I want one, too!" Jason feigned disappointment, extracting fits of laughter from the children. "Can't a grown-up qualify?"

"No, no!" the Grands shouted gleefully.

"Besides," Jennifer added slyly, "you must be very, *very good* to get an under-the-pillow gift."

Jason caught his wife's amused eyes, "Well, that probably counts me out!" He winked at her.

After breakfast, Jennifer carried plates to the sink then turned back to the kids. "Now run upstairs to change into play clothes for our woods walk."

"Is Gwandaddy coming, too?" asked Milo.

"No," Jason answered. "But I want to see what you find. And be careful. You might see a *snake*."

They giggled nervously at this possibility before hurrying toward the stairs.

To Jennifer he added, "...and that includes the human kind as well. I'll watch after you from the sun porch. Take your cell phone and call if anything seems suspicious."

CHAPTER FIFTY-EIGHT

SUNDAY, 7:05 AM

The Grands scampered upstairs and Jennifer followed to get dressed also. When they met again in the kitchen, each child held the handle of a plastic bucket before they headed across the yard, out the back gate and down the partially overgrown path leading into the woodsy Fairfax County parkland. An active stream coursed beneath huge, spreading trees. Clinging fall leaves and bushy evergreen foliage muted the nearby traffic sounds enough to hear melodic birdcalls.

In only a hundred steps from their back door they transitioned from the fenced yard of their residential world into a natural one. As they trooped along a downhill path, pushing back branches to make way, Jennifer thought she saw and heard movement in the bushes—as if something or someone were running away. Probably retreating wildlife: a red fox, possum, raccoon or even coyote.

They knew deer lived in these woods, having seen them grazing often just outside their back fence in the grassy strip before the woodland's tree line began. Surprising a wary deer on a walk with three boisterous children to spook it away seemed unlikely; yet as they walked together along an area of dense thicket, a deer exploded out of the bushes, rocketed past them and disappeared into foliage on the other side of their path.

"Wow, did you see that?" Christine exclaimed.

"Wait 'til I tell Mommy and Daddy," Milo marveled.

"They'll be amazed," Alicia agreed. "Why are you wearing your garden gloves, Gran?"

"They protect my hands when I pick up trash to keep the woods clean — things like this." She reached down for an empty plastic bottle and a piece of weathered newspaper in bushes edging the trail. "Anybody find special nature study items yet?"

"Here are some acorns attached to a branch with dried oak leaves," Christine said.

Alicia added, "And here's a cicada shell. Look how the claws hang on to my sweater."

Not to be outdone, Milo picked up something from the ground, announcing, "I found a wock, a gway wock. With pride, he dropped it into his bucket.

"That's the best gray rock I've seen." Jennifer patted his head. They wandered beneath the sheltering trees for half an hour, collecting nature's treasures.

"Okay, kids. Time to start back now to show Granddaddy your collections." They exerted extra energy to hurry uphill on the last leg home. Pretending she could barely keep up, Jennifer reached the back gate last.

"Run on ahead to the house to show Grandaddy what you found while I pick up this last bit of litter. I'll catch up in a minute," she called.

At the edge of the woods near their back fence, she added an empty beer bottle and a dirty, leatherette, pocket-size case to her litter trashbag before hurrying home behind the others.

After the children's nature show-and-tell for Jason, Jennifer said, "Grandaddy and I want to read the newspaper. Guess what: today's a 'Sponge Bob' TV marathon. Isn't that your favorite?"

Two said "yes" but not Christine. "Mommy said not to watch TV all the time we're here."

"She's right and you haven't. Would she really mind if you watch 'Sponge Bob' awhile?" Christine agreed and Jennifer settled the children on the den couch before selecting their channel.

After poring over the voluminous Sunday *Washington Post* and *The Times*, Jennifer emptied her litter collection bag, pulled out bottles and soda cans to recycle and trashed the rest. The leatherette case landed on top in the wastebasket and, judging it new enough to put in her Goodwill box, she put it aside to take to the garage later.

Just then, Alicia returned to the kitchen and tugged at Jennifer's sleeve. "Gran, I remember something," she said. "Watching 'Sponge Bob' reminded me because he has one in his show."

"One what?"

"One elephant. In a garden by the front porch of the house where I bought my doll is the statue of an elephant about this high." She touched her waist. "I remember giving my doll a ride on it while the rest of you shopped there. The lady giving the sale is the same one who traded the new doll for my old one last night."

Jennifer hugged Alicia. "Thank you, Honey, for such an excellent memory."

Pleased at Jennifer's praise, Alicia skipped back to her place on the couch in the other room.

"All right, Jen, what are you up to now?" Jason asked, wary.

"I'm getting an idea."

"That's another danger phrase from you." He sighed with resignation.

"Jay, I couldn't find addresses for Hussein or Witherspoon in the phone book but, thanks to Alicia, I know how to find Zayneb's house, where this Ahmed who owns the diamonds is staying. I knew the community, but it's huge and without a street address I'd never remember the house."

"Okay, and...?"

"And if we looked for the house in your car, nobody could recognize us since I shopped those sales in *my* car. The house where we bought the doll has an elephant in the front yard. We could wear sunglasses for disguise." She snapped her fingers. "I even have a Halloween wig I could wear so nobody could recognize me. Therefore, safe."

Jason moaned audibly, "Does this mean you want to borrow my car?"

"Actually, I thought maybe we could go together—a little Sunday adventure. Becca could watch the children. Aren't we *both* trying to figure out this diamond situation?"

"Geez, Jen, I have a lot of computer work to do this afternoon with my company's merger coming up." He sighed and cocked an eyebrow. "Will the marriage suffer if I say no?"

Trying not to laugh, she pretended to examine her nails? "Are you willing to risk it?"

"All right, I know blackmail when I hear it." But he only faked annoyance. Although swept into this potential danger by default, as usual, he recognized that he needed to know as much as possible to protect his family.

CHAPTER FIFTY-NINE

SUNDAY, 7:37 AM

Ahmed's subconscious sifted through his many problems as he slept. He awoke with two clear plans: one for disposing of Mahmud's body and the other for recovering the diamonds.

This Jennifer Shannon woman had the gems or knew who did. The sleeper cell would get to her, use torture as leverage to get her cooperation, or threats to kill a loved one, or both, until she produced the treasure. They could burst into her house or follow her when she left and abduct her elsewhere. To avoid a witness to inform police, they'd kill her, making that appear a random incident.

He mentally rehearsed his story of Mahmud's sudden "trip" as he went downstairs for breakfast, where a double surprise awaited him. The lovely Khadija stood at the foot of the stairs, melting his heart with her pleasant smile and friendly disposition.

"You have a guest this morning," she said. "My mother isn't well today, so I answered the doorbell. He's waiting for you in my father's study."

"Thank you, Khadija. Will you join me at breakfast later?"

"I...I don't think my father will allow that. But if not, maybe we can talk together later today." She led him to the study door. "Here he is," she said to the guest and backed away as they closed the door.

The men exchanged God's blessing. "You may remember I am Abdul, who hosted our cell meeting on Friday. Perhaps Mahmud would like to sit with us while I speak with you?"

Ahmed cleared his throat. "An excellent idea, but Mahmud is not here. He returned yesterday afternoon to his home country for a family emergency. He may be gone for an extended time, so we must proceed without him."

Abdul hid his shock well, but Ahmed saw it and continued quickly. "This timing is unfortunate, as we are down from eleven to nine men without Ali and Mahmud. But we will manage. I will stay in this house to protect his family in his absence. I will, however, need a new driver since my presence here is undocumented and I cannot risk a police stop."

"May I have that honor, Ahmed?"

"Thank you, Abdul, but the honor is mine if you will accept the job. Have you had breakfast? No? Then why don't we go to the dining room to eat while we talk?"

"A fine idea and thank you for the invitation."

They seated themselves in the dining room. Ahmed called, "Heba, we would like breakfast now."

She appeared instantly, more subdued than ever, wearing her usual long sleeves, long skirt and hijab. She poured coffee and placed fruit, bread and jelly on the table.

After she returned to the kitchen, Ahmed spoke. "Thank you for dealing with Ali."

"Allah solved that problem for us with an explosion leaving them all dead. I did nothing but report this to you," he admitted modestly.

"But you were prepared to solve it yourself otherwise."

"Of course," Abdul confirmed. "And now may I speak in confidence about quite another matter?"

"Speak then, for no ears will hear but mine."

CHAPTER SIXTY

SUNDAY, 7:46 AM

W hen Ahmed confirmed they spoke privately, Abdul relaxed. "At our cell meeting you told us American Jews killed your parents. Then the Great Leader arranged your rescue, educated you and selected you to lead this project?" Ahmed nodded. "You said you were five then?" He nodded again.

"You said two men came to take you to the madrassa."

"Yes."

"And were you the only child of your parents?"

"No, they also killed my infant sister. My twin sister visited another village that day. My mother's dying words begged me to take care of her, but at school, my rescuers would not tell me my origins and punished my questioning. So I gave up. Without knowing the name of my village — or even my country — I'll never find her."

"And at the meeting two days ago did I see above your shirt a red birthmark on your neck? Is it a stain that runs across your shoulder?"

Ahmed sat up straight. "Yes, but how could you know this?"

"And did you tell those men your Baba said Allah marked you with this stain to show your special importance to Him?"

"Yes!"

"And those two men who rescued you, was one older and one younger?"

Speechless with surprise at these intimate revelations from a stranger, Ahmed nodded.

"Then I was that younger man, fifteen years old at the time and in training to rescue boys like you. I can't remember them all, but you were my first so I remember you well."

Ahmed jumped to his feet. "Do you speak the truth, Abdul?"

"As my witness is Allah, peace unto His name."

"Then you know my country? My village?"

"Yes." He named them for Ahmed. "Your village was too small for many maps, but places with as few as 200-500 inhabitants worked well for our tactics."

"Praise Allah, I prayed for this knowledge. Thanks to you, I feel rooted to the earth at last."

"You have a special hate for the Americans and the Jews, as you explained at the meeting."

"Yes, revenge for their murder of my parents."

"Your hate for them is worthy, but you know only what you were told. There's more to the story."

"What do you mean?"

"At that time, our new cause hungered for recruits. Our Great Leader's unique multi-purpose plan designed future world domination earlier than any other sects imagined. We needed many soldiers for our army of action. Our Great Leader, whose forward-looking brilliance constantly amazed us, conceived another clever plan. In each village lived many people supporting our cause but a few troublemakers who did not. He said culling out the opposition meant everyone left agreed with us. We'd eliminate the opposition and harvest their children to train as soldiers for our new army."

"But how does that apply to me?"

"Your parents objected to our ideas. They spread dissent against Islamic radicalism to all villagers who listened. Eliminating them sent a powerful message to other villagers—join us or die. So our Great Leader sent men to dispose of your parents who we knew had three children, a boy, a girl and an infant. When we came for you, your sister had disappeared. This was no loss to us, for we trained only boys."

"But the American Jews..."

Abdul grinned, pleased to impart important news. "We told that story to all the boys we harvested to focus their hatred on our enemy and secure their loyalty to our cause. Not knowing their villages of origin, they could never return to learn otherwise. So we rescued you twice: first, by saving you from your parents' blasphemous rantings and, second, by providing you education and training to fight for Allah's grand purpose. Fortune smiled two times on you, Ahmed."

Ahmed stared at Abdul, dumbstruck. This man's words changed all he thought he knew about his early life. He believed what the school told him but saw now that all of it was false.

Was anything he believed true? All his information came from other people. He had accepted this until Khadija urged him to question authority and think for himself.

His mother's voice pushed forward in his consciousness: "Avenge our undeserved deaths." Yet rather than avenging his parents, he'd furthered their murderers' goals with every breath he drew.

Ahmed stood with effort, holding the edge of the table for support. "Thank you, Abdul for...for telling the true story and...for your rescue."

But deep in his mind the recipients of vengeance for his parents' murders now wore new faces: Abdul and the Great Leader for whom Ahmed saw he'd become a terrorist errand boy. "Please allow me a moment to absorb this information."

His mind raced. He couldn't show any behavior changes or the cell would eliminate him. He must appear as dedicated as ever while evolving into a different person.

He sat down again, wiping his hand across his brow. "This is a remarkable story, Abdul. I did not realize the depth of our Great Leader's planning. I am more dedicated than ever since you told me this today."

"And I am twice honored by Allah, blessings upon Him, first to play even a small role in guiding that five year old on a path to his position of such leadership and, second, to fight by his side to strike mortal blows against the great Satan's side."

"Please pick me up here at 8:30 for our meeting at 9:00 with the entire cell again tomorrow at your place of business. I will reveal more information about our plot against America, for the time comes very soon now. I will phone the others to attend."

* * * *

Heba leaned against the kitchen wall beside the closed door. Once again, she'd heard everything said in the adjacent dining room.

CHAPTER SIXTY-ONE

SUNDAY, 8:03 AM

"Do we smell bacon?" Hannah asked as she and Adam strolled into the kitchen fully dressed. "Morning, Mom...Dad."

Jason waved a slice of toast in the air as Jennifer said, "Good morning to you. Yes, it is bacon—the special applewood smoked brand Dad likes." She pointed along the counter to fruit and Krispy Kreme donuts, "And here's more you might add to it."

"You look dressed and ready to roll," Jason observed.

"Busy day ahead for us at the farm," Hannah said as they filled their plates. "We're heading home soon to accomplish what we can."

"Thanks again for rushing over here last night. Funny how it worked out; we baby-sat the Grands and you police-sat us." They laughed at this twist.

Adam spoke with concern. "When we leave, so will the police cruiser out front. Even if it discouraged somebody last night, you're on your own today. Please be careful. Hannah will give me no peace if she thinks you're in danger. Your decisions in the next few days could affect your safety. Make good ones."

"We certainly don't want trouble," Jason agreed. "Once we figure this out we can better reduce risks. You might be a key player here, Adam, telling us if-and-when police learn more clues."

They finished breakfast and exchanged good-bye hugs. Jennifer walked them to the car and waved as they drove away. Back inside, she resumed reading the Sunday *Washington Post* as she waited for Becca to appear.

"Maybe we could just take the Grands with us," she suggested to Jason.

"Where?"

"On the elephant hunt."

"Oh, that. I thought you planned to press Becca into nannying. Did I get that right?"

"What if she sleeps 'til noon? I'm getting antsy already. Why don't we take the kids on a Sunday ride? Alicia might even recognize the house after remembering the elephant."

"Are you serious about this?"

"Afraid so."

"Can we rip them away from 'Sponge Bob' without consequences?"

"Why don't I watch with them until this episode ends and then introduce the ride? I'll take along car-bingo cards to prevent boredom."

"Do we still have those from when our kids were little?"

"No, I found six yesterday at a garage sale."

"Jen, Jen. Is there nothing you can't find at one of those sales?"

"Not love, but I already found that somewhere else." She planted a kiss on his forehead and joined the children.

Fifteen minutes later when she appeared with the children at the kitchen door, he lay down the newspaper and said with false enthusiasm. "Okay, gang, let's go for a drive."

Jennifer directed Jason to the community sale neighborhood, where they cruised the streets looking for the statue in each yard. They were about to give up when Jennifer cried, "Jay, is that it? Do you see an elephant?"

He looked where she pointed. "Yes, I do." The Grands looked up from their bingo cards.

"My card has stop signs and houses and trees and other things to cover if I see them—but no elephants," said Christine. The other Grands murmured agreement.

Jennifer couldn't hide her excitement as they drove past the house. "That's it! Now we know where we bought the...er, doll." She wouldn't mention diamonds in front of the children.

"Now we know," he agreed. "But aren't we interested in a house next door?"

She thought about this as he drove several streets away and pulled the car to the curb.

"What next?" she wondered aloud.

"Good question!"

"I know, let's drive by slowly going the other way and I'll snap pictures of all three houses."

"What will that accomplish besides giving us more risky exposure?" Jason asked.

"We'll have physical proof to flesh out our story when we tell the police."

"Is telling them the next step?"

"In a way, we already have, unofficially, by letting Adam know. Should we make what we know official? I'm not sure, Jay. What do you think?"

"I think one step at a time."

"But a photo becomes another fact in proving our case, wouldn't you agree?"

"Proving our case? What case? If the place means trouble, it's something we don't need."

"I guess you're right, but then what makes me think we need this picture?"

"Because you're totally crazed?"

They both laughed, but she noticed he laughed longer... "If I don't get the pictures now, I'll just come back to do it tomorrow."

"I was afraid of that. Okay, let's get it over with." He changed the subject. "Look, kids, there's a dog by a mailbox. Are either of those on your bingo cards?"

The Grands concentrated. "*Yes,* I have a dog. Thanks, Gwandaddy," said Milo, shutting the window over that picture on his card.

"And I have a mailbox," Alicia added. "Good job, Granddaddy."

Jennifer put her hand on Jason's knee. "And I have a sweetheart husband willing to play Batman while Robin uses the camera."

Batman smiled.

CHAPTER SIXTY-TWO

SUNDAY, 9:15 AM

When Abdul left, Ahmed went to his room, phoned his cell members on an untraceable phone and announced tomorrow's meeting. He also mentioned Mahmud's sudden "trip" to the Middle- East.

Now he needed tools for his next task. He searched the garage without success. Who to ask? He doubted he would see Zayneb this morning and Khadija had disappeared back upstairs. He hadn't told her about her father's "trip," nor Safia or Heba.

He made his way to the kitchen. Heba busied herself at the sink, looking out the kitchen window when he approached. At the sound of his voice, she immediately withdrew into her submissive shell, averting her face from him by looking at the floor.

"You don't speak but you listen and understand. Is that right?"

She nodded.

"I am looking for some yard tools: a rake, some buckets, a shovel, a tarp and so on. I don't see them in the garage. Could you please show me where to find them? Before he left last night on an extended trip to his homeland, Mahmud asked me to make new gardens in the back yard where his wife can grow vegetables. I'd like to start them this morning."

Grabbing paper and pencil Heba wrote, "To the Middle-East? For how long?"

"Yes, he went early today. He won't be back for a long time, maybe a year or more."

Heba nodded and scurried ahead of him out the back door. She pointed to a shed.

"Thank you, Heba."

As she returned to the house, he found what he needed in the garden tool storage area. First he measured the existing raised gardens, then selected two symmetrically pleasing locations next to them and positioned eight stakes in the ground, four for each garden and identical in size to those already there. Not wanting to alert neighbors to his project by pounding in the stakes, he wiggled them into the soil as far as he could and braced each with bricks from the shed. Then he connected each set of four stakes with string, forming two four-foot-by-six-foot rectangles.

He skinned off the top layer of lawn in each staked area with a spade, piling the resulting sod on a plastic tarp. As quietly as possible, he used a shovel to dig one work area down about two feet, piling that soil on another plastic sheet.

He returned to the kitchen and asked Heba, "Is Khadija upstairs?" The servant nodded.

"Would you please tell her I will speak with her in the study?" Heba nodded again and hustled away, head down.

She returned with Khadija. "Good morning, Ahmed. Did you want something?"

"Yes." He led the way to the study and closed the door after them. They sat in opposite chairs.

"Khadija, I have news about your father. An emergency in his home country needs his attention. He left early this morning on an extended trip. He doesn't know when he will return. It may be a long time, but I will protect your family in his absence for...as long as I can stay."

Khadija couldn't hide her surprise but hoped she masked relief that her contentious father was temporarily out of their lives. In his absence, perhaps she and Ahmed could develop their friendship without his sour interference.

Her face lighted. "I understand."

"Also may I ask for your help? Could you please take me to a store this morning?"

"Of course. What kind of store?"

"A store that sells nails, boards, bags of dirt and vegetable plants."

"A hardware store, but perhaps what you need is already here at the house."

He forced a smile. "Your father promised your mother to build two raised vegetable gardens in the back yard, but he didn't have time before leaving. To soften the news of his sudden long trip, he asked me to build them for her. I need materials to do so."

"I'm happy to drive you there, but is fall the best time of year to start such a garden?"

He hadn't considered this question. "Yes, because the soil I mix will settle over the winter to be ready for planting in the spring."

"When would you like to go?"

He looked at his watch. "This morning. I am ready now."

"I'll get my purse. The place I will take you opens Sundays at ten, so we can leave now." But as they left the study, Safia appeared on the bottom stair step.

Khadija crouched beside her to explain their father's trip. The little girl began to cry, for she loved him and her privileged life as his favorite. Khadija hugged and consoled her sister. "We will have new kinds of fun together while Baba is away. For instance, after lunch we'll go for ice cream."

This was a treat her father didn't allow. Even Safia grasped this immediate advantage.

"And when your Baba returns you will be his special girl just like always." Mollified, the child dried her tears and headed for breakfast with Heba.

Already their communication felt more relaxed in her father's absence. "Other hardware stores nearby open earlier on Sundays, but I'd like to use McLean Hardware Store. My family has shopped there for decades and I know the manager."

Minutes later, he stifled automatic shock at riding in a car with a woman driver. He convinced himself no disapproving Muslim would see him in the passenger seat and, besides, this driving arrangement was common in America. He chafed at the inconvenience of his mandate not to drive but accepted the reason. He didn't ask Abdul for this transportation because this was a personal matter.

SIXTY-THREE

SUNDAY, 10:04 AM

As they drove toward the hardware store, Ahmed made conversation. "A Middle-Eastern business friend asked me what to do if he wants to stay in this country."

"That depends upon why. He could apply for citizenship to become a legal immigrant. If he's afraid to return to his own country because he fears his government, he might defect and ask for political asylum."

"Would your government hide him from those he fears?"

"Hiding him is different. I think if the federal government needs evidence to prosecute certain criminal cases where a witness's testimony causes life-threatening danger, they trade his testimony for the witness protection program."

"Where would my friend go to find out?"

"Let's see, if I recall correctly from my course preparations, I think witness protection comes under the Justice Department, administered by federal marshals, but a local police station should get him to the right people."

They parked in front of McLean Hardware. "This store has two mottos," she said. "The first is 'if we don't have it, you don't need it' and the second is 'stop in for the things you need from the people you know.' I tell my students about stores like this because many have nothing similar in their countries. Do you?" He shook his head.

"Here, I'll introduce you to the manager." A pleasant man greeted them as they came inside. "Hello, this is Mike Cannon. Ahmed wants to build two raised gardens like these." She showed him a picture of the original two. "Could you please help him find what he needs to match them and maybe some construction advice?"

"Sure thing." Mike studied the photo. "This looks easy enough." He and Ahmed discussed dimensions and Mike assembled the needed materials.

"My family started shopping decades ago at your Old Dominion Drive store, but this new location is fabulous," Khadija said.

Mike laughed, "After fifty years there we just needed more room."

When they finished, Ahmed said to Mike, "You know what you are doing. I respect that."

He laughed. "I've been with the company since 1982, so I've learned a few things. Here, I'll get somebody to load it into your van."

Back home, Khadija changed clothes to help with the construction project. "I looked out the window. You've been busy: the outline's staked, grass removed and even some excavation."

"Yes, but I'll dig down another foot to get more old dirt to mix with the soil bags they sold us." In fact, he dug down almost three feet on one garden, piling shovelfuls of dirt onto a tarp.

"If this one's the experiment, maybe you won't need to dig as deep for the second one. Didn't Mike say some people put the bags of dirt into the framework with no digging at all?"

"You are right, Khadija. I learned from the first." He put his shovel aside. "Now let's assemble the wood sides and then I'll mix the dirt. Let us fill this shallower garden first." He poured, alternating contents of different bags and the tarp soil into the enclosure, mixing them together with a rake. "How does it look?" he asked.

"Good. Shall we finish the other one now?"

"No, I will finish it tomorrow. You could put some of the plants we bought in this one." He thought for a moment: It would be nice to see them sprout and thrive in the spring but his destiny ruled that out.

When she finished planting, they sat on patio chairs to survey their work over glasses of iced tea.

"You haven't been in this country very long, but is it what you expected?" she asked.

"No. They said to expect capitalistic greed in which the rich hurt the poor, a corrupt imperialist government that meddles uninvited with their armies in our homeland countries, vices like alcohol and wanton sex, women who dress immodestly and flaunt themselves in public and hordes of unbelievers in Islam, the one true religion. Worse, they are in league with our enemies, the Jews."

"And do you still believe all you were told?"

"I am not sure now. You tell me to question what I was told, to think for myself. This is new and uncomfortable for me. I see appeal in this freedom idea but also danger. How do you know what is right or wrong without religion to make those decisions clear for you?"

"A person here could live a useful, moral or ethical life with no religion whatsoever—unless he chooses one."

"You do not choose Islam. Islam chooses you and, once chosen, you are committed to it for life."

She explained, "Here that happens only with your consent. Freedom of religion means nobody has the right to force you if you question and disagree."

He thought about this, wishing he had freedom to choose something else instead of a desperate need to retrieve the diamonds at all costs. The powerful web maker who was their Great Leader, the impatient McLean cell members he was sent to unleash on Americans and the ruthless Russians—all exerted strangle-hold controls over his life. He must succeed. Failure meant only one outcome: a coward's death, not the martyr's death guaranteeing reward forever in Paradise. But was that even a guarantee?

Now that he questioned everything, what could he believe?

CHAPTER SIXTY-FOUR

SUNDAY, 11:00 AM

Jennifer answered the ringing phone. "Hi, Mom. It's Kaela. How are the children getting along?"

"They're having a wonderful time and so are we. Would you like to speak with them?"

"Sure, but first we have a big favor to ask. Would you mind keeping them until Tuesday morning? We're having a great time and it's a beautiful place. We met some old friends who happened in at the same time. We'd like to stay a little longer, if that works for you."

"Let me check my calendar." Jennifer took a look. "No problem. What time Tuesday morning?"

"How about ten? We'll have an early breakfast before we drive back."

"Do you think the children want to stay longer?"

"Mom, I haven't a doubt in the world, but I'll ask to be sure. But before you get them, thanks for being such an understanding mom."

"You're welcome, Honey. I well remember those hectic years with demanding little ones day and night. You need a break once in awhile. Hang on, I'll get them."

Jen listened to enough of the Grands' phone chatter to learn they'd like to stay. Later she'd prepare extra under-the-pillow gifts. This "tradition" created work for her, but garage sales supplied most surprises. Relishing their anticipation and delight justified her efforts.

The doorbell rang. Cautious, she first peeked out the front door's sidelights and, seeing Tony, opened the door wide. They hugged and she gave him a concerned look. "How are you?"

He sighed. "Okay. The funeral this afternoon is small, just for family." His expression took on a different intensity. "But I wanted to come by to see you, to thank you and Jay for all your help, to tell you how much I value you..." he reached for her hand and looked into her eyes, "...as marvelous neighbors and precious friends." This emotional outpouring left him near tears.

Jennifer gave him a reassuring hug. "We're here for you just as you would be for us, dear Tony."

"You can count on me. If Jason's here, I'd like to work out details for our deer hunt Tuesday."

"Oh?" Jennifer looked surprised. "That's news to me, but I know you two venture out every fall and it's that time of year. Think you'll bring venison for Thanksgiving dinner? You're joining us, I hope, plus your children if they're still here. It's only a few days away."

"The kids will be gone by then. Thanksgiving with them seemed awkward under the circumstances, but sharing time with you and your family sounds great, Jen."

Jason wandered in. "Thought I heard you, Tony. Did someone mention deer hunting?"

"Yes, we're all set for Tuesday. No shooting before the light of dawn, but it's at least an hour's drive so we should leave at 5:30 to see the sun rise from our stands."

"Count me in. I'll bring coffee for the drive. Can you stay awhile?"

"No. We're getting ready for the funeral. I just took a minute to escape the black cloud at home."

Tony left. They waved and closed the door. Jason locked it. "Why take chances?"

CHAPTER SIXTY-FIVE

SUNDAY, NOON

Celeste didn't normally work weekends, but a real estate company offered double pay to clean a house new on the market and she jumped at the chance. Fred's janitorial team worked 10:00 to 6:00 night shifts after stores and offices closed for the business day. He'd have dinner waiting.

She loved Fred, an improbable development considering she met him while she was the girlfriend of his older brother Ralph. She remembered the day she met dashing Ralph Forbes at a McLean garage sale. Their instant attraction fanned her heart—and his whim to add her to his household. And his burglary team.

In those days, Fred lived in the shadow of the flamboyant older brother he idolized. Shrinking from independent thought or action to avoid Ralph's biting criticism, Fred followed Ralph's orders, vainly hoping to please his brother. From the outset he worked the residential thefts Ralph masterminded, obediently but without enthusiasm, until the addition of sixteen-year-old Celeste to their criminal web.

In Ralph's clever plan, he and Celeste attended estate or indoor garage sales, afterward making blueprint sketches of the interiors. Using these layouts, Ralph returned days or weeks later to burglarize the houses. Fred drove the get-away car.

Too intimidated by low self-esteem to date, Fred found constant fascination in Celeste's sharing their house. She thought his intense stares "creepy," not realizing they reflected adoration of this dream woman he'd never have. Never, that is, until their traumatizing arrests for what the media dubbed "Blueprint Burglaries."

Guilt at ruining their lives prompted Ralph Forbes to make the first selfless decision of his life. "I'll take the rap," he told his inventive court-appointed attorney, "if you can get them off." Ralph testified convincingly that he terrorized Celeste and Fred with threats of disfigurement and death if they failed to comply. Only the horror of his retaliation forced them to cooperate. For this lie, he received a harsher sentence while a cringing Fred and frightened Celeste drew probation. He'd caused their downfall but balanced the scale.

After the trial, the judge warned Celeste and Fred, "I'm giving you each fifty hours of community service. You must report to a parole officer once a month. Stay out of trouble. If you're brought before me again, you'll show a pattern of criminal behavior pointing you straight to jail."

Narrowly escaping prison frightened the two enough to turn their lives around, find honest jobs and go straight. Having no other friends, they hung together by default.

When she'd fled her mountain home on the first bus out, Celeste met Amanda Rochester. This sympathetic older woman took pity on the vulnerable young runaway in the seat beside her, inviting Celeste to stay at her Arlington house until the girl "landed on her feet." But Celeste never thought Amanda's home her final destination. When she met Ralph three weeks later, her path forked in a new direction. "Come back if it doesn't work out," Amanda offered.

After the arrest with nowhere else to turn, Celeste brought Fred to Amanda. Concerned over Celeste's new predicament, Amanda said, "You could rent my basement apartment: two bedrooms, a living room, kitchen, bathroom and separate entrance." This solved the "acceptable" address for their parole officers. But they needed jobs. Penniless, with high school educations and crime their only skill, what could they offer employers? After trying menial restaurant jobs, they applied as maids at a Tyson Corner motel, using public transportation in lieu of a car.

Omitting the arrest, Celeste told the motel manager, "Look, we don't have work references 'cause we're just out of high school, but we're hard workers and really need the job."

"At least let us show you what we can do," Fred pleaded.

The manager eyed them warily but liked their determination and energy. And the girl had that cute West Virginia drawl.... He rubbed his chin; three of his housekeeping staff had quit yesterday for better jobs, without giving the standard two weeks' notice. This put him on the spot since his motel rooms needed daily cleaning. Hiring these two saved running an ad and interviewing prospects. And if they worked out... He made a snap decision.

"Okay, I'll try you. Work is 8:00 AM to 5:00 PM. Half an hour per room means eight rooms in the morning and eight in the afternoon. Here's the checklist showing what to do in each room. The first day you train with one of our regular maids. The second day you're on your own. More hours are possible if we have a full house but that'll be at the usual rate, no overtime pay. One hour lunch. Wear black slacks and black shirt. We issue you a blazer with the motel name on the pocket. Friday is payday." He then described the hourly wage—without benefits.

A month later, as they ate a meager dinner in Amanda's basement apartment, Celeste said, "You know, Fred, the motel pays basic wage less federal deductions. What if we cleaned houses on our own? We could charge more per hour than we're getting now and keep what we earn."

Fred considered. "The motel taught us how to clean rooms, but how do we find these other jobs?"

"We could try those fancy neighborhoods near Tyson Corner and charge less than their current help. If we prove ourselves in one home, we'd ask for referrals to others."

"I like it, working the same hours for better pay. But what about supplies? The motel provides everything we use now."

Celeste thought. "We'd start out using the customer's mops, Windex and so on, just providing muscle. Once we buy a car, we bring equipment and supplies and charge more."

After work, they walked to single-family neighborhoods fanning around Tyson Corner to ask if owners needed domestic help or knew someone who did. "We're a team. We clean faster and better than anyone. It's the American dream: have a good idea, work hard and live a decent life. We learned our skills at a Tyson Corner hotel. Just try us. You'll see."

Most residents in these neighborhoods used domestic help, often hiring a housekeeper via a friend's referral. The sincerity of these two young people gleaned two job offers the first day. Enthusiastic referrals followed their conscientious work at those homes. A month later the pair worked ten jobs a week, two houses a day. They used public transportation, paid their rent and began saving money. Soon they hired others to help them and bought a used van to ferry their crews. Celeste concentrated on residential cleaning while Fred branched out to commercial janitorial service, where he quickly rose to crew foreman. Besides the labor side, his new position exposed him to management, where he learned much they'd used to grow their own operation.

Housemates by chance, Celeste and Fred slept in separate bedrooms in Amanda's basement apartment. Over time, their work relationship transformed their energy and focus into admiration and trust. "Why, we've become really great friends," Celeste noticed one day with surprise.

Fred gazed at her. "I adored you the first day you walked into my life." Her eyes widened as he reached for her hand, pulled her into a gentle embrace and their lips met for the first time. Was he the kind, dependable man missing in her life? Tears of happiness spilled as she returned his embrace. Soon they transformed the second bedroom into an office.

Celeste found cleaning homes different from motel work. She told Fred, "Motels are predictable, but homeowners can save nasty chores for us like crusty cooking pans or filthy utility sinks. Motel rooms are cleaned daily while dirt in homes builds for a week or more. At motels we please one supervisor, but in homes no two employers are alike. Our good efforts satisfy some while others never like what I do. Most motel maids barely see guests, while in homes the owners' lives show in every room. We get to know them, even some of their problems."

"Like...?"

"Like rebellious teenagers leaving food, dirty clothes and wet towels around their rooms for me to pick up before I clean. Or pet poop deliberately left for me, or a reeking sickroom where an aging parent lives. I see children and pets neglected and hear door-slamming and arguments."

Fred added, "You're right. You think houses neat on the outside would also be neat on the inside, but we know you don't always get what you expect."

"Some treat you like a servant and others like you're almost a family member. With them you feel involved. It's like acting in a weekly soap opera. For instance, I work for two nice, lonesome people who should meet each other. One's a widow, the other a widower. If I could get them together, both their lives could be happier."

"I don't know...isn't it better not to get involved? I mean, we're just day workers on the fringe of their lives, and we depend on their referrals. What if something you think is a good idea backfires instead? We get a bad reputation for meddling, not a good one for caring."

"I hear you," Celeste agreed, yet she often sensed good or bad feelings about houses where she worked. Miss Jennifer's felt like a good house, but across the street, Mr. Tony's did not. She couldn't explain, but she felt something was wrong there.

Then she found an item hidden in his closet to prove her right. Should she keep this information quiet as Fred suggested or should she tell Miss Jennifer on Tuesday?

CHAPTER SIXTY-SIX

SUNDAY, 4:46 PM

The three Grands bustled in from the yard where they'd played for a couple of hours inside the wrought-iron fence. "Could we have the second Learning Surprise now?" asked Christine.

"Could we have it on the sun porch?" Alicia wanted to know.

"Could we have a snack?" Milo chimed in. "Maybe one with chocolate?"

Jennifer smiled. "Let's do them all. I'll bring you each a chocolate chip cookie on the sun porch and we'll talk right there."

When they settled onto the wicker couches and chairs, she held up her cell phone. "Today let's talk about dialing 911. You only do this if you ever really, really need special help from police or an ambulance and no other adult is there to help you. Can you all read numbers?" Christine and Alicia nodded with confidence. "You, too, Milo?" Jennifer asked.

"Yes, I weed numbers 'cause Mommy taught me how. I can count to twenty-eleven."

They all laughed.

"Okay then, Milo, will you please point to the 9 and the 1 on this phone?" Jennifer asked. She nodded approval as he pointed. "We dial 911 only for a very *serious* emergency because when we call this number, police or firefighters come to help us if nobody else is nearby who can. So don't call 911 if a parent or baby sitter or teacher is nearby to help. Don't call 911 if you break a toy or stub your toe or can't find your crayons. The trusted adult taking care of you would help you solve those problems. But let's think of a serious emergency when no adult is nearby to help you."

The children exchanged puzzled looks. "Could you give us an example?" Christine suggested.

"You went to the fire station yesterday. Can you think of an emergency that might need their help?"

"A fire," they each volunteered.

"Yes, any fire burning where a fire shouldn't be. A fire inside the fireplace is okay but what about a fire on the floor or in a bed?"

"Call 911," they agreed with excitement.

"Okay, what if your Mommy falls on the floor, can't breathe and her lips turn blue? You say, 'Mommy are you okay?' but Mommy is too sick to answer. You need help but no other adult is at home. That's a time to call 911. Or what if a neighbor is cut by a lawn mower and bleeding and can't talk when you ask if he needs help? If another adult is nearby, you run to them for help to save the injured person, but if no adult is there you call 911 to send help. Any questions?"

The three Grands shook their heads.

"Okay, here's the test. If you lose your ball do you find a nearby adult to help you or call 911?"

"Find an adult," they chorused.

"If a thief steals your car with you inside and your parents are not nearby to save you but you have a phone in your pocket, do you call 911?"

"Yes," they shouted.

"If your grandmother falls down the stairs and you ask her if she's okay but she's too hurt to answer you and no other adult is in the house to help, what do you do?"

"Call 911," they squealed with glee.

"Now, would each of you please give me an example when not to call 911 and another example when you should call 911?"

Milo spoke first. "If you bwake some glass and your gwanmudder can clean it up for you, don't call 911. But if you bwake some glass and your gwandmudder gets cut so bad she falls down and can't talk and gwandaddy isn't home to help, then you call 911."

"Very good, Milo. Who's next?"

Alicia jumped to her feet. "If you're at a garage sale and lose your money but your grandmother helps you find it you do not call 911. But if you're at a garage sale and someone starts shooting people and they're falling down dead then you call 911."

"Right." They high fived. "Chris, how about you?"

"If I'm by the fishpond in your back yard and my doll falls in the water, then I find an adult to help me get it out. But if I'm by the fishpond and a real baby falls in and no adult is nearby to help get him out then I call 911." Chris gave a satisfied smile at her recitation.

"Good," Jennifer said. "So let's summarize. Part One is knowing when to call 911. Part Two is knowing *what to say* when they answer your call. When they answer they'll say, 'Where is your emergency?' You tell them the emergency *and* your name *and* your age *and* where you are so they know where to send help. Do you know your home phone number and address in case something happens when you're there?"

"We do," announced Alicia, "because Mommy put those words and numbers in the 'Row, row, row your boat' song." Jennifer laughed as they sang the song together.

Alicia asked, "What do I tell 911 if I'm not sure where I am? What if I'm in a store but I don't know which store. What if I say I'm at my Gran's house? Do they know where that is?"

"Good questions. You answer the 911 operator the best you can. You could say you're in a restaurant or a parking lot or a store. Sometimes 911 can trace a phone location. If you're holding the phone and they find where it is, they know where you are."

Satisfied smiles all around.

"Oh, look, here's Grandaddy." Jennifer turned toward him. "Today's learning surprise is about when to call 911 and what to say. Grandaddy, would you like to take the test?" He nodded compliance. "Can you give us an example when not to call 911 and another when you should call?"

Jason considered. "Well, if three smart grandchildren visit you and bake cookies with their grandmother and the cookie smell fills the house, you can ask Grandaddy to help you eat the cookies. But if the house catches on fire while the cookies bake and no adult is there to help you solve the problem, you call 911 and ask them to send firemen." He thought a moment. "Then get out of the house and wait for the firefighters."

Delighted, they all clapped hands and cheered approval.

Jennifer hugged each of the Grands then shooed them with her hands. "Now, all of you hustle down to play in the basement playroom because Grandaddy and I need to talk for a few minutes before he comes down to play ping-pong with you."

Off they scampered.

CHAPTER SIXTY-SEVEN

SUNDAY, 5:14 PM

"You volunteered me for ping-pong with the little ankle-biters without my knowledge or consent? Thanks a lot, partner," Jason chided. "And what triggered this 911 thing?"

"Today's newspaper story about a five year old grabbed my attention. He called 911 when his mother had a seizure. Medics arrived and saved her life. Our Grands should know how to use 911 and I needed a Learning Surprise, so..."

"I might have known." He chuckled. "Jen, Jen. Now let's hope it doesn't come back to bite us."

"What do you mean?"

"The Grands may know what to do but have they the judgment to identify a real 911 situation? I doubt police or firemen like irrelevant calls from small kids no matter how sincere the little tykes are about their so-called emergency."

"Well, here's a so-called emergency of our own. Hannah and Becca know about the diamonds. Should we tell our other three about them so nobody feels left out?

Jason considered this. "Or just wait until Thanksgiving. It's close and we might know more then."

"Okay. By the way, how about taking the Grands and me to McLean Family Restaurant tonight? Their menu has things for kids and adults plus your own cook gets a night off."

"Good idea. I'll make a reservation in case they're extra busy. By the way, a golfing buddy told me that restaurant's been here forty years and the father of tennis player Pete Sampras was one of the three original Greek owners."

"I know it's a McLean landmark but the rest is news to me. Remember when our kids were young how we crossed our fingers to get a table at their Sunday brunch?"

"Geez, Jen, that takes me back a lot of years. Then we couldn't imagine our kids grown up or us in our sixties and grandparents besides." He pulled her into his arms. "All those dreams came true, didn't they?"

They held each other close. "I love you, Jay."

"Love you, too, dear Jen."

"I said it first."

They both laughed. "Type-A's should never marry each other."

She hugged him. "Is the ping-pong champ about to dazzle the small fry with his remarkable skills?"

"You mean will he endlessly chase the ball fired in all directions but the right one?"

"That, too."

Jason winked and left the kitchen.

She sat, contemplative for a moment, then unloaded the dishwasher and wiped the counters. As she did, her eye fell upon the worn leatherette case, scruffy from the woods where she'd picked it up with other litter and set it aside till later. Now she'd clean it up for a charity resale.

She brushed away surface dirt and wiped it clean. Opening the folder she saw a crescent moon with a star embossed on the leather. One flap of the inside was empty but tucked into the other side lay a folded piece of paper. She opened it and gasped, staring at her name, address and license plate information. What was this doing in a case dropped in the woods behind her house?

And then she knew. Someone had deliberately watched the back of her house. Who else but the diamond owner?

Jennifer's eyes widened and her throat constricted in fear.

CHAPTER SIXTY-EIGHT

SUNDAY, 8:31 PM

*" . . . a*nd that's the end of the bedtime story." Jennifer closed the book and went to each child's bed to hear their "best thing" and "good deed" for the day.

"I really liked my under-the-pillow gift tonight," Christine said.

"I really like staying at your house." Alicia said as she snuggled under the covers.

"I weally like lollipops. Will you have more for us tomowwow?" asked Milo.

"We'll see about that when you wake up in the morning. Now happy dreams, children."

She tiptoed out, closed the door and joined Jason in the bedroom, where he watched news on TV. She turned on the bedside lamp and lay the leatherette case on his chest.

"What's this?" He opened it up and read the paper inside. "Where'd you get this?"

"The children and I apparently surprised someone in the woods when we took our walk this morning. Looks like he dropped this when he ran."

"Geez, Jen, someone's stalking the house and I've got to go out of town tomorrow to the damn merger talks. I can't leave you here under these circumstances. But Hell, I can't cancel this meeting either. I'm the company president so I have to be there. How can I solve this?"

"Don't worry, we'll be fine. The kids wore me out today. How about you?"

"Yeah, the whole day wore me down. Where did we get the energy to deal with our own? Glad those days are over and we somehow lived to tell about them." He laughed weakly.

"Indeed we did." She smiled and gave him a kiss. "This is a wonderful time of life, isn't it, Jay?"

"It might be if we had less excitement, like this voyeur watching us from the woods."

"I mean I'm glad we're both here to share it. Think about Kirsten, here one day, gone the next."

"Then get your shower and hurry back. A new episode of *Law & Order* starts in twenty minutes."

"Do you want popcorn?"

"No, Jen, just you."

CHAPTER SIXTY-NINE

SUNDAY, 11:59 PM

Zayneb paced anxiously in her room, glancing periodically at the clock on the dresser. She awaited the midnight hour. She no longer anguished over right or wrong: it was *all* wrong. She knew the law directed citizens to call police right away for any murder case, even self-defense. But instead she fell for their guest's seductive logic: to erase the incident as if it never happened.

She shrugged, realizing she locked herself into this dangerous new situation last night by agreeing to wrap her husband's body in the shower curtain and leave it on the floor until Ahmed resolved the problem. But she hardly knew Ahmed. He'd been at their house only four days, and he was from an entirely different culture. What passed as "right" in his world? Would she open the door to find Ahmed with a hallway full of policemen ready to arrest her? Or would he bring cronies along to *kill* her for daring to strike, never mind kill, her husband? Or finding her defenseless without a husband to protect her, might he rape or murder her? With no idea what to expect next, Zayneb choked back an apprehensive sob.

Her head snapped up at a rap on the bedroom door. She hurried across the carpet, pressed her forehead against the door and mustered courage to face whatever fate held on the other side.

"Zayneb?"

"Yes."

"Ahmed here. Please open the door."

Holding her breath in fear, she unlocked the door and edged it open. To her relief, Ahmed stood alone in the hallway. She backed away for him to enter.

He spoke forcefully. "Listen carefully. You must be strong. This is what we are going to do." He described his plan. When he explained the last part, her eyes widened in shock. But what choice had she at this point? She could only do what he said.

Ahmed opened the door from the bedroom to the upstairs deck before guiding her into the bathroom, where her husband's body lay wrapped in the shower curtain.

"Everybody sleeps now, but we must be quiet. I'll lift the heavy part." He indicated the torso of the wrapped corpse. "You take the legs."

He and Zayneb took their positions and bent to the burden of carrying the lifeless body's weight. Ahmed walked backward, leading the way through the bedroom door onto the deck. Maneuvering their burden slowly down the wooden stairs brought them at last to the bottom, where Ahmed whispered they should put the body on the ground. There they secured edges of the shower curtain, which had loosened in transit. Ahmed showed Zayneb their destination. They carried their heavy bundle to the empty raised garden frame with the three-foot excavation. With effort, they coordinated lifting the body up over the edge, then lowering it into the pit.

For a moment they both stared silently into the grave. "I washed him in the traditional Islamic way," Zayneb whispered.

"Good," Ahmed said. "We can each say our own prayers for him later." Ahmed slit open a plastic bag of hardware soil and emptied it into the pit. He opened another for Zayneb and, though she lifted the bag with difficulty, she managed to pour out its contents. They both added soil until it filled around the body and a light layer of dirt covered the shrouded figure. He slit open more bags of hardware dirt for Zayneb before quietly shoveling in excavated dirt dug earlier from a tarp next to the new garden. They alternately added the two kinds of soil until it came even with the top of the frame.

He indicated they'd done enough, gathered the empty bags into a pile and lay the shovel on top to prevent them blowing away. He took Zayneb's arm, guided her up the wooden stairs and followed her into the bedroom. He closed and locked the deck door.

"Have you cleaned the bathroom?" he asked. She nodded. "Show me," he said. After she did, he nodded in approval. "Our work is finished. May he sleep in peace."

He looked at Zayneb. "You are a strong, brave woman." He turned and left the room.

She locked the door.

Zayneb stood numb in the dark bedroom, the room she'd shared for a quarter of a century with her husband. She could hardly grasp the past twenty-four hours' chaotic events. Yet an unexpected peace crept into her soul, freed at last from the fear and dread with which she'd lived so long.

Ahmed returned to his room. Myriad thoughts crisscrossed his mind: Mahmud's burial, his growing need for Khadija, Abdul's childhood rescue story, his doubts about the jihad he planned and how to recover the diamonds.

On the main floor, Heba stood alone in the dark kitchen. Often restless at night, she frequently came up from her cell-like room to look out the kitchen window, but tonight's scene outside defied belief. She saw Ahmed and Zayneb bury something in the new garden, something shaped like a human body. Her evil master Mahmud, now presumably on a long trip, was the only person missing from the household.

Or was he?

DAY FIVE

MONDAY

CHAPTER SEVENTY

MONDAY, 7:11 AM

"Grands sleeping late this morning?" Jay asked his wife as she poured their coffee.

"I haven't checked, but they're not shy about reporting for breakfast. You'll be out of town today?"

"Yes, but with the madness here, I won't stay over. I wouldn't go at all, but it's the biggest thing our company has ever done and I'm the pivotal decision maker. I'll definitely drive back tonight but will get home late. Who could I call to stay here with you. One of our kids? Adam?"

"Thanks, Jay, but they have their own busy lives. We have an up-to-date security system and phones all over the house to call for help. We should be fine..."

Jason wondered if he should insist. Her schedule might influence that decision. "What's on your list today?"

"Herding the Grands until Kaela collects them tomorrow about ten o'clock, plus getting organized for Thanksgiving in only three days. We're having twenty adults and ten children and..."

"Geez, Jen, that's thirty people for a sit-down dinner? What were you thinking?"

"Celeste and Fred will help in the kitchen, wash dishes and clear the tables. Most are family, but the list mushroomed with kids' friends plus a few neighbors like Tony plus Adam's mother and father. By the way, weren't you going to discuss finders-keepers with Greg Bromley?"

"Yeah, but today is tough. With a full work morning of preparation plus that trip, I can't today. And tomorrow morning is Tony's deer hunt. Maybe tomorrow afternoon or, worst case, when he comes for Thanksgiving." He looked at his watch. "Gotta go. Love you, Hon." He kissed her goodbye and headed toward the garage.

"Please remember to repair the garage door before it crushes somebody," she called after him.

She sighed, hoping he'd heard her, put the kitchen Rolodex by her coffee cup, dialed the grocery and reserved two large turkeys for Wednesday pick up. Grabbing a pencil to write down the order number, she noticed the psychic's phone number Adam had left yesterday.

Becca appeared in her PJs and said in a bleary voice. "Morning, Mom. Coffee needed." She shuffled her way to the counter and poured herself a cup.

"You're up early. Anything going on?"

"No, just couldn't sleep any longer. Thought I might take Chris and Alicia to a movie and dinner today if you don't mind having Milo to yourself. He's too little to keep it together that long."

"The girls will love it. By the way, could you baby-sit all three a couple of hours around lunchtime? I'd like to meet this psychic who visited the police station, if she's available." Becca nodded. "And Thursday morning could you help me with Thanksgiving details?"

"Count me in, Mom."

The Grands appeared at the kitchen door. "The good news is we're ready for breakfast."

"What's the bad news?"

"Milo wet the bed."

CHAPTER SEVENTY-ONE

MONDAY 7:30 AM

Hannah stepped out the kitchen door to enjoy morning birdcalls from the huge trees nearby. She loved the country feel of this old farmhouse. Even when they built their new house here, the surrounding multi-acre lots assured this continued closeness to nature.

Adam's police shift began at noon, so a busy morning at home lay ahead for them. Transforming the old home's interior exhilarated them. Her first project today: installing the new medicine cabinet. Only her mom could produce so specific a garage-sale item so fast.

Hannah found a Phillips screwdriver, got the cabinet out of the box and carried it to the bathroom. Adam still slept, so she'd work quietly, surprising him with a finished project when he awoke.

Emptying the cosmetics and pills from the old medicine cabinet, she found two screws on each side fastening the old cabinet to the studs. She removed the lower ones first, then the upper with greater care, bracing the cabinet to prevent its crashing to the floor. She eased the old one out and leaned it against the wall.

But as she lifted the new cabinet toward the vacated space, something caught her eye. Unlike wallboard or insulation, the unfinished opening behind the old cabinet revealed antique lathe-and-plaster construction found in civil-war era buildings. Stranger still, a small, rusted nail fastened a yellowed envelope to the lathing. On the envelope she read one faded word: "Mathis."

Hannah put down the new cabinet and gently touched the envelope. Brittle around the edges, might it crumble if she removed it? Adam had been called Mathis when he lived here as a little boy—before his later adoptive parents renamed him. She tried to remember what her mother had learned about the people living here then.

Hannah tiptoed back to the kitchen, closed the door, dialed a phone number and spoke quietly.

"Mom, it's Hannah. Have you a minute to talk about the old Yates house?... Good. When Mathis was born, weren't his parents the only adults living in this house?... Okay. And didn't you say the father was a tyrant who abused his wife and sons until sent to a booby-hatch where he later died?... So after the boys left didn't the mother live in the house by herself like a hermit?... Wasn't she trained as a school teacher?... Well, we just found something unusual and I'll call you back when we know more about it...." Hannah laughed, "Yes, I know the suspense is killing you. Be brave, Mom."

Hannah tiptoed back to the bathroom and studied the envelope. In the bedroom, she smiled at her husband's peaceful sleep before gently nudging him awake. His eyes opened with the "where am I" expression until he saw her standing over him. He reached for her arm, pulled her into the bed, pinned her down beside him and kissed her well.

To her half-hearted protest he said sheepishly, "Hey, it's not my fault. I am a newlywed."

She giggled before extricating herself. "Adam, be serious. I just found something incredible you need to see right away."

He traced a finger along her arm. "Can't it wait?"

"No, it can't. Hurry, you'll see." He followed her to the bathroom, where they stared at the envelope. "It's hung there a long time," Hannah said. "Your mother taught school. Doesn't this flawless cursive look like a teacher's writing?"

"Slow down, Hannah. Who's the detective here? Or are you turning into your mother?" They shared a laugh. He removed the envelope carefully. "Let's see what this is about."

Part of the faded envelope crumbled away as he unsealed it, revealing better preserved paper inside. He opened the tri-folded letter carefully. Hannah peeked over his shoulder as he read.

My Precious Child,

I hope you're all grown up when you read this even though now you are my beautiful, perfect baby. Tobias frightens me every day, threatening to break my spirit, whatever it takes. Strange, because my parents valued my spirit. I think my spirit must be who I am. If he succeeds, will my body be an empty place with nobody home?

If Tobias finds this letter he'll surely kill me. He's acutely jealous of my deep love for you, dear little Mathis, so I show you my adoration when he is outside and can't see me rocking you, cuddling you or humming songs to you. If I sing aloud he might hear me. I live in constant fear of what he'll do next to me or to you. I must obey him, for what would happen to you if I died during one of his brutal tirades? He regularly threatens to maim you if I cringe at his evil whims or cry when he beats me. I live in terror of your safety.

This letter's purpose is for you to know when you grow up that you are my proudest achievement, created in happiness with the only man I ever loved. A problem kept us from sharing our lives together, but in our hearts and your genes we're irrevocably interlaced.

My heart is yours alone. I'll shield you the best I can as long as I can. Whatever happens to me, my dearest wish is for you to grow into a bright, capable, loving man filled with your own unique, precious spirit.

My heart overflows with love for you, my sweet little boy,
Your devoted mother,
Wendey.

Choking with emotion, Adam folded the letter with trembling hands.

Hannah knew from their intimate talks he'd never understood his mother's cruelty to him. How could he have angered her enough to cut off his little finger? Why did she hate him? Had she ever loved him? Was it his fault? Had he been an unlovable person from the start?

The letter's wrenching words answered those questions, proving beyond any doubt she'd cherished him — until Tobias drove her mad.

Suddenly Adam threw his arms around Hannah, clutched her and sobbed. She'd never seen him like this and winced at the depth of festering, repressed anguish at last unleashed. Her heart ached as she comforted the man she loved, grappling with such emotional chaos. Swept into his experience as if it were hers, Hannah choked back her own sobs and hugged him tightly as they wept healing tears together.

CHAPTER SEVENTY-TWO

MONDAY, 8:17 AM

"**G**ood morning," Ahmed said to the women at the breakfast table as he came inside from the yard. "I wakened early to finish the second garden this morning so you can add more plants whenever you like," he announced.

"Will you join us for breakfast?" Khadija invited.

"Yes, thank you." He sat down at the dining room table.

"Shall I drop Safia at school on my way to work this morning?" Khadija asked her mother.

"Yes, please," Zayneb answered.

Heba entered the dining room, poured coffee and brought breakfast.

Did she seem more relaxed than in the past or was this only Ahmed's imagination? Others at the table also appeared relieved at avoiding Mahmud's overshadowing dark presence. Even Zayneb smiled and talked. Only little Safia seemed downcast, but the others cheered her until she seemed happy as she headed toward the car with her sister.

As they watched the car drive away, Zayneb said, "Thank you, Ahmed, for helping me."

"We solved it together." He purposefully changed the subject. "Abdul will drive me to my business appointments today. May I have a key to the house to use as needed, please?"

"I have an extra one in the office."

"Also I might come and go at unusual hours, so do not expect me for meals." Realizing he often saw Khadija when they ate, he added quickly, "On the other hand, if I chance to be here at mealtime, dining with your family is always a privilege."

Ahmed's cell phone rang. "Abdul here," said the voice. "I am close to your house. Will you lift the garage door for my arrival?" Ahmed said he would.

"I must open the garage now. I also need to keep an opener with me if you have another."

"Yes, we have three, one for Khadija, one for me and one for..." She looked away. "The third one is for you now. I will bring you the key and the garage door opener."

As Heba refilled his coffee cup, he thought he saw the trace of a smile. Because she always looked away modestly, he wasn't sure. He didn't look forward to the emergency meeting he called for five members of his cell, but he needed help regaining the diamonds so crucial to their plot. As their leader, he must maintain his men's respect without admitting he'd lost the source of the mission's funding. He crafted a plausible story.

Abdul drove him to the nearby meeting place, and he joined the men inside.

"Thank you for coming today. We have an unexpected problem to solve. The Great Leader knew the risk of bringing a large amount of cash into this country to fund our operation. In his wisdom, he sent me instead with valuable diamonds, untraceable and easily converted to cash for weapons through our special contacts. Upon arriving, I hid the diamonds for safety until the money exchange. In a serious misunderstanding, the item containing the stones accidentally fell into another person's hands. Today we will get them back."

Noticing quizzical looks on his comrade's faces, Ahmed continued. "A woman in McLean had the item in which the diamonds were hidden. We know she removed the stones. We do not know where she put them. We will *persuade* her to tell us and then eliminate her as a witness. We will wear balaclava disguises to prevent her recognizing us."

"Does she live alone?"

"No, but we surreptitiously installed tiny surveillance cameras on a lamppost and two trees across the street from her house. We know who lives at her house, thus we will know when she is alone and the time is right. Stay close in McLean today. When I call you on our special cell phones, immediately stop other activity and assemble here. I will have masks and weapons. Here is the plan."

He unfolded a hand-drawn sketch showing a house with cul-de-sac in front and parkland in back and along one side. "We arrive through these woods, break into the house, torture her and leave with the diamonds. Any questions?" Nobody spoke. "Then may Allah be with us, peace be upon Him."

The others murmured assent and left.

CHAPTER SEVENTY-THREE

MONDAY, 11:46 AM

"I'll be at Serbian Crown if you need me, Becca. Back around two o'clock. You'll find lunch for you and the Grands in the fridge. Have fun and remember to keep the doors locked. Probably overcautious, but why not?"

On impulse, Jennifer tucked into her pocket one of the diamonds she and Jason had found two days ago during their basement search. She drove toward her lunch date with Adam's mysterious contact. The woman had sounded normal enough on the phone when Jen suggested lunch today, but who knew what lay ahead?

Driving along Route 7, Jennifer turned onto Colvin Mill Run, glancing as she drove past at the historic old Colvin Mill stone building with the large wooden waterwheel. Built circa 1811, the grain mill seemed a water-powered wonder then. She'd toured the restored mill with her own kids and made a mental note to bring the Grands soon. Those owners from two hundred years ago would marvel at the unimaginable changes since to McLean, Tyson Corner and environs. The original agricultural, dirt-road countryside with a few modest country stores had morphed into upscale residential communities and glass high-rises at Tyson Corner.

She turned at the restaurant and parked. Jennifer's natural spontaneity had led her to rich friendships but also—she drew a nervous breath at the memory—into terrifying danger. Following Adam's cautionary police advice, she'd meet with Veronika in this public place. Were legit psychics possible? She had her doubts.

When a woman matching Adam's description of Veronika stepped from a car, Jennifer hustled toward the entrance and introduced herself outside the front door.

Entering Serbian Crown, Jennifer felt like Dorothy going from Kansas to Oz, but in this case from McLean to Europe. The old-world décor and artifacts provided the convincing backdrop for their well-known Russian and continental cuisine. The host knew both Veronika and Jennifer but seemed surprised they knew each other. He showed them to a window table.

"Jennifer, I thank you for coming today." Veronika smiled. "Curious?"

Jennifer chuckled at the woman's candor. She liked this direct approach. "Curious for sure," she agreed. "What's this all about, Veronika? You must think it important."

The older woman frowned. "Important, yes, and together we may understand why. First let's order vodka. They serve it frozen almost to slush. Do you like flavored or plain?"

"Not my normal drink but today with you it is vodka at noon." She selected a flavor. Imbedded in a bucket-size chunk of ice, the vodka bottle lay heavily on the waiter's arm. He poured the chilled liquid expertly, filling the small glasses to the very top where surface tension created a slight bulge above the rim of the glass.

"The challenge is to spill not a drop as you bring the drink to your lips. 'Za zdorovye.' To your health." They lifted their glasses together and she demonstrated a perfect first sip.

"To your health also." Jennifer spilled a drop en route to her lips and, after swallowing, made a face as the powerful liquid stung her mouth. After a moment to savor, Jennifer said, "Why do you want to talk with me?"

"As a child," Veronika began, "I often knew about events happening elsewhere or anticipated happenings before they did. In Russia they call me 'yasnovidyaschaya.' You would say 'clairvoyant.' I don't understand it. I don't even like it, but we play the cards fate hands us."

"That we do." Jennifer nodded, wondering if she could handle another sip of the fiery vodka.

"Shall we study the menu? The wild boar is very good but a little heavy for lunch." They discussed the merits of several choices and ordered.

"When you saw my picture at the police station..." Jennifer coaxed again.

"Why did I insist upon talking with you? Because I sense this growing danger includes you in a special way. Before we met, I didn't know how you were part of the danger, but now I think you fell into it by accident."

"Danger?"

"Yes, in my first vision of ten angry men, I realized they used certain foreign words that spell trouble. When the visions became more frequent and stronger, I vacillated between doing nothing and warning authorities. In past experience, telling someone about a vision could postpone or stop what will happen if different choices are made than those leading to what I saw. After 9/11's horror, the chance to defuse another terrorist mission drove me to tell the police. Even if they thought me a lunatic, at least they know what I fear comes this way."

"And..."

"And I believe terrorists very soon plan a terrible attack close by."

Jennifer stared disbelieving at her companion, but Veronika's serious expression told her this was no joke to her. But did that make it true?

"When?"

"I don't know yet. More information may come to me any time. But I think soon—maybe only days or a week. So," she gave a wry laugh, "think about taking your family on a quick trip away from here to avoid the coming calamity."

Jennifer studied Veronika's serious expression. No question she believed what she said. Jennifer took a small sip of vodka. An imminent terrorist threat seemed harder to swallow than this burning drink, yet this woman's compelling sincerity coupled with her own bizarre diamond discovery...

"You also could escape the danger with a journey, Veronika. Will you?"

Veronika's appealing laugh animated most of her wrinkled face. "My life nears the end one way or another. Which way matters, but I'd as soon face the finale in the home I love than traveling in a strange place."

A sudden idea popped into Jennifer's mind. She groped in her pocket and found it. "Veronika, if you close your eyes, I'd like to put something in your hand. This may be another piece of information."

"That's called psychometrics: receiving psychic information by touching an object."

"How would you know that?" Jennifer hid an edge of suspicion.

"If psychic messages bombarded you, wouldn't you try to understand the phenomenon? The study of parapsychology suggests some individuals interact with the environment in ways not yet explained by science. For some, psychometry is a tool for remote viewing, of seeking impressions about a distant or unseen target using paranormal means—ESP—or sensing with the mind."

"What are others you've studied?"

"Psychic information through tasting is called clairgustance, through smelling is called clairalience, via hearing or listening is clairaudience, via feeling or touching is clairsentience or psychometry. Psychometry is not my way, but I will try it if you like."

She closed her eyes, extended a hand and Jennifer placed the item in her palm.

What happened next baffled them both. When Veronika's fingers closed on the diamond, she uttered a sharp cry and flung it away. The gem skittered across the table, hit the wooden floor and rolled ten feet away before coming to rest at a baseboard.

"My God, what was it? Look, it seared my hand." But as she opened her fingers, they saw no mark. "I could have sworn it left a blister."

"Maybe you felt it in your mind."

Veronika looked up. "You do understand. But what was that hot ingot you gave me?"

Was Veronika's display bona fide or was it skillful theatrics? Jennifer retrieved the stone and showed it to her.

"A piece of glass? No, cut like a gem. A diamond? No, please don't give it to me. I'll look at it in your hand. Yes," she nodded with certainly, "this is part of the problem. But how does it fit? Maybe it belongs to the terrorists, but why? What could they do with one diamond, even a big one like this? And if it's theirs, how could you have it?"

Jennifer downed another sip of vodka and decided to share the truth. "Sewn inside the body of a cloth doll bought at a garage sale we discovered 289 high-quality diamonds like this one. When a jeweler appraised them at about $3 million, I hustled them to a bank lockbox until we understood the situation. The next day, two women arrived asking to trade a nicer doll for the original. They seemed happy enough to take it, apparently knowing nothing about the treasure sewn inside. But we knew when whoever sent them to me got the empty doll, that person would know they were missing.

"Next, in the woods behind my house I found a folder, dropped in haste, with a paper showing my name, address and car license letters. Obviously, someone studied the back of my house as they surely must have studied the front. And they know my car. If your visions are right and the diamonds are related to them, doesn't this confirm that the people knowing I have their gems are terrorists?"

"And they need them back immediately because their destructive plan won't wait long."

"But what if your vision and my diamonds are unrelated? How can we find out?"

Veronika looked thoughtful. "Two possible ways," she answered. "Either I receive a vision which links them or separates them or..." She fell silent.

"Or?" Jennifer prompted.

"Or the terrorists will take them from you very soon."

Jennifer's eyes widened. "Can you invite these visions to come?"

"No, it doesn't work that way with me. I'm so sorry, Jennifer. I want to help you, but I can't make them happen."

Their food arrived. They ate and drank more vodka, which tasted better and better. Jennifer liked this pleasant older woman but wondered about her strange gift. Along with logic, Jennifer reflected, her own problem-solving included intuition, hunches and gut-feelings, but not precognition or future sight.

When they finished their meals, exclaiming over the high quality and rich flavors, Jennifer said, "Here's my phone number, Veronika. Please call me the minute you receive more information. I have your number to tell you about developments on my end."

As they parted, Jennifer hugged Veronika goodbye. "By the way, have you plans for Thanksgiving afternoon?"

"You mean three days from now?"

"Yes. Would you like to join my big family and friends for a meal at 1:00?"

Veronika beamed as she nodded. "Why yes, I would. Thank you very much, Jennifer."

CHAPTER SEVENTY-FOUR

MONDAY, 2:07 PM

R eturning home, Jennifer looked around suspiciously as she drove up to her house and pulled into the gated driveway. As she parked and opened her door she heard something hit the garage floor but didn't see it when she got out. She pressed the automatic garage door button. As it rumbled to a stop, she heard a splat and hiss. Taking a look, she realized the door had smashed open a full soda can, which probably fell from her car and rolled across the floor. She must remind Jason again to repair that door.

"Did you bring us something?" Christine asked as soon as Jennifer walked inside.

"Let's see. Did they eat good lunches, Becca?" Her daughter nodded. "Then how about Drumstick ice cream cones from the freezer?" This suggestion met with great enthusiasm.

"I'll have one, too," Becca said, "and let's eat them outside in the gazebo." An hour later, Becca announced she and the girls were ready to leave on their shopping-movie-and-dinner outing. "Be extra careful today, Honey," Jennifer told her daughter before distracting Milo as they left so he wouldn't feel left out. When the girls trooped out the front door to load into Becca's car, Jennifer locked the door behind them and activated the alarm.

"Let's play cawds," Milo suggested.

"What card game would you like?"

"Waw."

"Have you ever played the game 'War' before?" Jennifer asked. He nodded confidently.

"Good." She brought cards and they played at the sunroom table. She turned on the TV's Easy Listening channel for soft background music. When they finished the first game, Jennifer shuffled and counted the cards into two equal stacks. When they both turned over tens, the war began. Jennifer noticed Milo stopped playing. He stared open-mouthed at something behind her. She turned to look.

Two men wearing masks faced them, guns drawn. How was this possible with the alarm engaged? Jennifer cried out, jumped to her feet and pushed Milo behind her.

"Where are the diamonds?" asked the first man.

"The diamonds?" she stalled.

"The diamonds inside the garage-sale doll. *Those* diamonds," he sneered.

"Those diamonds are not here."

One of the men walked over and grabbed her arm roughly. "We're not here to play games. We will leave with the diamonds one way or another. *Where are the diamonds?*"

"They're at the bank."

The men exchanged looks. "What do you mean at the bank?"

"I have a bank security box to store valuable things in their vault."

The first man dropped Jennifer's arm and stepped away to talk to the second man before returning to stand in front of her. "We must know you tell the truth. We can hurt you to help your memory or we can hurt the boy. I think we will start with the boy."

"No," Jennifer said quickly. "Leave him alone. I *am* telling the truth. This house has no safe place, so my husband told me to take them to the bank until we found the owner."

"We are the owners," the first man spoke forcefully. "We want our property back now."

He lurched forward, slapping her so hard across the face she nearly lost her balance. She screamed and Milo began to cry. Treated well all her life, Jennifer couldn't believe the pain from one blow. She fought tears while her mind raced. What should she do? What *could* she do?

In a voice she hoped sounded steady, she said, "Look, this isn't the way you want it, but this is the way it is. The diamonds are at the McLean Bank. If you want them, I must go there to get them."

"You say they are locked inside a box there?" She nodded. "You have the key?"

"Yes, but I must sign my name to get into the vault to use the key. They compare my signature with the one already on record. You can't get the diamonds without me."

The two men conferred again. The first man stepped into the foyer, spoke quietly on his cell phone and reported to the second man. He then opened the sunroom door to the patio. A few minutes later, three more masked men pushed into the house. As the five talked together, Jennifer tried to think of an impromptu weapon or escape route. With Milo to protect and one-against-five odds, she saw no options.

The first man grabbed her arm. "Okay, get your key. We go to the bank. You ride in my car."

She retrieved the key from the study. "Come on, Milo, let's go."

"No," the first man indicated the three men. "The boy stays with them. You go with us."

As the two men hustled her outside, she called, "Don't worry, Milo. I'll be back soon."

The stricken look on his little face engraved itself indelibly in her mind.

CHAPTER SEVENTY-FIVE

MONDAY, 2:21 PM

The men pushed Jennifer out the back door of her house and prodded her through the woods to their car. When they exited the parkland, they pulled off the masks that made them conspicuous in public. Throwing her roughly into the back seat, one man climbed in beside her while the other drove.

An evil smile crossed the face of the man next to her. "You see my face and think now you can ID me for the police." His cruel laugh told Jennifer that would never happen. As their car entered traffic in mid-Mclean, she tried to signal fellow motorists until the man beside her twisted her arm behind her back, immobilizing her. Now her slightest movement shot excruciating pain into her shoulder.

"Tell us where to find this bank," the driver demanded.

They followed her directions, by-passing the front entrance to park instead in a lot next door. The man released her arm. "We only want our diamonds. We don't want to hurt you or the nice little boy, but we will if you try any tricks. Go in, get the diamonds, come out, we take you home, you and the boy are safe. I will walk to the bank with you and wait outside. We watch you every moment. The boy will pay for any of your mistakes."

Using the arm he hadn't twisted, she got out, gathered her strength and walked toward the bank. The man followed a few paces behind. She went in alone.

"Hello, Mrs. Shannon." She heard Heather's friendly voice fill with concern. "Are you all right?"

How did they read her distress? Was she disheveled from the manhandling? Did her fear and desperation about Milo show in her face? She must think faster and clearer than ever before in her life. Milo's life and her own depended upon her making the best decision, though she had no idea what to do.

She heard herself say, "I need to get into my lockbox, Heather, and once we're in the vault, could we please talk for a minute?"

Heather nodded soberly, got the bank key and the two walked into the vault, out of sight of the bank lobby. "Is something wrong, Mrs. Shannon?"

"Yes. I need your help. Five men just broke into my house. Three are holding my four-year-old grandson hostage there while the other two brought me here to get lockbox items for them. Once they get them, they'll kill us both. We must call the police, but the five men talk with cell phones. If police come here first, the men here will tell the others to kill my grandson. The police must make simultaneous raids here and at my house to prevent the men from warning each other. That means no sirens, no warning. Here is my home address. My only chance is calling the police."

"We have a phone right here inside the vault, Mrs. Shannon. I'll get the police on the line and you can tell them about this yourself."

Jennifer held her arm. "If the man comes into the bank when we're in the lobby, please act cheerful and I will also. We mustn't let him know we have a plan. Maybe you could call me over, pretend to talk about some new bank product you're selling. Anything to stall for time if that's what we need to do."

"I understand. Once you're on the phone, I need to tell my manager we have an incident underway so the bank is prepared as well." She dialed 911, explained who she was and gave the phone to Jennifer, who repeated her story, stressing identical timing for the two raids.

"Can you describe the two men and the car they're driving?" the operator asked. Jennifer did, adding that one stood outside the bank and the other sat in the parked car in an adjacent lot.

She described the car as best she could.

"Stay by this phone in case we need to call you back, and don't leave the bank until a policeman comes inside to get you."

Jennifer agreed.

As Heather returned to the vault, Jennifer held up the sock of diamonds. "If something goes wrong and the men get this after all, I'd like to leave what's valuable in the box but fill the sock with something else. Can you think of anything handy to produce this same bulge?"

Heather laughed good-naturedly, reached into her sweater pocket and held up a bag. "M&Ms?"

"Perfect," Jennifer said gratefully. She emptied the sock's contents into the lockbox and substituted the candies.

"Did they say how long until they'll be here?" Heather asked.

"No, but a policeman will come inside to get me when it's over."

"We could watch out the window."

"No, we don't want to spook the man waiting outside. If he thinks something's wrong, he'll phone the others to harm my grandson."

This thought reminded her how frightened Milo must feel. When she saw him next, how could she make it up to him?

She hoped he was still alive.

Seeing two policemen approach the bank, the manager pressed the front door release button.

He showed them where Jennifer waited inside the vault.

"Don't worry, Ma'am, we got both men outside the bank and impounded their car and cell phones for evidence."

"Oh, thank you so much. And at my house?"

"We nabbed two men there all right, but no sign of a third man...or your grandson."

Jennifer's heart sank. But she knew what she had to do.

"Can you excuse me just a moment please," she asked the policemen. "I need to close my lockbox and then I'd appreciate a ride home."

Jennifer found herself alone in the vault. She scooped something from the box into the M&M-filled sock before calling Heather to replace her security box.

CHAPTER SEVENTY-SIX

MONDAY, 3:17 PM

A t home, Jennifer answered questions for the police. Adam arrived, joining them at the dining room table. When the others left, he stayed on.

"Milo's kidnapping is a high profile case in McLean. They're assembling a task force to find him. They should arrive any minute."

"Wave them off, Adam. The diamond people may have a way to watch the house because they knew when I was there alone, except for Milo. They know police made arrests today and must be fuming, but I may have a chance to get Milo back unless more police swarm the house. Tell this task force to phone me instead of coming here. I'll cooperate with them, but I don't want the diamond people to panic while they have Milo."

Adam hurried to the phone to relay her message to his chief. "I gave them your message, but I doubt they'll accept it."

"Let's think about this, Adam. The kidnappers need to contact me to tell me where to exchange Milo for the diamonds. They'll assume police tapped my phones to intercept their calls, so they must find another way to let me know. What could it be?"

"As a sworn police officer, I offer my professional and personal advice, which are identical now. Don't try this alone. Besides skill and experience, police have electronic tools to track and observe these people's phones and computers. They want what you want: Milo safe at home. You're my mother-in-law and I love you, so please don't take offense at this, but do you really think you're smarter than the entire Fairfax County police force?"

Jennifer chuckled. "Thanks for speaking your mind, Adam. I always admire that and you've made your points well. You're a fine policeman and I appreciate your advice and protection. I'll think carefully about what you've said. I can't set the house alarm because the kidnappers cut the connections. Could you stay another ten minutes to guard the place while I lie down to figure this out? I'll set my bedside alarm and not take longer than ten."

"Of course. You must be exhausted."

"Thanks, Adam. See you in ten...."

Upstairs, she stretched out on her bed, put her forearm over her eyes and concentrated hard. Nine minutes later she had decided what to do.

CHAPTER SEVENTY-SEVEN

MONDAY, 4:03 PM

Jennifer thanked Adam for staying. "I feel focused now."

He heard the determination in her voice. "Please take my advice. Milo's safety depends upon your wisest decisions."

"You pulled out the big cannons for that volley, but thanks, Adam, for wanting to *help*."

When he left, she removed some things from her purse, added note paper and envelopes, combed her hair, applied lipstick, grabbed her keys, wrote one note to Becca and another to Jason, locked the house except for the door where the men broke in and drove away. Once out of her neighborhood, she headed toward her destination.

Parking next door to the "elephant house," she knocked on the door. When it opened, she said, "Hello, Zayneb. Do you remember me? May we talk for a minute?"

The woman couldn't hide her shock. "Yes," she said hesitantly. "Come in."

"I'm sorry to involve you but I don't know where else to turn, so I must ask for your help."

Zayneb nodded politely but said nothing.

Jennifer studied the woman's face for clues as she talked. "You know we bought your daughter's doll at your neighbor's sale, but you may not know we found hundreds of large, valuable diamonds hidden inside." She saw Zayneb's flicker of surprise. Jennifer described what she'd gone through that afternoon. "While they forced me to go to the bank, one of them kidnapped my four-year-old grandson."

Zayneb's lips parted in shock as Jennifer continued. "I think you know the owner of the diamonds. To get my grandson back, I must trade the diamonds for the child. Clearly, the owner wants them back, but he doesn't know how to contact me because police became involved by capturing some of his men. So now it's up to me. I must contact the diamonds' owner. Is he here now?"

Zayneb shook her head.

"But you know how to find him?"

The woman dipped her head slightly.

"Then I'd like to give you a letter telling him how to contact me for the exchange. I don't want to die and I certainly don't want my grandson to die. I never wanted these diamonds. They came to me by accident, and the danger they've caused terrifies me. I've told you my story. What can you tell me to better understand what's going on?"

Zayneb looked very uncomfortable. She stared at her lap, nervously twisting the edge of her skirt. She saw this Jennifer had problems, but she did, too. Ahmed helped her bury Mahmud's body. Smitten with Khadija, he might join her family one day. Since Mahmud no longer provided money, perhaps Ahmed would. She had no loyalty to this woman but several ties to Ahmed.

"I know nothing of this," Zayneb said. "I knew about the doll but nothing inside. Our houseguest of five days was very upset about the missing doll. I could give him your note."

"What can you tell me about your houseguest?"

"He is my husband's business associate. He is polite and speaks English well. He hasn't told me how long he plans to stay and I know nothing of his business here. My husband respected him and I have no reason to think him unworthy of my respect too."

"You said 'respected' him. Was that past tense?"

Zayneb flinched at her mistake. "My husband left two days ago on an extended trip to his homeland. I meant to say before he left he showed respect for this man. He called him 'our honored houseguest,' but in their country they sometimes speak flowery language."

"And what country is that?"

"The Middle-East."

"That's a large area. Where in the Middle-East?"

"I don't know. We never discussed it. My husband was...is Muslim, as am I."

"Yes...your head scarf.... Can you think of any reason your houseguest would own or hide these diamonds?"

"No." But she wondered now. Did that make him a wealthy merchant? If so, and if he married Khadija, might he appreciate Zayneb's role in getting back his diamonds? Her reverie stopped at Jennifer's next question.

"And what is his name?"

"His name?" Zayneb backed off, not wanting to reveal more about him.

"Yes, so I can address my letter to him."

"Ah, his name is Ahmed."

Jennifer wrote this on her note pad. "And his last name?"

"I wasn't told his last name," she admitted truthfully.

"Okay. May I take a minute to write my letter to him?"

"Of course."

Jennifer took paper and envelope from her purse and wrote:

Dear Ahmed,

In an unwelcome accident, I bought the doll containing your diamonds. You want them back and I want my grandson. Let's trade your treasure for my treasure. To avoid police interference, please leave an untraceable cell phone sealed in an envelope with Zayneb's neighbor, Roshan. Tell Roshan to call me at home (Zayneb has my phone number), saying "your order has arrived at Bloomingdale's." When I get that message from Roshan, I'll drive to her house, pick up the phone and await directions on it to a place you choose. At that place, you get your diamonds and I get my grandson. Let us both give this unwanted situation a positive ending in which we all win.

Thank you, Jennifer Shannon

Jennifer folded the letter, sealed it in the envelope, wrote "Ahmed" on the front and handed it to Zayneb along with her phone number on a post-it note.

"Thank you for helping me. You have children so I'm certain you understand the deep bonds that unite all women."

Zayneb showed her to the door.

Jennifer drove away praying Milo could endure whatever was happening to him.

CHAPTER SEVENTY-EIGHT

MONDAY, 5:01 PM

Jennifer snapped up the phone when it rang. "Hi, Mom, its Hannah," said the voice.

"Hannah, let me call you right back on my cell. I'm trying to keep the land line open."

She found her cell phone and dialed her daughter. Hannah described the letter behind the medicine cabinet. "Mom, Adam has a whole new understanding about his mother, one that's helped him get his early childhood in perspective. It's a miracle. And it all happened because you found that medicine cabinet at a garage sale."

"Who'd think of such an unusual place to hide something? Thank goodness you found her letter rather than losing it forever."

"What can I bring or do for Thanksgiving?"

"The meal is at one o'clock. Maybe come early to help set tables and get food ready in the kitchen? We're having a big crowd."

"Ambitious, but you can do it."

"'With a little help from my friends,' as the song says."

"Okay, we'll come early. See you Thursday. Love you, Mom. Say hi to Dad for us."

She hung up and considered calling Greg Bromley, but if the diamonds ransomed her grandson, once they were gone, finding legal ways to keep them became irrelevant.

Jennifer jumped when the phone rang. "Hi, Sweetheart, it's your loving husband. How are you and the Grands doing?"

She ached to tell him about the unfolding nightmare, but he was out of town and helpless. He'd be sick with worry but unable to make a difference. "All is well," she lied. "How about your meetings?" He described some highlights for her. "Still coming home late tonight?" He was. "Jay, I love you so very much. We've had a terrific life together. I cherish every minute."

"Don't know what brought that on but I like hearing it. Take care of your sweet self, darling Jen."

"I...I'll do my best."

"You always do your best. Oh, gotta go. Love you, Hon."

"Love you, too, Jay." She hung up, surprised to find tears in her eyes.

Were these their last words if things went wrong tonight?

She no sooner hung up than the phone rang again. "This is Detective Felts with the task force. We need to talk with you right away about finding your grandson."

"Please give me your phone number, Detective, and I'll call you back on my other line."

Jennifer sighed and looked out the window. Typical of this time of year, dusk had fallen at only five o'clock. Soon it would be black outside.

The phone rang again. "Hello, your order has arrived at Bloomingdale's," said a voice with a British/Indian accent.

Jennifer froze momentarily, then managed, "Thank you."

She needed to return the detective's call, but what would she tell him?

A long conversation with him about using the police force robbed precious time from finding Milo. She'd call him later.

Was she making the right decision? She again adjusted items in her purse, some in, some out. On the way to the car she took one last look at her beautiful home. She'd been so happy here. Would she ever see it again or lie dead in a ditch before the night ended?

With resignation, she locked the door, got in her car and drove away.

CHAPTER SEVENTY-NINE

MONDAY, 6:03 PM

"Nine-one-one. Where is your emergency?" A whimper. "Hello, can you hear me? Where is your emergency?"

Sniffle. "My name is Milo and...and I am fowah yeahs old. They put me inside the black closet for a long time but then I twied to open the handle and it wasn't locked so I opened the closet doah and came out into this woom. On the mattwess next to the magazine and the pizza box I found this cell phone and I'm calling you for help."

"Milo, can you tell me where you are?"

"I'm where the bad men taked me."

"Do you know your address, Milo?"

He sang the row-row-row-your-boat ditty his mother taught them, with new rhyming words giving their address and phone number. "But I'm not at my house. I'm at this scawy place."

"All right, Milo. Who put you in the black closet?"

"The bad men did. They had guns and they taked me from my Gwan's house. The police came but one bad man gwabbed me and wan into the woods and put me in his caw. He maked me lie down on the flowah."

"Milo, do you know your last name?"

"Milo Kwuse."

"Milo Kruse. Milo, did the men hurt you?"

Sniffle. "They slapped me lots of times, weally hawd."

"They slapped you hard. Did they do anything else?"

"They have mean faces. They shouted and pushed me. I'm afwaid. I wanna go home." A sob.

"Milo, you did the right thing to call 911 and I'm sending help. Can you tell me about the room you are in?"

"It's diwty and it *stinks*. They taked me down the steps to get here."

"Can you see out a window?"

"No...no window."

"Can you hear any noises like a train or a bell?" Silence. "Milo?"

"No."

"Can you tell me what you see in the room?"

"Mattwess. Pizza. Magazines. Potty. Sink. Walls. Doah. Closet. TV."

"Okay, Milo. You're doing fine. How did you know to call 911?"

"My Gwan taught us if something *weally* bad happens and no adult is close to help, we call 911. The men *aw* adults but they aw *bad* adults 'cause they hitted me."

"Okay, Milo. Do you have a pocket big enough to hold the cell phone?"

"...My new cawgo pants have lots of pockets."

"Here's what to do. Do not turn off the cell phone when we finish talking. Leave it turned on and put it in your pocket. Then get back in the closet and close the door so they won't know you found the cell phone. They'll think you stayed in the closet the whole time they were out of the room. Our policeman will follow that cell phone signal to find you. Don't tell the bad men you have the cell phone even if they ask you, because they will turn it off. Do you understand?"

"I...I think so."

"Have you any questions about what to do?"

"When will the policeman come?"

"He's on his way right now. Milo, even if the bad men take you somewhere else, the policeman will follow your cell phone signal as long as it's turned on. He will find you wherever you are."

"Okay."

"Be brave, Milo. You're a good boy."

"Thanks." Sniff.

"Are you back in the closet yet?"

"No."

"Go there quickly and close the door. Leave the cell phone turned on. Hide it in your pocket. Don't tell anybody it's in your pocket. Help is coming soon."

CHAPTER EIGHTY

MONDAY, 6:11 PM

Jennifer knocked on Roshan's door. "Hello again. Do you remember me?"

"Of course I do. Would you like some tea? Your envelope is here on the table."

"No tea, thank you, but may I sit long enough to read my letter?"

"Go right ahead. I'll be in the kitchen if you need me."

Jennifer opened the padded manila envelope. Inside lay a cell phone and a phone number. She called to Roshan. "Thank you, I'm going now." Roshan appeared and Jennifer added, "Nice seeing you again and thank you so *very* much for your help getting this letter tonight." Roshan nodded and Jennifer slipped out the door and into her car.

From habit, she locked her car door, realizing afterward this safety measure was ludicrous against the risks ahead for her tonight. She turned on the interior car light and used the new cell phone to call the number in the envelope. "This is Jennifer."

A voice-distorted monotone answered. "We will give you turn-by-turn directions and observe your progress as you follow them. Make a U-turn now. Then after two blocks, turn right."

She steered with her right hand, holding the cell phone to her ear with her left hand as she headed into the dark night. She heard the voice say, "Turn left at the next intersection." Had they spotters along the way to radio her progress or had they a way to track her car? A glance in the rearview mirror showed an empty street behind her. She passed numerous intersections without receiving new instructions. Had they lost contact? What would she do if that happened?

"Turn right at the next intersection." She turned, squinting at the street sign. Her headlights provided the only illumination except for weak glows from houses set back from spacious front yards. No streetlamps lighted these main roads—in an unrealistic effort to "keep the country feel," although this area was more residential than rural.

Driving through darkness, she took her hand off the wheel long enough to touch the sock of diamonds stuffed into her inside jacket pocket to be *certain* she brought it. She passed enough intersections in cell phone silence to fret again about losing contact with the kidnappers. They had her little Milo. His fate depended upon her. She must reach the destination.

The distorted voice spoke again. "Slow down to twenty mph." Jennifer did. "Prepare to stop soon." Her car crept along a wooded, uninhabited section of road. "Stop. Now inch along until you see a stick with yellow cloth tied at the top. Immediately past that stick is a path in the tall grass just big enough for a car. Turn right into that path, immediately after the stake."

She almost passed the place described, halting abruptly and backing up a few feet until she saw the yellow tie. She hesitated, not wanting her front wheels mired in the storm ditch that ran along these roads. Then she noticed they'd filled that section of trench with logs. She rolled roughly across this improvised "bridge," pulled into a field, bumped over grass and peered into her headlight's beam for human figures. She saw none.

"Turn your headlights off and your interior car light on so we know you brought no one else with you," the cell phone instructed. She obeyed. Suddenly masked people moved around her vehicle. Now came the tough part. She might die right here, tonight, but this was the best way she knew to try to save her precious grandson.

CHAPTER EIGHTY-ONE

MONDAY, 6:41 PM

"Home again, home again, jiggety jog," Becca sang to Chris and Alicia as they trooped in the front door with sacks of shopping trophies and bags of leftover movie popcorn. Becca saw a note, taped to a dining room chair placed in the foyer. "Put your things away now, girls. I'll be with you in a minute."

She opened the note:

Becca,

I'm away with Milo. Not sure when we'll return. Don't worry. No matter what happens, always remember how much I love you.

Mom

Odd note; it seemed almost as if her mother thought she wouldn't see her again.

The phone rang. Becca picked it up with one hand, still holding the note in the other.

"This is Detective Felts again, Mrs. Shannon. You didn't call back and it's urgent that we speak with you about the kidnapping. When can I come to the house?"

Becca's jaw dropped. *Kidnapping?* "This is her daughter, Becca. She isn't here right now. What's going on, Detective?"

"You say you are her daughter? How old are you?"

"Twenty-one. For God's sake, Detective, what's going on?"

"You don't know?"

"I've been out all afternoon and just got home. Please tell me, what's this about?"

He filled her in. "We need to come over now to plan strategy to get the boy back safely."

"I hear call-waiting. Give me your number. I'll call you right back."

Becca scratched his number on the note her mother had left then switched to the incoming line.

"Hello, this is Veronika Verontsova. May I speak to Jennifer's husband?"

"He's not here but this is her daughter. May I help?"

"I'm the Russian woman she met for lunch today."

"The psychic?"

"Yes. I...I've had another vision and I'm calling to warn you. She is in perilous danger tonight. She's in a field trying to save a little boy from dangerous men who plan to kill them both."

Becca gulped.

"Please listen carefully. We have very little time to save her and you must play an important role. In my vision she left information about where she went. A letter? A note for her husband?"

"Hold on while I run upstairs to look. She rushed into her parents' master bedroom, glanced into each of their walk-in closets and then into their bathroom. Between their double sinks she found an envelope addressed to "Jason." She tore it open. "Veronika, are you still there?"

"Yes, what did you find?"

"Her note to my father. Here, I'll read it aloud:

Jay, Sorry to do this without you, Love, but I couldn't wait for your return tonight.

I contacted Milo's kidnappers today and got a cell phone, which they'll use to give me directions.

They said to bring the diamonds to exchange for him, but I'm only taking half because if they get them all, Milo and I won't come back. I made this decision myself, knowing you'd stop me otherwise. I created this problem so I should solve it. If things go wrong, remember how much I have always loved you and that you and our family are most precious to me in all the world.

If I'm not home by your return, please rescue me. I gave OnStar advance permission to share my GPS location with you and the Fairfax County police. Call 1-888-For-OnStar. My member number is on the enclosed card. Maybe Adam can help you with OnStar. Nice to have a police detective in the family when we need one!

My love always, Jen

Veronika's voice filled with urgency. "Now you must alert this Adam about the OnStar so he can find her, and you must call OnStar to confirm your authorization for him to use this information to save her life. Do you understand?"

"Yes. Thank you, Veronika."

"Hurry!"

She hung up the phone.

CHAPTER EIGHTY-TWO

MONDAY, 6:52 PM

"Hello, Hannah? Please let me talk to Adam right away. I don't have time to explain. It's urgent. ...Adam, it's Becca. We have an emergency. I found a note from Mom saying she contacted Milo's kidnappers. They gave her a cell phone to receive directions to some place where they'll exchange the diamonds for Milo. She planned ahead by giving OnStar permission to tell Dad and the police her vehicle's tracking location. Dad's out of town, so it's up to you. Can you start right away?"

"Yes, ready to copy."

She read the numbers. "Call me with any news. I can't believe she'd try this by herself."

"Really?" he asked and hung up.

* * * *

"Hello, Onstar? I'm Detective Adam Iverson of the Fairfax County Police. This is about your member, Jennifer Shannon." He read her member number. "She gave you her permission to tell us the location of her vehicle per your GPS. Do you find that?"

"I'll refer you to a different department and..."

"Wait a minute, is Brad Billings on duty tonight? He's familiar with...."

"Just a moment, I'll check."

"Hello, this is Brad Billings."

"Hi, Brad, here's a voice from the recent past. I'm sure glad you're on duty tonight." Adam identified himself and reminded him of their past work on the other case.

"I remember it well; glad it worked out. How can I help you now, Detective?"

"Jennifer followed directions from kidnappers to trade a ransom for her grandson. In order not to endanger other loved ones, she went herself. As backup, she left her permission with OnStar to let police track her vehicle and that's exactly what we're doing now."

"I'm searching for her permission to give you this information... yes, it just came up on the screen. Since I know who you are because we've worked together before, let's waste no time."

Adam heard the tap of computer keys.

"Okay, looks like her vehicle is parked along the McLean/Great Falls border in an area that's not commercial, residential or parkland but maybe agricultural. Here are the coordinates."

Adam copied numbers, thanked Brad and hung up.

As he stared at the coordinates and their significance registered, he jumped to his feet. "Geez, Hannah, I know these numbers by heart from subdividing our property. *Her car is parked on our land.*"

"We've got to hurry to save your Mom and Milo. Grab the rifle, your cell phone and a warm jacket. Climb into the deer stand halfway across the property. When I call you on your cell, fire the rifle into the air three times. By then I'll be close to the perps. Your gunshot will distract them so I can make my move."

Used to dressing fast for police work, Adam whipped on his Kevlar bullet-protective vest, jerking a black long-sleeved t-shirt over it. With no idea the size force he'd encounter, he slipped on a camouflage vest containing pepper spray, box cutter and taser. He pushed his pistol into his belt, thrust his cell phone into a vest pocket, grabbed night-vision goggles, blew a kiss to his startled wife and rushed from the house into the dark.

He ran along the same abandoned farm road used a year earlier by his deranged brother, Ruger, who took flight from police after Jennifer escaped. From the OnStar coordinates, Adam knew exactly where he headed on his property, two miles from his house but along a completely different country road.

He ran quickly but with little noise. From frequent walks around the property, he knew this grass-covered road well, even in the dark. Always volatile, kidnapping scenarios moved unpredictably. Would either family member still be alive when he reached the spot? He pushed himself to run faster, covering the two miles quickly. Nearing the target area, he slowed, heard voices and crept forward with stealth. He donned night-vision goggles and scanned the scene before him.

CHAPTER EIGHTY-THREE

MONDAY, 7:13 PM

Aware of masked people moving around her car, Jennifer heard the cell-phone voice drone, "Step out of the car and put your hands in the air."

She dropped the phone on the seat and climbed out into the darkness, palms raised.

Rough hands grabbed her, frisked her, removed the sock of diamonds and threw her on the ground face-down. A man's heavy boot ground into the small of her back, pinning her painfully flat on the ground. Fear and pain combined with the shock of this onslaught to warn her with certainty they intended to grab the diamonds and kill them both. She screamed, "You won't get the rest of your diamonds if you hurt me or the boy."

More rough hands pulled her to her feet. One grabbed her hair, jerking her head back. "What did you say?" he growled.

She shouted, "I said you won't get the rest of your diamonds if you hurt me or the boy."

The masked man holding the sock looked up sharply. "The rest of the diamonds? You didn't bring them all?"

The ringleader poured the sock's contents into one huge hand, studied them and dropped them back inside.

"Of course not," Jennifer said loudly, "I cannot trust you. You'd kill the boy and me if you got them all now. The rest are at the bank and only my key and signature can get them out."

"Well, now," came the oily voice of a second man. "You *are* a troublemaker, but we know how to deal with that. After what we do, you will beg to bring us to the diamonds."

"I beg to bring you the rest of the diamonds now. The bank is a public place where I must walk in to sign for them. Everybody will see me. If I am hurt in any way, they will all know."

"Hmm," the man purred, "we have many techniques showing no outside marks but which make you cry to do whatever we ask if only we stop the pain. You'll gladly get the diamonds for us."

"But I'll gladly get the diamonds for you now, anyway. After you return the boy."

"Or we keep the boy and give you a last chance to exchange the remaining diamonds for his life."

"Maybe you've already killed him, so none of this matters. Let me see him."

The voice behind the mask fell silent as an anxious moment passed. "Show her the boy."

Jennifer heard a car door slam in the darkness, followed by a child's whimpers. One of the men directed a flashlight beam on Milo. Held in a man's tight grasp, the child stood about thirty feet from her. He winced as the light played upon his little face, blinding him with brightness.

"Or another useful method is to chop off small pieces of the boy's body while you watch—until you bring us the remaining diamonds. First a fingertip, then an ear, then the nose, then..."

She hoped Milo missed this grisly incantation. She fought anxiety and steadied her voice to avoid further alarming the frightened child. "Milo, I've come for you," she shouted, holding her arms out to him. He wriggled to break away and run to her, but the man held him fast.

"No," said the voice behind the mask. "First we take the diamonds you brought tonight and you get the boy only when you produce the rest."

"But then we're right back to tonight. You'd have the diamonds while the boy and I have no protection and then you kill us." In defiance, she raised her body as high as it would go. "No."

The man spoke next in a condescending sing-song voice one might use with a toddler. "Well, then, I guess you must learn to trust us."

Jennifer choked back a semi-hysterical laugh of derision welling in her throat but which would only enrage the man. She'd read that a woman's public scorn equaled humiliation for a man in his culture, particularly with such ridicule delivered in the presence of his peers.

"We do not trust each other, but let's make a plan in which we both win," she said.

She heard the impatient snarl of one not used to having his desires questioned, but she must save Milo. "You trade me the boy for half the diamonds that I brought tonight. That's fifty percent more than you had and you're halfway to where you want to be. Tomorrow, I go to the bank to get the rest. I will put those diamonds anywhere you say and you can get them any time you want."

"And if you decide not to get the diamonds at the bank? You have the boy but we don't have all our diamonds. Or what if you tell police where you put them? They'd arrest the one who gets them."

"Kidnapping Milo showed me you can harm my family. I get that. Why would I call police to risk it again?"

He conferred with the others. Several nodded.

"All right. We have half the diamonds. Take the boy and go. You still have the cell phone directing you here tonight. We will use it to tell you where to leave the diamonds tomorrow. Fortunate for us your family is large, offering many easy targets if you make a mistake."

He made a gesture. "Release the boy."

No sooner than Milo began running toward her outstretched arms than the sharp report of three gunshots shattered the silence of the night.

CHAPTER EIGHTY-FOUR

MONDAY, 7:41 PM

In Adam's night-vision goggles, Jennifer and Milo glowed green as they hugged each other near her car. Adam saw the kidnappers nearby — at least three balaclava-masked men. They had the advantage of numbers, he of surprise. He could take down one, maybe two by himself but three or more changed the odds. More important, the government always wanted them alive for interrogation.

He called for backup before racing out of the farmhouse but doubted a cruiser would reach the scene in time. The three men he could see moved toward their car and opened the doors. Adam couldn't let them escape. "Shoot into the air now, Hannah," he whispered into his cell phone.

The crack of three rifle shots broke the night as she responded. At the kidnap scene, all heads snapped toward the sound. When no follow-up came, the men jumped into the vehicle and roared toward the road.

Adam shot out two tires on the side of the car visible to him in the goggles and as the car squared off to leave, he disabled the other rear tire with more bullets. A car could ride on flat tires, but not fast. As their vehicle reached the road, Adam saw the scene flicker with blue cruiser lights. How could police cars dispatched for backup arrive that fast?

Running up behind their fleeing car, Adam held his pistol steady. Seeing police in the road, the kidnappers bailed from their vehicle and rushed into the field, away from the arriving cops and directly toward Adam.

"Police! Stop or I'll shoot!"

A bullet zinged past him. He responded by shooting toward the legs of two of the men. When they screamed and fell, the third stopped, putting his hands in the air.

Alongside Jennifer, in the split second before one of the kidnappers raised his hands, he threw something at her. Reaching for it in the gloom, she realized he'd tossed back the bag of diamonds she'd brought tonight. "Now we know where to find them again," he said. "If police take them, they are gone for good."

Adam focused his weapon on the two men still standing when a surprising number of cops closed in from the road to overwhelm the kidnappers. Their cruiser headlights illuminated this corner of the dark field. With the three perps face down on the ground and cuffed, Adam called out to the uniforms, "Police officer here. Don't shoot." Hurrying over to the cops, he identified himself. "How the hell did you know about this crime scene?"

"911 traced the kid's cell phone. Fixed him at a house in McLean, but when the perps brought him here we followed his cellular IP. Are they okay, the woman and the kid?"

"Let's find out."

While several policemen wrestled the two injured men into an ambulance and the other into a cruiser, Adam and other cops strode over to Jennifer and Milo.

"You and the boy okay, Ma'am?" asked one of them.

"Glad to be alive and not hurt. Thank you for saving us. Milo says they pushed him around and scared him, but I think he's all right. He's been through a lot for a four year old."

"We'll drive you home right now, Ma'am."

"What about my car?"

"Give us your keys and one of our men will follow us there in it."

"Adam, how did you get here?" Jennifer asked in amazement.

"OnStar gave me your vehicle location and—you won't believe it— you're standing on a piece of my farm property."

"*What?*"

"They must have scouted an empty field away from residential scrutiny and picked mine. Hannah's here, too. She'll want to see you before you leave."

The policemen helped Jennifer and Milo into their cruiser.

"Wow," Milo marveled. "Are we going to wide home in this police caw?"

"We sure are, Son," confirmed the driver. "Shall we use the siren?"

Milo's smudged little face beamed. "Yes, yes!"

Hannah rushed up, gasping for breath. "Mom...I've been so worried. Are you and Milo...all right?"

They exchanged reassurances all around.

"Tomorrow we'll tell you Hannah's role in saving you and Milo," Adam said. Hannah beamed as his arm went around her shoulder.

"Thank you *both* for rescuing us. Love you so much."

As the police car bumped across the farm road to the pavement, Jennifer hugged Milo close. The little tyke said, "It's lucky you told us about calling 911."

Tears of relief sparkled in her eyes. "Yes," she agreed, smoothing his hair, "...very lucky."

When the cruiser reached the road, the policeman driving said, "Are you ready for the siren, Milo?"

He sat up, wiggling with excitement. "You bet I am."

"Here goes."

The distinctive wail filled the air. Jennifer marveled. They'd made it through alive and she still had the diamonds. But after the series of arrests, these people had even more reason to hate her. Would their ruthless companions add revenge to their previous zeal to get their diamonds?

She leaned her head back against the cruiser seat and closed her eyes. With tonight's rescue, was her terror over or was this only round one of a long bout yet to come?

CHAPTER EIGHTY-FIVE

MONDAY, 8:16 PM

Zayneb thought Ahmed did not look well tonight. He and Abdul, the man acting as driver since Mahmud's absence, had closed themselves in the study, intently discussing business.

She sat in the dining room, allowing her mind to wander. Mahmud's absence lifted a huge burden from her heart. She no longer feared his beatings, his looks of disgust, his loathing of her friends, his anger at her outside interests or his cutting indifference to Khadija.

Her family home was safe again now that he couldn't legally take half from her. She needn't anguish over the complications, expense and repercussions of divorce. While she still embraced Islam, she'd like to be called Phoebe once again.

Now she need only solve her money problems and wanted to find an independent solution different from asking Khadija to contribute from her salary. Maybe she could move Heba upstairs, finish the basement into an apartment and rent it out. Maybe she could get a job at the school where her hours dovetailed with Safia's, earning money while continuing as a stay-at-home mother. Who could imagine so much good came from her spouse's accidental death? According to the newspaper and TV detective programs, many people wished their spouse dead or tried to make it happen. In her case, Allah indeed worked his plan for each person's fate in unusual ways. Life was looking up.

In her room, Khadija thought about Ahmed. How was it possible for a practical, rational person like herself to fall in love this fast? She couldn't explain their instant attraction or how she seemed to know from the start that he'd play an important role in her destiny. And her genuine affection superseded smug retaliation against her father. Mahmud's departure on the extended trip clarified that for her. This relationship with Ahmed would last. She could tell. Life was looking up.

In the basement, Heba smiled. Her life had changed again with the last of the cruel, insensitive men in her life gone. Ironically, in the process she'd found a family and become an accepted member. Her admiration for Zayneb grew daily. She knew Mahmud didn't go on a trip. She didn't know how he died but she watched him buried. The day Mahmud left, something else had happened, something she practiced in her room, something new and wonderful. Life was looking up.

In the study, Ahmed and Abdul coped with their situation. Their greatest bafflement lay in Allah's reason for subverting their heroic, selfless efforts to glorify Him. Why wouldn't he smooth their way rather than destroy every effort? Questioning the Supreme Being amounted to blasphemy, but how could God's will lead them to this inglorious end?

"Summarizing," Ahmed said at last, "our cell of sleepers is reduced from ten to the two of us. Our funds are gone, we don't know how to get them back and we haven't manpower to implement our mission. Without our original cell's unique skills and connections, the mission we envisioned is unworkable. Worse, the enemy captured all seven freedom fighters alive. What might they reveal during interrogation?"

Abdul, elbows propped on thighs, nodded. "Thanks to the Great Leader's wisdom, each of us knew only what you told us. In that respect, you are most valuable to the enemy, for you know the most about this mission, the connection with the Russians and the Great Leader himself. Have you told him our situation?" Abdul asked.

"Not yet, but I will tonight."

"At the very least, the two of us can perish in glory. We can arm ourselves, hide our weapons and explosives beneath our coats, go to the shopping center and earn our path to Paradise in a glorious blaze of infidel deaths."

"Yes, we can," Ahmed agreed, but he seemed to have a dreamy, far-away expression.

"You said such spectacles will occur all over America, in every state on the same day at the same hour. So beyond our explosions here will flow a ripple of terror to frighten their whole nation."

"To frighten them or unite them against us?"

Abdul stared aghast at his companion. "You are joking, right?"

Ahmed forced a smile. "Of course, I am joking."

CHAPTER EIGHTY-SIX

MONDAY, 10:33 PM

Jason felt old and weary as he extricated himself from his car in the garage. The three-hour drive in each direction plus hectic merger meetings in Delaware took their toll. Staying overnight made sense, but the diamond danger pressed him to hurry home instead—to protect his loved ones.

"Hi, Dad. Glad you're home." Becca greeted him as he poked his head into the family room where she watched TV.

"Anything exciting happen today, Becks?"

Becca gave him "the look." She sighed. "Where to begin, Dad? Mom's asleep. She had several glasses of wine and took a pill besides, so I guess I'm the one to tell you."

"I'll get a glass of wine myself and then let's talk. Would you like one?"

"Sure, a wee chardonnay before bed would taste good."

He returned with two glasses. "Okay, let's hear it."

"Do you want the big news first or the little news?"

"Start me with the little news and work up."

"Mom had lunch today with the psychic. Mom handed her a diamond from the ones in the doll, which burned the psychic's hand—not a real burn but a mental burn, whatever that is. The psychic confirmed the diamonds are part of the danger. Well, duh! We knew that. But she impressed Mom enough to get invited to our Thanksgiving dinner."

Jason felt nervous already. "So...ah, what's the big news?"

As she described the break in, the bank and the kidnapping, Jason grew pale and clenched his fists. "That's Part One," Becca said. "Part Two is even better."

"Before you finish, skip to the bottom line. Is everybody okay now?"

"Yes."

Jason drained his glass. "Then pause a minute. I'm getting a refill." When he returned, he paced the floor with growing dismay as Becca described brushing off the police, arranging the cell-phone directions, Veronika's alert, Milo's 911 call, Adam's involvement and the final police rescue. "Dad, are you all right?"

"Of course, I'm not all right. How could I be all right, knowing my wife and grandson were nearly murdered tonight? I... 'overwhelmed' hardly covers it. True, I'm always leery to ask about a day in your mother's life, but this..."

He sat on the edge of the couch, his head in his hands, cursing his absence when this family needed his protection.

Becca strolled over and gave him a hug.

Getting his anxiety under control, he changed the subject. "And what about you? How are you handling all this?"

She giggled. "Actually, it's kinda fun being home for the holiday. Nothing this exciting happens at college."

He kissed her cheek. "Sleep well, Becks. If nothing crazier happens yet tonight, I'll see you tomorrow. Be sure to lock all the doors and set the alarm before bed."

"Forgot one detail: the alarm wires were cut."

Jason groaned.

"Night, Dad. Love you."

"Love you, too, Honey."

CHAPTER EIGHTY-SEVEN

MONDAY, 11:03 PM

"Blessings upon you, Great Leader. It is I, your servant Ahmed."

"May Allah smile on you and all your endeavors, Ahmed. What have you to report?"

"Alas, calamity changes our plans. We need your guidance to find a new path to the oasis."

"Yes, my son, speak."

Ahmed told his mentor what he needed to know, ending with the undeniable fact their cell was reduced to two men, entirely inadequate for the plans. "Without funds or freedom fighters, how can we complete our task?"

"Ah, my son, these are indeed grave problems. But Allah smiles on you and your mission. You did well to consult me. Did you make successful contact with the Russians?"

"Yes, Great Leader."

"Then I will deal directly with them myself, arranging another way to pay them for what we need. You need only coordinate where it is stored, when it is used and how."

"But Great One, how can I fulfill our mission with no men?"

"My faith in you is strong. I will send you ten new men tomorrow morning. They are sleepers in nearby states, eager to play roles in this wondrous mission. Now twelve instead of ten, this team exceeds your previous force. They will arrive in a van at the house where you stay, the home of Mahmud Hussein. The van will drive into that garage tomorrow morning at 10:00. Tonight you make arrangements for them at a nearby motel. Get six rooms, two men per room. When the van arrives, take them to the motel and describe their assignments for Friday."

"You say six rooms with two in each room?"

"Yes, you have two men left. You and the other man stay in one of those rooms. Having all of you in one place simplifies logistics and bonding in the short time remaining."

"But we can't reproduce the specific talents and contributions of our original cell members—access to trains and metro, to HVAC, janitorial service, computer hacking, explosive laden semi-trucks in tunnels, chemical lab toxins, heavy construction equipment and knowledge of explosives."

"Ah, then you improvise; that was one of the skills for which I chose you to lead this assignment."

"Thank you, Great Leader. I did not fully appreciate your limitless vision and resources."

"How could I fail to make your glorification of Allah a reality?"

"Blessings upon you, Great One."

"And upon you, my son. Oh, and one more thing."

"Yes?"

"This woman responsible for taking our diamonds and the arrests of our men?... Kill her."

"It shall be as you wish, Great Leader."

Ahmed lay back on his bed and moaned. He did not want to kill Jennifer Shannon, who had the diamonds only because of his mistake. He didn't want to push forward this murderous plan at the mall to kill unarmed innocents, despite their being non-believers. He didn't want to leave this house where Khadija lived, or the family atmosphere he enjoyed, the first he'd known since childhood. He didn't want to live out his remaining few days with men he didn't know in a motel—a lonely place like the other impersonal surroundings he'd recently learned to hate.

DAY SIX

TUESDAY

CHAPTER EIGHTY-EIGHT

TUESDAY, 4:58 AM

Jason spent a tormented night agonizing about the kidnapping. Trying to fall asleep, he looked often at the clock to mark his progress. At last he turned off the alarm just before it rang at 5:00. Why disturb Jennifer so early after what she'd been through?

Slipping out of bed, he gazed at her peaceful expression as she slept. How close he'd come to losing her. To guard his family, he longed to scratch today's hunting trip, but with Tony's life in shambles and this trip so important to him, he hated to disappoint his old friend. They'd need only six early hours and when they returned at 11:00, the bulk of the day lay ahead for his family.

Even before yesterday's kidnap shocker, Jason had asked Adam for extra surveillance due to the threat. Adam said neighborhood patrols would give their house special attention and he'd drop by himself. According to Becca's account last night, police arrested seven of the diamond owner's men, a feat that must have put a dent in their terrorist operation, whatever it was.

He tiptoed across the bedroom and closed the door. Donning the hunting clothes he'd assembled the night before, he crept downstairs. When Tony's pickup backed out of his driveway, Jason crossed the circle to pile his gear into the truck.

"Good morning. Takes focus to get up before dawn to shoot deer."

"But worth it, and a clean shot beats seeing the animals ripped to pieces on the road."

"And, if we're lucky, we bring home dinner. Going to that same place out past Great Falls?"

"Yeah. The farmer has so many deer on his land now that instead of us paying him to shoot there, he said he'd like to hire us. Bottom line, we hunt today — free — with his blessing."

"Want coffee?" Jason offered.

"Sure. Cream and sugar, if you have some. I brought breakfast and snacks for later."

Jason laughed. "You covered the bases." As he handed Tony a mug, he patted the cell phone in his jacket's outer pocket, a handy location if needed in a hurry. "About an hour to get out there?"

"Right. Little traffic this early so we'll move right along."

Not wanting to single out Tony's grief, Jason asked instead, "How's the family doing?"

"Glad the funeral on Sunday is behind us. The kids left Monday. They miss their mother and are taking her sudden death hard."

"Again, let us know if we can help out," Jason offered.

"Hey, see that doe on the side of the road? They're herd animals, so when you see one, expect more. Without natural predators to control the deer, Fairfax County has 5,000 DVCs a year; 54,000 in Virginia."

"DVCs?"

"Deer Vehicle Collisions. And deer aren't the only casualties; people are killed or injured, too."

"Yeah, I know it's a big problem. You're up on this stuff, aren't you?"

"Well, vets get the literature and the public brings us the hurt ones. Right now in November, during the rut, the White Tails are fearless and crazy. You'd be surprised how many road-injured deer are brought to vets' offices."

They drove awhile in silence. Tony looked preoccupied. Why not, burying his wife only two days ago? Jason yawned. "Forgive me if I doze off before we get there. Insomnia for hours plus leaving so early this morning made it a pitifully short night."

"Go ahead and grab a few winks."

The truck's rocking motion lulled Jason to sleep quickly, and he didn't wake up until Tony turned off the motor at their destination. Outside looked pitch black.

"We're here. You take the closer stand this time and I'll use the one about 150 feet further. We've been here before so you'll recognize it. We can't shoot until sunrise at 7:00. If we bag a deer, we field-dress it right here and drag it back to the truck later. Like before, if we hear the other one shoot, we stay put in the stand in case the noise steers deer your way. If we get no shots, I'll pick you up here about 10:00 and we'll head for the truck. Three daylight hours should be enough if we're waiting for them at dawn. Here's a sack with breakfast. Got your flashlight?"

"Yeah." Jason turned it on. They walked together to the first stand. Jason climbed up and Tony continued on.

Jason liked the woods — a contrast from northern Virginia's urban life. Still warm from the heated truck, he relaxed in the stand, rifle across his knees, and waited. Late November nudged winter in Virginia. The longer you sat in a deer stand, the colder you got.

An hour later he felt quite cold as he peered out from the stand, again scanning the farmer's field and the clearing below him. And then he saw it. A doe appeared in the clearing beneath him, followed by a buck focused on mating.

Jason lifted his rifle, sighted one through the scope and gently squeezed the trigger. The shot's loud crack echoed in the quiet morning. The doe skittered away but the buck fell in his tracks, motionless on the ground. Jason descended with his bag of equipment. He liked this part least, but knew field-dressing a deer was necessary to put venison on the table.

When he climbed back into the stand, another hour passed, during which he heard three shots from Tony's direction. Shots weren't necessarily hits, but he hoped his neighbor downed at least one.

By 9:30 Jason had had enough. Only thirty minutes until Tony's proposed departure, but Jason felt half frozen and ready to roll. He climbed down and dragged his deer to the truck. He loaded it and his equipment bag before starting toward the second stand. He had a pretty good idea where it was but used his compass as backup. Morning sun lighted the area. When he spotted the big rock, he knew the second stand lay just ahead.

He moved forward slowly. "Tony," he shouted. No answer. "Tony, it's Jason. If you're as cold as I am, let's go on home."

As he spoke, the compass slipped from his hand. When he bent over to get it, a bullet whizzed over him.

What the...?

He stood. "Tony," he bellowed, "don't shoot. It's me. We need to talk."

As he heard a second gunshot, a bullet pinged off the big rock and ricocheted into the bushes. "Tony, stop shooting," he yelled, slipping out of his neon orange vest and crawling away from it. Spotting a long branch, he hooked the vest with it and bobbed it up and down. A third shot rang out, this one puncturing the vest.

My God. He's trying to kill me!

What were his options? He had no keys to escape in the pickup. Should he run for his life from the man shooting at him? Attempt a citizen's arrest? Call 911? He reached for his cell phone, startled not to find it in the jacket pocket. He patted other pockets in case he forgot where he'd put it. Had Tony slipped it out while Jason napped en route?

Just then a buck exploded out of the bushes into the second stand's clearing. Tony fired. He must have operated on instinct, Jason thought, with his rifle already up in position firing at me! He heard the deer whoosh out of the clearing. Tony had missed. From behind a tree, Jason shouted a command. "Tony, enough. It's over. I've got you square in my sights. I don't want to hurt you, man. Throw down your weapon and get down here."

He peered cautiously around the tree. He saw Tony's rifle barrel edge out of the stand, turn toward Jason, waver uncertainly and fall out of the stand onto the ground.

Nothing stirred for a moment. Finally, Tony dropped his equipment bag and slowly descended the ladder. Avoiding eye contact, he mumbled, "Sorry, Jason, didn't see you. Made a mistake. Glad you're okay."

Jason had already scooped up Tony's fallen rifle, ejected the last cartridge and hung it over his shoulder. He held his own rifle in both hands, prepared to shoot defensively. "You walk ahead," Jason instructed.

Back in the truck, Jason held his rifle across his knees in the passenger seat, safety off, hands positioned to fire. Both knew the carnage such a short-range blast inflicted. They drove in silence a few miles before Jason cleared his throat. "Do you want to tell me what's going on, Tony?"

Silence. Jason stared at this man who'd been his neighbor and friend for over twenty years, now an unpredictable, lethal stranger. Was he mistaken or did Tony's eyes glisten with tears?

With morning rush hour over, they barreled down Old Dominion Drive toward McLean. Tension filled the truck. Tony seemed in a trance as Jason warned him several times of sighting deer along the roadside. Suddenly one hurtled from nowhere directly in front of their vehicle. The truck slammed it hard at full speed. The animal flew upward, smashing their windshield and peppering them with small glass chards. One end of the deer's body pushed in on the driver's side, striking Tony in the face. Jason felt the vehicle whip around in a semi-circle as it careened off the road and flipped. He saw a huge tree rushing closer...then blackness...

CHAPTER EIGHTY-NINE

TUESDAY, 9:58 AM

Kaela and Owain arrived to pick up the Grands at ten as promised. Jennifer asked Becca to distract the children while she told them a sanitized version of the weekend's events—from the doll to Milo's rescue.

Her daughter and son-in-law sat thunderstruck. "Just another happy ending," Jennifer summarized cheerfully, "but I thought you ought to know in case the girls talk about finding diamonds or Milo mentions his adventure."

Owain glanced nervously at his wife. "We thought this the safest place we could imagine for the kids while we were gone...." His voice trailed away.

"And you were right. We took wonderful care of them—except for the unexpected parts—and now they know how to call 911, so that's a plus." Jennifer smiled, hoping her positive attitude was contagious.

Kaela still looked stunned. "I...I don't know what to say, whether to be angry about putting my kids in danger or grateful they're fine and think they had a good time."

"Life's full of surprises, Kaela. Our attitude about what happens makes the difference for us and the ones around us. However you feel about it yourself, why not keep it positive for the children?"

Kaela hugged her mother. "You're nuts, Mom, but I really love you anyhow."

Just then the children raced in, all smiles and eagerness.

"We have lots to tell you," said Christine. "Becca took us for shopping, a movie and dinner."

"And Gran took us to garage sales where I got the first doll and this one I traded for it."

Milo could hardly wait to tell his news. "I wode in a police caw with a weal policeman and a siwen. It was so much fun."

"Told ya," Jennifer laughed.

After thanking her for babysitting, they left. As they pulled away, she still waved goodbye on the front porch when Adam's car arrived. He strode to the door. "Let's go inside where it's warm. I just heard some news at the station. A deer/pickup-truck accident in Great Falls on Old Dominion Drive sent Dad and Mr. Donnegan to Fairfax Hospital. They're okay but under observation. Do you want me to take you or can you drive?"

"You're on duty. I'll drive. Thanks, Adam. You're a good son." She hurried to alert Becca.

"If Dad's hurt, I want to come, too."

"Becca, I know you do, but won't you please stay here for the workmen coming this morning to repair the door where those men broke in and the security system they disabled? Getting the house secure again is so important right now. I promise to call you with everything I learn. And Celeste comes in an hour to clean for the Thanksgiving party. Someone needs to let her in."

Grudgingly, Becca agreed and Jennifer left. At the hospital she parked, hurried inside and identified herself at the ER desk.

"Have a seat. You can see them soon, after they're diagnosed and cleaned up. "

Fifteen minutes passed, then twenty. Anxious, Jennifer returned to the desk. "Just reminding you, I'm here to see Jason Shannon and Tony Donnegan."

"The doctor will be out to talk with you soon. I know it's hard to wait when you're worried. Would you like coffee or a soda?"

"No, thanks." She flipped through magazines for fifteen minutes more before the doctor appeared.

"Mrs. Shannon?" She nodded. "Your husband's cuts, bruises and sprained wrist are minor. He also has a concussion. We'll keep him overnight for observation. He's luckier than the other guy."

"I'm here for Tony also. He's our neighbor. His wife died a few days ago, so he's alone now. I'm his advocate as well, and I'm the one to tell his grown children."

"Okay, then. He has a fractured femur. He's all right now, but if it takes a worse turn, it could be serious. So he'll also stay for observation."

"When will you know?"

"Hard to tell. Meantime, we're putting him in ICU."

"And my husband?"

"He goes to the Neurology Ward. We hope to release him tomorrow and expect his symptoms to dissipate in a couple of days."

"Thank you, Doctor."

When he left, Jennifer asked the desk how soon she could visit Jason in Neuro. The half hour they mentioned gave her just enough time to make her calls. After her own children, she'd call Tony's family. She'd stored their contact numbers in her cell phone.

CHAPTER NINETY

TUESDAY, 11:18 AM

In the Neuro Ward, Jason lay quietly, eyes closed, as Jennifer entered his room.

"Are you awake?" she whispered. He nodded, opening his eyes. "How do you feel, Honey?"

"Blinding headache and can't focus. Everything's fuzzy. What happened?"

"As you returned from your hunting trip this morning, Tony's pickup hit a deer and ricocheted into a tree. You were knocked cold. You're feeling concussion symptoms. They say a few more tests, then bed-rest and taking it easy at home after that."

"Like we do a lot of that in our lives..."

"We will now, at least until you're better."

"When do I get out of here?"

"The doctor thinks tomorrow. The accident was serious, so you're very lucky."

His brow furrowed. With difficulty, he tried to think back to the crash. "How...how's Tony?"

"Don't know yet. He's in ICU. I came to see you before checking on him."

"Thanks, Sweetheart. This close call reminded me I didn't say I love you when I left before dawn. You were asleep and I didn't want to disturb.... Who knew it was almost my last chance?" He clutched her hand, blinking back tears.

"You won't get away from me that easily," Jennifer soothed.

He smiled. "I'm going to rest now. Bet they gave me something to make me drowsy."

His eyes closed. She stood beside him, holding his hand, until his snores signaled he slept.

In the ICU, Jennifer followed a nurse through the maze of privacy curtains shielding supine patients attached to beeping machinery. When asked about Tony's condition, the nurse said, "Stable at the moment. He's on morphine, so he may ramble a bit."

Tubes and life-monitoring wires linked Tony to a lot of equipment. He seemed asleep until she touched his hand. "Tony, it's Jennifer.

His eyes snapped open. He grabbed her hand and held on tight. "Thank God, Jennifer. You're here with me at last. It was all worth it for this reward."

Confused, she said, "Yes, I'm here with you now, and I'll stay close until your children arrive. But what do you mean, 'worth it for this reward'?"

"When I fell in love with you years ago, I...I wanted to divorce Kirsten but my lawyer said she'd get the house and then I wouldn't see you across the street every day."

"*What?*"

"So I had to think of another way to end my marriage for us to be together."

Jennifer couldn't believe her ears. Must be the morphine talking, she figured. Yet Tony sounded lucid, just very relaxed, as if he'd lost all inhibitions. And he looked at her clearly when he spoke.

"Finally I made a plan. At my clinic we use a drug called pentobarbital to euthanize animals. It took me a year to figure out the right dosage for a person of her size and weight, one that wouldn't kill outright as we do at the clinic but a dose she couldn't survive for long."

Jennifer's mouth gaped.

"I gave her a sedative first and when she slept I injected the drug slowly, a little between each of her toes where it left no bulge and nobody would look for it. Right on schedule, she had trouble breathing. When rescue arrived, the respiratory difficulties progressed into cardiac arrest and death at the ER, exactly as I'd calculated."

Jennifer's surprise turned to shock as he continued. "She didn't want cremation but I had no choice in case anyone looked later for evidence. The drug's detectable in an exhumed body and I couldn't risk it. Kirsten's death left me free at last. But not you. With Jason alive, you remained trapped in your own marriage."

Shock changed to horror. She stood, trembling, beside the hospital bed, hating to hear more but too fascinated to leave.

Tony spoke again. "I tried to stage an accidental shooting on the hunting trip but when that failed, the crash was the only way. If I brought the truck to a stop he'd be alive and you beyond my grasp. Instead, I hit the accelerator to crash the truck — to get rid of him. It was my last chance. If he died, you and I could start our life together. If I died instead, that would be better than facing the future without you, my darling.

"I did it all for you...for us. And now we can stay together all the rest of our lives." He looked deep into her widened eyes. "I love you, sweet Jennifer. Let me hear you say it to me. I've waited so long to...hear you say those...beautiful words."

"I...I," she gasped. But his eyes had closed as he fell into a deep sleep with a smile on his lips.

Jennifer staggered out of Tony's curtained enclosure, hurried back toward the Neurology Ward and reached her husband's room just as several of their children arrived to visit their dad.

CHAPTER NINETY-ONE

TUESDAY, 12:46 PM

"The workmen are here, Miss Jennifer," Celeste informed her as she hurried into the house. "Becca says the Mister is at the hospital. Is he all right?"

"Yes. Thanks for asking. He comes home tomorrow. What about you, Celeste? Are you well and happy?"

She laughed. "I am both."

"Are you still planning to help us here on Thanksgiving?"

"Oh yes, Fred and I will both be here."

"Good. Let's see..." Jennifer consulted her list. "I need to take something to the bank, pay the workmen, figure out dinner, make more phone calls, get groceries for Thursday and get back to the hospital."

"I can see you are busy, but..." She looked uncomfortable.

"What is it, Celeste?"

"You have been very good to me, and I found something I think you should know about."

"What?"

"It's something at Mr. Tony's house across the street. I clean for you Tuesday mornings and for him Tuesday afternoons. His wife used to let me in, but now that she's gone, he gave me a key. We could go there now or whenever is good for you on a busy day."

"This sounds important, but can it wait until this afternoon?"

"Yes."

"Good. We'll do it before I leave for the hospital."

Jennifer ran upstairs, grabbed the sock, poured out the contents and separated the diamonds from the M&Ms, leaving the candies in a dish on her vanity. The lockbox had proved a smart place to keep the diamonds before so she'd put them back. She checked the refrigerator and pantry supplies against her Thanksgiving menu shopping list. With Becca visiting her dad at the hospital, she left Celeste in charge of the workmen and hurried to complete her errands in town.

At the Giant grocery store, she chose a bouquet, took it to the bank and presented it to the manager before returning the diamonds to the vault. The card read: "Thanks to all of you at McLean Bank who safeguard your clients as well as their valuables."

Understandably curious about what happened yesterday, they had many questions. Because they'd played so important a role, she felt she owed them an explanation and outlined the police arrests—but excluded the diamonds.

After her other errands, she returned home. Celeste and crew had just finished their work. Jennifer paid her.

"Now my team goes to Mr. Tony's house. While they work downstairs, we could go upstairs."

Celeste led her to Tony's master bedroom, opened his closet door and pointed toward the back to a thin bulletin board. "He hid this here behind his clothes. Because it faces against the wall, I always vacuumed around without moving it. But Miss Kirsten said to pretend I'm spring cleaning even though it's fall and move things usually left in place. So last time I cleaned here, I took this out. Look what's on the other side." Celeste pulled out the large bulletin board and spun it around.

Jen gasped, eyes wide. Photos of her covered the surface, some cropped from group scenes eliminating all but her, and several of her and Tony, again culled from larger group shots. This discovery reinforced his drug-induced rambling confession in the ICU. Had he murdered his wife, Jennifer's close friend, to further a relationship existing only in his mind?

She shuddered.

"Thank you very much, Celeste. I value your loyalty to me and appreciate your decision to show me this. You knew something was wrong here. What you don't know is Mr. Tony's in the hospital, very sick. If he doesn't get better, his children shouldn't find this. Let's slip it inside a big trash bag and I'll get rid of it at my house."

"Oh, Miss Jennifer, I hope I did the right thing."

Jennifer hugged her. "You did. You were very brave to make this decision."

CHAPTER NINETY-TWO

TUESDAY, 12:57 PM

Ahmed had met with the Russians—Natasha and Boris—earlier that morning to confirm the Great Leader's promise they'd receive payment from another source, in currency rather than diamonds, for vests with explosives, Uzi's, canisters of Sarin gas, a few rockets and miscellanea. Delivery of said inventory to the warehouse Ahmed selected tomorrow afternoon by 5:00.

When "Mustafa" was forced to identify himself as Ahmed to qualify himself to the Russians as spokesperson for his side of their arrangement, "Natasha" revealed her name was really Anna. This provided the two otherwise-guarded conspirators their first laugh together.

Anna handed Ahmed an envelope. "Since we received our payment in a different form, here are your ten diamonds." Surprised at her unexpected honesty, Ahmed nodded his thanks.

The original ambitious list of supplies had narrowed to meet the terrorists' more modest needs. They'd no longer use mega explosives to ignite loaded semi-trucks at loading docks or to implode part of the metro tunnel or to bring down an elevated rapid transit train. The objectives had tamed, but twelve well-armed men with weapons, grenades and strapped-on explosives could still create dramatic destruction and carnage in a mall crowded with Black Friday shoppers.

As the Great Leader instructed, Ahmed guided the van-load of men arriving at 10:00 to a local motel, where they occupied adjacent first-floor rooms. Abdul drove separately in his own car. Gathering in one of the rooms, the ten men, who had met for the first time when they boarded the van in Maryland, introduced themselves to Ahmed and Abdul and described their skills.

Exuberance united them upon learning they targeted a large shopping mall on Friday at 1:00. Abdul distributed maps, the kind available to any mall shopper, showing the basic layout of stores and restaurants. Until the wee hours last night, Ahmed had worked out who would carry what weapons to which locations and now conveyed this battle plan to them.

Friday morning they were to appear clean-shaven, wearing accurate watches. They would board the van at 9:00 and synchronize their timepieces. Abdul arranged with motel management for late departure, but they'd never pay for the rooms since they'd be dead by that checkout time.

They'd drive their twelve-person van to the weapon warehouse, eat breakfast there and assist each other in concealing their assigned guns and explosives under bulky winter coats brought with them. At noon the van would drive to the mall, dropping them off singly at entrances near their destinations. The last man would park the van, never to return, before also entering the mall. Each man would be given a newspaper and a magazine. At their target points they'd inconspicuously window-shop or sit down to read until one o'clock. Then the jihad would begin.

During their stay at the motel, at mealtime one man would bring the rest carryout food, which they'd eat in their rooms. They'd become virtually invisible at the motel, drawing no attention to themselves individually or as a group. Nothing could go wrong.

But for Ahmed, everything had gone wrong. Stuck in this miserable motel, he couldn't say goodbye to Khadija or the others at her house. He thought of the wife he would never hold, the children he would never love and the gentle old age he would never reach. He questioned the carnage he planned, its purpose, its uncertain result and even its instant path to Paradise.

Why had Allah tortured him by throwing boulders across this path to righteousness? What had Ahmed's questioning achieved? Was Maury Rosenblum right when he said after the Frisbee game that Jews and Arabs in America could live and work productively together? If that were true, had Ahmed exerted his life's energy in exactly the wrong direction?

He wanted out of this nightmare but realized with a shudder that the walls inexorably tightening around him imprisoned him totally.

CHAPTER NINETY-THREE

TUESDAY, 2:04 PM

The Great Leader's kill order for Jennifer Shannon weighed heavily on Ahmed's mind. Did she deserve to die for innocently buying a doll at a garage sale with no idea about the treasure inside? Once she found it, she acted logically to protect it. On the other hand, her actions drastically impaired their grand mission by stealing its funds and reducing their manpower. Only the Great Leader's ingenuity and resources restored their ability to attack.

He'd like to spare the woman, but that defied a direct order. Who knew where the Great Leader positioned eyes to watch his every move? His choice: mercy for the woman or defiance of his mentor. Which path did Allah intend? In the end, with no way out of his cage, he saw no choice.

Ahmed knew Abdul's car provided flexibility the rest didn't have, so Abdul would carry out the order to kill Jennifer Shannon.

He did not question the assignment when Ahmed told him to eliminate her. From the start, Abdul thought her an insufferable, meddling woman. Her actions to destroy their original magnificent plans *deserved* punishment. Death after painful torture seemed best, but death in any form repaid her infidel wickedness.

"At your house you already have a pistol, a rifle, knives and grenades. Choose the method you think best to dispose of her, close or at a distance. Do it today and report to me when you finish."

"It shall be as you say," Abdul responded before driving home to get the equipment he'd need.

If Abdul were a passenger with a driver, killing her as she drove would be easy, but shooting accurately at someone while driving yourself was hard—he knew from experience.

He would do the job at her house.

He parked near the tennis court in her residential neighborhood, hid his gun beneath his coat, threaded his way past the community tennis courts and crept into the parkland to reach her house as he had done before. Hidden behind a tree at the edge of the woods, he watched for her to appear in front of any window. He waited. Half an hour passed. This, he knew, was one of his last three days on earth and he wished to spend the time differently than shivering in the woods. He waited. Another thirty minutes went by. Enough. Could he just tell Ahmed he'd done it? Would his leader learn the truth in the time left?

He stood up to leave. But wait. She had just walked into the kitchen.

He centered her head in his rifle scope, but she seemed constantly in motion. At last she stopped for a moment and he pulled the trigger just as she turned to do something else.

Three things happened at once: the crack of the rifle shot, the shattering of the windowpane and Jennifer falling like a rock to the floor. He must leave quickly. Neighbors watched out for each other in these communities. After the recent police presence here pursuant to the kidnapping, they'd be alert for the unusual.

He hurried back through the woods to his car, drove to the motel and reported his success.

CHAPTER NINETY-FOUR

TUESDAY, 2:43 PM

Typing at her computer upstairs, Becca heard a gunshot and shattering glass. She jumped to her feet.

"Mom? *Mom?*" she shouted, rushing down the stairs two at a time. She glanced into each room as she hurried past: the study, living room and dining room. In the kitchen, she saw her mother sprawled face down on the floor with blood in her hair. A glance at the spider web cracking around the hole in the window confirmed her worst fears.

"My God," she cried, kneeling beside her mother, trying to remember the first-aid mantra, "A-B-C: Airways, Breathing, Circulation." As she rolled her mother over, Jennifer's arm reached up weakly to pull her to the floor.

Her mother's hoarse voice desperately whispered, "...Down, Becca. Shooter outside..."

"Mom, there's blood. You're hurt. We need help."

"Blood?"

"Yes." Becca whipped out her cell phone. "I'm calling 911. We need medical help and there's a sniper in our back yard." She held her mother's hand and dialed.

Becca gave the emergency operator the address. "My mother's been shot in the head. She's on the floor bleeding but alive. Her name is Jennifer Shannon. I'm her daughter, Becca. Please send help, hurry!"

"What phone number are you calling from?" Becca told the operator. "Is the shooter still there?"

"I don't know. He shot through the window from our back yard or the woods behind."

"Get down low yourself in case he's still out there. Stay on the phone with me until help arrives."

"All right. *Please hurry.*"

"Help is on the way, Becca. Is your mom awake?"

"Yes."

"Is she breathing?"

"Yes."

"Has the bleeding stopped?"

"I think so but it's hard to tell. The wound's in her hair."

"Is she talking?"

"Yes." Becca began to cry. "Oh, Mom, this can't be happening." Into the phone she said, "I think I hear sirens. Yes, they're getting louder."

"Good. Stay on the phone until help has arrived. Has her condition changed in any way?"

"I don't think so. The sirens are loud now. Hold on. I'll crawl to the front door." She stood at the door to open it. "Hurry, she's in here," she directed the first responder. And into the phone, "Thank you for sending help fast."

She barely heard the operator's "You're welcome" as she hurried to the kitchen.

The medics went straight to work, blocking Becca's view as they evaluated and treated her mother. When a deep voice said, "We can't go on meeting like this," she spun around to look into Lt. Nathan Sommer's face. She nodded agreement.

Becca knew to stay out of their way as the EMTs worked on their patient but smiled with relief at her mother's lucid responses to their questions.

Ten minutes later, Nathan took Becca aside. "Your mother is one lucky lady. She faced away from the window when the pane shattered, propelling some glass fragments into her hair and skin. Miraculously, the bullet only grazed her scalp with a superficial flesh wound. Because head wounds tend to bleed a lot, it looked worse than it was. She didn't lose consciousness and she's talking normally. So far, so good."

Becca's relief showed on her face. "Thank you, Nathan."

"We've done our job." He looked at the broken window. "Police will arrive any minute to deal with this. Meantime, where's a couch for your mother to rest? She's okay physically but pretty shaken up."

"There's a couch in the study."

They helped Jennifer stretch out there. "Feeling better, Mom?" she asked, holding her mother's hand.

"Much better, Dear." Jennifer's voice was thin but steady.

When Becca and Nathan reached the foyer, he asked with concern, "Do you think you're safe here?"

"I did until yesterday and today," she said wryly.

"Wouldn't want anything to...to interfere with that Thanksgiving meal you invited me to attend. That's in just two days. Can you and your family stay afloat that long?"

"Not if today's an example. Seriously, Nathan, I hope we'll be okay. Mom looks forward to this event every year. It would take more than a shot in the head for her to cancel it."

Her sarcastic laugh at this absurdity covered her anxiety. "See you Thursday at one o'clock." As he turned to go, she touched his arm. "Nathan, thanks for being here to help us through this."

He squeezed her hand. "I hope you'll get used to having me around. Until Thursday, then?"

As he and the other firefighters and medics gathered their equipment and trooped out the front door, two policemen passed them on the way in.

Becca explained the situation, made a chalk outline showing where her mother had fallen and answered their questions.

"First we want to defuse any immediate danger. Then a detective will come out to investigate further. Is your mother up to talking with us about this?"

"Let's find out." She led the way to the couch.

By the time Jennifer explained the bank and kidnapping arrests followed by today's incident, they advised police protection. She agreed.

"We want to check the back yard before dark. We'll do that now. Then one of us will stay until the detective arrives. A patrolman will park his cruiser in front of your house during the time you need protection."

"Thank you, gentlemen. Now I think I'll rest a few minutes because Becca and I need to visit someone at the hospital tonight."

The policemen gave her a quizzical look. "My dad," Becca explained in the foyer. "He was injured in an auto accident earlier today."

"Sounds like your family better start taking life a whole lot easier."

CHAPTER NINETY-FIVE

TUESDAY, 6:04 PM

After the detective came and went, Becca and Jennifer drove to the hospital. "Honey, let's not tell Dad about the gunshot," Jennifer suggested before they entered Jason's room. "He'll just worry while stuck here in the hospital, and we know I'm fine and the situation is under control until he returns. Okay?"

Under control? Still, Becca agreed reluctantly, led the way to her father's room and hugged him.

Jennifer gave him a kiss. "You seem much livelier now. Do you feel as good as you look?"

"No more dizziness, my balance is back, the headache's gone and my vision's normal. I feel great. Don't know why they won't let me out right now."

"Your impatience is good, but we want you strong and steady for Thanksgiving. After all, you're our trusty wine steward."

"I'll be more than ready then. Heck, I'm ready now. Any news about Tony?"

Was there ever! She scarcely comprehended Tony's murderous tale herself, never mind telling anyone else. "No, we just got here but I...I'll check with the nurse while you and Becca visit."

The Neuro station nurse made a phone call. "He's still in ICU," she told Jennifer.

At ICU Jennifer identified herself to a nurse and explained her relationship to Tony. "One of his children is with him. He's a very sick man. We allow two visitors at a time, so I'll take you in."

They started down the hall of curtained cubicles but stopped when a flurry of activity ahead sent medical personnel scurrying to one of the patients. "Code Blue," one shouted and the nurse accompanying Jennifer hurried to help, leaving her standing awkwardly in the corridor.

As the others rushed into the cubicle, one woman stepped out and stood frozen while activity and commands punctuated the air from the curtained room. The woman looked familiar, but at this distance Jennifer couldn't be sure so she waited, uncertain what to do next. Then a nurse came from behind the curtain, put her arm around the woman and spoke to her.

Suddenly the woman collapsed in sobs and Jennifer hurried toward her. Approaching close enough to recognize Tony's grown daughter, she said, "Catherine? Honey, what is it?"

"He's *dead*," she sobbed. "Dad's *dead*. First Mom, then Dad — all in one week. I can't believe this. It's just too much." She buried her face against Jennifer's shoulder and wept as Jennifer tried to console her. When the crying lessened, Jennifer found a place for them to sit.

The doctor came out, shaking his head. "I'm so sorry," he said. "We had him stabilized, but I think the femur fracture he sustained in the car accident must have released bone marrow into his blood. This can cause a fat-embolism. The resulting clots travel up through the venous system to block the entrance to the lungs. When that happened, we couldn't stop it. We did everything medically possible to save him, but we can't control every outcome. All I can say is that we tried.... These things happen."

Catherine sobbed as the doctor and Jennifer exchanged looks and he left.

"Let's sit here a few minutes," Jennifer suggested. When Catherine quieted, she said, "Becca and I are visiting Jason in another ward. Would you like to spend a little time with us? Could we help you call your brothers about this?"

"Yes, thank you. Mom would be so glad you're here just when I need you most."

"Your mom was a wonderful person and my dear friend. It's the least I can do."

A nurse approached them. "You can go in now." She gestured to the curtained cubicle.

Catherine reached for Jennifer's hand. "Please, will you come with me?"

Steeling herself to view the man who told her he was a murderer, Jennifer put an arm around the grief-stricken girl. "Of course. Let's go in together."

290 - *Garage Sale Diamonds*

CHAPTER NINETY-SIX

TUESDAY, 7:03 PM

"**M**ay I have your car keys, Abdul?" Ahmed asked.

"But you told me you can't run the risk of driving. I can take you wherever you wish to go."

"You are correct I said this, but things have changed." Abdul looked nervous.

"Do you...have you had practice driving?"

"Of course. Choosing not to drive here was a matter of tactic, not skill."

"I...I planned to leave my extra keys with a note for my wife telling her to find the car here after the jihad. She will need it when I am gone."

"Don't worry, I will take good care of your car. Now, please, the keys."

Ahmed drove straight to Khadija's house, used the garage door opener and parked inside. Zayneb met him in the house. "Will you have dinner with us?"

"Yes, thank you."

He basked in the family atmosphere missing most of his life. He smiled at Safia, chatted with Zayneb and looked lovingly at Khadija. Heba seemed pleased to see him also. With time running out, he risked bolder conversation than in the past.

When Heba returned to the kitchen after serving them dinner, he asked Zayneb, "Do you know this woman's story?"

"She arrived here as my husband's servant, but she and I became friends. She said as a young child she visited relatives and for some reason stayed with them instead of returning to her family. Life was hard in that village so when an older man offered a dowry for her in marriage and a job for the father, as was custom in her country, they basically sold her to him when she was eight years old. He kept her for a time, but as a plaything not a wife. When he finished with her, he sold her to someone else. In both these cases she was raped and treated with scorn."

Ahmed blanched. "Life is sometimes cruel."

"The second owner sold her to the sex trade. Her life was unspeakable. One group smuggled her to the U. S., forcing her to work as a prostitute until someone bought her. Then she passed from owner to owner until Mahmud brought her to our household. She's had a horrible life, but she tells me the last twenty-four years here were the best since she was a child. She's intelligent. With my husband...away...she wants to get an education. I can help her do that. She has survival skills and shows an amazing spark of life, considering all she's been through."

"I see. Thank you for telling me this." They talked amiably as they finished their meal and at the end, Ahmed said, "May I speak privately with Khadija for a short while?"

They all looked at him in surprise but Khadija stood and nodded to him. "I'd like that. Shall we go into the study, Ahmed?"

Once seated there, Ahmed didn't know how to begin what he wanted to tell this beautiful woman about whom he cared so much. His future rode on what he said next.

"Khadija, tonight I speak from the heart. First, you must give me your oath you will never repeat what I'm about to tell you...to anyone...ever."

She looked puzzled. "I promise to tell no one else."

"You will hear good and bad things. Please remember, as I talk, that I love you and ask you to be my wife." She beamed. "You are the most intelligent, kind, remarkable person I have ever known. Your beauty encircles my heart. Your mind touches my thinking in ways I could not imagine possible. This is good news, but I also bring bad news. I share with you now secrets I have sworn to keep but cannot hide from you if our lives are to intertwine."

She smiled her love and reached out to hold his hand.

"Growing up, I knew only what others taught me, so I believed those teachings true and right. The man controlling my life groomed me to become a terrorist."

Khadija flinched at these words.

Ahmed rushed on before he lost his nerve.

"He and those around him convinced me and others like me that we were fighters for Allah, bravely escalating the coming of the one Islamic world. But you showed me terrorism is only one possibility in a larger group of choices. I do not want to blow up women and children even if they are infidels. I want to build, not destroy. I want to live, not die. I want to offer my love to you, to build a happy family like the one stolen from me by the leader, his liars and his murderers. I am a man at a crossroads, a man wanting to walk a new path with your hand in mine."

Khadija gave him a thin smile.

"Shall I stop now or do you wish to hear more?"

"I...I want to hear what you have to say."

"My job here is to lead a cell of terrorists on a jihad right here in northern Virginia. The Great Leader provided money to do this and men to accomplish it. If he heard me speak these words he would strike me dead himself or have others do it in the most painful way possible. They would think me too weak to carry out my task, a frightened coward afraid to sacrifice himself. Worse, they would label me a reviled traitor."

Khadija swallowed hard but said nothing.

"This is what I propose: I would like to defect, tell my story to the authorities and ask for the witness protection program. I would like to ask you to come with me as my bride. We could make a new life together in a new place. We could use our love to create precious children. We will teach them to 'question everything.' But this means you must leave your home and your family. You could not see them or communicate with them again, for our new location must remain forever a secret. Why? The all-powerful Great Leader will scour the earth to find and punish me. He ruthlessly eliminates those who embarrass him, defy his wishes or interfere with his plans."

Khadija's eyes filled with tears. She stared at her hands as he continued.

"Normally, a man offers the bride of his dreams positive rewards. Sadly, I offer you nothing positive...and, worse, I introduce risk and danger into your life along with my love and loyalty to you forever."

She cried softly, dabbing at her eyes with a tissue.

"I cannot blame you for choosing instead to continue a normal life with your mother and sister. I understand you may not love me enough to share this meager, uncertain life I offer you. Then I will disappear from your life, but wherever I am, you will always live in my soul."

Khadija now wept openly. He hated bringing such grief to the woman he loved, but only if she knew the truth could she make an informed choice.

He squeezed her hand. When she stopped crying enough to speak, she managed, "Ahmed, thank you for telling this incredible story. In the week since we first met, I found you an appealing person who I care very much about, but this future you describe...you're asking me to leave all that's familiar—plus everyone I know and love—for a life with you in which we're always looking over our shoulders for danger. That fear would increase for our children, who we'd never want harmed or at risk. Our strong attraction makes it seem we know each other well, but in only one week we're still more strangers than friends. Marrying someone under perfect circumstances is risky enough but under *these* circumstances..."

His eyes brimmed at the answer he'd feared. "I apologize for creating this impossible situation, but because of my love for you, I had to ask if you could make this difficult choice. You are right. You are young, beautiful and smart. You will find an American well-suited to you and live a good, safe life with your family's blessings. I wish you many children and great happiness."

He stood. "As for me..." he choked with emotion, "...no woman could ever measure up to you."

"I'm so sorry, Ahmed." She circled her arms around him and they stood, holding each other. After a moment, she broke away.

"Wait," he said. "Here is my cell phone number. If...if ever you want to reach me. I will answer it if I can. Also I have a strong warning for you and your family: Don't go to any shopping malls in three days—on Black Friday. Do you understand?"

She nodded, grateful at his parting gift— protecting her from danger.

He fought for composure. "I must speak now to your mother."

They walked to the dining room and found Zayneb. "I leave your house now. Good-bye and thank you for your kind hospitality."

Their eyes locked in a shared secret of their own about something hidden outside beneath a raised garden. "I will go upstairs to make sure I left nothing in my room."

When he drove away, determination alone prevented him from looking back.

Arriving at the motel, he thanked Abdul for the use of his car. Then, noticing Abdul's visible relief at seeing his vehicle returned intact, Ahmed added, "However, my friend, you would make a very bad camel trader."

CHAPTER NINETY-SEVEN

TUESDAY, 11:58 PM

Thunder rumbled in the distance as Adam crunched across the gravel parking area at the top of the driveway. Pushing open the barn door, he flipped on the light to locate a crowbar and ax. He tested the blade with his thumb. Not razor sharp but adequate for what he had in mind.

When he turned off the light, darkness closed in — almost as dark as last night when he and Hannah helped foil the kidnapping on the other side of their farm property. He glanced up at ominous clouds moving swiftly across the moon before blotting it from view. In the darkness, he felt the air freshen as the wind picked up. Branches in surrounding trees began to rustle and sway. Distant flickers of lightning accompanied a rising wind as the storm moved closer. The TV weatherman had forecasted severe thunderstorms tonight. Good, the countryside needed rain.

He remembered Nathan's warning: "Brush fires are a worry now in current drought conditions. Not only a problem for firefighters like me but for police like you who might need to evacuate residents from threatened homes." Considering the woodsy profile of this part of Fairfax County, Adam hoped the lightning fizzled fast but the rain poured hard.

Inside the house, he gazed lovingly at his sleeping bride before quietly closing the bedroom door and crossing the hall. A bright burst of lightning flashed outside the window shades as he counted one-one-hundred, two-one-hundred and three-one-hundred before a huge thunderclap rattled the windows. A close strike, only three miles away, if the old formula held true. Like most residences, theirs had no lightning rod, but knowing this wooden house had withstood over a hundred years of just such storms reassured him.

He moved quickly to the closet, climbed the stepladder positioned there, wiggled through the ceiling trapdoor access and again surveyed his childhood attic Punishment Room. He turned on the flashlight he'd left there yesterday, illuminating the claustrophobic wallboard enclosure. He focused the beam on the bloody four-digit handprint he'd made as a child when his mother shoved him up here after cutting off his little finger to punish spelling mistakes.

Though he saw no lightning through the makeshift room's four solid walls, the crashing rolls of thunder reverberated even louder in the attic as the storm stalled overhead. He'd felt pathetic gratitude at finding his mother's letter, proving she'd adored him once. That loving letter helped balance her later cruelty to him after she was driven insane by the monster she married.

Still, the memory of those horrible hours — those terrible days unable to defend himself as an abused child — welled over him, fueling anger at the injustice that took place here. He could let that tormented little boy escape by destroying this hated room now in a way he couldn't then. He lifted the ax and, using all his strength, hacked into one of the walls. The blade tore a long gash in the wallboard. A second blow widened the initial hole. After the third blow, he glimpsed some of the old attic on the other side. In a frenzy, he chopped and slashed at the wallboard until only the room's vertical studs remained.

As the resulting debris lay on the floor around him, he saw that someone had amateurishly planked the floor in this small area and erected a closed room around it with the closet's ceiling trapdoor the only access. His mother could not have built this. Maybe Tobias, or even his father? How many souls over how many generations had suffered punishment in this miserable hole? But he'd changed that. Nobody would ever suffer here again.

He had just squeezed through the destroyed room's studs into the larger attic, when he cringed involuntarily at an ear-splitting crash of thunder, so powerful the house shook beneath his feet. He steadied himself, clinging to a joist. He recalled his police training taught that when lightning strikes wood, the flow of current through it can splinter or shatter with such force the heat generated often ignites. Had a bolt struck the house? No. What was the chance of that?

In the larger attic, he swept his flashlight beam from one end of the old house to the other and across the floor. He stood a third of the distance from one end of the attic. He breathed in the ancient odor of long-abandoned space, as if he'd stepped backward through a time warp.

Attic insulation, once filling the spaces between the cross beams, spilled unevenly now across the floor, below beams in some places and over them in others. Walking across would be dicey. Adam stopped to sniff the air again. Something new, something beyond the stale attic odor he first noted. Maybe smoke? But the sight of an old trunk pushed against the rafters about twenty feet away caught his eye. He moved toward the eaves, hanging onto rafters for support as he moved clumsily across the trusses toward the trunk. But as he neared it, he sniffed again.

Yes, definitely smoke. He turned the flashlight beam toward the trapdoor. Although chunks of wallboard from his demolition efforts covered most of it, a wisp of smoke wafted through. He stared, immobile. Smoke meant fire.

Hannah.

Galvanized into action, he held onto rafter supports to retrace his steps across the beams. Pressing his way through the old room's skeletal studs, he kicked away the wreckage accumulated over the trapdoor. More smoke rose as he uncovered the opening. He cleared the hole and looked down, saw a smoke-filled room below, crouched on his hands and knees and dropped a leg through the ceiling opening to feel for the ladder.

Smoke choked him. By the time both feet settled on the top rung, the intense heat in the room forced him to scramble back into the attic. He slammed the trapdoor shut behind him.

Clearly he couldn't rescue Hannah from here, but if he got outside he could run around the house, break her bedroom window and pull her to safety.

He must make the right choices. Thin smoke hung in the attic now, increasing by the minute. If he could get to one end of the attic, maybe he could punch a hole in the gable vent, push it out and crawl through. He'd still have to drop fifteen feet to the ground but he would gladly venture that to save Hannah. He looked toward the vent at the end of the short distance but saw a tiny speck of flame licking at the attic insulation. He must go the long way instead.

Feeling for the rafters in the thickening brown-black smoke and coughing as its acrid chemicals stung his nose and lungs, he pulled off his shirt to tie around his lower face. He'd have a better chance if he could wet it but had no water. Remembering a wet-nap in his pocket, he tore its envelope open and pressed the damp paper over his nose and mouth inside the shirt-mask.

The smoke stung his eyes. He could barely see.

He groped his way in blackness along the rafters, measuring the truss distances in his mind and directing his unseen feet as best he could. Then he slipped. His foot drove through the insulation and sank through the ceiling of a room below. Searing heat caused him to jerk the foot up fast. He teetered on the cross beams, struggling to regain his balance and stumble onward.

Moving blindly in the smoke-filled attic, he forced himself mechanically from rafter to rafter, truss to truss, with no idea how far he had yet to go. His hands touched a solid wall. He'd reached the end of the attic. Now, to find the gable vent. He felt along the wall for the octagonal shape. Touching it, he pushed hard but it wouldn't budge. He'd need brute force to punch it out. He'd have to draw lungfuls of super-heated air to fuel that effort, a luxury he didn't have. This way out would become oxygen's way in, oxygen that would fuel the fire. The scorching smoke burned his lungs when he breathed.

His mind knew what he needed to do, but his body wouldn't respond.

He kicked at the vent with his last shred of strength and lucidity. To his amazement, the rotted wood around it gave way as a chunk the size of a door fell outward toward the ground. Air rushed in through this opening, sucked by the ravenous fire. He felt energy radiation rocket across the ceiling above him as the instant rush of heat and flame blended into a super-heated force igniting the space. In a horrific flashover explosion, the entire attic burst afire in a split-second conflagration.

The blast's powerful concussion hurled Adam's body out into the black night.

DAY SEVEN

WEDNESDAY

CHAPTER NINETY-EIGHT

WEDNESDAY, 12:32 AM

As Adam lay unconscious on the ground beside the burning house, sirens filled the air. Pieces of the burning structure fluttered down around him, one chunk landing on his arm.

McLean Volunteer Fire Department's ladder truck and ambulance appeared first on the scene. Aware of this fire's remote location, they called the Great Falls tanker for needed water. The firefighters arrived prepared, unloaded quickly, readied their equipment and got to work.

The lead medic jumped out of his vehicle to find Hannah sobbing hysterically in the driveway.

"Anyone inside the house?"

"My husband!" she wailed. "I don't know where he is. What if he's burning up in there?" Sobs shook her.

The medic grabbed her shoulders. "Ma'am, you need to calm down. We need your information *right now* to find your husband. Tell me exactly what happened."

"We were asleep in the bedroom. The lightning strike sounded like an explosion. The whole house shook. I woke up terrified. He wasn't in bed beside me or in the bedroom or the bathroom. I screamed for him down the hall but he didn't answer. The fire spread so fast I couldn't go after him. I climbed out a window and came straight to the driveway because we said we'd meet here in case of fire and..." she wept again, "*and he isn't here.*"

"Could he have left in the car?" They hurried to the barn and found both vehicles there.

"Okay, then. We'll try to get people inside and send someone to look around outside. What's your water source here? Do you have a pond?"

"Just a well, but that's not enough water for what you need."

"A tanker's already here and we've called other stations for more. Meantime, you stay put here in the ambulance. Don't leave. We have no time to look for you, too. Hear me?"

"Yes." She fought tears. "Oh, find my husband, *please* find Adam."

They all knew what to do and hurried to their tasks.

"A tree caught fire right next to the house," reported one fireman. "If it spreads to the woods we have a major problem. Do we need Brush Trucks?" He referred to large pickup trucks loaded with hand tools and small water pumps to deal with fire that spread to trees and ground cover.

"Not yet," came the answer. "It's just the one tree closest to the house right now. But we could use another tanker. They can refill at fireplugs along the main road. The storm brought plenty of lightning but no rain here. The adjacent woods are bone dry. We need to contain this blaze. At least the wind died. That helps."

Another firefighter hustled over. "This old place is a tinderbox, a hundred percent on fire. We got our men out, but nobody else could survive inside. Hope the husband got out."

"The overgrown bushes make it tougher to get near the house, never mind that radiant heat. We got guys looking for him in both directions."

Despite protective clothing, one fireman dodged fiery "floaters" as he trudged outside as close as heat and shrubbery allowed. Experience told him the missing man's chance for survival was poor from a fast-moving, roaring fire like this one. Didn't the wife call him Adam?

When the first smoke entered the air, the firefighter thought, the room where Adam stood would have contained twenty-one percent oxygen, allowing him to think clearly. But as thickening smoke displaced oxygen and that level dropped, Adam would become disoriented, as if drunk. Worse, when smoke increased and oxygen diminished, heat soared, often to several hundred degrees. Besides a fire's damage to a human body's exterior, breathing heated air singed the respiratory system inside.

The aged, dry wood in this house burned so hard from every angle that unless Adam had found a way out, he was cooked.

Glancing toward the roof, the fireman noticed a chunk missing from the triangular wall at the end of the attic. His eye followed its trajectory to the ground below.

"I think I found him," he said into the microphone clipped on his gear. The radio pack in his chest pocket beamed the message to the rest. Forcing his way through thorny bushes, he pushed aside smoldering debris and knelt beside Adam.

Seeing the hypoxic blue lips and comatose state, the medic feared he was dead. But when he checked, the man showed very weak vital signs. Smoke inhalation or fire-seared lungs made it hard to guess if recovery was even possible. Some fire casualties appeared undamaged on the outside but smoke inhalation killed them. His job: try to keep him alive until they reached the hospital.

Hannah waited at the ambulance. When two firefighters hurried a yellow-and-black stretcher around one end of the house, she jumped to her feet. Would Adam's charred body come next?

She steeled herself for the worst.

Moments later, the two firemen rushed the stretcher to the place Adam lay, heaved his dead weight onto it and carried him to the ambulance. They worked in sync, wasting not a second in strapping on an oxygen mask, attaching a BP cuff on his arm and pulse-oximeter on his finger, starting IVs and treating his burns.

"Oh my God," Hannah cried in anguish, staring at her deathly still husband and his raw burns. "Is he dead? Can you save him?"

"We'll do all we can. Then Fairfax Hospital ER takes over." He turned to the next firefighter. "Do we take him to Medstar for the burns or Fairfax ER? They're about equidistant."

"Only one looks third degree. I say Fairfax."

"Okay."

"Could I ride with him?" Hannah pleaded. The medic considered the hour, the rural location and the seriousness of the victim's condition. Poor kids, he thought.

"We're driving the bigger unit tonight so I think there's room, but only if you promise to stay out of our way while we work on him."

"I promise," she pledged.

"Then get in here. Let's go."

The door slammed shut and sirens filled the air as the vehicle whisked down the long driveway and, once at the road, zoomed toward their destination.

CHAPTER NINETY-NINE

WEDNESDAY, 3:34 AM

Wakened from a sound sleep by the chirping phone, Jennifer fumbled for the receiver. "Mom, I'm sorry to bother you in the middle of the night but...but I had to. Are you awake?"

"Hannah, what is it?"

"It's so awful, Mom, I can hardly say it."

Jennifer sat up, wide awake. "Honey, take a deep breath and tell me."

"Lightning struck our house in the big thunderstorm and it...it burned to the ground."

"Oh, Hannah. Are...are you both okay?"

"I am, but Adam fell out of the attic and while unconscious he couldn't push away some burning stuff that fell on his arm. We're at Fairfax Hospital now. The firemen saved him, but he broke his right leg and three ribs in the fall and has lots of small burns plus the big one on his arm. And his throat and lungs may be burned inside. They say it's a miracle he survived. Mom...oh, Mom...he's going to be *okay*."

"Precious Hannah, you must be in shock. But you're alive. Did you lose everything in the fire?"

"We hadn't moved in much furniture, just one bedroom and some kitchen stuff, but it's all gone plus our clothes. They saved the barn so we still have our cars."

"Have you had time to think what you'll do next?"

"Adam's sleeping so we haven't talked it over yet, but I guess we'll move back into his bachelor apartment in McLean. I'll have to scramble together some bedroom furniture and linens to replace what we lost. Otherwise, the rest of his apartment is still furnished."

"Have you told Adam's mother yet?"

"No, it's the middle of the night and he's going to be all right, so no point in waking her up. But I had to call you."

"You did exactly the right thing, Honey. Do you want me to come be with you?"

"No, you've had enough trauma lately. There's a reclining chair in Adam's hospital room. I'll sleep there tonight. They gave me a pillow and blanket. I want to be near if he needs me."

"I understand. Is your car there?"

"No, that's another thing. I'll need a ride home but I don't know when he'll get out."

"Well, that's easy. I get Dad tomorrow so when he's released, you can ride back with us."

"Oh, this is so embarrassing. With all that's happened I forgot Dad's even here in another ward."

"Dad was very lucky, Hannah, because Mr. D didn't make it."

"He's dead?"

"I'm afraid so. His children lost both parents in less than a week."

"Oh no. How awful." Silence. "But Mom, I just realized...we almost did too."

"What do you mean?"

"Well, Dad in the car wreck and you...shot by a sniper."

"Gee, you're right. I hadn't put it together that way."

"Sorry to wake you up, Mom, but hearing your voice helped me a lot tonight. It always does."

"I'm always here for you, Sweetie. Now try to get some sleep. Tomorrow will be a busy day."

"And a happy day, too, since we're all alive."

"Amen! Night, Honey."

"Night, Mom. I love you."

"Love you, too, Hannah."

CHAPTER ONE-HUNDRED

WEDNESDAY, 8:03 AM

"**Y**ou're back, I see," Veronika said to her younger half-sister. "To what do I owe this honor?"

"Perhaps because I miss my family ties?" Anna answered.

"Perhaps..." Veronika's voice sounded dubious.

"The...real estate business...has been very good to me recently," Anna volunteered, thinking of the nice bonus due soon for arranging the Islamic connection for her Russian arms-dealing friend. "So good that I brought you a special present." She placed a box in her sister's hands.

Veronika eyed her warily. Not typical for Anna to appear considerate, let alone generous. She knew her sister still resented their father willing his estate to his first child, property she knew Anna coveted for herself.

Veronika opened the box. Inside lay a small, silver ornately-engraved pistol. Beneath the gun she found a smaller box of bullets. Veronika looked at Anna, eyebrows raised in a question.

"It's an antique," Anna said, stopping herself from adding *just like you.*

"Are you concerned for my safety?"

"Well, you're isolated out here on the estate and your staff dwindled to nothing in recent years. When I found this unique piece of history, I thought you might value a treasure that's also practical."

"History?"

"Yes, the dealer says it belonged to Catherine the Great."

"Hmmm. She had an intriguing career, so it must have served her well."

Anna's polite laugh had a nervous edge. "You have plenty of room here on the estate for target practice, so become proficient if you like."

"Good advice and thank you, Anna, for the present. Will you stay long this time?"

"No, in fact I have a very busy day ahead—a big project to oversee before five o'clock. I'll leave in a few minutes, but I had to pick up a few things here at the house. I can't spend Thanksgiving with you because I'll be out of town on Thursday."

"Don't worry about me. I have an invitation to join friends tomorrow."

"Good. Then I'll say goodbye for now. Enjoy your gift."

As she walked away, the click of her high heels echoed in the hallway of the large house. Then a door closed, followed by silence.

While she had no vision to confirm this, Veronika felt instinctively uncomfortable about her sister. She sensed the girl dabbled in something dangerous but exhilarating, certainly not real estate. Though she wasn't close to this blood relative, she felt empathy for anyone living on the edge of peril—a high price to pay for whatever rewards the risky thrill brought.

Staring at the pistol, Veronika mused. Was this gift to buy forgiveness for her behavior or had Anna a sinister reason for arming her sister? Did she plan a shoot-out with Veronika in which Anna alone would survive to sue for ownership of the estate she envied and desired?

Veronika waited for insight but smelled no lilacs.

But enough of Anna. Veronika picked up the pistol. It fit her hand perfectly. Lightweight and small, it could slip into a purse or a pocket. Perhaps Catherine the Great had tucked it into her bodice for quick access.

Veronika aimed the gun. Hard to resist pulling the trigger. She hadn't checked to see if bullets were inside. She didn't know how to open it to find out.

But before the day ended, she would.

CHAPTER ONE-HUNDRED ONE

WEDNESDAY, 9:31 AM

"Oh, Adam, what an experience? How do you feel?" Jennifer asked the next day, eyeing his cast and bandaged arm.

"Glad to be alive, a fact I owe to my firefighter brothers and this hospital's doctors. Want to sign my cast?"

"You bet I do. You say they're discharging you today?" Jennifer looked surprised.

Hannah grinned. "Yes, apparently he was super lucky. They think he can heal at home as well as in the hospital, with a few doctor visits thrown in."

"You've heard the phrase, 'it only hurts when I laugh?'" He pointed to his ribs. "Well, it's true."

"Then take it easy at home to heal faster. I'll pick up Dad and we'll meet you in the lobby."

Jennifer hurried to the Neuro ward, found Jason ready to go, received last minute instructions from the nurse and they were off. In the elevator she told her husband about the fire and who would ride home with them.

Jason absorbed this news. "My God, it's always something with this family." He shook his head and changed the subject. "Let me know how I can help get ready for tomorrow's event. You've turned this holiday into quite a party. Can we handle thirty people?"

"Guess we're going to find out."

She drove her car from the lot to the front door. The rest climbed in. "First stop Sally's house?"

"We have no bedroom furniture there," Hannah admitted. "Could we stay with you tonight?"

"Yes, but the other out-of-town kids come tomorrow night, so let's try to locate some furniture for you today. Maybe from this morning's *Washington Post* classified or craigslist? Or maybe you'd prefer shopping at furniture stores."

"I don't think so," Adam volunteered. "With the farmhouse gone, my plan to subdivide the property and build our house speeds up. While this leg heals, I won't be on duty for awhile, so I'll have time to plot that out even sooner. Since we don't know how to furnish the new house yet, good used furniture makes sense now. Luckily, my laptop was in my car."

"If you have your keys, "Jason said, "why don't we go by the farm now to get your cars? Hannah could drive one and I'll bring the other. I think we'd all like to see the aftermath."

As they pulled up the long, overgrown driveway, Jennifer shivered, feeling an unpleasant déjà vu, because this part of the property looked exactly as it had the night she escaped Ruger Yates. But when they reached the gravel parking area at the top, her apprehension fell away.

While the barn showed scorch marks from floaters, the house existed no longer; only remains of jagged, charred wood that once had been walls surrounded the water-logged burn debris. Here and there a glimpse inside the basement's concrete shell showed where portions of damaged upper floor collapsed through.

They stood in funereal silence, comparing what once had been to what it had become.

Jason hugged Hannah, who sniffled, "We had such plans..."

Adam put an arm around her, "...and we still do, Honey. This old house was always a temporary step. Fate just cheated a demolition company out of taking it down."

"Will you keep the basement footprint for your new house?" Jennifer asked.

"Too early to make that decision," Adam said, "but I doubt it. I think we want to put the past behind and start brand new."

Hannah hugged her husband. "Good idea."

The sound of tires on gravel drew their attention as a car sped up the driveway. A man got out.

"Hello," he said. "You taking a gawk at the fire scene, too? It's my third time up here. We might even be on TV if the stations come to film while we're here. A fire like this is news in McLean."

The others exchanged looks. Adam weighed the intrusion and its liability implications.

"Did you know this is private property?" Adam asked.

Hands on hips, the man shook his head. "Hell, nobody lives here. Place was abandoned before it burned to the ground. It's a neighborhood spectacle now. Lots of curious people already came and will keep coming. It's public domain now."

"Actually, it isn't." Adam explained. "I'm the owner and only people I invite are welcome on my land. The property is posted 'No Trespassing' so you're actually here illegally."

Uncomfortable now, the man became defensive. "Unless you're going to camp right here to wave them off, you better get used to the idea that you're going to get a lot of rubber-neckers."

"I appreciate your letting me know about this."

"Yeah, well, if you're the owner, were you here during the fire?"

"Thanks for asking but that's privileged information. Please tell all your friends this is still private property. They can come only if I invite them, but I'm not inviting anybody now."

The man harrumphed. "Well, if you want to be rude about it..."

"Not rude, sir, just explaining this is private property. Can you find your way back to the road?"

Rebuffed, the man grudgingly strode to his car and, tires spewing gravel, drove away.

"In the barn, do you have what I need to block the driveway?" Jason asked.

"I think so." Adam turned to Hannah and Jennifer. "Could you two transform a piece of wood into a sign saying 'Private Property, No Trespassing'?"

"You bet." Jennifer reached into her purse. "Here's a magic marker."

Half an hour later, a chain attached to metal posts stretched across the farm's driveway entrance at the road. No one could mistake the message on the sign dangling from the chain's links.

CHAPTER ONE-HUNDRED TWO

WEDNESDAY, 10:06 AM

As Jennifer served them lunch, Hannah asked, "Mom, now that I'm running my own household, I'd like to know how you plan a meal for thirty people."

She tented her fingers under her chin. "Let me see...I guess it takes seven steps. First, you need places for people to sit; second: table decorations; third: menu; fourth: buy food; fifth, prepare food; sixth: serve; and last: clean-up."

"How about number eight?" Jason smiled. "Selecting, buying, uncorking and serving the wines?"

"You're right, Jay. By the way, I bought all the wines on your list. The cases are in the garage."

"So, what stage are you in now, Mom?" Becca wanted to know.

"Well, three stages today: some food purchase, some food preparation and some decorating."

"How can we help?"

"Why don't I write a to-do list so you can choose what you want? One item will be a grocery run to pick up turkeys and last-minute perishables. Another is assembling tables and chairs, which involves some furniture rearranging before setting those tables. That plus a few make-ahead dishes and voila!...this day will evaporate before you know it."

After lunch when the others busied themselves with to-do's, Jennifer said, "Jay, why don't you lie down a few minutes? The nurse said you should rest and...well, I'd like to talk about something."

"Uh-oh, it's another phrase that strikes fear in my heart. Can my concussion withstand this?" he joked, but with a nervous edge.

"I hope so." They went upstairs, where he relaxed on the bed and she sat beside him. "It's about Tony. I know he's dead, but his problem isn't, and I don't know what to do." She repeated their neighbor's startling ICU room confession. "And then Celeste found this hidden in Tony's closet and showed it to me yesterday. We decided to get it out of his house so his children wouldn't find it. Good thing we did." She unveiled the bulletin board. They both stared, speechless.

Finally Jason spoke. "There's more to this than you know. Tony shot right at me on the hunting trip, not once but three times. Jen, he tried to kill me. If we hadn't hit the deer on the way home, I would have had to turn him in. Who knows what he'd try next?"

"Seriously? My God, Jay. His imagined relationship with me drove him to kill his wife to free him...and to kill you to free me."

Jason studied her. "Was it an imagined relationship?"

She turned quickly. "You mean could he have mistaken my friendship for something more?"

To Jason's questioning look she said testily, "Wait a minute, isn't this called 'blaming the victim'?"

"Just trying to understand the situation."

"The situation to understand is Tony murdered Kirsten and tried to kill you, twice, once with the gun and then with the truck. What...what should we do with this information?"

Jason shook his head. "I guess we tell Adam. He's the detective."

They pondered this a few minutes. Finally, Jennifer shook her head. "I'm thinking about his children. They're distraught at losing their parents. If they learn their father killed their mother and tried to kill a neighbor, won't it destroy them, Jay?"

"But we have proof."

"Do we? The only real evidence is this bulletin board. Nobody witnessed what he told me in the ICU. Kirsten's cremation eliminates the pentobarbital evidence. He's already dead, so the law can't punish him any further."

"What are you saying, Jen?"

"I'm saying maybe one option is to reveal nothing."

"*What?*"

"Was Tony a Jekyll/Hyde person? By day, he was the good vet with an enthusiastic following, a nice neighbor, a good father and a well-liked contributor to his community. By night, he had an aberrant blind spot about an imagined, deluded love affair that didn't exist."

"You're really into this scenario, aren't you?"

Ignoring him, she continued. "If we tell nobody, his orphaned children have decent memories of their parents and the community mourns the loss of a fine vet, which he was. In a way, you might say justice has already been served since his crimes led to his death. What do you think?"

"I think you're totally insane. What's worse, I can actually follow your reasoning, which means I'm insane too. So this would be our secret?"

"If that's what we decide. Any other ideas about it, Jay?" He shook his head. "Then shall we vote? Thumbs up or thumbs down?"

"You use two hands and I use one?" he laughed.

Jennifer joined in. "So are we co-conspirators furthering the greater good?"

"How have I lived with you all these years and remained sane?" he wondered aloud. "It's a good thing for you that I have a concussion and am not thinking clearly because I vote thumbs up with both hands, too. That means four thumbs for conspiracy."

She threw her arms around him and planted kisses on his smiling lips.

He whispered in her ear. "I like the way you seal a bargain."

CHAPTER ONE-HUNDRED THREE

WEDNESDAY, 1:37 PM

"Put the explosives over here," Ahmed instructed as he supervised the Russians delivering weaponry at the warehouse. His phone rang. "Here, Abdul, take over please while I answer." "Hello."

"Ahmed, it's Khadija. I...I thought about our talk and...and I'd like to know more of your plan."

"I will come right over." Assuming a business-like expression, he said to Abdul, "I must borrow your car again. Please oversee the remaining delivery. I will return very soon."

Abdul scowled but produced the keys. Ahmed drove directly to Khadija's house.

She met him at her front door. "Come, let's sit in the study."

"You want to know more of my plan? Have you spoken of this with anybody else, dear one?" She shook her head.

"I've thought it all out. I plan to begin the defection process this afternoon. If all goes well and if you chose to go with me, I would return for you tomorrow. I would call before I come to get you. For your own protection, I don't think I should tell you more unless...unless you want to start this new life with me."

He looked inquiringly into her expressive hazel eyes. Her serious expression dampened his hope she would share his future.

"Khadija? Have you made a decision?"

She spoke with difficulty. "Yes, I have."

"What is it?"

"I would like to come with you, Ahmed."

"Praise Allah, peace be upon His name," he cried. "Oh thank you, beloved Khadija, for your brave and loving choice."

In a spontaneous move, he embraced her. But his mind swam with surprise as much as desire when she lifted her lips to gently brush his mouth.

CHAPTER ONE-HUNDRED FOUR

WEDNESDAY, 2:13 PM

Ahmed parked at the McLean police station on Balls Hill Road. The fewer people who saw what he did now, the better. He searched for prying eyes before going inside, for the Great Leader's tentacles entwined everywhere. Might he have placed a sleeper in the Fairfax County Police force? Ahmed must stay alert. Every step involved terrible risk.

Without ID papers or a driver's license, he knew he couldn't drive into Homeland Security's compound, though that was his destination. His entire future depended upon making the right choices now. He needed another way in.

"Hello," he said into the lobby phone indicated by the man behind the glass window. "I would like to speak to the highest ranking officer here today. This is urgent. Can you help me?"

"Your name?" asked the uniform. Ahmed told him. "What's the problem so I know how to direct your inquiry?"

Ahmed cleared his throat, buying time to think of the answer. "It is a personal matter. The timing is urgent. I must talk now with the officer I mentioned."

"Just a minute," the uniform said.

Ahmed watched him speak into another phone. He knew the uniform noted his accent and Middle-Eastern features. He understood too well their reason to proceed with caution.

The policeman behind the window gestured impatiently as he spoke words unheard in the lobby. A moment later a policeman came through the door and said, "What can I do for you, Sir?"

This man was young, not an experienced, silver-haired veteran who'd heard it all. "This is a serious matter I cannot discuss in the lobby. Can we please talk in a private place?"

The policeman shot a guarded look toward his associate behind the glass window. "There's nobody here right now, so this is a private place, Sir."

Ahmed's disappointment showed. "Perhaps I made a mistake in coming here. I thought you would help me." He stood to leave.

"I want to help you, but first I need to know your problem."

This seemed reasonable. Ahmed sat again. "I need to speak immediately with Homeland Security. I know details of a terrorist attack planned very soon. I risked my life to come here. If other operatives see me here, I am a dead man. Please get me out of this lobby fish bowl."

The policeman read a mix of determination and fear on Ahmed's face. Probably a crank, but you never knew. The word "terrorist" meant he'd have to hear him out.

"Come with me." The policeman led the way through the door to an interrogation room, flipping on the light as they entered. "We can talk here. Have a seat." They faced each other across a small table. "I am Officer Eatmon. What is your name?"

Ahmed told him. "My name means nothing to you nor will it to Homeland Security, but my knowledge has crucial value for them. In your newspaper, I read that county and federal governments share information in emergency situations. You are county and Homeland Security is federal, but you can contact them to talk to me. This is correct? They must talk to me tonight to stop this horror from happening only days away. It is, as you say, Flash Red."

Officer Eatmon looked confused a moment then brightened. "You mean Code Red?"

"That is it, Code Red." Ahmed looked relieved. "You understand, then."

Eatmon searched the man's face. No question that he believed what he said, but that didn't make it true. "Excuse me a minute."

The officer left, closing the door behind him. In the next room he picked up a phone, consulted his Rolodex and dialed a number.

"Hello, is this Steve Wolf ?... Ken Eatmon here, Steve. How do you like working over at the new spook building?... Yeah, pretty much the same here at the station since you left, but here's something that might interest you. I got a guy here says he knows all about a terrorist attack in a few days. He looks scared enough and says he's dead if the terrorists find him. He asked to talk to the highest-ranking person at the station, which happens to be me right now. I could have called the official Homeland number on our list but thought I'd run it past you first....

"No, he looks Middle-Eastern but clean-shaven, regular haircut, good English but foreign accent.... I'd say thirty to thirty-five, but I can ask his age if you want.... Yeah, he's a hundred percent believable or I wouldn't call.... No, he says it's urgent. Code Red, he says.... Do I bring him there or you come here?...You want the conference room? Okay, see you in ten."

Officer Eatmon returned to Ahmed. "They're sending some people from Homeland Security in ten minutes. You want coffee, a soda or water while you're waiting? Water? Okay, we'll wait for them in a bigger room. Follow me."

CHAPTER ONE-HUNDRED FIVE

WEDNESDAY, 3:03 PM

Steve Wolf arrived with three associates. Introductions over, he asked, "May I call you Ahmed?"

He nodded.

"How can we help you?"

"I wish to trade detailed information about terrorist attacks coming very soon in northern Virginia and elsewhere in exchange for safety in your witness protection program—safety for me and my fiancé, an American in McLean."

"The witness protection program?"

"My fiancé and I wish to start a new life as Americans somewhere in the United States."

"But you said she is an American."

Ahmed smiled. "You are correct. I should have said I wish to start a new life as an American with my American fiancé somewhere in the United States. Can you provide this for the two of us?"

Steve and the men with him exchanged looks. Now that he'd delivered himself to their control, they each mentally reviewed their options: arrest him, interrogate him, imprison him; maybe even turn him, creating a mole to feed vital information until his own people discovered his duplicity and killed him. Meantime, they'd use a different strategy.

"Let's say we agree to this. How do we know your information is true?"

"You have already arrested seven of my men, two at a bank, two at a McLean woman's house and three in a field with a boy. If you accept my plan, you will soon arrest more whose names and locations I provide, thus wiping out my entire cell. In the process, you prevent a terrible calamity."

"How many more are there?"

"Eleven besides me in this area; more elsewhere."

"And if we don't agree?"

"My lawyers will hand-deliver my letter to a certain famous reporter at *The Washington Post*. It says I am going to warn Homeland Security about the disaster. If I do not contact him within thirty-six hours, my lawyer delivers the letter. The attack you don't know about will take place in your back yard, showing the public your organization's incompetence. If you agree to my trade, your signed document assuring me witness protection will stay in his vault until I contact him in one month that my new life is in position. I will contact him each month thereafter to ensure you don't change your mind."

"And you need this protection because..."

"The Great Leader will post a fatwa for my life the moment he learns I meet you today. Even without his direction, my own cellmates would turn on me like jackals. In my country, what I do now is unthinkable."

"This is a serious, life-altering change for you. How did you decide to break from them?"

"My fiancé showed me that murdering defenseless people doesn't glorify God; it shames him."

"And how did you decide to come to us?"

"Because my wife-to-be and I believe my god wants us to live long, peaceful, productive lives. We want children and a safe life for them. That future is impossible without the trade I propose."

"You want to defect?"

"Yes."

"Have you told anyone else your plan?"

"No, we wanted to avoid danger for her family when we're gone. The Great Leader will learn *what* happened but not *how*. With no one left to tell, he won't know who to punish."

Steve stood up. "Will you excuse us for a moment?"

Ahmed nodded.

When the men returned, Steve faced Ahmed and nodded. "We like what you've told us. We want to know more. Let's talk further at our building."

Ahmed lifted a warning hand. "You must know more before we go. If I fail to appear somewhere in two hours, the others will know something is wrong. If I fail to appear at all, they will consult the Great Leader, who could accelerate or alter our current plans. I guarantee my information only if I continue to lead my cell. Timing is critical. You must hide my defection with an accident in which I appear to die. This must happen tomorrow, on your Thanksgiving Day. Can you do this? If not, we have no more reason to talk. I have been trained to withstand brutal interrogation."

Steve and the others looked uncomfortable. Reading their faces, Ahmed added, "Look, I came to cooperate. I bring you a well-designed plan, in which you stop multi-terrorist acts, arrest the men involved and fake my death to avoid the Great Leader's reprisals. *I hand you this ready-made plan.* You need only to say yes."

"Yes," Steve said suddenly.

As they prepared to leave, he turned to Ahmed. "Just out of curiosity, how did you come up with the ideas of faking your death and stashing documents with a lawyer for insurance?"

Ahmed smiled. "I saw it on American TV."

CHAPTER ONE-HUNDRED SIX

WEDNESDAY, 4:53 PM

Ahmed pulled up to the warehouse, found Abdul and returned his keys. "Thank you. Are all the weapons on the list accounted for?" He nodded. "Then today's work is finished. Well done."

Anna walked up to Ahmed, extending her hand. "Good to do business with you. Until next time."

As she left, all male eyes followed her well-formed body as she clicked across the warehouse on her stiletto heels, climbed into her sports car and zoomed away.

Abdul and Ahmed locked the warehouse and returned to the motel. They'd kept their relationship at a business level, so Abdul felt surprise when Ahmed asked, "Would you like to say goodbye to your family tonight?"

"I'll do that tomorrow."

"Then I will use your car to bring in the meals tonight and afterward for a brief errand."

Feeling trapped into this, Abdul didn't respond. They drove to the motel in silence.

On the drive into Vienna to buy the eleven dinners, Ahmed phoned Khadija. "May I join your family for dinner tonight? I have news." Breathless, she agreed.

After delivering meals to the motel, Ahmed drove to the house. Zayneb greeted him warmly.

As they ate, Safia asked, "Do you know when my Baba comes back from his trip?"

"No, I don't." Instead he asked, "Do you have holiday vacation now?" The child nodded.

"And you, Khadija?" They smiled at their secret: her work vacation wouldn't matter, for tomorrow they'd be on the way to their future.

"Yes, vacation for me also," she said.

As Heba replenished the vegetables, Ahmed said to her, "This food is very good." Again, she gave a brief nod and flicker of a smile as she modestly averted her face. What was it about this woman that puzzled him? If he could look squarely into her face...but he saw no polite way to do so.

As Khadija passed him the sauce, the bowl slipped from his hand, and the contents splashed across the front of his shirt. He pushed back his chair, gathered up what he could in his napkin and blotted the rest with napkins handed him by the others.

On her feet, Khadija said, "Come into the kitchen. Take off your shirt so we can wash out the spot in the sink and put it in the dryer. You'll have it back like new very soon." He followed her.

Had they been alone in the kitchen, they might have embraced, but Heba stood at the sink. One look at Ahmed's shirt and she understood the problem, took the shirt he handed her and began to wash the stain.

As she did, the other two stepped across the kitchen, where Ahmed whispered to Khadija, "We're all set for tomorrow evening at six. Drive your car to the community center near the library in McLean. Bring only two suitcases and..."

His words were cut short by a gasp behind him.

He and Khadija spun around to see what had happened. Heba stood in shock, her eyes wide, her mouth forming an "O," her finger pointing at Ahmed. They hurried over to her.

"What is it, Heba?" Khadija asked with concern.

"*You*..." Heba spoke the first word any of them had ever heard her say; indeed, it was the first word anyone had heard her speak since her cousins sold their eight-year-old relative.

Khadija and Ahmed exchanged startled looks. Heba pointed to herself and said, "Amina. I...am...Amina."

Ahmed frowned in confusion. He stepped closer, looking straight into Heba's face for the first time. Green eyes stared back at him.

"Amina?" he exclaimed in disbelief. "Can this be *true?* Is it you, my sister?" They clutched each other like the two children they'd been, twins lost to each other all these years. Amina wept with happiness while Ahmed swiped away his own tears of relief.

Hearing the commotion, Zayneb and Safia hurried to the kitchen.

Oblivious to the others in the room, Ahmed spoke only to Amina. "But how did you know?"

"The red mark on your shoulder, the one our Baba said Allah drew to show your importance to him. I could never forget it because I longed for one also to show my importance to Allah. I added this to some things I overheard and...I just knew."

Zayneb took Amina's hands in hers. "You can speak. How is this possible?"

"When Ahmed arrived a week ago the voice sounds began to return. I practiced saying words in my room and...now I can speak again." Her face beamed.

"It's a miracle," Zayneb said to Khadija.

"Only one of many miracles today," Khadija replied, her eyes sparkling.

DAY EIGHT

THURSDAY

CHAPTER ONE-HUNDRED SEVEN

THURSDAY, 6:01 AM

Jennifer pressed the clock alarm "off " button, jumped from bed and hurried downstairs in her pajamas. She started the coffee maker, assembled stuffing ingredients and pulled out the two big turkeys. They must be in the ovens by seven to roast in time for the meal.

Jason sauntered in a few minutes later to unwrap and rinse the turkeys before settling them into roasting pans to await stuffing. "How did you sleep, Hon?"

"Very well. I was really tired last night. How's your concussion this morning?"

"Completely normal."

"You're sure?" She looked at him with concern. He nodded. "That's wonderful news because we have lots to do today."

"Just give me commands and I'll be your devoted servant. That's DS for short."

She laughed. "How about bringing in the morning paper then, DS?"

When he returned, they slid the stuffed turkeys into heated ovens at 6:59. "Right on schedule," Jason said; "steady as she goes."

Jennifer turned suddenly, considering him with new eyes. That phrase seemed a perfect metaphor: his level-headedness kept the ocean-liner-of-their-lives on course, no matter the storm. He'd become an accomplished ship's captain, inventing hands-on how to foil what came along during their forty-one years together. Moreover, his balanced approach to threatening waves allowed her latitude for more whimsical pursuits.

He even gripped the wheel bravely when rogue waves smashed them broadside, like Ruger Yates a year ago, and now, this diamond fiasco.

She crossed the room, put her arms around his shoulders and kissed him. "I love you very much," she whispered.

"Whatever brought that on, have some more." He winked and squeezed her hand.

"Jay, an idea came to me in the night."

"Geez, here we go again. Remember I'm in recovery, just home from the hospital. Be gentle."

"Not an idea so much as an intuition," she added.

He hung his head as if waiting for the next blow. "I'm afraid to ask," he mumbled to himself, then raised his head and smiled. "Okay, let's hear it."

"I don't think our family should mention the diamonds to our guests at today's party. I can't give you a logical explanation and I know it's on all our minds, but it's a strong feeling. If you agree, should we tell them so we're all on the same page before company comes?"

"I see no reason but don't object. If it makes you more comfortable, that's what we'll do. By the way, when *do* the guests arrive?"

"I told them one o'clock to get acquainted before the meal at 1:30." Of course, the kids and Grands will drift in throughout the morning. You shouldn't exert too much the next few days, so when some of those strong, young men arrive, ask them to help you bring in the tables and chairs."

Becca shuffled into the kitchen. "Did I hear the phrase 'strong, young men'? I'm a girl in my prime tuned for compatibles."

"Morning, Becca. I meant to ask you: How were the Donnegan kids when you took over the dinner we sent last night?" Jennifer asked.

"Sad but pragmatic. Besides planning the funeral, they met with their lawyer yesterday about the estate and need to decide what to do with the house."

"Did you invite them to our Thanksgiving?"

"Yes, but they said no. Understandably, they're not feeling too thankful...and not up to dealing with a happy crowd."

Hannah strolled into the kitchen and they heard the rhythmic thump of crutches descending the stairs behind her. "Hello all," she said. "Adam had a bad night. Guess the painkillers wore off. We'll grab a quick breakfast, then dash over to Sally's so I can get the bedroom settled before we move in there tonight. Adam can rest there while I return to help out here. Then I'll get him about noon and we'll return in time for the party."

Adam crutched in, settled onto a chair, rested his bandaged arm on the table and greeted them. "Sorry I wasn't much help yesterday with the furniture, but luckily the seller loaded it on his end and Greg, er, Dad was at my mother's house when we arrived, so my two dads made it happen."

Jason sighed. "Took two trips but it all fit into the van. Teamwork triumphs again."

"A real craigslist bargain," Hannah added. "Two dressers, two night tables and a king-size bed with like-new mattress and springs, all for $400."

Jennifer put out breakfast choices buffet-style. They helped themselves.

"I'll be back in about an hour to help out here. Our sheets from last night are in the washer. Transfer them to the dryer, Mom, and I'll make the bed when I return...to get it ready for new guests tonight," Hannah called over her shoulder as she and Adam left.

"Where do we start, Mom?" Becca asked.

"The dining room table for twelve is already in position. We'll decorate it first as a model for the other three."

They piled the tablecloths, napkins, centerpieces and utensils for the other three tables on a rocker in the sunroom. "We'll put a buffet line of food across these two credenzas with two stacks of fifteen plates each at one end; then the wine bar goes there and desserts over here. Each place at the table needs a water and wine glass except the children get tumblers instead of goblets. Each spot needs a place card to mix guests and family. I'll write names on the cards and you can decide who's compatible. If I'm distracted later this morning when someone else offers to help, you can show them the ropes."

"Mom, its 8:30 and you're still wearing your pajamas."

Jennifer laughed. "Just hope I'm not still wearing them when the company arrives."

CHAPTER ONE-HUNDRED EIGHT

THURSDAY, 12:29 PM

Jennifer answered the door to a slew of arriving guests. "Hello, Sally and Greg. Welcome. Come right in. Celeste will put your coats in the study. Tina MacKenzie, it's so long since we've seen you. Becca," Jennifer called, "Tina's here. Veronika, thanks for sharing this holiday meal with us. We hope our boisterous family doesn't overwhelm you. Celeste, please take her coat."

Becca hurried to the foyer to greet her friend and introduce her to Nathan.

Several asked Jennifer, "Did you see the police cruiser? Do you know why it's parked in the cul-de-sac?"

"Later. I'll explain after everyone's here."

Fred circulated among the guests offering wine and sodas while Jason and adult family members mingled and chatted. Nearby, Grands ran about squealing with excitement as they played.

In the kitchen, Jennifer coordinated last-minute details, asking her girls and Celeste to help put food on the buffet. "Tina, will you be Salad Girl?" From previous meals here, Tina knew Salad Girl combined and tossed the ingredients. Celeste spooned stuffing from the turkeys into serving dishes and Jason carved the birds with an electric knife.

With all ready at 1:30, Jennifer handed the dinner bell to the nearest Grand, who rang it throughout the main floor and in the back yard. Guests moved toward the tables, found their places and passed through the buffet line. Burdened with his cast, Adam let Hannah prepare his plate while parents selected acceptable morsels for finicky small children.

As the meal ended, Jason stood. "If you haven't finished dinner, please continue your meal while I make a few announcements. Then the floor is open to anyone with news to share.

"First, on this Thanksgiving Day let's each take thirty silent seconds to consider what we're thankful for in our lives." After that pause, he continued. "Next, I'll introduce our guests with a short description about who they are." The introduced visitors each waved a jaunty hand. "Since I'm already on my feet, my announcement is how grateful I am to survive yesterday's traffic accident." Much applause. "Has anyone else an announcement?"

A hand went up and Greg Bromley stood. "Sally Iverson..." he rested his hand on her shoulder, "and I are both delighted to be here today and we want to announce we're getting married on December 15."

Sharp intakes of breath, murmurs of surprise.

"That makes it easy for Adam and Hannah and for all of you to visit the two of us, since soon we'll live in the same house." He sat down to applause, cheering and congratulations.

Getting up with effort because of his cast, Adam stood. "Yesterday our house at the farm burned to the ground, but thanks to firemen like Nathan over there, Hannah and I lived to tell about it. But another person here today warned me a week ago that this very farmhouse was a dangerous place for me. Unfortunately, I wasn't smart enough to listen. I thank Veronika for trying to protect my bride and me by using her gift of clairvoyance. I'll pay very close attention to any future predictions."

More enthusiastic response from the crowd.

Smiling, Veronika stood. "It doesn't take a psychic to sense positive energy around this table. I am grateful to share this occasion with all of you. Thank you for inviting me to your family holiday."

More applause.

Kaela stood. "Owain's too modest to tell you himself, but this past weekend at his business meeting at The Greenbriar...turns out the big-wigs studied their staff for promotions. He learned yesterday he's the new regional manager for his company." She grinned. "I'm very proud of him."

Clapping and atta-boys followed.

"Wait, there's more. Dad and Mom babysat our children for four days while we attended that meeting, which was brave enough, but in the process Mom helped Milo through some excitement with heroic assistance from Veronika, Becca, Hannah and Adam. So we're thankful for lots today."

Wild cheering ensued.

Tina rose. "Some of you may know I took a year off from college to... to get my act together, but I started back this fall and will complete my senior year in June."

Everyone cheered her courageous recovery from the brutal attack she'd endured.

Becca raised a hand and stood up. "Dad introduced Nathan earlier, but besides being a brave firefighter, the kind who rescued Adam, he's also an EMS lead medic. So if anyone feels faint today, the timing is perfect."

Chuckles interspersed with applause.

Dylan rose, wine glass in hand. "As the family's oldest child, I toast Dad and Mom, the makers of today's feast."

The diners stood, applauding their appreciation.

Jason lifted his wine goblet, "And another toast...to family and friends with us today. Please help yourselves to dessert."

Jennifer asked Celeste to take a plate of food out to the policeman in the cruiser guarding the house. As Celeste replenished buffet platters and Fred filled empty glasses, the guests talked about neighborhood news, including the Donnegan family's two untimely deaths.

Keeping the story short, Jason underplayed the police car out front as providing temporary protection against someone who took a potshot at Jennifer through the sun porch window. This triggered uneasy discussion about a shooter in the community. Several examined strips of clear tape covering the crackled spiderweb of glass around the bullet hole in the kitchen window.

Many guests lingered long after the meal to trade stories and nibble second desserts. Adam hobbled over to Veronika. "We're leaving early, doctor's orders, but before I go might you answer a question for me?"

"Gladly, if I can."

"At the police station, remember when you warned me about the house? You also mentioned an important career decision for me soon. Can you shed any light on that?"

She looked at Adam, closed her eyes, then opened them again. "No, nothing more. Do you know what it's about?"

"I'm a police detective now, but my newly discovered father, Greg Bromley over there, is a lawyer who needs a detective in his firm. He also offered to help me through law school if I decided to join his practice. Have you a sneak preview of what's to come?"

"No, but perhaps it's just as well. You and your lovely wife must make these decisions together."

"Good point. Thanks for joining our family today and for your critical help with saving lives at the kidnapping. Trust we'll see you here often."

"I'd like that." Her infectious smile showed she meant every word.

CHAPTER ONE-HUNDRED NINE

THURSDAY, 4:47 PM

Khadija smiled broadly. "Ummi, I have wonderful news. I am in love with Ahmed. We want to marry and have a family. I ask for your blessing."

This announcement coming as no surprise, Zayneb said, "You have my blessing, sweet daughter, whatever you choose. Like any parent, I wish for your happiness and hope this is the right choice. During your life, you've given me so many reasons to be proud of you. Because you are precious to me, it is important that he be gentle and loving with you."

She thought of her own dreadful marriage, unimaginable in her starry-eyed courtship days. "If for any reason this does not work out, I welcome you home with loving arms...and no questions."

She reached for Zayneb's hand. "You must never discuss what I'm about to say. Something's going to happen very soon that is not what it seems. If a foreigner with important information is given political asylum in the U.S., before hiding him in the witness protection program they may make it appear he died instead—to leave a cold trail for anyone pursuing him. So if someone you know well appears to die, it might not be so. You might even see a body bag that doesn't contain a person, or the government may substitute a different body for a funeral, all done so it seems the person really died. Meantime, this person and his wife or family would disappear to begin a safe and happy life somewhere else with a brand new identity."

Zayneb stared at her daughter. What was this senseless talk from her child? "I...I don't understand. Why should I know this?"

"You must use your imagination when and if the time comes. I love you, Ummi, and will always love you. Every time you see a butterfly, let it remind you that I am well and happy."

She hugged her mother tightly, knowing after today she would never see her again. The pain of leaving this beloved woman who had given her life and cared for her since the day she was born nearly overbalanced her desire to share her future with Ahmed.

This is odd behavior, Zayneb thought, from a daughter whose every mood she'd known since infancy. "Sweetheart, you're crying. What is the matter?" she asked with concern.

Khadija forced a smile despite tears and fought for composure. "I'm so happy life is good."

Before hugging her loved ones, Kadija had stashed her suitcases in the car's trunk. She walked one last time through the familiar rooms of the house where she'd lived her whole life. When the known was good, was it not expected that exchanging it for the unknown would hurt so much?

"I'm going out on errands now," she said. As if drawn by an invisible force, her mother, Amina and Safia all appeared in the kitchen to wave goodbye.

"Wait," she said, "this is perfect." She snapped a photo of them with her cell phone, waved one last time and was gone.

* * * *

Abdul spent Thanksgiving Day with his family. No need to hurry back to the motel, though he'd sleep there tonight to ride the van with the others the next morning. He wouldn't have returned to the motel at all tonight, but he shared a room with Ahmed, who expected him there.

Abdul loved his family enough that saying goodbye, while appearing not to say goodbye, was more difficult than he'd imagined. However, his duty to Allah had never faltered. He believed deeply in the holy jihad, grateful to serve Islam even if it meant sacrificing his life. While he enjoyed worldly life, it compared poorly to Paradise, where he envisioned unspeakable pleasures picking luscious fruit, sitting with the prophets, having the seven doors of Heaven open to him and, penetrating willing virgins. He would savor those wonders tomorrow after their appointment with destiny.

* * * *

Unseen by the other terrorists, at 5:30 Ahmed walked quickly, carrying his valise through the motel lobby, out the front door, across the parking lot and into the back seat of a blue car.

"Go!" Steve Wolf told the driver. Then he asked Ahmed, "All unfolding as expected?"

"I think so," Ahmed replied, hoping Steve didn't notice the beads of sweat on his forehead.

At the community center, Khadija sat in her van parked in a far corner of the lot. As Steve and Ahmed pulled up beside Khadija, a third car waited in the lot. Ahmed opened Khadija's door and helped her out. Men in the third car put her suitcases and Ahmed's valise in the trunk of the blue car. One of those men asked for Khadija's keys. The three vehicles caravanned a few miles to a commercial building, passed through security points and parked underground.

"Do you understand what you are doing? If you enter witness protection, you must cut off all ties with the world you've known. *All ties*. You will never communicate with people from your past again. Are you prepared to do this?"

"Except for telling my lawyer to sit on the letter," Ahmed said.

Steve nodded.

Ahmed and Khadija exchanged encouraging looks. She fought tears for the loved ones she knew she'd lose, while he fought worry for the hated ones he hoped to lose.

"Okay, then someone here will do your orientation and explain your new identities while we defuse the attack planned by your cell tomorrow morning. Later tonight we will fly you to your new life. In about an hour, Khadija's car will explode in an accident burning all 'occupants' beyond recognition. That's your safe ticket out of here."

Kadija nodded. "We understand."

When Steve left the room, they had a few minutes alone. Khadija touched Ahmed's hand for strength, her distress still apparent in her tears. Despite programming to the contrary, he reached out spontaneously to take her small hand in his.

"My dearest Khadija," he said gently, "looking at all that has happened with fresh eyes, I understand it in a new way. If a Muslim's destiny lies always in Allah's hands, maybe this is exactly what He planned for us from the start. You, born in America to a Middle-Eastern father and American mother, both Muslim, educated to teach the very studies to enlighten me when I arrived from halfway across the world at *your house* — of all the houses in the world. The next miracle was your choice to teach your knowledge to the stranger in your house, thus opening his mind to totally new ideas. A final miracle is our love for each other."

Her hazel eyes gazed into his as he continued speaking.

"This strange journey brought answers to questions tormenting me my whole life. I know who destroyed my parents. I know who thrust me into a military life I did not choose or want but undertook mistakenly, thinking it God's plan for me. Many around me reveled in the slaughter, but I never liked killing. When they made us wring the necks of chickens and strangle small dogs and torture people, I forced myself because they said this was my destiny. I had no reason to think otherwise, despite longing for a peaceful life and a family to love."

Touched by this knowledge about his life, she felt herself drawn into his revelation. Soon they'd braid their individual chapters into the story of their future. She smiled encouragement.

"As my mother lay dying, she told me my path would be difficult but Allah would guide me. She said to seek truth, use my mind to sift what I see and hear, to think for myself and listen to my heart. You urged me to do the same and showed me how. My mother asked me to protect Amina, the sister lost to me forever, until suddenly there she was in your house. Another miracle.

"The last thing my mother asked was to avenge my parents' undeserved deaths. In reporting the people who murdered them to Homeland Security, at last I avenged them. My entire life and all the events occurring here pointed me toward my life's true fate in this strange land with you. I think hiding the diamonds in the doll happened by divine guidance, my Khadija."

She lowered her eyes and caressed his hand in hers. "This many miracles added together do seem like signs pointing to our new direction," she said gently. "But now you look sad. What is it?"

"With very little to give up except the violence I detest, starting a new life without looking back is easy for me. But you, sweet Khadija...you give up your dear family, your job and your happy life. You are the brave one here. I will spend all my days making sure your new life is worth this sacrifice. I love you, my dearest one."

"I love you, too, Ahmed. From now on, our life—our destiny—is together."

CHAPTER ONE-HUNDRED TEN

THURSDAY, 6:01 PM

"Hello, we're with Homeland Security." The two men at the motel registration counter showed their badges. "How many of your staff are on duty tonight?"

"Two of us," the desk manager said. "We're the 3:00 to11:00 shift."

"An incident will take place at your motel tonight. We have the authority to take over your facility, but we'd prefer your cooperation so nobody gets hurt."

Panic clouded the desk manager's eyes. "I don't have the authority to..."

"Correct. *We* have the authority here. Is your motel full?"

"Far from it. We have guests in," he consulted his computer, "only twenty-three rooms."

"Good. I need your motel map, the one showing guests their room location." He studied this map and circled several units. "Listen carefully. You must evacuate people in every room except these six." He tapped the circle.

"Call all other occupied rooms and tell them to come to the lobby immediately while you investigate a gas leak. For anyone who doesn't answer the phone, presumably because they're not there, freeze their door locks so they must come to the lobby to refresh key cards. Tell the people warned of the gas leak to check in with you at the desk when they reach the lobby. Then mark them off by room number and freeze their locks also. When the rooms are empty or lock-frozen, except for these six, give me that list. Do it now and thank you for your cooperation."

Wide-eyed, the clerk complied. Disgruntled, concerned guests began filtering into the lobby demanding to know what was going on. Some brought their suitcases.

"Here is the list," the clerk said fifteen minutes later.

"If these people press you for information, say you won't know until the gas company techs report to you. You're going to hear some bangs and when you do, tell the guests not to worry, that the gas company has everything under control.

"All your hotel rooms have one door and one window facing the parking lot, correct? Okay, so only one way out of a room... through the door. Right?"

The desk clerk nodded like a dashboard doll.

"Fine. This man is going to stay with you. He'll say he's from the gas company and help with crowd control. On the chance your facility is damaged during this incident, the government will make swift repairs at our expense."

He spoke into his phone. "Go."

At his command, teargas canisters fired through the windows of the six rooms produced quick results. As the terrorists stumbled out coughing and gagging, operatives tasered them, cuffed their hands behind their backs and taped their mouths. They loaded the subdued men into waiting vehicles and drove away.

The operatives outside the sixth room reported that no one came out. "That's the room Ahmed shared with..." he looked at his clipboard, "Abdul. Call Ahmed and ask why that man isn't here."

The waiting repair team had already begun window replacement after which guests would be allowed to return to their rooms. Some checked out on the spot, others after retrieving belongings from their room. Some stayed when told the problem was solved.

When the teargas abated, another team searched the six rooms, removed the terrorists' belongings and drove that gear away in another van. Within an hour, the scene had returned to normal.

"Ahmed says Abdul has his own car and planned to spend the day with his family with no curfew for returning tonight. We could pick him up at his house or wait until he returns here."

"Okay, freeze his lock. We'll wait for him."

TV evening news didn't mention the motel incident, but did report a fiery car crash off the GW Parkway near Turkey Run Park, identification of victims withheld until notification of relatives.

CHAPTER ONE-HUNDRED ELEVEN

THURSDAY, 7:04 PM

She answered the ringing phone. "Hello, Ma'am. Are you Zayneb Hussein?"

"Yes."

"This is Highway Patrol calling. Is your daughter Khadija Hussein and is your husband Mahmud Hussein?"

"Yes."

"There's been an auto accident. We have some bad news. There are casualties."

Silence.

"Are you still there?"

"Yes."

"Another man was in the car with them. His name is Ahmed Jalaal. Do you know him?"

"Yes, he is our houseguest."

"I'm very sorry to tell you none of them survived the fire that engulfed their car."

Zayneb screamed and dropped the phone. She bent forward, keening and rocking in place.

Later, as her initial denial slid away, she tried slowly to process the information. How could Mahmud perish in that car when she *knew* he lay under the garden in the back yard? Or was that the hideous dream, not this? Had she lost the ability to distinguish reality from fantasy? She rushed outside to see for herself but found the garden's soil undisturbed and the new plants in their same positions.

Was this a terrible mistake or...what had her daughter said earlier that made no sense?

She hurried upstairs to Khadija's room. On the bed beside an envelope lay the most beautiful reproduction of a butterfly she'd ever seen. It was formed of delicate feathers with exact markings of a monarch butterfly so skillfully reproduced that for a moment she thought it real. Opening the envelope, she read,

My dearest Ummi,

Remember I told you to look for things not necessarily what they appear to be?

Remember I said every time you see a butterfly, let it remind you I am well and happy?

Remember those things now, dear mother, and remember how much I love you, always.

Your grateful daughter, Khadija"

P.S. These five very valuable diamonds are my wedding dowry for you from Ahmed. Spend them well.

Zayneb tilted the envelope. Five large, shimmering diamonds tumbled onto the bedspread. She brushed away tears as she remembered more her beloved Khadija had said this afternoon—that she loved Ahmed and they wanted to marry. She mentioned new identities for people entering a witness protection program and the importance of leaving a cold trail so that enemies couldn't follow. Did this mean her daughter lived after all?

Since Mahmud couldn't have been in that car, why include his name? Perhaps to tell her the fiery death of her daughter wasn't real?

Or was it something else? Ahmed and her husband worked closely together. If Ahmed made dangerous enemies, perhaps Mahmud had also. Maybe those enemies wouldn't come after her if they thought him dead?

But either way, her grief reflected wrenching loss. Perhaps her daughter hadn't died, but even if she lived, Zayneb would never see her or speak to her again, exactly as if she were truly dead.

DAY NINE

FRIDAY

CHAPTER ONE-HUNDRED TWELVE

FRIDAY, 7:03 AM

"At least we didn't start at midnight when the first stores opened for Black Friday." Becca sipped breakfast coffee, fully dressed and ready for mall action. "Tina and Hannah should arrive any minute and the gals who stayed over last night should come down to go with us."

Jennifer buttered toast. "Are you really going to brave those huge crowds for a bargain?"

"Mom, you do this all the time at garage sales. It's even harder to resist Black Friday bargains. Sure you don't want to come along?"

"No, thanks. After yesterday's dinner party excitement, I'm in recovery-mode today."

When the doorbell rang, the girls joined up in the foyer then left in a wave of chatter and giggles. "Bye, Mom," was the last Jennifer heard from them.

Jason strolled in carrying the newspaper and put it on the table. "Brrrr, it's chilly outside this morning. I'll wear a coat to get the paper tomorrow. Jen, did you notice the police car's gone?"

"No. Why, do you suppose?"

"Don't know, but if this means we're back to looking scared over our shoulders and keeping a loaded gun handy, then I don't like it."

Jennifer clicked on the TV's morning news. After traffic, weather and a commercial, the newscaster said, "Highway Patrol reported an auto accident yesterday evening on the George Washington Parkway near Turkey Run Overlook. Three passengers perishing when fire engulfed the vehicle are identified as Khadija Hussein, Mahmud Hussein and Ahmed Jalaal."

"Wasn't Hussein the last name of the woman who came here to trade dolls?" Jason asked.

The phone rang and Jason answered. "Who? That's what I thought you said.... Why? Well, I guess so. How about four o'clock?... Thanks."

Jennifer raised her eyebrows expectantly. "Weird call." Jason looked confused. "Says he's from the U.S. Department of Homeland Security and wants to talk to the two of us. I figured the last of the family would be gone by late afternoon."

"The Homeland Security that tracks terrorism?"

In a thunder of footfalls, the ten visiting Grands rushed upstairs from the basement. "We're ready for breakfast now," Rachel announced. "Since I'm the oldest, they wanted me to let you know."

"You announced the situation well, Rachel. Shouldn't the oldest also have the first piece of bacon?" Jennifer winked at Rachel as the girl beamed with importance. "After all, you'll be a new teenager next week on your birthday,"

Rachel munched her bacon slice. "Thirteen at last..."

"I'm foah," Milo announced, holding up the correct fingers. The remaining Grands reported their ages as well.

"Okay, everybody. Have a seat to hear about breakfast choices." They ordered. She delivered.

"What's our learning surprise today?" asked Christopher.

"It's a combination learning surprise and contest. Put on coats to see who can find the prettiest fall leaves on the ground in the back yard. The wind blows lots of them there from the woods, so you'll have plenty of choices. Afterward we'll identify the leaves and have prizes."

After they scurried away, she turned to Jason. "With the police gone, should you watch them from the sun porch to make sure they're safe?"

"I'll do better than that. I'll throw a coat over my pajamas and go leaf-hunting with them."

"Hope it works out better than your deer-hunting."

He gave a cynical laugh. "Yeah, I hope so, too."

CHAPTER ONE-HUNDRED THIRTEEN

FRIDAY, 9:58 AM

The haunting lilac fragrance had wafted around Veronika several times during the past twenty-four hours. Her anxiety rose with the first troubling vision: an industrial space full of deadly weapons for delivering death to thousands. But her second vision showed those weapons swept away. With them went the dread they'd instilled in her. When the intoxicating lilac scent crossed her nostrils later that day, she envisioned a shopping mall where she *knew* deadly killers lurked in the crowd, but in a second vision the mall felt placid and safe.

Then she saw a scene in which her sister lay in a street with blood seeping from a terminal chest wound. She looked past her sister to another bloody body. A cloth covered the second person's face. As she pulled the cloth away she screamed, staring at her own face.

Had she foreseen her death? Previous visions always related to others, never herself. She understood, at her age, death would come one day, but why the blood and how did this relate to Anna? Had she and Anna harmed each other?

With this confusion filling her mind, she lunged forward in her chair when her sister appeared in the doorway. "Hello, Anna." She hid her surprise.

"I'm back but not for long. I...I'm in trouble. Of all people, I hate to come to you for help, but I've nowhere else to go." She sighed. "I thought Russians stuck together no matter what, but now I see in business it's only until they need someone to blame for a problem."

"And what *is* the problem, Anna?"

Her sister sank into another chair in the estate's living room and slipped off her stiletto heels. "Why don't I just tell you the whole story? Maybe you can even offer advice."

"Maybe..."

"I've been working for a Russian arms dealer. He's magnificent— imaginative, fearless, brilliant and irresistibly handsome. He took a shine to me...." She smiled, twirling a curl of her hair around her finger. "... And the attraction was mutual. He is rich, powerful and charismatic. He adored me. When I identified a lucrative contact for him with a group of hungry terrorists, he made millions from the deal and promised me a large cash bonus."

"This sounds like a positive story."

"No, because suddenly the situation went to hell. An anti-terrorist task force took out the entire cell. During interrogation, the authorities must have forced them to tell who supplied the weapons for their strike against America. They confiscated the armaments and now my Russian friend is running for his life. The Americans' clever surveillance makes his escape doubtful. Although this isn't my fault, he blames me anyway. I tried to reason with my love, but he said business is different from pleasure. He must punish me as an example for others who bring him trouble."

"You didn't think this possible?"

"No, and it isn't fair, Veronika. He's gone mad. He won't listen to reason." She gave a wry laugh. "Due to our relationship, he promised my death would be quick and painless."

"You sound resigned."

"Oh, no, I am going to run. But this changes my life forever. I will never see you again or this beautiful place, which I dreamed one day might be mine—this place I coveted for the memories of my mother and the legacy of my father...our father."

"Where will you go?"

"You must not know. If they thought you did, they'd torture you for that information. They're ruthless, but I thought I was the exception."

She sighed and stood. "I'll pack now and if you'll give me some money, I'll be on my way. I'm sorry we haven't been better friends. It's my fault. I tried not to hate you, but Father clearly loved you more and had for all those years before I was even born. My jealousy grew as I did, ruining any chance for our relationship. I apologize for that. Try not to remember me too harshly, my sister."

As she stepped across the room to leave, high heels dangling from her fingers, they heard a noise out in the hall. A large man materialized in the doorway in front of her. She gasped in disbelief and held up a protective hand. "Not you, Boris. I thought you were my friend." She watched him lift a gun.

"Sorry," he said, firing a bullet into her heart. The impact spun her around and as she crumpled to the floor. The shoes flew from her fingers through the air, landing at her assailant's feet. He stared at them a moment before lifting the gun again, aimed at Veronika.

A second explosion echoed in the room. Caught by surprise, Boris gazed in disbelief at the hole ripped in his own chest. Before lurching forward to sprawl dead on the floor, he lifted his gaze long enough to see a very old woman with a small, ornately-tooled silver pistol in her hand and a smile on her face.

CHAPTER ONE-HUNDRED FOURTEEN

FRIDAY, 1:30 PM

"Quick, turn on your TV for breaking news."

This tweeted message hit Mike's cell phone first. He alerted everyone in the house to turn on TVs. Every station covered the same story.

"To summarize the news crossing our desk for the past half hour, in an unprecedented move, terrorist attacks took place in every one of our fifty United States except Virginia. They happened simultaneously at 1:00 PM Eastern Standard Time. Those on the west coast, at 10:00 AM and in Hawaii, at 5:00 AM. None of these attacks approximated the scale of 9/11. Most are not in big cities but large suburbs or towns. This required sophisticated planning to accomplish them at the same time, drawing attention not only from each individual state attacked but from the nation as a whole, since this affected our entire country."

"Nothing in Virginia?" Jason marveled. "Right next to the nation's capital? They missed us?"

"In the District of Columbia, three gunmen opened fire on the main-floor concourse of Union Station. A fourth man, wearing a vest of explosives, detonated himself in the station's multi-tiered parking garage. Authorities speculate his destination was Union Station but his equipment malfunctioned, resulting in a premature explosion before he reached the shopping area. Inside the station, the building's security team wounded three gunmen and arrested them. Despite no fatalities among the shoppers, travelers and diners in the station, the gunmen injured eight people, one seriously, before authorities subdued them.

"Now, state by state, here's what took place."

A rustle at the door caused Jennifer to look there. "Gran, could you please back your car out of the garage so we can get the bikes and scooters?" Ethan asked.

"Sure, Honey." Jennifer tore herself away from the newscast long enough to find her keys and back her car halfway out of the garage. She took a quick look to make sure no one unsavory lurked around the driveway or the front and back yards before hurrying back inside.

"What did I miss?" she whispered as she sat down again in front of the TV.

"Not much, just what happened in each state."

The newscaster droned on. "The majority of attacks occurred in stores or malls where crowds of shoppers gathered on Black Friday. Homeland Security had issued Code Red alerts last night to every state, providing them time to increase protection in such areas on Black Friday."

Someone switched to another channel. "Some ask why no attack occurred in the state of Virginia. Homeland Security states they broke up a well-armed terrorist cell targeting a mall in northern Virginia. We now have a bulletin from NTAG, the National Terrorism Advisory Group.

"'We urge citizen alertness wherever you are, today and every day. We ask you to report suspicious activity or behavior to the toll-free number now on your screen. Our agency values responsible citizen input in our common effort to increase public safety through awareness and cooperation.'"

Mike shook his head. "Hard to believe all these attacks happening nationwide at the same moment. None of them very big, but so many at once makes you very uneasy."

Jason put an arm around his son. "Which is exactly what the terrorists had in mind."

CHAPTER ONE-HUNDRED FIFTEEN

FRIDAY, 2:47 PM

Though a few still watched news coverage, repetitive by now, most visited together in the kitchen. They all heard the whine of the descending garage door, punctuated mid-cycle by a crash. Jennifer and Jason exchanged quick looks before heading out to see what happened, but doubled their pace when Christine and Alicia rushed in shouting *"broken glass."*

Several other adults followed on their heels. "Bwoken glass," Milo said, shrinking back in fear as he hovered below the button controlling the automatic garage doors. They all gaped at the trauma to Jennifer's Cadillac, parked half-way out of the garage. The bottom edge of the garage door Milo lowered had smashed the windshield and planted itself firmly on the car.

"Oh, no!" Jennifer cried.

Jason's face reddened. "Geez, if only I'd fixed that door mechanism earlier."

A small, familiar voice next to them whimpered, "I didn't mean to do it, Gwan. You said we should keep our doahs closed so bad people can't get in and this doah was open and I wanted us safe so I pushed the button and…" He buried his face against her skirt.

Still staring at her car, she smoothed her little grandson's hair as he clutched her tight. "Thank you, Milo, for wanting to help our family be safe. I parked my car in a silly place, forgetting this garage door doesn't bounce up the way it's supposed to. It's okay."

"Sowwy, Gwan," he looked up at her, tears on his cheeks.

"You meant to do a good deed, Milo. It's ok. I still love you, ya little monkey." She kissed his cheek. "Now run back inside and get a surprise from the kitchen treat jar as a reward for trying to protect your family."

Relieved, the child sped inside.

Jennifer hugged Jason. "Isn't it kinda touching, Jay? He wanted to keep the family safe."

"You're becoming a pretty good grandmother. Glad to be on your team." His lips touched hers. "But now," he added brusquely, "my engineer side says to assess the damage."

Jennifer marveled, "The little guy actually remembered I taught them to find an adult to resolve a problem with broken glass. Maybe my learning surprises are useful after all."

Jason gestured toward Jennifer's SUV. "This particular broken glass would be hard to hide for long."

Their sons lifted the door off the windshield, pulled the car into the garage and lowered the door safely again. Their meaningful glances told Jason they knew he'd repair that door very soon.

With the others back inside, she said, "At least it is broken glass this time and not diamonds."

"Maybe we should take a closer look." Jason suggested. The shattered windshield's tempered glass bowed in the middle but clung to its surround. Still, a sprinkle of chunky glass fragments lay scattered across the front seat.

Jennifer gathered up a few in one hand. "They do resemble those diamonds in the basement."

He reached down to pick up a chunk, but when he turned his hand over Jennifer's eyes widened and her mouth formed an O.

"Jay..."

"Why, what's this?" he exclaimed with mock surprise.

She reached for the shimmering item in his palm with a quizzical look.

"It's your memento of this diamond escapade. When I moved heavy furniture downstairs, I found this lone diamond hidden back under a bookcase. I know you like rings and had a jeweler choose a setting showing the stone well. But he'll gladly change it if you prefer something different."

"So this is buried treasure, Jay?"

"Buried under the bookcase, yes."

"You pirate, you."

An impish look crossed his face. "And why are pirates pirates?"

She shrugged, eyebrows raised.

"Because they *ARRRRRRRRRRRRR.*"

She giggled with delight at this boyish part of his personality, one too often kept in check.

After all, he was an engineer.

CHAPTER ONE-HUNDRED SIXTEEN

FRIDAY, 3:49 PM

A mid warm farewells and hugs at the door, the children and Grands left as Jennifer and Jason waved goodbye. Ten minutes later, the doorbell chimed promptly at four. They answered it together.

"Mr. and Mrs. Shannon? I'm Steve Wolf from Homeland Security." He showed his ID.

"Come in," Jennifer said. "Let's sit in the living room. A drink, anyone?" They shook their heads.

Steve wasted no time. "Here's the background for my visit today. The U.S. government tasks Homeland Security to prevent terrorist attacks in this country, to reduce our terrorism vulnerability and, for attacks that do occur, to minimize damage and to speed recovery. I ask you to treat the information I bring you today on a need-to-know-basis. I imagine you'll want to tell your immediate family, but explain that the story doesn't go beyond them. Okay?"

Jennifer nodded and Jason said, "Okay."

"Good. I guess you've heard today's news about terrorist attacks across the country excluding Virginia?" They nodded. "That's because last night we cracked our local case wide open, subverting the attack they planned here and alerting authorities in every state about simultaneous shopping-venue attacks scheduled across the nation at 1:00 EST today on Black Friday. This alert enabled them to beef up security, minimizing what could have taken place."

"So what we heard was bad enough," Jennifer said, "but it could have been worse?"

"Yes, *much* worse. A mastermind, let's call him 'Foreign Leader' imbedded about a dozen men in every state, twenty to thirty years ago. A week ago he smuggled operatives into each state to lead those sleeper cells in terrorist attacks. Let's call the one arriving in Virginia last week 'Local Leader.' He moved into a sleeper's house in McLean with diamonds to fund this attack. Local Leader hid the diamonds, and you know what happened next."

They nodded, knowing all too well.

"You know the events taking you to the bank, where you wisely called police, enabling us to nab cell members there and at your house. Those still at large tried trading your grandson for the diamonds. Fortunately, only terrorists were injured in that confrontation and we captured more cell members. One of them revealed during interrogation you brought only half the diamonds, which he threw back to you before his arrest. Yours was a smart move."

"Yes, he did. They were tied in a sock."

"Furious that you caused them to lose many cell members, that you kept the diamonds, that you compromised their attack here and that you humiliated them at every step, Foreign Leader told Local Leader to eliminate you."

Jason sat forward in alarm. "You mean a fatwa?"

"In Islamic faith, a fatwa is a legal judgment made by a qualified mufti on an issue pertaining to Islamic law. An Islamic death sentence is only one example but has become the one commonly thought of here. We believe this wasn't a fatwa but a simple hit—because you stood in the way of their mission and made them really mad in the process. When he got the order, the Local Leader assigned a cell member to do the job. That man shot at you through the window, Mrs. Shannon, and when you fell down, he thought he'd killed you. Fortunately, luck was on your side."

Jason muttered, "And I only learned what happened when I asked about the hole in the window."

Steve continued. "That's when we asked Fairfax County Police to protect you with a cruiser parked in front of your home. The patrolman checked the perimeter of your house twice an hour.

"Once we destroyed the cell, we told police to remove protection because the threat was over."

Jennifer reached for her husband's hand. "The threat is over, Jay. That's why the cruiser left."

But Jason seemed edgy. "Steve, how did you learn about this local terrorist cell in the first place?"

354 - Garage Sale Diamonds

Steve remembered Ali. "A sleeper placed in McLean twenty-five years ago decided not to join the terrorists even though he was sent here specifically for that purpose. At their first meeting, they asked if anyone wanted out. One did but knew defying them meant death. He approached us that morning for witness protection. That afternoon he bailed with his wife and kids, and we arranged an explosion at his home that, as far as anyone knew, killed the entire family.

"He told us at that first meeting he saw ten others, nine of them sleepers sent to blend seamlessly into the population. A brilliant, long-term plot implemented by Foreign Leader, whose true identity we now know, by the way."

"*Thirty years?*" Jennifer marveled. "What planning and patience."

"Oh, yes. Thirty years is nothing. They feel time is on their side. "About then, your son-in-law, Adam, alerted us to a psychic's vision. Though not verifiable, it underscored details close to what we knew. We learned more yet from the seven members we captured, thanks to Mrs. Shannon's involvement. That left two at large. Then Local Leader also defected. He told us Foreign Leader substituted cash for the lost diamonds and sent ten replacement cell members for the seven we caught, so the attack was back on again. But we got them all and confiscated the military weapons in their warehouse. They bought them from a Russian cartel, giving us another unexpected link to a group working against us."

Jason smiled, "It's the story behind the story, as Paul Harvey would say."

"Now the bottom line," Steve said. "The good news is I bring the gratitude of Homeland Security and your country, Mrs. Shannon, for the role you played to help us deal with these terrorist attacks. We can only guess how many thousands of lives you saved across the nation. Predictably, several government organizations, including ours, initially ginned up 'valid' reasons to confiscate those diamonds. But considering your service to our country, we unanimously decided you should keep them, with the full blessing of your government.

"And the bad news..." Jason asked warily.

"We strongly advise you not to bring unwanted attention to your diamonds. You don't want the terrorists to know you still have their treasure. Like the Mafia, they have big ears and long memories for revenge. You don't want them to pick up your trail again."

"Just a minute now," Jason said. "They tried to kill her once, so they already know who she is and where she lives. Why do you think they won't use that knowledge to harm her again?"

"Local Leader gave us two reasons: first, Foreign Leader didn't ask for her name, and second, when the assassin the Local Leader sent to do the job said he killed her, the Foreign Leader was told she is dead. If he doesn't know who she is and he thinks she's deceased, she should be safe."

Jason and Jennifer exchanged uncomfortable looks.

Steve shrugged. "Look, they're a secretive organization. We don't really know what eyes and ears they have in the U.S. This cell operating right under our noses exemplified that. But if you hush the diamonds, we think you'll be okay. If we hear anything different, we'll tell you immediately.

"Any questions? If not, I thank you for your time and, Mrs. Shannon, for your remarkable contribution. Here's my card if you need to contact me about this."

He stood to go. They thanked him and showed him out. After he left, they stood awkwardly in the foyer, looking at each other.

"He says it's over at last, Jay, so why don't I feel relieved?"

He shook his head as if to clear it and said sarcastically, "Well, enough happy time. I need to deal instead with something I *can* control—your broken windshield. Do you suppose our insurance company covers us for an act of grandchild?"

CHAPTER ONE-HUNDRED SEVENTEEN

FRIDAY, 5:30 PM

J ennifer stood at the foot of the stairs to call her husband, but a car circling the cul-de-sac caught her eye and she looked out the front window instead. She half expected to see firefighters or medics or a protective police cruiser. Hard to accept a threat's end once you're geared for fear.

She studied the empty Donnegan house across the circle, remembering early days when both their houses rocked with boisterous family activity. No happy holiday ahead for the Donnegan children this year, but at least they wouldn't wrestle with their father's misdeeds. She glanced down the street at the other houses, so similar on the outside, so different on the inside.

Turning, she called up the stairs, "Jay, it's the cocktail hour. Want a glass of wine?"

"I'm on my way down." By the time he reached the kitchen, she'd poured two glasses and handed him one. "Cheers. Actually, three cheers." He grinned and, at her questioning look, explained. "First, you're a national hero, Jen. Homeland Security says so. True, you can't tell anyone but me, but I think it's incredible and salute your service to our country with a toast."

She smiled her surprise as they clinked glasses and sipped.

"Mmm, a good Malbec." He continued. "Second, we toast your windshield repair at ten o'clock tomorrow and third, repair of the broken garage door an hour later at eleven."

Into the swing she added, "And fourth, shouldn't we also toast becoming three million dollars richer with the government's blessing?"

"We are but we aren't, Jen."

"What exactly does that mean?"

"If we hush up the diamonds as directed, how can we sell them? How can we declare them as a financial asset? Where did they come from? Who knows where the terrorists' eyes and ears he mentioned may hide? In the back room of a jewelry store, in our CPA's office, with the IRS? And if we make a mistake, murder could be the payoff. Who knows when the future knock on a door signals they discovered you're alive and are making the hit? If anyone else is at home that day, what do you think is their fate? Jen, Jen, I don't want to scare you but I don't know how to protect you." He shifted uneasily. "It's gnawing at me."

"Look, Jay, the situation isn't ideal, but unless they tell us differently, I'm going to assume we're safe to live normally. We'll figure a way to make the diamonds pay off. Here's your first brilliant solution." She wiggled her fingers so the flashing stone in her new ring dazzled with light. "I know you'll think of others. Thank you, Sweetheart, for this thrilling gift, a fabulous surprise you schemed up all by yourself."

"Guilty as charged." He smiled and slid his arms around her. He pulled her close, smelling her perfume. "White Diamonds?"

"When you gave me this perfume for Christmas last year we didn't dream the name would fit this new page in our lives."

He held her out at arms' length. "You are the rose in my garden of life. I love you, Jen."

"Still?" She looked up into his eyes. "Even after all these years and risky adventures?"

"Still." But as an afterthought, "Although you could make life easier for me in the future."

And then a new thought struck her. "Guess what, Jay, I have an exciting idea."

"Jen, I adore you, but I'm not brave enough now to face one of your exciting ideas. These days they strike terror in my heart." He blanched. Did that mean he lived with his own terrorist?

She smiled. Today was Friday. Tomorrow the weekend garage sales began in earnest.

"Now what's that Cheshire Cat look on your face?" he asked.

Her smile broadened. She put her arms around him and whispered. "He who loves the rose must respect the thorns...and even the knock on a door."

ACKNOWLEDGEMENTS

Here's my chance to thank those who graciously gave their time and shared their knowledge to improve accuracy in this novel. If errors exist in my novel, they are my mistakes alone.

Veronika Viktorovna Bardonner, a native of St. Petersburg, Russia, now an American citizen in Indiana, told me about her native land, language, culture and proper names.

President and CEO **John J. Brough, Heather Schoeppe** and **Mubeen Baig** walked/talked me through my bank scenes at **Chain Bridge Bank** in McLean.

Cyndee Cannon, wife (and co-employee) of **Mike Cannon**, manager of McLean Hardware, filled me in on the company's history, mission and community service.

Margo Gibbs, my sister and a former ESL teacher, provided important references and education about this subject. An avid reader herself, she made many useful suggestions, edited typos and urged my writing forward.

Carole Greene, my invaluable, ingenious editor, literary agent and cherished friend, masterfully coaxed my manuscript to show its best face.

Chief Investigator **Terry Hall**, assigned to Fire & Hazardous Material Investigation in 1983 and with **Fairfax County Fire & Rescue** for the last 42 years, gave my fire scenes his crucial insights.

Wink Harned, a hunter since age nine and many years a deer hunter, edited my hunting scene.

Bob Maurer arranged an enlightening tour of staff insights about **Tyson Corner Shopping Mall**.

Mutahara Mobashar, a Muslim friend and librarian at **Central Rappahannock Regional Library** in Virginia, guided me with Islamic names, insights and references.

Rabbi James H. Perman of Naples, Florida, a professor of Jewish Studies at **Florida Gulf Coast University**, read and commented on the accuracy and legacy of my Genesis chapter.

L. Tod Ross, a professional jeweler for thirty-five years, shared his engaging knowledge of diamonds and the jewelry business.

Dr. Paulette Salmon, Doctor of Veterinary Medicine, answered my veterinary drug questions.

Nicola Tidey, RPL, E-911 Director for Orange County, Virginia, gave me input about operators' responses to emergencies.

Doctors **Julie and Bill Wilson** checked my medical scenes for believability and, authors themselves, made other helpful suggestions.

Lt. David Winter, veteran of the fire service since 1999, member of the **Fairfax County Fire & Rescue** since 2005 and practicing lead medic, supplied information about their techniques.

REFERENCES

I borrowed ideas and direct quotes from *American Ways: An Introduction to American Culture*, 3rd Edition, Datesman, Crandall and Kearny, 2005 by Pearson Education, Inc.

In *The Holy Quran*, 2003, Goodword Books, West Market, New Delhi, translated by Abdullah Yusef Ali, I read the story of Ibrahim.

In *The Torah: A Modern Commentary*, 1981, Union of American Hebrew Congregations, New York, I read the story of Abraham.

The Clash of Fundamentalisms: Crusades, Jihads and Modernity by Tariq Ali, 2002, Verso (London, NYC)

Islam: A Short History by Karen Armstrong, 2000, Modern Library Edition (Random House)

A Brief Illustrated Guide to Understanding Islam, 1997, Darussalam Publishers and Distributors, Houston, TX

Now They Call Me Infidel: Why I Renounced Jihad for America, Israel and the War on Terror by Nonie Darwish, 2006, Sentinel (Penguin Group)

Standing Alone in Mecca: An American Woman's Struggle for the Soul of Islam by Asra Q. Noman, 2005, Harper (San Francisco)

Growing Up bin Laden: Osama's Wife and Son Take Us Inside Their Secret World by Najwa bin Laden, Omar bin Laden and Jean Sasson, 2009, St. Martin's Press, NYC

The Terrorist Next Door: How the Government is Deceiving You About the Islamist Threat by Erick Stakelbeck, 2011, Regnery Publishing Inc., Washington, D.C.

Religion of Peace? Islam's War Against the World by Gregory M. Davis, 2006, World Ahead Publishing, Inc., Los Angeles, CA

The True Believer: Thoughts on the Nature of Mass Movements by Eric Hoffer, 1951, Harper & Row Publishers

READING GROUP QUESTIONS

1. Discuss whether we accept what we're told rather than fact-finding on our own.
2. Discuss the pros and cons of profiling in the current times.
3. How do you think we should balance trust and vigilance as individuals? As a nation?
4. Discuss trying to solve a kidnapping situation yourself versus turning it over to police.
5. Did this story make you uncomfortable? Why?
6. Which of the story's characters do you find most believable? Explain.
7. Discuss what you think the future holds for Khadija and Ahmed.

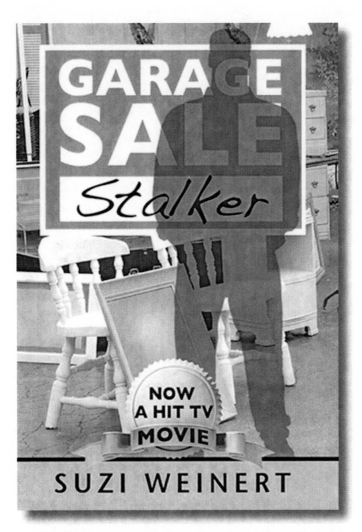

We hope you enjoyed reading Suzi Weinert's book, *Garage Sale Diamonds*. Did you have the opportunity to read *Garage Sale Stalker*, the first story in her series? If not, you can purchase *Garage Sale Stalker* through BluewaterPress LLC online at www.bluewaterpress.com/GSS. It is also available through Amazon.com and other online retailers.

JUL 2 9 2015

CPSIA information can be obtained at www.ICGtesting.com
Printed in the USA
LVOW07s1708080715

445447LV00003B/448/P

9 781604 520651